12/95   4 50

I. B. S.

ISAAC BASHEVIS SINGER

A Crown of Feathers

AND OTHER STORIES

 NEW YORK

FARRAR, STRAUS AND GIROUX

Library of Congress catalog card number: 73–81055
ISBN 0–374–13217–8
Printed in the United States of America
Published simultaneously in Canada by Doubleday Canada Ltd., Toronto
Design by Herb Johnson

The following stories in this collection appeared originally in *The New Yorker*: "A Crown of Feathers," "A Day in Coney Island," "The Cabalist of East Broadway," "The Bishop's Robe," "Property," "The Briefcase," "Her Son," "Lost," "The Son from America," "The Magazine," "The Third One," "On a Wagon," "Neighbors," and "The Egotist." "Grandfather and Grandson" appeared originally in *The Southern Review*, "The Captive" in *Intellectual Digest*, and "The Lantuch" in *Yiddish* and subsequently in *Intellectual Digest*. Other stories have appeared in *Hadassah Magazine*, *Nimrod*, *Present Tense*, and *Union Seminary Quarterly Review*

Contents

Author's Note

A S THE READER CAN SEE, there are in this collection as many stories dealing with life in the United States as stories about pre-war Poland. Because I have now lived in this country longer than in Poland, I have developed roots here too. Just the same, my American stories deal only with Yiddish-speaking immigrants from Poland so as to ensure that I know well not only their present way of life but *their* roots—their culture, history, ways of thinking and expressing themselves. In spite of these self-imposed limitations, I feel that my field is large and my responsibilities even larger. Some of these people have helped to build Warsaw and New York and are now helping to build Tel Aviv. They lived in the midst of almost all the social movements of our time. Their illusions were the illusions of mankind. The vandals who murdered millions of these people have destroyed a treasure of individuality that no literature dare try to bring back.

The fourteen stories published in *The New Yorker* and a few others were edited by Rachel Mackenzie, and all of them were edited by Robert Giroux. Most of them were translated by me with the help of my co-translators. Since in the process of translation I do quite a lot of editing and revising, I do not exaggerate when I say that English has become my "second original language," paradoxical as these words may sound.

I dedicate this book to my late friend, Maurice Winograd, a fellow writer for *The Jewish Daily Forward*, a gifted poet and a psychical researcher in his own fashion. Of course I am grateful to my editors and translators. God bless them all.

I. B. S.

New York
July 9, 1973

A Crown of Feathers

AND OTHER STORIES

A Crown of Feathers

REB NAFTALI HOLISHITZER, the community leader in Krasnobród, was left in his old age with no children. One daughter had died in childbirth and the other in a cholera epidemic. A son had drowned when he tried to cross the San River on horseback. Reb Naftali had only one grandchild—a girl, Akhsa, an orphan. It was not the custom for a female to study at a yeshiva, because "the King's daughter is all glorious within" and Jewish daughters are all the daughters of kings. But Akhsa studied at home. She dazzled everyone with her beauty, wisdom, and diligence. She had white skin and black hair; her eyes were blue.

Reb Naftali managed an estate that had belonged to the Prince Czartoryski. Since he owed Reb Naftali twenty thousand guldens, the prince's property was a permanent pawn, and Reb Naftali had built for himself a water mill and a brewery and had sown hundreds of acres with hops. His wife, Nesha, came from a wealthy family in Prague. They could afford to hire the finest tutors for Akhsa. One taught her the Bible, another French, still another the pianoforte, and a fourth dancing. She learned everything quickly. At eight, she was playing chess with her grandfather. Reb Naftali didn't need to offer a dowry for her marriage, since she was heir to his entire fortune.

Matches were sought for her early, but her grandmother was hard to please. She would look at a boy proposed by the marriage brokers and say, "He has the shoulders of a fool," or, "He has the narrow forehead of an ignoramus."

One day Nesha died unexpectedly. Reb Naftali was in his late seventies and it was unthinkable that he remarry. Half his day he devoted to religion, the other half to business. He rose at daybreak and pored over the Talmud and the Commentaries and wrote letters to community elders. When a man was sick, Reb Naftali went to comfort him. Twice a week he visited the poorhouse with Akhsa, who carried a contribution of soup and groats herself. More than once, Akhsa, the pampered and scholarly, rolled up her sleeves and made beds there.

In the summer, after midday sleep, Reb Naftali ordered his britska harnessed and he rode around the fields and village with Akhsa. While they rode, he discussed business, and it was known that he listened to her advice just as he had listened to her grandmother's.

But there was one thing that Akhsa didn't have—a friend. Her grandmother had tried to find friends for her; she had even lowered her standards and invited girls from Krasnobród. But Akhsa had no patience with their chatter about clothes and household matters. Since the tutors were all men, Akhsa was kept away from them, except for lessons. Now her grandfather became her only companion. Reb Naftali had met famous noblemen in his lifetime. He had been to fairs in Warsaw, Kraków, Danzig, and Koenigsberg. He would sit for hours with Akhsa and tell her about rabbis and miracle workers, about the disciples of the false messiah Sabbatai Zevi, quarrels in the Sejm, the caprices of the Zamojskis, the Radziwills, and the Czartoryskis—their wives, lovers, courtiers. Sometimes Akhsa would cry out, "I wish you were my fiancé, not my grandfather!" and kiss his eyes and his white beard.

Reb Naftali would answer, "I'm not the only man in Poland. There are plenty like me, and young to boot."

"Where, Grandfather? Where?"

After her grandmother's death, Akhsa refused to rely on anyone else's judgment in the choice of a husband—not even her grandfather's. Just as her grandmother saw only bad, Reb Naftali saw only good. Akhsa demanded that the matchmakers allow her to meet her suitor, and Reb Naftali finally consented. The young pair would be brought together in a room, the door would be left open, and a deaf old woman servant would stand at the threshold to watch that the meeting be brief and without frivolity. As a rule, Akhsa stayed with the young man not more than a few minutes. Most of the suitors seemed dull and silly. Others tried to be clever and made undignified jokes. Akhsa dismissed them abruptly. How strange, but her grandmother still expressed her opinion. Once, Akhsa heard her say clearly, "He has the snout of a pig." Another time, she said, "He talks like the standard letter book."

Akhsa knew quite well that it was not her grandmother speaking. The dead don't return from the other world to comment on prospective fiancés. Just the same, it was her grandmother's voice, her style. Akhsa wanted to talk to her grandfather about it, but she was afraid he would think her crazy. Besides, her grandfather longed for his wife, and Akhsa didn't want to stir up his grief.

When Reb Naftali Holishitzer realized that his granddaughter was driving away the matchmakers, he was troubled. Akhsa was now past her eighteenth year. The people in Krasnobród had begun to gossip—she was demanding a knight on a white horse or the moon in heaven; she would stay a spinster. Reb Naftali decided not to give in to her whims any more but to marry her off. He went to a yeshiva and brought back with him a young man named Zemach, an orphan and a devout scholar. He was dark as a gypsy, small, with broad shoulders. His sidelocks were thick. He was nearsighted and studied eighteen hours a day. The moment he reached Krasnobród, he went to the study house and began to sway in front of an open volume of the Talmud. His sidelocks swayed, too. Students came to talk with him, and he spoke without lifting his gaze from the book. He seemed to know the Talmud by heart, since he caught everyone misquoting.

Akhsa demanded a meeting, but Reb Naftali replied that this was conduct befitting tailors and shoemakers, not a girl of good breeding. He warned Akhsa that if she drove Zemach away he would disinherit her. Since men and women were in separate rooms during the engagement party, Akhsa had no chance of seeing Zemach until the marriage contract was to be signed. She looked at him and heard her grandmother say, "They've sold you shoddy goods."

Her words were so clear it seemed to Akhsa that everyone should have heard them, but no one had. The girls and women crowded around her, congratulating her and praising her beauty, her dress, her jewelry. Her grandfather passed her the contract and a quill, and her grandmother cried out, "Don't sign!" She grabbed Akhsa's elbow and a blot formed on the paper.

Reb Naftali shouted, "What have you done!"

Akhsa tried to sign, but the pen fell from her hand. She burst into tears. "Grandfather, I can't."

"Akhsa, you shame me."

"Grandfather, forgive me." Akhsa covered her face with her hands. There was an outcry. Men hissed and women laughed and wept. Akhsa cried silently. They half led, half carried her to her room and put her on her bed.

Zemach exclaimed, "I don't want to be married to this shrew!"

He pushed through the crowd and ran to get a wagon back

to the yeshiva. Reb Naftali went after him, trying to pacify him with words and money, but Zemach threw Reb Naftali's banknotes to the ground. Someone brought his wicker trunk from the inn where he had stayed. Before the wagon pulled away, Zemach cried out, "I don't forgive her, and God won't, either."

For days after that, Akhsa was ill. Reb Naftali Holishitzer, who had been successful all his life, was not accustomed to failure. He became sick; his face took on a yellow pallor. Women and girls tried to comfort Akhsa. Rabbis and elders came to visit Reb Naftali, but he got weaker as the days passed. After a while, Akhsa gained back her strength and left her sickbed. She went to her grandfather's room, bolting the door behind her. The maid who listened and spied through the keyhole reported that she had heard him say, "You are mad!"

Akhsa nursed her grandfather, brought him his medicine and bathed him with a sponge, but the old man developed an inflammation of the lungs. Blood ran from his nose. His urine stopped. Soon he died. He had written his will years before and left one-third of his estate to charity and the rest to Akhsa.

According to the law, one does not sit shivah in mourning after the death of a grandfather, but Akhsa went through the ceremony anyway. She sat on a low stool and read the book of Job. She ordered that no one be let in. She had shamed an orphan—a scholar—and caused the death of her grandfather. She became melancholy. Since she had read the story of Job before, she began to search in her grandfather's library for another book to read. To her amazement, she found a Bible translated into Polish—the New Testament as well as the Old. Akhsa knew it was a forbidden book, but she turned the pages anyway. Had her grandfather read it, Akhsa wondered. No, it couldn't be. She remembered that on the Gentile feast days, when holy icons and pictures were carried in processions near the house, she was not allowed to look out of the window. Her grandfather told her it was idolatry. She wondered if her grandmother had read this Bible. Among the pages she found some pressed cornflowers—a flower her grandmother had often picked. Grandmother came from Bohemia; it was said that her father had belonged to the Sabbatai Zevi sect. Akhsa recalled that Prince Czartoryski used to spend time with her grandmother when he visited the estate, and praised the way she spoke Polish. If she hadn't been a Jewish girl, he said, he would have married her—a great compliment.

That night Akhsa read the New Testament to the last page. It was difficult for her to accept that Jesus was God's only begotten son and that He rose from the grave, but she found this book more comforting to her tortured spirit than the castigating words of the prophets, who never mentioned the Kingdom of Heaven or the resurrection of the dead. All they promised was a good harvest for good deeds and starvation and plague for bad ones.

On the seventh night of shivah, Akhsa went to bed. The light was out and she was dozing when she heard footsteps that she recognized as her grandfather's. In the darkness, her grandfather's figure emerged: the light face, the white beard, the mild features, even the skullcap on his high forehead. He said in a quiet voice, "Akhsa, you have committed an injustice."

Akhsa began to cry. "Grandfather, what should I do?"

"Everything can be corrected."

"How?"

"Apologize to Zemach. Become his wife."

"Grandfather, I hate him."

"He is your destined one."

He lingered for a moment, and Akhsa could smell his snuff, which he used to mix with cloves and smelling salts. Then he vanished and an empty space remained in the darkness. She was too amazed to be frightened. She leaned against the headboard, and after some time she slept.

She woke with a start. She heard her grandmother's voice. This was not a murmuring like Grandfather's but the strong voice of a living person. "Akhsa, my daughter."

Akhsa burst into tears. "Grandmother, where are you?"

"I'm here."

"What should I do?"

"Whatever your heart desires."

"What, Grandmother?"

"Go to the priest. He will advise you."

Akhsa became numb. Fear constricted her throat. She managed to say, "You're not my grandmother. You're a demon."

"I am your grandmother. Do you remember how we went wading in the pond that summer night near the flat hill and you found a gulden in the water?"

"Yes, Grandmother."

"I could give you other proof. Be it known that the Gentiles are right. Jesus of Nazareth is the Son of God. He was born of the Holy Spirit as prophesied. The rebellious Jews refused to accept the truth and therefore they are punished. The Messiah will not come to them because He is here already."

"Grandmother, I'm afraid."

"Akhsa, don't listen!" her grandfather suddenly shouted into her right ear. "This isn't your grandmother. It's an evil spirit disguised to trick you. Don't give in to his blasphemies. He will drag you into perdition."

"Akhsa, that is not your grandfather but a goblin from behind the bathhouse," Grandmother interrupted. "Zemach is a ne'er-do-well, and vengeful to boot. He will torment you, and the children he begets will be vermin like him. Save yourself while there is time. God is with the Gentiles."

"Lilith! She-demon! Daughter of Ketev M'riri!" Grandfather growled.

"Liar!"

Grandfather became silent, but Grandmother continued to talk, although her voice faded. She said, "Your real grandfather learned the truth in Heaven and converted. They baptized him with heavenly water and he rests in Paradise. The saints are all bishops and cardinals. Those who remain stubborn are roasted in the fires of Gehenna. If you don't believe me, ask for a sign."

"What sign?"

"Unbutton your pillowcase, rip open the seams of the pillow, and there you will find a crown of feathers. No human hand could make a crown like this."

Her grandmother disappeared, and Akhsa fell into a heavy sleep. At dawn, she awoke and lit a candle. She remembered her grandmother's words, unbuttoned the pillowcase, and ripped open the pillow. What she saw was so extraordinary she could scarcely believe her eyes: down and feathers entwined into a crown, with little ornaments and complex designs no worldly master could have duplicated. On the top of the crown was a tiny cross. It was all so airy that Akhsa's breath made it flutter. Akhsa gasped. Whoever had made this crown—an angel or a demon—had done his work in darkness, in the inside of a pillow. She was beholding a miracle. She extinguished the candle and stretched out on the bed. For a long time she lay without any thoughts. Then she went back to sleep.

In the morning when she awoke, Akhsa thought she had had a dream, but on the night table she saw the crown of feathers. The sun made it sparkle with the colors of the rainbow. It looked as if it were set with the smallest of gems. She sat and contemplated the wonder. Then she put on a black dress and a black shawl and asked that the carriage be brought round for her. She rode to the house where Koscik, the priest, resided. The housekeeper answered her knock. The priest was nearing seventy and he knew Akhsa. He had often come to the estate to bless the peasants' bread at Easter time and to give rites to the dying and conduct weddings and funerals. One of Akhsa's teachers had borrowed a Latin-Polish dictionary from him. Whenever the priest visited, Akhsa's grandmother invited him to her parlor and they conversed over cake and vishniak.

The priest offered Akhsa a chair. She sat down and told him everything. He said, "Don't go back to the Jews. Come to us. We will see to it that your fortune remains intact."

"I forgot to take the crown. I want to have it with me."

"Yes, my daughter, go and bring it."

Akhsa went home, but a maid had cleaned her bedroom and dusted the night table; the crown had vanished. Akhsa searched in the garbage ditch, in the slops, but not a trace could she find.

Soon after that, the terrible news was abroad in Krasnobród that Akhsa had converted.

Six years passed. Akhsa married and became the Squiress Maria Malkowska. The old squire, Wladyslaw Malkowski, had died without direct heir and had left his estate to his nephew Ludwik. Ludwik had remained a bachelor until he was forty-five, and it seemed he would never marry. He lived in his uncle's castle with his spinster sister, Gloria. His love affairs were with peasant girls, and he had sired a number of bastards. He was small and light, with a blond goatee. Ludwik kept to himself, reading old books of history, religion, and genealogy. He smoked a porcelain pipe, drank alone, hunted by himself, and avoided the noblemen's dances. The business of the estate he handled with a strong hand, and he made sure his bailiff never stole from him. His neighbors thought he was a pedant, and some considered him half mad. When Akhsa accepted the Christian faith, he asked her—now Maria—to marry him. Gossips said that Ludwik, the miser, had fallen in love with Maria's inheritance. The priests and others persuaded Akhsa to accept Ludwik's proposal. He was a descendant of the Polish king Leszczyński. Gloria, who was ten years older than Ludwik, opposed the match, but Ludwik for once did not listen to her.

The Jews of Krasnobród were afraid that Akhsa would become their enemy and instigate Ludwik against them, as happened with so many converts, but Ludwik continued to trade with the Jews, selling them fish, grain, and cattle. Zelig Frampoler, a court Jew, delivered all kinds of merchandise to the estate. Gloria remained the lady of the castle.

In the first weeks of their marriage, Akhsa and Ludwik took trips together in a surrey. Ludwik even began to pay visits to neighboring squires, and he talked of giving a ball. He confessed all his past adventures with women to Maria and promised to behave like a God-fearing Christian. But before long he fell back into his old ways; he withdrew from his neighbors, started up his affairs with peasant girls, and began to drink again. An angry silence hung between man and wife. Ludwik ceased coming to Maria's bedroom, and she did not conceive. In time, they stopped dining at the same table, and when Ludwik needed to tell Maria something he sent a note with a servant. Gloria, who managed the finances, allowed her sister-in-law a gulden a week; Maria's fortune now belonged to her husband. It became clear to Akhsa that God was punishing her and that nothing remained but to wait for death. But what would happen to her after she died? Would she be roasted on a bed of needles and be thrown into the waste of the netherworld? Would she be reincarnated as a dog, a mouse, a millstone?

Because she had nothing to occupy her time with, Akhsa

spent all day and part of the night in her husband's library. Ludwik had not added to it, and the books were old, bound in leather, in wood, or in moth-eaten velvet and silk. The pages were yellow and foxed. Akhsa read stories of ancient kings, faraway countries, of all sorts of battles and intrigues among princes, cardinals, dukes. She pored over tales of the Crusades and the Black Plague. The world crawled with wickedness, but it was also full of wonders. Stars in the sky warred and swallowed one another. Comets foretold catastrophes. A child was born with a tail; a woman grew scales and fins. In India, fakirs stepped barefooted on red-hot coals without being burned. Others let themselves be buried alive, and then rose from their graves.

It was strange, but after the night Akhsa found the crown of feathers in her pillow she was not given another sign from the powers that rule the universe. She never heard from her grandfather or grandmother. There were times when Akhsa desired to call out to her grandfather, but she did not dare mention his name with her unclean lips. She had betrayed the Jewish God and she no longer believed in the Gentile one, so she refrained from praying. Often when Zelig Frampoler came to the estate and Akhsa saw him from the window, she wanted to ask him about the Jewish community, but she was afraid that he might hold it a sin to speak to her, and that Gloria would denounce her for associating with Jews.

Years rolled by. Gloria's hair turned white and her head shook. Ludwik's goatee became gray. The servants grew old, deaf, and half blind. Akhsa, or Maria, was in her thirties, but she often imagined herself an old woman. With the years she became more and more convinced that it was the Devil who had persuaded her to convert and that it was he who had fashioned the crown of feathers. But the road back was blocked. The Russian law forbade a convert to return to his

faith. The bit of information that reached her about the Jews
was bad: the synagogue in Krasnobród had burned down, as
well as the stores in the marketplace. Dignified householders
and community elders hung bags on their shoulders and went
begging. Every few months there was an epidemic. There
was nowhere to return to. She often contemplated suicide,
but how? She lacked the courage to hang herself or cut her
veins; she had no poison.

Slowly, Akhsa came to the conclusion that the universe
was ruled by the black powers. It was not God holding domin-
ion but Satan. She found a thick book about witchcraft that
contained detailed descriptions of spells and incantations,
talismans, the conjuring up of demons and goblins, the sacri-
fices to Asmodeus, Lucifer, and Beelzebub. There were ac-
counts of the Black Mass; and of how the witches anointed
their bodies, gathered in the forest, partook of human flesh,
and flew in the air riding on brooms, shovels, and hoops, ac-
companied by bevies of devils and other creatures of the night
that had horns and tails, bat's wings, and the snouts of pigs.
Often these monsters lay with the witches, who gave birth to
freaks.

Akhsa reminded herself of the Yiddish proverb "If you can-
not go over, go under." She had lost the world to come; there-
fore, she decided to enjoy some revelry while she had this life.
At night she began to call the Devil, prepared to make a
covenant with him as many neglected women had done before.

Once in the middle of the night, after Akhsa had swallowed
a potion of mead, spittle, human blood, crow's egg spiced
with galbanum and mandrake, she felt a cold kiss on her lips.
In the shine of the late-night moon she saw a naked male
figure—tall and black, with long elflocks, the horns of a
buck, and two protruding teeth, like a boar's. He bent down
over her, whispering, "What is your command, my mistress?
You may ask for half my kingdom."

His body was as translucent as a spider web. He stank of pitch. Akhsa had been about to reply, "You, my slave, come and have me." Instead, she murmured, "My grandparents."

The Devil burst into laughter. "They are dust!"

"Did you braid the crown of feathers?" Akhsa asked.

"Who else?"

"You deceived me?"

"I am a deceiver," the Devil answered with a giggle.

"Where is the truth?" Akhsa asked.

"The truth is that there is no truth."

The Devil lingered for a while and then disappeared. For the remainder of the night, Akhsa was neither asleep nor awake. Voices spoke to her. Her breasts became swollen, her nipples hard, her belly distended. Pain bored into her skull. Her teeth were on edge, and her tongue enlarged so that she feared it would split her palate. Her eyes bulged from their sockets. There was a knocking in her ears as loud as a hammer on an anvil. Then she felt as if she were in the throes of labor. "I'm giving birth to a demon!" Akhsa cried out. She began to pray to the God she had forsaken. Finally she fell asleep, and when she awoke in the pre-dawn darkness all her pains had ceased. She saw her grandfather standing at the foot of her bed. He wore a white robe and cowl, such as he used to wear on the eve of Yom Kippur when he blessed Akhsa before going to the Kol Nidre prayer. A light shone from his eyes and lit up Akhsa's quilt. "Grandfather," Akhsa murmured.

"Yes, Akhsa. I am here."

"Grandfather, what shall I do?"

"Run away. Repent."

"I'm lost."

"It is never too late. Find the man you shamed. Become a Jewish daughter."

Later, Akhsa did not remember whether her grandfather had actually spoken to her or she had understood him without words. The night was over. Daybreak reddened the window. Birds were twittering. Akhsa examined her sheet. There was no blood. She had not given birth to a demon. For the first time in years, she recited the Hebrew prayer of thanksgiving.

She got out of bed, washed at the basin, and covered her hair with a shawl. Ludwik and Gloria had robbed her of her inheritance, but she still possessed her grandmother's jewelry. She wrapped it in a handkerchief and put it in a basket, together with a shirt and underwear. Ludwik had either stayed the night with one of his mistresses or he had left at dawn to hunt. Gloria lay sick in her boudoir. The maid brought Akhsa her breakfast, but she ate little. Then she left the estate. Dogs barked at her as if she were a stranger. The old servants looked in amazement as the squiress passed through the gates with a basket on her arm and a kerchief on her head like a peasant woman.

Although Malkowski's property was not far from Krasnobród, Akhsa spent most of the day on the road. She sat down to rest and washed her hands in a stream. She recited grace and ate the slice of bread she had brought with her.

Near the Krasnobród cemetery stood the hut of Eber, the gravedigger. Outside, his wife was washing linen in a tub. Akhsa asked her, "Is this the way to Krasnobród?"

"Yes, straight ahead."

"What's the news from the village?"

"Who are you?"

"I'm a relative of Reb Naftali Holishitzer."

The woman wiped her hands on her apron. "Not a soul is left of that family."

"Where is Akhsa?"

The old woman trembled. "She should have been buried head first, Father in Heaven." And she told about Akhsa's conversion. "She's had her punishment already in this world."

"What became of the yeshiva boy she was betrothed to?"

"Who knows? He isn't from around here."

Akhsa asked about the graves of her grandparents, and the old woman pointed to two headstones bent one toward the other, overgrown with moss and weeds. Akhsa prostrated herself in front of them and lay there until nightfall.

For three months, Akhsa wandered from yeshiva to yeshiva, but she did not find Zemach. She searched in community record books, questioned elders and rabbis—without result. Since not every town had an inn, she often slept in the poorhouse. She lay on a pallet of straw, covered with a mat, praying silently that her grandfather would appear and tell her where to find Zemach. He gave no sign. In the darkness, the old and the sick coughed and muttered. Children cried. Mothers cursed. Although Akhsa accepted this as part of her punishment, she could not overcome her sense of indignity. Community leaders scolded her. They made her wait for days to see them. Women were suspicious of her—why was she looking for a man who no doubt had a wife and children, or might even be in his grave? "Grandfather, why did you drive me to this?" Akhsa cried. "Either show me the way or send death to take me."

On a wintry afternoon, while Akhsa was sitting in an inn in Lublin, she asked the innkeeper if he had ever heard of a man called Zemach—small in stature, swarthy, a former yeshiva boy and scholar. One of the other guests said, "You mean Zemach, the teacher from Izbica?"

He described Zemach, and Akhsa knew she had found the one she was looking for. "He was engaged to marry a girl in Krasnobród," she said.

"I know. The convert. Who are you?"

"A relative."

"What do you want with him?" the guest asked. "He's poor, and stubborn to boot. All his pupils have been taken away from him. He's a wild and contrary man."

"Does he have a wife?"

"He's had two already. One he tortured to death and the other left him."

"Does he have children?"

"No, he's sterile."

The guest was about to say more, but a servant came to call for him.

Akhsa's eyes filled with tears. Her grandfather had not forsaken her. He had led her in the right direction. She went to arrange conveyance to Izbica, and in front of the inn stood a covered wagon ready to leave. "No, I am not alone," she said to herself. "Every step is known in Heaven."

In the beginning, the roads were paved, but soon they became dirt trails full of holes and ditches. The night was wet and dark. Often the passengers had to climb down and help the coachman push the wagon out of the mud. The others scolded him, but Akhsa accepted her discomfort with grace. Wet snow was falling and a cold wind blew. Every time she got out of the wagon she sank over her ankles in mud. They arrived in Izbica late in the evening. The whole village was a swamp. The huts were dilapidated. Someone showed Akhsa the way to Zemach the Teacher's house—it was on a hill near the butcher shops. Even though it was winter, there was a stench of decay in the air. Butcher-shop dogs were slinking around.

Akhsa looked into the window of Zemach's hut and saw peeling walls, a dirt floor, and shelves of worn books. A wick in a dish of oil gave the only light. At the table sat a little man with a black beard, bushy brows, a yellow face, and a pointed nose. He was bending myopically over a large volume. He wore the lining of a skullcap and a quilted jacket that showed the dirty batting. As Akhsa stood watching, a mouse came out of its hole and scurried over to the bed, which had a pallet of rotting straw, a pillow without a case, and a moth-eaten sheepskin for a blanket. Even though Zemach had aged, Akhsa recognized him. He scratched himself. He spat on his fingertips and wiped them on his forehead. Yes, that was he. Akhsa wanted to laugh and cry at the same time. In a moment she turned her face toward the darkness. For the first time in years, she heard her grandmother's voice. "Akhsa, run away."

"Where to?"

"Back to Esau."

Then she heard her grandfather's voice. "Akhsa, he will save you from the abyss."

Akhsa had never heard her grandfather speak with such fervor. She felt the emptiness that comes before fainting. She leaned against the door and it opened.

Zemach lifted one bushy brow. His eyes were bulging and jaundiced. "What do you want?" he rasped.

"Are you Reb Zemach?"

"Yes, who are you?"

"Akhsa, from Krasnobród. Once your fiancée . . ."

Zemach was silent. He opened his crooked mouth, revealing a single tooth, black as a hook. "The convert?"

"I have come back to Jewishness."

Zemach jumped up. A terrible cry tore from him. "Get out of my house! Blotted be your name!"

"Reb Zemach, please hear me!"

He ran toward her with clenched fists. The dish of oil fell and the light was extinguished. "Filth!"

The study house in Holishitz was packed. It was the day before the new moon, and a crowd had gathered to recite the supplications. From the women's section came the sound of pious recitation. Suddenly the door opened, and a black-bearded man wearing tattered clothes strode in. A bag was slung over his shoulder. He was leading a woman on a rope as if she were a cow. She wore a black kerchief on her head, a dress made of sackcloth, and rags on her feet. Around her neck hung a wreath of garlic. The worshippers stopped their prayers. The stranger gave a sign to the woman and she prostrated herself on the threshold. "Jews, step on me!" she called. "Jews, spit on me!"

Turmoil rose in the study house. The stranger went up to the reading table, tapped for silence, and intoned, "This woman's family comes from your town. Her grandfather was Reb Naftali Holishitzer. She is the Akhsa who converted and married a squire. She has seen the truth now and wants to atone for her abominations."

Though Holishitz was in the part of Poland that belonged to Austria, the story of Akhsa had been heard there. Some of the worshippers protested that this was not the way of repentance; a human being should not be dragged by a rope, like cattle. Others threatened the stranger with their fists. It was true that in Austria a convert could return to Jewishness according to the law of the land. But if the Gentiles were to learn that one who went over to their faith had been humiliated in such a fashion, harsh edicts and recriminations might result. The old rabbi, Reb Bezalel, approached Akhsa with quick little steps. "Get up, my daughter. Since you have repented, you are one of us."

Akhsa rose. "Rabbi, I have disgraced my people."

"Since you repent, the Almighty will forgive you."

When the worshippers in the women's section heard what was going on, they rushed into the room with the men, the rabbi's wife among them. Reb Bezalel said to her, "Take her home and dress her in decent clothing. Man was created in God's image."

"Rabbi," Akhsa said, "I want to atone for my iniquities."

"I will prescribe a penance for you. Don't torture yourself."

Some of the women began to cry. The rabbi's wife took off her shawl and hung it over Akhsa's shoulders. Another matron offered Akhsa a cape. They led her into the chamber where in olden times they had kept captive those who sinned against the community—it still contained a block and chain. The women dressed Akhsa there. Someone brought her a skirt and shoes. As they busied themselves about her, Akhsa beat her breast with her fist and recounted her sins: she had spited God, served idols, copulated with a Gentile. She sobbed, "I practiced witchcraft. I conjured up Satan. He braided me a crown of feathers." When Akhsa was dressed, the rabbi's wife took her home.

After prayers, the men began to question the stranger as to who he was and how he was connected with Reb Naftali's granddaughter.

He replied, "My name is Zemach. I was supposed to become her husband, but she refused me. Now she has come to ask my forgiveness."

"A Jew should forgive."

"I forgive her, but the Almighty is a God of vengeance."

"He is also a God of mercy."

Zemach began a debate with the scholars, and his erudition was obvious at once. He quoted the Talmud, the Commentaries, and the Responsa. He even corrected the rabbi when he misquoted.

Reb Bezalel asked him, "Do you have a family?"

"I am divorced."

"In that case, everything can be set right."

The rabbi invited Zemach to go home with him. The women sat with Akhsa out in the kitchen. They urged her to eat bread with chicory. She had been fasting for three days. In the rabbi's study the men looked after Zemach. They brought him trousers, shoes, a coat, and a hat. Since he was infested with lice, they took him to the baths.

In the evening, the seven outstanding citizens of the town and all the important elders gathered. The wives brought Akhsa. The rabbi pronounced that, according to the law, Akhsa was not married. Her union with the squire was nothing but an act of lechery. The rabbi asked, "Zemach, do you desire Akhsa for a wife?"

"I do."

"Akhsa, will you take Zemach for a husband?"

"Yes, Rabbi, but I am not worthy."

The rabbi outlined Akhsa's penance. She must fast each Monday and Thursday, abstain from meat and fish on the weekdays, recite psalms, and rise at dawn for prayers. The rabbi said to her, "The chief thing is not the punishment but the remorse. 'And he will return and be healed,' the prophet says."

"Rabbi, excuse," Zemach interrupted. "This kind of penance is for common sins, not for conversion."

"What do you want her to do?"

"There are more severe forms of contrition."

"What, for example?"

"Wearing pebbles in the shoes. Rolling naked in the snow in winter—in nettles in summer. Fasting from Sabbath to Sabbath."

"Nowadays, people do not have the strength for such rigors," the rabbi said after some hesitation.

"If they have the strength to sin, they should have the strength to expiate."

"Holy Rabbi," said Akhsa, "do not let me off lightly. Let the rabbi give me a harsh penance."

"I have said what is right."

All kept silent. Then Akhsa said, "Zemach, give me my bundle." Zemach had put her bag in a corner. He brought it to the table and she took out a little sack. A sigh could be heard from the group as she poured out settings of pearls, diamonds, and rubies. "Rabbi, this is my jewelry," Akhsa said. "I do not deserve to own it. Let the rabbi dispose of it as he wishes."

"Is it yours or the squire's?"

"Mine, Rabbi, inherited from my sacred grandmother."

"It is written that even the most charitable should never give up more than a fifth part."

Zemach shook his head. "Again I am in disagreement. She disgraced her grandmother in Paradise. She should not be permitted to inherit her jewels."

The rabbi clutched his beard. "If you know better, you become the rabbi." He rose from his chair and then sat down again. "How will you sustain yourselves?"

"I will be a water carrier," Zemach said.

"Rabbi, I can knead dough and wash linen," Akhsa said.

"Well, do as you choose. I believe in the mercy, not in the rigor, of the law."

In the middle of the night Akhsa opened her eyes. Husband and wife lived in a hut with a dirt floor, not far from the cemetery. All day long Zemach carried water. Akhsa washed linen. Except for Saturday and holidays, both fasted every day and ate only in the evening. Akhsa had put sand and pebbles into her shoes and wore a rough woolen shirt next to her skin. At night they slept separately on the floor—he on a mat by the window, she on a straw pallet by the oven. On a rope that stretched from wall to wall hung shrouds she had made for them.

They had been married for three years, but Zemach still had not approached her. He had confessed that he, too, was dipped in sin. While he had a wife, he had lusted for Akhsa. He had spilled his seed like Onan. He had craved revenge upon her, had railed against the Almighty, and had taken out his wrath on his wives, one of whom died. How could he be more defiled?

Even though the hut was near a forest and they could get wood for nothing, Zemach would not allow the stove to be heated at night. They slept in their clothes, covered with sacks and rags. The people of Holishitz maintained that Zemach was a madman; the rabbi had called for man and wife and explained that it is as cruel to torture oneself as it is to torture others, but Zemach quoted from *The Beginning of Wisdom* that repentance without mortification is meaningless.

Akhsa made a confession every night before sleep, and still her dreams were not pure. Satan came to her in the image of her grandmother and described dazzling cities, elegant balls, passionate squires, lusty women. Her grandfather had become silent again.

In Akhsa's dreams, Grandmother was young and beautiful. She sang bawdy songs, drank wine, and danced with charlatans. Some nights she led Akhsa into temples where priests chanted and idolators kneeled before golden statues. Naked courtesans drank wine from horns and gave themselves over to licentiousness.

One night Akhsa dreamed that she stood naked in a round hole. Midgets danced around her in circles. They sang obscene dirges. There was a blast of trumpets and the drumming of drums. When she awoke, the black singing still rang in her ears. "I am lost forever," she said to herself.

Zemach had also wakened. For a time he looked out through the one windowpane he had not boarded up. Then he asked, "Akhsa, are you awake? A new snow has fallen."

Akhsa knew too well what he meant. She said, "I have no strength."

"You had the strength to give yourself to the wicked."

"My bones ache."

"Tell that to the Avenging Angel."

The snow and the late-night moon cast a bright glare into the room. Zemach had let his hair grow long, like an ancient ascetic. His beard was wild and his eyes glowed in the night. Akhsa could never understand how he had the power to carry water all day long and still study half the night. He scarcely partook of the evening meal. To keep himself from enjoying the food, he swallowed his bread without chewing it, he over-salted and peppered the soup she cooked for him. Akhsa herself had become emaciated. Often she looked at her reflection in the slops and saw a thin face, sunken cheeks, a sickly pallor. She coughed frequently and spat phlegm with blood. Now she said, "Forgive me, Zemach, I can't get up."

"Get up, adulteress. This may be your last night."

"I wish it were."

"Confess! Tell the truth."

"I have told you everything."

"Did you enjoy the lechery?"

"No, Zemach, no."

"Last time you admitted that you did."

Akhsa was silent for a long time. "Very rarely. Perhaps for a second."

"And you forgot God?"

"Not altogether."

"You knew God's law, but you defied Him willfully."

"I thought the truth was with the Gentiles."

"All because Satan braided you a crown of feathers?"

"I thought it was a miracle."

"Harlot, don't defend yourself!"

"I do not defend myself. He spoke with Grandmother's voice."

"Why did you listen to your grandmother and not to your grandfather?"

"I was foolish."

"Foolish? For years you wallowed in utter desecration."

After a while man and wife went out barefoot into the night. Zemach threw himself into the snow first. He rolled over and over with great speed. His skullcap fell off. His body was covered with black hair, like fur. Akhsa waited a minute, and then she too threw herself down. She turned in the snow slowly and in silence while Zemach recited, "We have sinned, we have betrayed, we have robbed, we have lied, we have mocked, we have rebelled." And then he added, "Let it be Thy will that my death shall be the redemption for all my iniquities."

Akhsa had heard this lamentation often, but it made her tremble every time. This was the way the peasants had wailed when her husband, Squire Malkowski, whipped them. She was more afraid of Zemach's wailing than of the cold in winter and the nettles in summer. Occasionally, when he was in a gentler temper, Zemach promised that he would come to her as husband to wife. He even said that he would like to be the father of her children. But when? He kept on searching for new misdeeds in both of them. Akhsa grew weaker from day to day. The shrouds on the rope and the headstones in the graveyard seemed to beckon her. She made Zemach vow that he would recite the Kaddish over her grave.

On a hot day in the month of Tammuz, Akhsa went to gather sorrel leaves from the pasture that bordered the river. She had fasted all day long and she wanted to cook schav for herself and Zemach for their evening meal. In the middle of her gathering she was overcome by exhaustion. She stretched out on the grass and dozed off, intending to rest only a quarter of an hour. But her mind went blank and her legs turned to stone. She fell into a deep sleep. When she opened her eyes, night had fallen. The sky was overcast, the air heavy with humidity. There was a storm coming. The earth steamed with the scent of grass and herbs, and it made Akhsa's head reel. In the darkness she found her basket, but it was empty. A goat or cow had eaten her sorrel. Suddenly she remembered her childhood, when she was pampered by her grandparents, dressed in velvet and silk, and served by maids and butlers. Now coughing choked her, her forehead was hot, and chills flashed through her spine. Since the moon did not shine and the stars were obscured, she scarcely knew her way. Her bare feet stepped on thorns and cow pats. "What a trap I have fallen into!" something cried out in her. She came to a tree and stopped to rest. At that moment she saw her grandfather. His white beard glowed in the darkness. She recognized his high forehead, his benign smile, and the loving kindness of his gaze. She called out, "Grandfather!" And in a second her face was washed with tears.

"I know everything," her grandfather said. "Your tribulations and your grief."

"Grandfather, what shall I do?"

"My daughter, your ordeal is over. We are waiting for you —I, Grandmother, all who love you. Holy angels will come to meet you."

"When, Grandfather?"

In that instant the image dissolved. Only the darkness remained. Akhsa felt her way home like someone blind. Finally, she reached her hut. As she opened the door she could feel that Zemach was there. He sat on the floor and his eyes were like two coals. He called out, "It's you?"

"Yes, Zemach."

"Why were you so long? Because of you I couldn't say my evening prayers in peace. You confused my thoughts."

"Forgive me, Zemach. I was tired and I fell asleep in the pasture."

"Liar! Convert! Scum!" Zemach screeched. "I searched for you in the pasture. You were whoring with a shepherd."

"What are you saying? God forbid!"

"Tell me the truth!" He jumped up and began to shake her. "Bitch! Demon! Lilith!"

Zemach had never acted so wildly. Akhsa said to him, "Zemach, my husband, I am faithful to you. I fell asleep on the grass. On the way home I saw my grandfather. My time is up." She was seized with such weakness that she sank to the floor.

Zemach's wrath vanished immediately. A mournful wail broke from him. "Sacred soul, where will I be without you? You are a saint. Forgive me my harshness. It was because of my love. I wanted to cleanse you so that you could sit in Paradise with the Holy Mothers."

"As I deserve, so shall I sit."

"Why should this happen to you? Is there no justice in Heaven?" And Zemach wailed in the voice that terrified her. He beat his head against the wall.

The next morning Akhsa did not rise from her bed. Zemach brought porridge he had cooked for her on the tripod. When he fed it to her, it spilled out of her mouth. Zemach fetched the town healer, but the healer did not know what to do. The women of the Burial Society came. Akhsa lay in a state of utter weakness. Her life was draining away. In the middle of the day Zemach went on foot to the town of Jaroslaw to bring a doctor. Evening came and he had not returned. That morning the rabbi's wife had sent a pillow to Akhsa. It was the first time in years she had slept on a pillow. Toward evening, the Burial Society women went home to their families and Akhsa remained alone. A wick burned in a dish of oil. A tepid breeze came through the open window. The moon did not shine, but the stars glittered. Crickets chirped, and frogs croaked with human voices. Once in a while a shadow passed the wall across from her bed. Akhsa knew that her end was near, but she had no fear of death. She took stock of her soul. She had been born rich and beautiful, with more gifts than all the others around her. Bad luck had made everything turn to the opposite. Did she suffer for her own sins or was she a reincarnation of someone who had sinned in a former generation? Akhsa knew that she should be spending her last hours in repentance and prayer. But such was her fate that doubt did not leave her even now. Her grandfather had told her one thing, her grandmother another. Akhsa had read in an old book about the Apostates who denied God, considering the world a random combination of atoms. She had now one desire —that a sign should be given, the pure truth revealed. She lay and prayed for a miracle. She fell into a light sleep and dreamed she was falling into depths that were tight and dark. Each time it seemed that she had reached the bottom, the foundation collapsed under her and she began to sink again with greater speed. The dark became heavier and the abyss even deeper.

She opened her eyes and knew what to do. With her last strength she got up and found a knife. She took off the pillowcase and with numb fingers ripped open the seams of the pillow. From the down stuffing she pulled out a crown of feathers. A hidden hand had braided in its top the four letters of God's name.

Akhsa put the crown beside her bed. In the wavering light of the wick, she could see each letter clearly: the *Yud*, the *Hai*, the *Vov*, and the other *Hai*. But, she wondered, in what way was this crown more a revelation of truth than the other? Was it possible that there were different faiths in Heaven? Akhsa began to pray for a new miracle. In her dismay she remembered the Devil's words: "The truth is that there is no truth."

Late at night, one of the Burial Society women returned. Akhsa wanted to implore her not to step on the crown, but she was too weak. The woman stepped on the crown, and its delicate structure dissolved. Akhsa closed her eyes and never opened them again. At dawn she sighed and gave up her soul.

One of the women lifted a feather and put it to her nostrils, but it did not flutter.

Later in the day, the Burial Society women cleansed Akhsa and dressed her in the shroud that she had sewn for herself. Zemach still had not returned from Jaroslaw and he was never heard of again. There was talk in Holishitz that he had been killed on the road. Some surmised that Zemach was not a man but a demon. Akhsa was buried near the chapel of a holy man, and the rabbi spoke a eulogy for her.

One thing remained a riddle. In her last hours Akhsa had ripped open the pillow that the rabbi's wife had sent her. The women who washed her body found bits of down between her fingers. How could a dying woman have the strength to do this? And what had she been searching for? No matter how much the townspeople pondered and how many explanations they tried to find, they never discovered the truth.

Because if there is such a thing as truth it is as intricate and hidden as a crown of feathers.

Translated by the author and Laurie Colwin

A Day in Coney Island

T ODAY I know exactly what I should have done that summer—my work. But then I wrote almost nothing. "Who needs Yiddish in America?" I asked myself. Though the editor of a Yiddish paper published a sketch of mine from time to time in the Sunday edition, he told me frankly that no one gave a hoot about demons, dybbuks, and imps of two hundred years ago. At thirty, a refugee from Poland, I had become an anachronism. As if that were not enough, Washington had refused to extend my tourist visa. Lieberman, my lawyer, was trying to get me a permanent visa, but for that I needed my birth certificate, a certificate of morality, a letter saying that I was employed and would not become a public charge, and other papers I could not obtain. I sent alarmed letters to my friends in Poland. They never replied. The newspapers were predicting that Hitler would invade Poland any day.

I opened my eyes after a fitful sleep, full of nightmares. My Warsaw wristwatch showed a quarter to eleven. Through the cracks in the shade a golden light poured in. I could hear the sound of the ocean. For a year and a half I had been renting a furnished room in an old house in Sea Gate, not far from Esther (that's what I'll call her here), and I paid sixteen dollars a month for it. Mrs. Berger, the landlady, gave me breakfast at cost.

Until they deported me to Poland, I was enjoying American comfort. I took a bath in the bathroom down the hall (at that time of day, it was not occupied), and I could see a huge boat arriving from Europe—either the *Queen Mary* or the *Normandie*. What a luxury to look out my bathroom window and see the Atlantic Ocean and one of the newest and fastest ships in the world! While shaving, I made a decision: I would not let them deport me to Poland. I would not fall into Hitler's paws. I would stay illegally. I had been told that if war broke out I had a good chance of becoming a citizen automatically. I grimaced at my reflection in the mirror. Already, my red hair was gone. I had watery blue eyes, inflamed eyelids, sunken cheeks, a protruding Adam's apple. Although people came from Manhattan to Sea Gate to get sunburned, my skin remained sickly white. My nose was thin and pale, my chin pointed, my chest flat. I often thought that I looked not unlike the imps I described in my stories. I stuck out my tongue and called myself a crazy *batlan*, which means an unworldly ne'er-do-well.

I expected Mrs. Berger's kitchen to be empty so late in the morning, but they were all there: Mr. Chaikowitz; his third wife; the old writer Lemkin, who used to be an anarchist; and Sylvia, who had taken me to a movie on Mermaid Avenue a few days before (until five o'clock the price of a ticket was only ten cents) and translated for me in broken Yiddish what the gangsters in the film were saying. In the darkness, she had taken my hand, which made me feel guilty. First, I had vowed to myself to keep the Ten Commandments. Second, I was betraying Esther. Third, I had a bad conscience about Anna, who still wrote me from Warsaw. But I didn't want to insult Sylvia.

When I entered the kitchen, Mrs. Berger cried out, "Here's our writer! How can a man sleep so long? I've been on my feet since six this morning." I looked at her thick legs, at her crooked toes and protruding bunions. Everyone teased me. Old Chaikowitz said, "Do you realize that you've missed the hour of morning prayer? You must be one of the Kotzker Hasids who pray late." His face was white and so was his goatee. His third wife, a fat woman with a thick nose and fleshy lips, joined in. "I bet this greenhorn hasn't even got phylacteries." As for Lemkin, he said, "If you ask me, he was up writing a best-seller the whole night."

"I'm hungry for the second time," Sylvia announced.

"What are you going to eat today?" Mrs. Berger asked me. "Two rolls with one egg, or two eggs with one roll?"

"Whatever you give me."

"I'm ready to give you the moon on a plate. I'm scared of what you may write about me in your Yiddish paper."

She brought me a large roll with two scrambled eggs and a big cup of coffee. The price of the breakfast was a quarter, but I owed Mrs. Berger six weeks' rent and for six weeks of breakfasts.

While I ate, Mrs. Chaikowitz talked about her oldest daughter, who had been widowed a year ago and was now remarried. "Have you ever heard of a thing like this?" she said. "He hiccupped once and dropped dead. It seems something ruptured in his brain. God forbid the misfortunes that can happen. He left her over $50,000 insurance. How long can a young woman wait? The other one was a doctor, this one is a lawyer—the biggest lawyer in America. He took one look at her and said, 'This is the woman I've been waiting for.' After six weeks they got married and went to Bermuda on the honeymoon. He bought her a ring for $10,000."

"Was he a bachelor?" Sylvia asked.

"He had a wife before, but she was not his type and he divorced her. She gets plenty of alimony from him—$200 a week. May she spend it all on medicine."

I ate my breakfast quickly and left. Outside, I looked in the letter box, but there was nothing for me. Only two blocks away I could see the house Esther had rented the winter before last. She let rooms to people who wanted to spend their vacations near New York. I couldn't visit her during the daytime; I used to steal over late at night. A lot of Yiddish writers and journalists lived there that summer, and they were not to know about my love affair with Esther. Since I didn't intend to marry her, why jeopardize her reputation? Esther was almost ten years older than I. She had divorced her husband —a Yiddish poet, a modernist, a Communist, a charlatan. He took off for California and never sent a penny for their two little daughters. He was living with an artist who painted abstract pictures. Esther needed a husband to support her and the girls, not a Yiddish writer who specialized in werewolves and sprites.

I had been in America for eighteen months, but Coney Island still surprised me. The sun poured down like fire. From the beach came a roar even louder than the ocean. On the boardwalk, an Italian watermelon vender pounded on a sheet of tin with his knife and called for customers in a wild voice. Everyone bellowed in his own way: sellers of popcorn and hot dogs, ice cream and peanuts, cotton candy and corn on the cob. I passed a sideshow displaying a creature that was half woman, half fish; a wax museum with figures of Marie Antoinette, Buffalo Bill, and John Wilkes Booth; a store where a turbanned astrologer sat in the dark surrounded by maps and globes of the heavenly constellations, casting horoscopes. Pygmies danced in front of a little circus, their black faces painted white, all of them bound loosely with a long rope. A mechanical ape puffed its belly like a bellows and laughed with raucous laughter. Negro boys aimed guns at metal duck-lings. A half-naked man with a black beard and hair to his shoulders hawked potions that strengthened the muscles, beautified the skin, and brought back lost potency. He tore heavy chains with his hands and bent coins between his fin-gers. A little farther along, a medium advertised that she was calling back spirits from the dead, prophesying the future, and giving advice on love and marriage. I had taken with me a copy of Payot's *The Education of the Will* in Polish. This book, which taught how to overcome laziness and do system-atic spiritual work, had become my second Bible. But I did the opposite of what the book preached. I wasted my days with dreams, worries, empty fantasies, and locked myself in affairs that had no future.

At the end of the boardwalk, I sat down on a bench. Every day, the same group of old men was gathered there discussing Communism. A little man with a round red face and white hair like foam shook his head violently and yelled, "Who's going to save the workers—Hitler? Mussolini? That social Fascist Léon Blum? That opportunist Norman Thomas? Long live Comrade Stalin! Blessed be his hands!"

A man whose nose was etched with broken veins yelled back, "What about the Moscow trials? The millions of workers and peasants Stalin exiled to Siberia? What about the Soviet gen-erals your Comrade Stalin executed?" His body was short and broad, as if his midsection had been sawed out. He spat into his handkerchief and shrieked, "Is Bukharin truly a German spy? Does Trotsky take money from Rockefeller? Was Kamenev an enemy of the proletariat? And how about your-self and the proletariat—you slum landlord!"

I often imagined that these men didn't stop to eat or sleep but waged their debate without interruption. They jumped against one another like he-goats ready to lunge. I had taken out a notebook and a fountain pen to write down a topic (perhaps about these debaters), but instead I began to draw a little man with long ears, a nose like a ram's horn, goose feet, and two horns on his head. After a while, I covered his body with scales and attached wings. I looked down at *The Education of the Will*. Discipline? Concentration? What help would that be if I was doomed to perish in Hitler's camps? And even if I survived, how would another novel or story help humanity? The metaphysicians had given up too soon, I decided. Reality is neither solipsism nor materialism. One should begin from the beginning: what is time? What is space? Here was the key to the whole riddle. Who knows, maybe I was destined to solve it.

I closed my eyes and determined once and forever to break through the fence between idea and being, the categories of pure reason and the thing in itself. Through my eyelids the sun shone red. The pounding of the waves and the din of the people merged. I felt, almost palpably, that I was one step from truth. "Time is nothing, space is nothing," I murmured. But that nothingness is the background of the world picture. Then what is the world picture? Is it matter? Spirit? Is it magnetism or gravitation? And what is life? What is suffering? What is consciousness? And if there is a God, what is He? Substance with infinite attributes? The Monad of Monads? Blind will? The Unconscious? Can He be sex, as the cabalists hint? Is God an orgasm that never ceases? Is the universal nothingness the principle of femininity? I wouldn't come to any decision now, I decided. Maybe at night, in bed . . .

I opened my eyes and walked toward Brighton. The girders of the "L" threw a net of sun and shade on the pavements. A train from Manhattan zoomed by with a deafening clatter. No matter how time and space are defined, I thought, it is impossible to be simultaneously in Brooklyn and Manhattan. I passed by windows displaying mattresses, samples of roofing shingles, kosher chickens. I stopped at a Chinese restaurant. Should I go eat lunch? No, in the cafeteria it might be a nickel cheaper. I was down to almost my last cent. If my sketch, "After the Divorce," didn't appear in the Sunday edition, nothing remained but suicide.

Walking back, I marveled at myself. How could I have allowed my finances to dwindle this way? It was true that a tourist wasn't permitted to work, but how would the Immigration and Naturalization Service know if I washed dishes in a restaurant, or if I got a job as a messenger, or as a Hebrew teacher? It was crazy to wait until you were completely broke. True, I had convinced myself that I could be sustained by the leftovers on cafeteria tables. But sooner or later the manager or cashier would notice a human scavenger. The Americans would rather throw food into the garbage can than let it be eaten without payment. Thinking of food made me hungry. I remembered what I had read about fasting. With water to drink, a man can live for sixty days or so. I had read somewhere else that on an expedition to the South or North Pole Amundsen had eaten one of his boots. My present hunger, I told myself, was nothing but hysteria. Two eggs and a roll contain enough starch, fat, and protein for days to come. Just the same, I felt a gnawing in my stomach. My knees were weak. I was going to meet Esther that night, and starvation leads to impotence. I barely reached the cafeteria. I entered, took a check, and approached the buffet counter. I knew that those who are condemned to death order last meals; people don't even want to be executed on an empty stomach. This, I thought, was proof that life and death have no connection. Since death has no substance, it cannot end life. It is only a frame for living processes that are eternal.

I had not yet become a vegetarian, but I was brooding about vegetarianism. Nevertheless, I picked out flanken in horseradish with boiled potatoes and lima beans, a cup of noodle soup, a large roll, a cup of coffee, and a piece of cake—all for sixty cents. Holding my tray, I passed tables littered with the remains of meals, but I stopped at a clean one. On a chair lay the afternoon tabloid. Although I wanted to read it, I remembered Payot's words: intellectuals should eat slowly, chew each bite thoroughly, and not read. I glanced at the headlines just the same. Hitler had again demanded the Polish Corridor. Smigly-Rydz had announced in the Sejm that Poland would fight for every inch of territory. The German ambassador in Tokyo had had an audience with the Mikado. A retired general in England had criticized the Maginot Line and predicted that it would be broken at the first attack. The powers that rule the universe were preparing the catastrophe.

After I finished eating, I counted my money, and I remembered that I had to call the newspaper and ask about my sketch. I knew that a call from Coney Island to Manhattan cost ten cents, and the Sunday editor, Leon Diamond, rarely came to the office. Still, I couldn't leave everything to fate. One dime wouldn't change the situation. I got up resolutely, found an empty telephone booth, and made the call. I prayed to the same powers preparing the world catastrophe that the operator wouldn't give me a wrong number. I pronounced my number as clearly as I could in my accent, and she told me to put in my dime. The girl at the switchboard answered and I asked for Leon Diamond. I was almost sure she would tell me he wasn't in the office, but I heard his voice on the line. I began to stutter and excuse myself. When I told him who I was, he said brusquely, "Your story will be in on Sunday."

"Thank you. Thank you very much."

"Send me a new story. Goodbye."

"A miracle! A miracle of Heaven!" I shouted to myself. The moment I hung up, another miracle occurred; money began to pour from the telephone—dimes, nickels, quarters. For a second I hesitated; to take it would be theft. But the Telephone

Company would never get it back anyway, and someone who needed it less than I might find it. How many times had I put dimes into the telephone without getting a connection! I looked around and saw a fat woman in a bathing suit and a wide-brimmed straw hat waiting for the booth. I grabbed all the coins, shoved them into my pocket, and left, feeling like a new person. In my thoughts I apologized to the powers that know everything. I walked out of the cafeteria and strode toward Sea Gate. I calculated: if I got fifty dollars for the sketch, I would give Mrs. Berger thirty to cover my rent and breakfasts and I would still have twenty dollars to spend. Besides, I would re-establish credit with her and could stay on. In that case, I should call Lieberman, the lawyer. Who knows, maybe he had news from the consul in Toronto. A tourist could not get a permanent visa while in the United States. I would have to go to Cuba or Canada. The trip to Cuba was too expensive to consider, but would Canada allow me to enter? Lieberman had warned me that I would have to be smuggled from Detroit to Windsor, and whoever took me across the bridge would ask a fee of a hundred dollars.

Suddenly I realized that I had committed not one theft but two. In my elation, I had forgotten to pay for my lunch. I still held the check in my hand. This was certainly the work of Satan. Heaven was tempting me. I decided to go back and pay the sixty cents. I walked briskly, almost running. In the cafeteria, a man in a white uniform was standing next to the cashier. They spoke English. I wanted to wait until they were finished, but they kept on talking. The cashier threw a sidelong glance at me and asked, "What do you want?"

I answered in Yiddish, "I forgot to pay for my meal."

He grimaced and muttered, "Never mind, get out of here."

"But—"

"Get out of here, you," he growled, and then he winked.

With that, I understood what was going on. The man in

the white uniform must have been the owner, or the manager, and the cashier didn't want him to see that he had let a customer get by without paying. The powers were conspiring to provide me with one stroke of luck after another. I went out, and through the glass door I saw the cashier and the man in the white uniform laughing. They were laughing at me, the greenhorn, with my Yiddish. But I knew that Heaven was trying me out, weighing my merits and iniquities on a scale: did I deserve to stay in America or must I perish in Poland. I was ashamed at having so much faith after calling myself an agnostic or unbeliever, and I said to my invisible critics, "After all, even according to Spinoza everything is determined. In the universe there are no large and small events. To eternity, a grain of sand is as important as a galaxy."

I didn't know what to do with the check. Should I keep it till tomorrow or throw it away? I decided I would give the money to the cashier without it. I tore it to bits and threw them into the trash can.

At home, I collapsed on my bed and fell into a heavy sleep, where I found the secret of time, space, and causality. It seemed unbelievably simple, but the moment I opened my eyes it was all forgotten. What remained was the taste of something otherworldly and marvelous. In my dream I gave my philosophic discovery a name that might have been Latin, Hebrew, Aramaic, or a combination of all three. I remembered myself saying, "Being is nothing but . . ." and there came the word that answered all questions. Outside, it was dusk. The bathers and swimmers had all gone. The sun sank into the ocean, leaving a fiery streak. A breeze brought the smell of underwater decay. A cloud in the form of a huge fish appeared out of nowhere, and the moon crept behind its scales. The weather was changing; the lighthouse fog bell rang sharply. A tugboat pulled three dark barges. It seemed unmovable, as if the Atlantic had turned into the Congealed Sea I used to read about in storybooks.

I no longer needed to scrimp, and I went to the café in Sea Gate and ordered cheesecake and coffee. A Yiddish journalist, a contributor to the paper that printed my sketches, came over and sat at my table. He had white hair and a ruddy face.

"Where have you been hiding these days? Nobody sees you. I was told you live here in Sea Gate."

"Yes, I live here."

"I've rented a room at Esther's. You know who she is—the crazy poet's ex-wife. Why don't you come over? The whole Yiddish press is there. They mentioned you a few times."

"Really? Who?"

"Oh, the writers. Even Esther praises you. I think myself that you have talent, but you choose themes no one cares about and nobody believes in. There are no demons. There is no God."

"Are you sure?"

"Absolutely sure."

"Who created the world?"

"Oh, well. The old question. It's all nature. Evolution. Who created God? Are you really religious?"

"Sometimes I am."

"Just to be spiteful. If there is a God, why does He allow Hitler to drag innocent people to Dachau? And how about your visa? Have you done anything about it? If you haven't, you'll be deported and your God will worry very little about it."

I told him my complications, and he said, 'There's only one way out for you—marry a woman who's an American citizen. That'll make you legal. Later, you can get the papers and become a citizen yourself."

"I would never do that," I said.

"Why not?"

"It's an insult to both the woman and to me."

"And to fall into Hitler's hands is better? It's nothing but silly pride. You write like a ripe man, but you behave like a boy. How old are you?"

I told him.

"At your age, I was exiled to Siberia for revolutionary activities."

The waiter came over, and I was about to pay when the writer grabbed my check. I'm too lucky today, I thought.

I looked toward the door and saw Esther. She often dropped in here in the evening, which was the reason I avoided the café. Esther and I had conspired to keep our affair a secret. Besides, I had become pathologically bashful in America. My boyish blushing had returned. In Poland, I never thought of myself as short, but among the American giants I became small. My Warsaw suit looked outlandish, with its broad lapels and padded shoulders. In addition, it was too heavy for the New York heat. Esther kept reproaching me for wearing a stiff collar, a vest, and a hat in the hot weather. She saw me now and seemed embarrassed, like a provincial girl from Poland. We had never been together in public. We spent our time in the dark, like two bats. She made a move to leave, but my companion at the table called out to her. She approached unsteadily. She was wearing a white dress and a straw hat with a green ribbon. She was brown from the sun, and her black eyes had a girlish sparkle. She didn't look like a woman approaching forty, but slim and youthful. She came over and greeted me as if I were a stranger. In the European fashion, she shook my hand. She smiled self-consciously and said "you" to me instead of "thou."

"How are you? I haven't seen you for a long time," she said.

"He's hiding." The writer denounced me. "He's not doing

anything about his visa and they'll send him back to Poland. The war is going to break out soon. I advised him to marry an American woman because he'd get a visa that way, but he won't listen."

"Why not?" Esther asked. Her cheeks were glowing. She smiled a loving, wistful smile. She sat down on the edge of a chair.

I would have liked to make a clever, sharp reply. Instead, I said sheepishly, "I wouldn't marry to get a visa."

The writer smiled and winked. "I'm not a matchmaker, but you two would make a fitting pair."

Esther looked at me questioningly, pleading and reproachful. I knew I had to answer right then, either seriously or with a joke, but not a word came out. I felt hot. My shirt was wet and I was stuck to my seat. I had the painful feeling that my chair was tipping over. The floor heaved up and the lights on the ceiling intertwined, elongated and foggy. The café began to circle like a carrousel.

Esther got up abruptly. "I have to meet someone," she said, and turned away. I watched her hurry toward the door. The writer smiled knowingly, nodded, and went over to another table to chat with a colleague. I remained sitting, baffled by the sudden shift in my luck. In my consternation I took the coins from my pocket and began to count and recount them, identifying more by touch than by sight, doing intricate calculations. Every time, the figures came out different. As my game with the powers on high stood now, I seemed to have won a dollar and some cents and to have lost refuge in America and a woman I really loved.

Translated by the author and Laurie Colwin

The Captive

THROUGH the twenties, during the period of expressionism, cubism, and other isms in painting, Zorach Kreiter remained a confirmed impressionist. He was one of those Lodzians who habitually lived in Warsaw, where he had a reputation for diligence and productivity. He even worked while he ate. At the Writers Club, Zorach Kreiter would sit munching a frankfurter and sketching the people around him on paper napkins or on the tablecloth. He was tall and swarthy, with yellow-green eyes, a pointed skull completely devoid of hair, and a wide mouth that never rested. Either he was boasting of his prowess with women or telling tall tales about Lodz and Paris, which he frequently visited. Somewhere in Lodz he had a wife but he semed to be separated from her. His father, he said, had been swindled out of a fortune by a business partner. He told so many lies I never knew whether he really had his own atelier in Warsaw, as he claimed, or boarded with someone; whether he earned big money or starved. I remember him always in the same brown suit, his pockets stuffed with drawing pads, charcoal, newspapers. He ran—never walked—on his long legs; a cigarette invariably clung to his lower lip. Kreiter didn't speak; he shouted, guffawed, banged his fist on the table, and bubbled with enthusiasm over things no one cared about. I paid him five zlotys apiece for a couple of drawings he made of me. Each time his comment was the same: "If I wanted to, I could sell them for one thousand zlotys."

"Why don't you?"

"What do I need so much money for? You take the drawing. Fifty years from now they will be worth a fortune."

Once, in the early thirties, he made arrangements for me to sit for an oil portrait, but he didn't keep the appointment. A short time later I learned that he had gone to France. Soon the news spread in the Writers Club that Zorach Kreiter had "conquered Paris." Articles about him appeared in the French press. Museums purchased his works. I was told that he didn't send a penny to his wife, so she followed him to Paris and created a scandal. In the midst of all this I departed for America, leaving Kreiter's drawings of me behind in the furnished room where I had lived.

World War II had begun. In 1945, word got around that Zorach Kreiter had perished. Though he had a chance to escape to Morocco, he had stayed on in Paris and the Nazis had sent him to a concentration camp. His wife, who managed to get to Palestine, survived.

All this information I heard from Tobias Anfang, another painter, who came to New York from Paris in 1940. Tobias Anfang was a quiet little man with a round face, blond curly hair, and the pink eyes of an albino. He had lived in Germany for years and had married a German woman, who bore him two sons. When Hitler came to power, the German woman swore in court that the children were not Anfang's, that their father was an Aryan. The marriage was annulled. Tobias Anfang fled to Paris, where he shared an atelier with Zorach Kreiter. He insisted that Zorach Kreiter was a genius. Anfang also knew Zorach's wife, Sonia. I asked him what type of person she was. "An aggressive piece of merchandise," he said.

This conversation took place in a cafeteria on lower Broadway; Tobias Anfang had recognized me from a picture in a Yiddish newspaper and suggested that we meet. He wore a beige corduroy jacket with a black ascot. While showing me his drawings in a sketch pad, he told stories about Zorach Kreiter. Kreiter could eat twenty rolls during a meal and fast for the next three days. He could lie down on a park bench and sleep without interruption for ten hours. Tobias Anfang had once watched him have intercourse with a half-dozen prostitutes, one right after the other. Sonia, Zorach's wife, he described as an ugly, hysterical nymphomaniac and a shrewd businesswoman.

After we had each consumed two portions of rice pudding and a good many cups of coffee, Tobias Anfang invited me up to his studio. It was a tiny room in a Greenwich Village boardinghouse. The furniture consisted of a broken chair, an iron bed stacked with canvases, palettes, brushes, frames, and rags. Cigarette butts littered the floor. The window faced a red-brick wall. He showed me paintings that baffled me—I had never seen such colors and forms. He listened to my praise, thanked me profusely, and then said, "It's all worth a shot in Hell."

"Don't you believe in art any more?" I asked.

"I don't believe in anything any more."

"So what should one do?"

"Nothing. Everything is lost—everything was kaput to begin with."

I liked him, and though I myself was poor, I wanted to order a portrait from him, but he put me off. "What do you need it for?" he said. "In a world where human beings are burned in gas ovens, what point is there in art? The whole nonsense should be ended."

One evening I invited him to have supper with me and we returned to the same cafeteria. Again his conversation reverted to Zorach Kreiter. "Where is he now? A handful of ashes. Do you believe in the existence of a soul? Yes, from reading what you write, I think you do. The soul is also ashes."

"Who created the world?"

"There was matter somewhere in the cosmos and for a long time it lay there and stank. That stench was the origin of life."

"Where did the matter come from?"

"What's the difference? The main thing is that we have no responsibility—neither to ourselves nor to others. The secret of the universe is apathy. The earth, the sun, the rocks, they're all indifferent, and this is a kind of passive force. Perhaps indifference and gravitation are the same." He spoke and yawned. He ate and smoked.

"Why do you smoke so much?" I asked.

"It keeps me indifferent."

For some time we continued to meet at the cafeteria or at the public library. He finally began to paint a portrait of me and spoiled a few canvases. I offered him an advance, which he refused. While he painted, he talked incessantly of Zorach Kreiter. It seemed that Zorach had had a wife before Sonia, a seamstress who committed suicide. In Paris, Zorach had a girl friend—a painter who lost her mind and ended up in an asylum.

Tobias Anfang said, "I know there's no such thing as a soul, but somehow I'm aware of Kreiter's presence. At night when I put out the light, he's there."

"Do you see him?"

"No. If I saw him, I'd be a candidate for an asylum myself. It's purely subjective. He had great hypnotic power."

"Why didn't he use it to improve his lot?"

"Those who possess such powers don't seek their own convenience. They're always running away from themselves and only begin to live once they're dead."

After many starts, Tobias Anfang gave up trying to paint me. No matter how many times he tried, he could not produce a likeness. His comment was, "Every day you have a different face. Your face even changes during a sitting. It would take a Zorach to capture it."

One day Tobias Anfang informed me that he was returning to Paris. "I have nothing to do there, either," he explained, "but it's easier to be indifferent."

In the fifties I visited Israel, and a note in the press announced my arrival. My phone rang one morning. When I lifted the receiver, I heard a murmuring and muttering. "Who is it?" I asked. "Please speak a little louder."

"My name is Tobias Anfang. I doubt that you remember me."

"I remember you very well."

"In that case you have a good memory."

"How long have you been in this hallowed land?"

He did not answer immediately. Finally, he said, "I've been here five years, but no one knows. It's a long story."

"Are you hiding?"

"You might call it that."

"For what reason?"

"Oh, it cannot be told so quickly, and I have to be especially careful at the place I'm calling from. I would like to see you very much. I'm, you might say, caught in a trap, and—" Tobias Anfang did not finish the sentence.

"Is it something to do with the government? Are you here illegally?"

"How can a Jew be illegal in Israel?"

"So what happened?"

"I can't tell you on the phone. Perhaps we can meet somewhere. I seldom go out, but I can pay you a visit. I'm not a complete prisoner," he said, and he chuckled.

"Come to my hotel."

"That's quite a trip from where I am. It will take me some time."

"All right. I'll be happy to see you."

"Don't speak of this call to anyone, I implore you. I'm a forgotten man here—actually a ghost, though not the kind of ghost you write about. Are you alone?"

"Yes, alone."

"Well, thank you. Forgive me for—I'll see you."

Tobias Anfang's words aroused my curiosity. What could have happened to him? Had his German wife returned and was he hiding from her? I went down for breakfast, bought a Hebrew newspaper and took it to an outdoor table shaded from the sun by a green awning. I sipped iced coffee through a straw. Across the street an Arab vendor was selling figs, dates, and grapes from a wagon harnessed to a donkey. I heard him speak Hebrew mixed with Yiddish and Arabic. Occasionally the donkey stamped his hoof, than again stood immobile. The sun poured dry fire. A butterfly came fluttering from somewhere and lighted on the tin pan of the Arab's scale. From a side street, a beggar walked toward me, his head twisted to the left, his rigid hand extended crookedly. I gave him a few piasters. In the paper before me I read about thefts, car accidents, border shootings. One page was full of obituaries. No, the Messiah hadn't come yet. The Resurrection was not in sight. Orthopedic shoes were displayed in a shop across the way.

After breakfast I returned to my room and tried to nap, as I had slept fitfully the night before. But the telephone kept disturbing me, and in less than an hour I got up, opened the shutters, and let the light in. On a balcony on the other side of the street an elderly, sickly looking man lay on a chaise, propped up with pillows, under a sun umbrella. He wore a black, silk-like robe and a matching skullcap. A young woman, probably his daughter, brought him some beverage, and I noticed that before drinking his lips moved in prayer. I gazed up at the pale blue sky unmarred by a cloud. Where was the God of Israel? Why was He waiting so long?

Shortly before three o'clock someone knocked at my door. I opened it and Tobias Anfang entered. He seemed even tinier than he had in New York—pale, aged, and stooped. What hair he had left had turned golden gray. He peered at me from under flaxen eyebrows, blinked his pink albino eyes, and said, "Really, you don't look a day older."

I suggested that we sit outside on the terrace but he refused. I called room service and ordered refreshments. Tobias Anfang scrutinized the room as though he suspected someone was hiding there to spy on him. "Are you sure no one can hear through these walls?" he askèd.

"No one can hear you."

We chatted about Israel and America. Then Anfang said, "What happened to me is strange, but the more I think about it the more I feel that it was inevitable. It's not even tragic—it's funny."

"What happened? Did your German wife come back to you?" I asked, to show him that I had an inkling of his story.

He became serious, almost angry, "I have heard from neither her nor the children. If they are alive they are grownups. They have vanished completely."

"Are you trying to find them?"

"No."

The Yemenite chambermaid tapped at the door and entered with tea and cookies. Tobias Anfang watched her suspiciously and shook his head. "No, this has nothing to do with my wife. I've been told that she married a Nazi and he was lost somewhere in Russia. Since she swore that she was unfaithful to me, what's the sense? To me they are absolutely dead. I came here, first of all to be a Jew, and perhaps to find a way to Jewish art. Where else could I have gone without a penny? And who do you think I found here? Zorach Kreiter's widow, Sonia. She told me she had been able to save a number of her husband's paintings and was selling them. It seemed unlikely to me—how could she have saved canvases in the fury of fleeing from the Nazis? What I'm telling you now is a secret— God forbid you should repeat a word of it. Naturally, I was eager to see Kreiter's last works, and I asked Sonia when I could come over. She put me off with all sorts of excuses. Finally, she confessed to me that the pictures she sold were not really Kreiter's."

"Whose were they?"

"She'd made the acquaintance of some smearer—a copier —and he delivered the fakes. How they passed the critics and so-called art experts is a riddle, but not such a great riddle. They're a bunch of idiots."

"And Sonia is a swindler," I said.

"I am also a swindler."

"What do you mean?"

"After that charlatan left—I think he went to Australia —I became the painter of Kreiter's works."

"Why did you do it?"

"I don't want to defend myself, but I was hungry and sick, too. I needed a woman. In New York you can be an ascetic; in this climate it's impossible. She took me in and gave me what I needed. I'm a man without ambition and now, it seems, without character."

"And they believe the paintings are genuine?"

"I have actually become a reincarnation of Zorach Kreiter."

We were silent, then Tobias Anfang said, "The moment I read in *Haaretz* of your arrival, the thought came to me to tell you the truth. Such a secret weighs on the mind. Sonia and I are involved in a real conspiracy. I take the canvases to her during the night. If anyone cared to make the effort, the deception could be discovered easily enough. She has already sold more Kreiters than he could have produced in his lifetime. But neither the art dealers nor the customers seem inclined to investigate. The owner of the gallery may have some idea, but why should he care? He's getting his percentage. I've heard that there are ghost writers in America, but a ghost painter must be Sonia's invention. I don't know why I confess to you. Of course I find excuses for what I do. I'm convinced that I give good value even though the signature on the paintings is faked. The dictionary calls this mystification, not fraud. Didn't Rabbi Moshe de Leon write the Zohar under the name of Rabbi Simon ben Yochai?"

"Yes, it's true."

"Do you have a little patience?"

"I have a lot of patience."

"I've read enough of what you've written to know you will understand my situation," Tobias Anfang said. "Often I feel as though Kreiter's soul had taken possession of me. You've seen my paintings in New York. When I did them, I was still myself—worlds away from Zorach Kreiter. Here I have become Kreiter. What I am doing now is not an imitation; it is organic. No artifice is needed. When I try to revert to my former self, it is impossible. I toyed with the idea of painting in two styles and exhibiting the things that reflected my own spirit, but it didn't work. Tobias Anfang doesn't exist any more—it's like something out of the books of the occult or cases of multiple personalities. It was difficult for me to go through this metamorphosis. True, I admired him, but we were diametrically opposite. By nature he was an extrovert, while I am introverted. In every respect he was an unusual man. I am living with his widow and hear facts about him that are so grotesque I am astounded. Sometimes I'm not even certain with whom I spend the night—her or him. I'm ashamed to admit it, but I'm her captive, literally. She doesn't permit me to go any place, not even to get together with other artists. We both live in Jaffa. She was given the large house of an Arab who fled—a sheik or God knows what. All I could get was a half-ruined hut, surrounded by Yemenites and paupers. There isn't even a café around. An Arab shoemaker lived there before and I guess you know the miserable conditions of the Arab workers. My room is windowless. Instead of a door, there's a curtain. The sun shines outside, but inside my room is as dark as Egypt. I paint in the darkness and I often think I do it automatically. A hand guides me. When I put a canvas on the easel, I don't know what I'm going to paint and often grasp the meaning of what I'm doing only when I'm about to finish it. The oddest thing is that a transformation has also taken place in Zorach. As a painter he used to be more or less realistic. Slowly, his style has become abstract—not completely so, but partially. I paint with fantastic ease and this frightens me. If I believed in the immortality of the soul and all that goes with it, I'd be less puzzled."

"It is your subconscious."

Tobias's eyes filled with laughter. "I was afraid you might say that. You should be ashamed of yourself. That is nothing but an empty word."

"No more empty than the words 'consciousness,' 'will,' or 'emotion.' "

"It's a hollow phrase. What is the subconscious?"

We drank tea, nibbled on the cookies, and sat in silence. Then I asked, "What kind of devil is this Sonia?"

Tobias Anfang pushed away his glass. "She is a witch. In Paris I hated her like the plague. Zorach ran from her. We used to sit in the Café La Coupole or Le Dôme and she would come to make scenes. More than once I saw him beat her up. I gave her hell myself a good many times. She was so repulsive to me it was beyond my understanding how Zorach could ever have fallen for her. Here she behaves differently. She is possessed by a dybbuk—like me, she has become a reincarnation of Zorach Kreiter. As a matter of fact, she really does not need me. I suspect she could continue Zorach's work herself, but she's lazy. During the daytime she is never at home. She spends her time sitting in the cafés in Tel Aviv. She has a good many cronies. She travels about to Jerusalem and Haifa, hobnobbing with professors, writers, politicians. There's a clique of important dowagers in this country, and she's their leader. No one here ever heard of Zorach Kreiter, but now because of her he is famous. They write her up in the newspapers—in the humor page on Friday. Somehow, with all this, Tobias Anfang no longer exists."

"Don't you have any relatives?"

"No one here. There are a few people with whom I was friendly in Paris and America, but they don't know where I am. I wouldn't have been able to meet you today, either, if Sonia hadn't gone to Safad. There's a colony of artists there and she tries to manage them. Really, it is funny."

"Don't let the tea get cold."

"No."

"How can you sleep with such a bitch?"

Tobias Anfang began to stir his tea. "That is a story by itself. I am really not with her but with Zorach, as if I had turned into a homosexual in my old age. We chatter only about him. Without this I could not be aroused. You mentioned the subconscious. I read Freud and the others. I know all the theories, but spelling things out isn't a cure. Besides, lying down on an analyst's couch is not in my nature. The whole of Israel is like a small village. If a fly settles on your nose, everyone knows about it. Sonia is careful enough not to send the paintings to an exhibition in case a reviewer might be suspicious. She has immense business acumen and always manages to get top prices. Just the same, I receive only a pittance from her. I'm treated like a cat or a dog—that's the truth."

"She can't force you to stay here. You could leave for Paris or the U.S.A."

"What? I have fallen in love with Israel. I'm fascinated with the land. Once I had a philosophy about indifference. But here one cannot be indifferent. At night, when the moon is shining and I walk through the narrow alleys, I am enraptured. If I moved to another country I would die from yearning. I stroll along the sea and literally hear the words of the prophets. It's in my imagination, I know, but I'm surrounded by the old Israelites and even the Canaanites and the other nations that preceded Joshua, the son of Nun. I've lived in both Algeria and Morocco. The ghosts there are wild apaches, murderers, maniacs. This land teems with saints and heroes. Although I do not believe in God, I hear His voice. An atavism has taken hold of us Jews and it is even stronger than the instinct for life. Don't you feel it?"

"I begin to feel it."

"For your own good, run before it's too late. If you stay half a year you won't be able to tear yourself away."

"And you still call yourself an atheist?" I asked.

"What difference does it make what I am? I'd like you to meet Sonia and see my paintings. She's read your books, and when the press notice about your arrival appeared, she became very excited. As a rule she sleeps little, not more than two or three hours a night. That night she lay awake and talked about you till dawn."

"What does she know about me?"

"Zorach told her. I often talked to her about you, too—why, I don't know myself."

"How should I get in touch with her?"

"Call her up, but don't mention my name. You're not supposed to know that I'm here. If she feels like it, she'll arrange a meeting of the three of us. But approach her as Zorach's friend, not mine. She's in constant fear that her secret may leak out. This is her phobia."

He stopped speaking, and I opened the door to the balcony. Heat struck me in the face. I stood looking out over the roofs, windows, balconies, stores In what way is all this different from Brooklyn? I wondered. No, this isn't just an ordinary khamsin but a flame from Sinai. The sky above is not just atmosphere but a heaven with angels, seraphim, God. That merchant of orthopedic shoes is a descendant of those who returned from the Babylonian exile and perhaps of those who were later expelled from Spain. The Lord has led him back to the land He promised to Abraham when He made a covenant with him. He and all the others here are captives, just like Tobias Anfang.

Sonia and I sat in the small car, with Sonia at the wheel, driving to Jaffa. She steered with her left hand only. Golden charms dangled from her wrist. In her right hand she held a lighted cigarette. Once in a while I glanced at her out of the corner of my eye. She was small, emaciated, dark complexioned, with high cheekbones; her flat, turned-up nose had nostrils as large as a bulldog's. Her hairy lower chin jutted forward. She had thick lips and large crooked teeth. She blew the horn steadily and cursed those who blocked her way.

"What do you need America for?" she asked. "This is a Jewish country. There will be anti-Semitism in America just like in Poland. It's there already. Sure, they may have a couple of Jewish senators and perhaps a governor, but for each senator there are thousands of Jews being discriminated against. Better stay here. You will be accepted with open arms."

She stopped the car at a building with a cupola. A dog ran out, barking. A short, dark-skinned man who might have been an Arab or a Yemenite Jew busied himself in the sandy garden. We entered a large hall, its walls full of pictures— like a museum. The shutters were closed and Sonia did not open them. In the dim light I recognized scenes of Poland, Paris, a Warsaw market, bewigged women, yeshiva boys, musicians playing at a wedding, Hasidim dancing.

"How I managed to save all this only God knows," Sonia was saying. "Miracles happen. In his last years Zorach painted day and night. He was never in his life as productive as then—as if he had a premonition that the end was near. He also wrote his memoirs, hundreds of pages. You probably didn't know it, but the last few years we lived together again. All our misunderstandings were resolved and he was a faithful husband. He dictated his autobiography to me. He often mentioned you with utmost admiration."

"I see he became more abstract," I interrupted.

"A different Zorach emerged in his last few months. He used to say the worst things about Chagall. Suddenly, without warning, he himself became a modernist. 'What is so wonderful about copying nature?' he asked me. 'The artist must create his own universe.' These were his very words. He explained it all in his autobiography. Unfortunately, my Yiddish is not on a literary level. My handwriting is one big scrawl. I am the only one who can read it, and sometimes it is too much even for me. I would need the help of a writer of your caliber to make order out of this chaos. I could give you a million details and together we would produce a book that would surprise the world."

"I am returning to America. Why don't you find someone here?"

"Who could I get? The Hebrew writers have forgotten Yiddish. Besides, there are very few who are any good. The best ones were killed off by the Nazis. What Yiddish writers we have are old, sick, and bitter. What's more, you loved Zorach and he loved you . . ."

"What happened to Tobias Anfang?" I asked. "He and Zorach used to be close friends. I met Tobias years ago in America. Suddenly he disappeared."

Sonia looked at me inquisitively with her bulging eyes. "He is in Israel, but he stopped being creative. He simply lost his talent."

"What's he doing? Did he marry?"

"Marry? I don't think so. Since he is not working, who would marry him? He's not the only one. The artists who settle here seem to go through a process of resurrection or they become paralyzed. I see him occasionally in Jaffa or Tel Aviv. I think he lives in this area. He is not the same Tobias Anfang but a phantom of his former self. Even so, they don't let artists starve in Israel. Somehow he manages. I don't want to boast, but I have helped him out more than once."

The telephone rang in another room. Sonia went to answer it and left me alone. I imagined that the smells of the Arabs who once lived here still pervaded the place. A sweetish spicy scent hung in the air. Perhaps this had been a harem. Sonia did not come back for some time. When she returned, she said, "Come, we are going to have dinner."

"Thank you, I'm not hungry."

"A guest of mine ought to be hungry. Besides, a man has to eat, if not—"

She took my arm and pressed it to her body, smiling shrewdly. The dining room we entered had a stone floor. Paintings were displayed on every wall here, too. On a marble-topped table there were bowls of fruit salad, sour cream, cottage cheese, and tomatoes, as well as a basket of pitta, the Arab bread. A fat Yemenite maid, with eyes as large as those of a horse, served coffee in tiny cups. There was something oriental and ceremonial about this meal—too late for lunch and yet too early for supper. A few times Sonia's leg brushed against mine. I could see her better now. Her face was sunburned, parched, wrinkled. Her scrawny neck, full of blue veins, was adorned with chains and strings of beads. She had eyes that were blacker than those of the Yemenite. A mysterious darkness gleamed in them. It was difficult for me to believe that such intense blackness could see the light of day. How strange—a sudden lust for that ugly creature seized me.

I heard myself ask, "How is it that you haven't remarried?"

Sonia pushed her cup of coffee away. "After Zorach? A woman who has had the good fortune or the misfortune to live with a true artist cannot—forgive me the expression—go to bed with a simple man, whether he's a doctor, a professor, or even Ben Gurion himself. Once an artist possesses a woman, she remains his captive forever. To me, Zorach is not dead—I continue to live with him, I admire his paintings, I listen to his words. The moment I close my eyes he is there. I could not have accomplished what I have without his guidance. He even told me about your impending visit here, possibly before you yourself decided on the trip."

"How does he speak to you?"

"Oh, in many ways. I own a ouija board, and sometimes I sit with it until late at night. The little planchette runs on with a speed that's uncanny. My finger barely touches it. It tells me things I never had an inkling of. I write automatically. I take a pencil, spread a sheet of paper, and Zorach directs my hand. I hear his voice, too. I want to tell you something and I hope you take it in good grace: you didn't come here just for a visit. You were sent here because Zorach wants his memoirs published and you're the only person who could see it through."

"I must go back to America."

"You mustn't. You can stay. I will give you a room and everything you need. You have no dependents in America— whom do you have to return to? There are a lot of interesting women here. Believe me, you won't have to fast." And Sonia winked at me. The phone rang again. She went to answer it. I noticed that her legs were bent and thin as sticks. Again she stayed out for quite a while. I could hear her murmuring into the telephone. When she returned she was all smiles.

"A strange coincidence. Tobias Anfang called me. I haven't heard from him for God knows how long! Isn't that queer? We were just discussing him. Such things happen to me all the time. When I told him that you were here, he became terribly excited. He simply invited himself and will be along later. Anfang needs encouragement. He hasn't a single friend in the country. If you remain in Israel, he will revive. Meanwhile, you and I can prepare Zorach's recollections for publication—"

I ate the sweets and washed them down with strong coffee. Sonia was saying, "Do you believe in the hereafter?"

"Yes, I do."

"This was my impression from reading you. Though you can't always be sure if a writer means it or whether it's there just for the reader's consumption. I believe in the soul. Zorach is with me right now. I see him in you."

"How can that be? We were completely different personalities."

"You only imagine so. When a man dies, his soul enters into his friends, those who were close to him and admired him. For a time he and Tobias Anfang were chums and when Tobias phoned just now, I thought for a moment that I heard Zorach's voice. These things cannot be explained. I sit near you and I feel Zorach's presence. You were his favorite author. He mentions you often in his recollections. A few weeks ago I lay awake one night and he spoke to me about you for an entire hour."

"What did he say?"

Sonia looked at me slyly and with suppressed amusement. "This is still a secret."

I knew that I was on the verge of committing a folly, an indiscretion, and an act of treachery, but I looked up at one of the pictures and asked, "Who painted that—Anfang?"

Sonia became tense. "What makes you say this? It is Zorach's. One of his latest works."

"It reminds me of Anfang," I replied in spite of myself. It was as if someone else spoke through my mouth.

"I have none of Anfang's works," Sonia said angrily. "I told you, he has stopped painting altogether. He's one of those who gave up here."

She threw me a furious look. I became alarmed. A woman like her was capable of poisoning me.

I rose and said, "It's all a fraud. Zorach didn't leave any pictures, neither did he write any memoirs."

I made for the door and she ran after me. I imagined that she threw a plate at me. I fumbled in the hallway before I found the door. Outside, the sweltering heat almost choked me. I felt dizzy. My legs buckled and I was bathed in sweat. I had the sensation that I had just managed to escape from a great danger. One moment more and I would have been lost. I looked up and at the far corner of the street I saw Tobias Anfang—bent, shabby, withered—an old man shuffling his feet. He saw me and greeted me. I looked back and there was Sonia. She stood waiting for me, her arms spread out, her face wrinkled with triumphant laughter, as if my running away were a prank and a sign of intimacy. She beckoned to me with her index finger, and I heard her call in a shrill voice, *"Meshugener literat, kum krik."* ("Crazy writer, come back.")

That night I slept at Sonia's. Tobias insisted that he had to leave early. At dawn the seasonal rains started. Lightning flashed and it thundered. The wind wailed like so many jackals. The sun rose—a smoking wick among the black clouds. The morning was as dark as dusk. The radio announced that the road to Tel Aviv was flooded. Porters had to carry pedestrians from one side of the street to the other. Late in the day, I sat down with Sonia before the fireplace, and from the ouija board she dictated to me the first chapter of Zorach Kreiter's memoirs.

Translated by Alma Singer and Ruth Schachner Finkel

The Blizzard

THE STUDY HOUSE stood on a hill and I imagined that more snow fell on it that winter than on any other house in the neighborhood. Its gabled roof gave it the appearance of a sugar cone. Those who came there to pray left around five o'clock, immediately after the evening prayer. The yeshiva boys went home about nine, but I stayed on. Later the study house was occupied by men who in larger towns would be found in a tavern. But in Bilgoray the tavern was open for the peasants only on market days.

Between nine and eleven I was alone. The brick oven was heated. Above the table where I sat hung a kerosene lamp with a tin shade. From the highest shelf where the rarely used volumes were kept I took down *The Tree of Life*, its pages yellowed, the covers made of oak. My pondering over the cabala texts alternated with my fantasies about girls. I carried a notebook with me in which I wrote down my thoughts and drew figures of people, animals, and whatever else crossed my imagination.

I heard heavy steps, a stamping of feet, and the wheezing of someone suffering from a shortness of breath. I knew who it was: Bendit the Daddy. Daddy was his nickname. He was the father of two girls who had become whores during the war. They had a brothel on the Sands which was frequented first by the Russian soldiers, then by the Austrians, and now by Poles. His older daughter Zevtel had a husband in America, and soon after the war he sent her divorce papers. I was present in the chambers of my Uncle Joseph, who inherited my grandfather's rabbinical chair, when the papers were served on her. She brought with her her younger sister Basha. Both wore kerchiefs over their heads and long dresses down to their ankles like modest women. Their mother had died in the cholera epidemic. Bendit was called Daddy because it was known that he took money from his daughters. In earlier years he had been a night watchman. Now he was too old for that job. But he hadn't lost the habit of late hours.

Bendit, small, unusually broad for his height, with huge hands and feet, a short nose, a long upper lip, and slanted eyes, had already passed his seventieth year. But his sparse beard showed only a few gray hairs. He was wearing a sheepskin coat, a hat of the same material, and heavy boots. He fell into the room with a puffing and a haste as if chased by thieves. He shook the snow from his clothing, rubbed his hands for warmth. His face, which was usually red, had a bluish color. He shouted in a gruff voice, "What a night! It would be a sin to let a dog out." He sat down near the hot stove sighing, coughing, mumbling to himself, and under his boots a pool formed. He called to me, "Are you studying so late?"

"I like to study."

"You take after your grandfather, he should intercede for us."

A little later Tevele Smearer entered. He was called Smearer because at the time of the Austrian occupation he became a chum of the commander of the town and an intermediary between him and the town smugglers, who brought tobacco from Galicia and carried back flour, groats, and meat. Tevele bribed the commander and the gendarmes, and took a good percentage for himself. For a time he also transported oxen from Bilgoray to the Italian front. Tevele was not yet thirty. He was tall, dark, and dressed like a dandy. Even now he wore a short jacket, riding breeches, boots with high uppers. He smoked a cigarette in an amber holder. He carried a bottle of vodka in one pocket and a bag of salt pretzels in the other. He entered as carefree as if we were in midsummer. The smile in his dark eyes was both sly and benign.

"Tevele, you're not cold?" Bendit asked.

"I'm heated inside," he replied, pointing to his belly. Under his jacket he wore a black blouse and a soldier's belt with a brass buckle.

The last to come was Shmuel Klepke, a bachelor of about forty, tall, dark, with black dreamy eyes. Shmuel Klepke was known for his laziness. His sister supported him. He had lived for years in Russia, where he went through the Revolution, the pogroms, the civil war. It was said in Bilgoray that he had been the lover of a policeman's wife. All sorts of stories were told about him. It was rumored that he had been about to be executed in Russia but obtained his freedom at the last moment. He surrounded himself with secrets. Many matches were proposed to him but he refused to marry. He would listen to the matchmaker's offer to the very end and then ask, "What for?"

And he would smile sadly. He rolled his own cigarettes, which he smoked without a holder. He had the sideburns of a Russian. His curly hair was so dark that it seemed blue.

They had their routine. Tevele Smearer took out the vodka, took one swallow, and handed the bottle to Shmuel Klepke. He drank and gave the bottle to Bendit. Bendit opened his mouth, showing one blackened tooth in his empty gums, and groaned as he drank. His eyes filled with tears. He emptied the bottle and grimaced as if he had made a mistake. He said, "In olden times vodka packed a punch. Today's vodka is water."

"It's ninety percent alcohol," Tevele Smearer said.

"Ninety shminety."

I was never offered any vodka, but Tevele gave me a few of his salt pretzels. Then they began to talk and their talk always led to stories. Bendit was saying, "After such a winter summer comes early. I'm afraid that when the ice melts, our river will be over its banks."

"The water never goes farther than Bridge Street," Tevele said.

"That's what you say. You're still a boy, what do you know? I remember a Passover when the water ran into the synagogue. The cantor was standing at the podium reciting the prayer for dew when suddenly a stream poured in from the antechamber and the congregation waded in water up to the knees."

"Did the cantor go on with the liturgy?" Tevele asked.

"The men might have continued but the women raised a commotion."

"Did they think that the water would come up to their balcony?"

"You know women. Give me a cigarette."

Tevele gave Bendit one of his fancy cigarettes. When Tevele lit a match, Bendit covered it with both hands as if to protect it from a wind. He blew out the smoke and said, "You don't fool around with water. This did not happen in your time. Near Kreshev there was a castle inhabited by an old squire. He was one of the Zamojski family. It happened before the serfs were freed. The fields and villages extended from Zamosć up to the River San. He was already on in years, but his wife was young and a great beauty. Most probably she stemmed from an impoverished house and had married a man about forty years older than she. The Polish squires were always engaging in lawsuits. If they lost in one court they appealed to a higher one, until it reached the Sejm or God knows where. It was all very costly and many noblemen went bankrupt even when they won the case. Drunkards they were all—from the smallest nobleman to the Radziwills and Czartoryskis. Many became sick from drinking. Every squire had his court Jew, and without him none of them would have had a shirt to his name. The court Jews took care of all the business of the nobles because their managers, commissars, marshals, and whatever they called themselves could only drink and whip peasants. The boss was actually the court Jew. Just the same, when the squire had a ball the court Jew was asked to disguise himself as a bear. They pulled his tail, made fun of him, but the Jew didn't seem to mind.

"This particular squire at Kreshev had a young wife whom he loved to distraction. He had a court Jew, Reb Zekele, with whom he used to play chess. Zekele knew the game better than the squire but he let him win. Once when Zekele let him win too easily the squire fell into such a rage that he tried to shoot him with a pistol. The squiress happened to be present and she tore the gun out of his hand. One day the squiress got sick. I think she had smallpox, and that was the end of her. The squire had summoned the greatest doctors from Lublin but they couldn't help her. As a rule Gentiles don't weep at a funeral as we do, but the squire howled so that you couldn't hear the priests chanting.

"In those years each squire had a family vault, a house with a roof over it. I don't know if the coffins were buried or just put inside the houses—what's the difference, the worms eat us all, whether we lie in the earth or in a golden casket. Am I right or not? Give me another cigarette."

"What has all this to do with water?" Tevele asked.

Bendit puffed on the cigarette and said, "There is a proverb,

'What the earth covers must be forgotten.' People thought that the squire would cry for a few weeks and then find himself another woman or else drink himself to death. But no, he fell into—what do you call it?—a melancholy. He called for Reb Zekele and asked him, 'What is the sense of a man's life if he is to end up rotting in the earth?' He said to him, 'We Christians know nothing. Perhaps the Jews have an answer.' Zekele told him what is written in the sacred books, but the squire fell into such a rage that he grabbed his whip and tried to beat up the court Jew. Zekele barely escaped with his bones unbroken. The squire also went to the rabbi—not to your grandfather but to the one before him. What could the rabbi have told him? 'This is God's will.' But for the squire that was not enough.

"I'm not going to draw it out. There was in Kreshev a carpenter, Meir, who made all the coffins in the region. The squire went to Meir and ordered, 'Make me a bed that looks like a coffin, so that when I die I can be buried in my own bed.' Meir probably thought the squire had lost his mind, but in those times a workman did as he was told. He made a coffin broad enough to contain a mattress, a pillow, and a quilt cover. The squire summoned the people of his castle and said to them, 'Since the end of every man is a coffin I'm going to start sleeping in a coffin right now.' In the winter he kept it in his bedroom. In the summer he put it in that little stone house and there he slept until it grew cold again. His friends asked him, 'What good does it do to sleep in a coffin?' and he replied, 'I don't want to forget my end. Also, I want to be as near to my wife as possible.'

You know the River San. In comparison to the Vistula it's a small stream. But that winter it kept on snowing day and night. After Passover the squire had his coffin carried over to the stone house and there he slept each night. In the middle of one of those nights the river overflowed. The squire slept and knew nothing. The door of the stone house stood open. The water rushed in, and soon the coffin was floating like a boat. It went out the door while the squire continued to snore—most probably he had tippled more than usual.

"When they realized in the castle what was happening, peasants were sent out to rescue the squire, but the water was deep and no boat was available. They waited for days until the water receded, and by then there was no sign of the coffin bed. Some said that it had reached the Vistula and from there had floated out to sea. Others believed that the demons had captured it. They even wrote about it in the newspapers of Lublin and Warsaw, and they talked about the event in half of Poland.

"But how long do people remember anything? Lost is lost. The squire had a nephew abroad, I think in Paris, and he was the heir. He came back and took over the whole estate. He was still a bachelor, but he soon married the daughter of a count who brought him a dowry of more villages and more peasants. The old squire was forgotten as if he had never existed. The crones who spun flax muttered that the squire had fallen to the creatures that are half women and half fish and succumbed to their songs.

"Ten years passed. Once when the squire's nephew sat with his family at dinner, a peasant woman came to the palace gate leading a little boy of eight or nine by the hand. The guard asked what she wanted and she said that she desired to speak with the young squire. The guard thought that she was crazy—who ever heard of a peasant woman talking to a squire? He lifted his stick as if to let her have it, but the peasant woman yelled, "I'm the old squire's wife and this is his child!" The guard took one look and saw that the boy resembled the missing man like two drops of water. There was a commotion in the court as they brought the peasant woman to the new squire. She told him that she lived in a village a day's walk from Kreshev. Her husband had been a forester in the woods of the squire of that region. The couple was childless.

On the night of the flood her husband happened to be in a small hut in the forest and he drowned there. The same night the water had also reached her house. She had no neighbors. When the water rose to her window she went up to the attic. The light of the moon was as bright as day and she saw floating in the water tables, stools, barrels, and even cradles. Suddenly she saw a floating-coffin. In it sat a man shouting for help. In the beginning she thought it was a mirage and a sign that her husband was dead. Then the man jumped out of the coffin and began to draw it toward her. If this had happened to a city woman she would have died of fright. But she was a hardened peasant. She screamed, 'What do you want? Who are you?' And he called back, 'I am Count Zamojski.' In the neighborhood it was known that he slept in a coffin or perhaps she recognized him. There was a granary near the house and the door stood open. The squire dragged the coffin into the granary, locked the door with a chain, and, half naked, climbed up to the woman in the attic. There they waited two days and two nights until the water receded. Soon after that the peasants found her dead husband. The squire remained in the attic until after the funeral."

"I'm sure in those two days the squire knew what to do with her," Tevele Smearer remarked.

"I think so. After the funeral the widow gave the squire her husband's clothes and made believe that she employed help. Not all the peasants were serfs then. Foresters and such had their own little properties. Many peasants were freed by the nobles or purchased their freedom. So she had a helper. She began to receive a pension from the court. When, after some months, she became pregnant and did not want to give birth to a bastard, the old squire married her. Their child was born. This was the boy the peasant woman brought with her."

"Why didn't the squire return to his court?" Tevele Smearer asked.

"This is what I'd like to know. There is a saying, 'One gets tired even of kreplech.' When you're a squire for sixty years you want something else. Besides, when a man sleeps in a coffin he's not in his right mind any more."

"What happened then?"

"In the beginning the young squire couldn't believe that all this was true. He asked, 'How long has my uncle been dead?' The woman replied, 'He died only yesterday, and he's lying in his coffin in the granary.' She also said that the squire had asked before his death that his coffin be placed beside the coffin of his first wife. The priest and the other noblemen had arrived, and the whole bunch of them got into carriages to go to the hut of the peasant woman. There they found the coffin with the dead squire dressed as a peasant. They all recognized him. They had him carried to church, where he lay in state for a night, and then he was buried near his first wife."

"What happened to the boy?" Tevele Smearer asked.

"They sent him to school somewhere in Lublin or Warsaw. There he got scarlet fever and died."

"Most probably they poisoned him."

"Who would poison a child in school? Although everything is possible."

"Didn't the squire ask that his son inherit his estate?"

"It seems he wanted him to grow up a peasant. He was never taught anything during the old man's lifetime."

"How about the mother?"

"She went back to her hut."

"It didn't come to a lawsuit?"

"No lawsuit."

"I never heard the story before," Shmuel Klepke said.

"What do you young people know, anyway?"

Bendit got up. He began to rub one hand against the other and look toward the door. After some hesitation he said, "I must go out."

"In this cold?"

"I can't do it here."

He opened the door and went out. Tevele Smearer winked. "He has his secrets."

"Does he still visit his daughters?" Shmuel Klepke asked.

"I saw him there myself. I had some business in Bujary and I returned late at night. Suddenly I saw Bendit. I hid behind a fence and watched him enter the brothel."

"Don't they have customers at night?"

"Not in the middle of the night."

"I wouldn't visit such daughters."

"A father is a father. Besides, what can he do in his old age? He would have to go to the poorhouse."

The door opened. Bendit entered with a cloud of steam. His clothes, his boots, his hat, everything was white from the snow.

"A blizzard."

"We may get snowed in and not be able to go home," Tevele Smearer said.

"For you it's a joke, hah," Bendit said. "Not far from Goray there is a forest, and once in the month of Heshvan two squires went to shoot hares. It was Sunday and they took their wives with them. It was as warm as a summer day. All day long they kept shooting animals and birds. Suddenly the sky became overcast and it started snowing. It also hailed. Pieces of ice the size of goose eggs fell from the sky. I remember that Heshvan like today. It thundered as if it were the middle of summer. All the paths disappeared and the squires lost their way. They would have frozen to death if they hadn't found a cave. They thought that the blizzard would stop during the night and they'd be able to go home in the morning. My dear friends, they remained in that cave almost a week. Later I saw the cave myself, and I couldn't imagine how four people could exist in there. They must have crawled one on top of the other like worms. They ate raw meat and drank snow. Peasants were sent to find them, but the peasants themselves lost their way. After a week the snow stopped falling and the sun reappeared. They got out of the cave and dragged themselves to Goray. By now they looked like savages. Their toes were frozen and the doctor from Janow chopped them off with an ax. Otherwise they could have gotten gangrene. Both couples returned to their courts.

"Don't interrupt me. One of the women became pregnant and around Tisha B'Av she gave birth. With an infant it's hard to see after whom it takes, but when the midwife took one look at it she knew it didn't come from this squire but from the other one who had been in the forest with them. She kept her mouth shut, but the older the child became the more people were aware of it. The squire who was supposed to be the father was dark and his wife was also a brunette, but the child had red hair like the other squire. The Polish squires all had bevies of poor relations who lived at their courts as hangers-on. Most of them were spinsters and they were forever fighting one another. When this child came into the world, the old maids began to whisper that it was a bastard. The talk reached the squire—besides, he wasn't blind himself. With the nobility honor is the most important thing. How was Poland torn to pieces? Every nobleman wanted to be king. In the Sejm when one nobleman said it was Sunday, another screamed it was Monday. When the Cossacks attacked Poland and slaughtered whole villages, the squires remained drunk in their castles, intriguing against one another. When the enemy approached, the squires twirled their mustaches, dressed up as for a ball in sable furs, put on swords each of which weighed a ton, and even wore golden chains around their necks. Their horses were fat and lazy. The squire would ride to war with his retinue blowing on trumpets. The Cossack was as light as a feather and his horse ran like an arrow from a bow. He moved like a demon, chopped off the squire's head, and carried it on his spear. This is how Poland fell apart.

"Yes, honor. The betrayed husband approached two of his friends and asked them to be witnesses at a duel. The redheaded squire was a giant, while the dark squire was small and wore mustaches down to his shoulders. When the witnesses informed the redheaded squire of the duel, his laugh could be heard over the whole estate. He said, 'What does he want? We were squeezed together in the cave like bedbugs. Who of us could know who we slept with? But if he wants a duel, let there be a duel. What does he choose to fight with, swords or pistols?' The two witnesses could easily have made peace. But what did they care? They chose pistols. The next morning both squires met in a meadow. First they greeted one another with compliments in the Polish manner. Then the little squire pulled the trigger and shot the redheaded one through the heart.

"The Russian government had forbidden duels, but the Russians themselves fought one another just for the fun of it. The little squire hid for a week or two. Then he came home and this made him honorable again.

"He was rich. He took good care of his possessions while the redheaded one had been a gambler and had had affairs with countless females. His widow was choked with debts and her estate was about to be auctioned off to the creditors. Women in such a position are not particular about their honor. She ordered the carriage and drove to her husband's murderer. She entered and said, 'Stanislaw'—this was his name—'you must help me.' She had slept with him in the cave and she could be familiar with him now. The little squire greeted her as one of his own and asked the maid to bring the baby. The visitor took one look at the baby and exclaimed, 'It is just like Zdzislaw.'

"Zdzislaw was what the red-haired squire was called.

"She began to kiss the child as if he were her own. The little squire said, 'If you love him so much, become his nurse and I'll take over all your debts.'

"To make it short, she agreed. She became the child's governess and the dark squire took over all her obligations. He was so shrewd that he was able to settle with the creditors to his advantage. He got the remainder of the other squire's fortune as well as his wife."

"And his own wife said nothing?" Shmuel Klepke asked.

"She feared him like the Devil."

"So he had two wives?"

"For a squire this was not unusual."

"What else?"

"I must go out again."

"Have you taken castor oil?"

"When one gets old one has difficulty urinating. I feel a pain in my bladder but when I go out—three drops."

"Don't fall into a cave," Tevele Smearer joked.

Bendit's face lit up. "If I had someone with me I'd stay there with her until Passover."

"A sturdy little man," Shmuel Klepke said after Bendit had stepped out.

"He was known for his strength," Tevele Smearer said. "Once the thieves of Piask came to Bilgoray at night. Bendit was the watchman. He blew his whistle, but the wind was also blowing and no one could hear. With his bare stick he beat unconscious three of the thieves and the others ran away empty-handed."

"Why didn't he marry again?" Shmuel Klepke asked.

"Why don't *you* marry?" Tevele Smearer asked back.

"If you see what I've seen, you lose the appetite."

"Just the same, a man cannot remain alone forever," Tevele Smearer said.

"You might as well marry one of Bendit's daughters."

Bendit opened the door. "Children, God has quarreled with his wife and she's tearing up the featherbed. The world is all white."

For a while all three were silent. Bendit looked at me. "Why do you sit here and listen? You should study, not pay attention to our chatter."

"I studied all day long."

"Your grandfather studied all day long and all night long. Right after the evening prayer he went home and your grandmother, peace be with her, gave him his supper. He ate only twice a day, morning and evening. He went to sleep immediately after the night meal, and at midnight he got up and began to study his books. I should know, I was the night watchman for thirty years, and I often passed Synagogue Street. Sometimes when it was cold I knocked on your grandfather's shutter and he opened the door for me. For some of our community elders a poor man is less than the mud under your nails, but your grandfather, the famous scholar, offered me a chair. A samovar was always boiling on his table and he poured tea for me.

"In Bilgoray there was a man called Melech Vishkower, a rich lumber dealer. He had a wife named Tsippa, and this Tsippa was a ball of Hell fire. They had no children. When Melech invited the congregation to his house on holidays, she locked the door and wouldn't let them in. She suspected all women of wanting to take her husband from her. Just the same, she cursed him vilely. She even let out her rage on God's creatures. When a dog or a cat passed her house, she was capable of throwing a stone at it. Her husband treated her well. She could have had maids all the time, but no maid could stay long in her house.

"Suddenly Tsippa got sick and went packing. One shouldn't say so but it made a holiday for the town. Immediately after the shivah her husband left for the forest. Everyone knew that he would not mourn for her very long. Only three months had passed when he reappeared with a new wife. He had married an eighteen-year-old girl, good-looking and an orphan, as peaceful as a dove. Her name was Ittele. The women of the town buzzed around her like bees on honey. A few months later the good tidings were heard that she was pregnant. I remember my mother, peace be with her, saying, 'Well, is Tsippa going to stand for this?'

"She did not stand for it. Once at night in the middle of the winter, when Ittele lay in bed, the feather quilt blew up like a lung and began to slap the orphan's face. The pillow bounced under her head. Ittele had a maid who was a relative of mine, Breindel. Ittele screamed for help and Breindel rushed in. She began to scream too, and both of them ran out to the street in their nightshirts. The town woke up. As a rule ghosts are afraid of people, but not Tsippa. Every night there was another commotion. Hot stones fell on the roof. The chimney spat fire. Dishes were broken. Once when Ittele went into the kitchen a potato grater struck her face. Forgive me, but Tsippa emptied out a night pot into Ittele's bed. When Melech came home and saw what was going on, he went to the rabbi of Turisk and the rabbi told him to summon Tsippa to a hearing.

"For such a proceeding three rabbis are needed. But your grandfather refused to attend. He said it was all witchcraft and idolatry.

"When the Hasids of Turisk heard what your grandfather had said, they all became his enemies. Two rabbis were brought from other villages. A quorum of ten men went out to Tsippa's grave, knocked at it with their canes, and summoned her to the hearing. The next morning a corner of the synagogue was fenced off with a sheet to be ready for Tsippa's soul. The synagogue was so full that a pin couldn't have fitted in. The rabbi of Turisk called out, 'Tsippa the daughter of Beila Dobba, since you refuse to rest in your grave and you bring anguish to your former husband and to his wife, we have summoned you to this court—' He used many Hebrew words and threatened Tsippa with excommunication, the blowing of the ram's horn, and black candles. The women wept as on Yom Kippur. I was there and saw everything. Suddenly the sheet began to shake and to bulge out as if someone were behind it, trying to come out. Better not ask me what happened. There was such an outcry and a stampede that three people were crushed to death."

"I heard the story." Tevele Smearer nodded.

"Was it really Tsippa?" Shmuel Klepke asked, smiling.

"It was the community he-goat. There were some wise guys in town who didn't believe in ghosts. The wall on the right side of the synagogue had a window leading to the antechamber. When the hearing began and the antechamber emptied, they dragged in the community he-goat and pushed him through the window into the synagogue behind the sheet. It was all planned. Before someone dared to lift up the sheet to discover the he-goat, half the women had fainted. The three were killed trying to get out of there. One of the tricksters went to prison. I mean to say that your grandfather was a wise man. He foresaw that nothing good could come of something like that."

"What became of Melech Vishkower and his new wife?" Shmuel Klepke asked.

"He sold his house and they left town."

"The hearing didn't help?"

"She kept on pursuing them."

It became quiet, and Bendit said, "Children, let's go home. It's already daybreak in Pintchev."

"I'm afraid to walk alone," I said.

Bendit smiled, showing his single black tooth. "What are you afraid of? Tsippa has been silent a long time."

The snow outside fell as dry and heavy as salt. The blasting wind whipped it into coils. Tevele Smearer and Shmuel Klepke turned into Lublin Street, where they both lived. Bendit walked with me. From time to time he stopped to catch his breath. "Does your mother let you study so late?" he shouted.

"Twice a week I study late."

"I could tell you a story about this but I'd rather not."

"Why not?"

"You'd be afraid of your own shadow afterward."

He took me to our house. The shutter in the kitchen was open and I could see Bendit through the window after I got inside. He stood there with hunched shoulders, shuffling his feet, writing letters in the snow with his cane, and looking to right and to left. He shook his head and seemed to be mumbling and giving signs to some unseen being. Then he began to walk in the direction of the Sands, where his daughters had their brothel.

Translated by the author and Herbert R. Lottman

Property

I SAT in the Café Royal with Max Peshkin—that's what I shall call him here. I was young, recently from Poland, and he was a former anarchist whose memoirs had just been published in three volumes. In the thirties, anarchism was already "played out" in the United States (it was Peshkin's own expression), but there was still a remnant of the old group, and they published a magazine in Yiddish. Max Peshkin had invited me to lunch and had brought me his books as a gift. He was small, with a head of milk-white hair, a round red face, and eyes that were not yet tired.

We ate onion rolls with sour cream, drank coffee in glasses, and Peshkin said, "What used to go on here—it's all over. Our Socialists have completely cooled off. They use the old phrases, but the spirit isn't there. As for our Communists, they read the Red sheet every morning and repeat it like gospel. Yesterday Bukharin was a great leader; today he is a traitor. If their paper came out saying that Stalin was an enemy of the people and a mad dog, they would repeat that, too. The anarchists were different. Anarchism always attracted people with individuality—even the ignorant ones had a kind of independence. When I came to America in the early nineties, active anarchism was already declining, though they went on talking about the protest meeting at the Haymarket in Chicago and about the four who were hanged:

Spies, Parsons, Fischer, and Engel. The Marxists had taken over. But in the Yiddish neighborhood on the Lower East Side anarchism still flourished. Not all of us wanted to wait until capital was concentrated and Kautsky or De Leon gave the signal that the hour of the revolution had arrived. It's true we had no important theoreticians or leaders in New York, but we had literature from London, where Kropotkin was king. Besides, guests used to come from Russia and Germany—sometimes even from Spain. Our meetings were always crowded. Most of the delegates from Russia spoke Yiddish. We were vain enough to believe that if a couple of bombs were thrown the masses would rise up like one man and abolish all governments.

"I don't have to tell you that anarchism is a name for many different theories and movements. There's a big difference between Proudhon and Bakunin. As for Stirner, he is a chapter by himself. Before I came to America, I was a student. I read all these theoreticians—first in Russia and then in England. But on the Lower East Side most of our people did not know one from another. They were emotional anarchists. They used to say, 'Let's get rid of the tyrants, then something will happen.' Alexander Berkman went to prison and was half forgotten, but Emma Goldman and her preachings of free love made a tremendous impression—especially on the women.

"When you read my memoirs, you will find the names of Maurice and Libby. I couldn't tell all the facts about those two, because there are still people alive who knew them and might guess whom I meant even if I changed the names. Besides, it would take a writer of fiction to do this story justice. I thought it might interest you. If you have time and nothing better to do, I would be glad to tell it to you."

"I have time and I have nothing better to do," I assured him.

"Good. Probably in fifty years nothing of this will be remembered. But you are still a young man. How old are you? Not thirty-five yet? I thought you would be older."

"I will be thirty-three in July."

"*Nu*—you are still a baby. With that Maurice I got acquainted around eighteen hundred and ninety-three, four —even five. Here in the United States the anarchists were just talking, but in Russia they were red hot with zeal. They were divided into a dozen groups: the Chernoye Znamia (The Black Flag), Chlebovoltsy (Demand for Bread), the Beznatchaltsy (Without Government). The most remarkable were the Bezmotivniki (The Motiveless). They claimed that man is allowed to kill, rob, and commit arson without any motive—simply to spite authority. I don't remember exactly when, but they threw a bomb at the Hotel Bristol in Warsaw. You might not have been born yet. In Odessa, they blew up a ship. In Bialystok, one of their bombs killed a Bundist leader, Esther Riskin. Later we learned that a number of the anarchists had become ordinary bandits—perhaps they were bandits to begin with.

"Maurice was a little man with black eyes and long curly hair. He also had a beard—a tiny beard. He used to hold forth at our meetings. I am ashamed to admit it, but of all our activities our infamous Yom Kippur balls were the most important. It was considered an atheist mitzvah to have a ball on Yom Kippur, to eat non-kosher food, preferably pork, just to annoy the Almighty. Maurice was the very soul of these undertakings—not as a dancer but as a propagandist. What did he do for a living? Nothing, really. His wife, Libby, was the provider. She sewed ladies' blouses for the shops. I think she made men's shirts, too.

"Even though I was a greenhorn, I taught English to foreigners at the Educational Alliance. I happened to be looking for a room. The place where I boarded was terribly dirty.

The food was unspeakable. Someone told me that Maurice had a room to let. He was a funny type. He always wore a pelerine, a black hat with a wide brim, and a flowing tie. Though he was small and frail, his speeches were fiery. Normally he had a soft voice, but when he got on the subject of capitalism he grew shrill. He attacked those anarchists who put their reliance on propaganda. He believed only in terror. His wife used to come listen to him, but I had the feeling that she didn't take him very seriously. She wasn't much taller than he—darkish, appealing. She wore her hair long, combed back in a bun—not cut short like the anarchist women's. When she smiled, there was a dimple in her left cheek. She often wore a pleated skirt and a blouse with a high collar. When Maurice raged against Rockefeller, she sat on a bench at the back of the room and yawned. Sometimes she had her knitting with her.

"One evening after his speech, I went up to him and asked if it was true that he had a room for rent. He seemed pleased and called Libby. They told me that they had a large apartment on Attorney Street and that they would be more than glad to have one of their circle as a boarder. In those days, for me to move was a small matter. All I had to do was pack my valise and carry it from Rivington Street to Attorney Street. The house where they lived was in an area that would be called a slum today—a third-floor walkup. The toilet was in the hall. If one wanted to take a bath, one went to the barber; the barber was also the bath attendant. The room they gave me was small, the window faced the street, and the furniture was an iron cot. What else did I need? Where I had been, we slept three in an alcove.

"There was a sign over the living-room door of the apartment: PROPERTY IS THEFT—a quotation from Proudhon. Pictures of Godwin, Proudhon, Bakunin, Kropotkin, Johann Most hung on the walls, and, of course, the Chicago Martyrs.

Perhaps Maurice wouldn't have left Stirner out, but no picture of him existed. A bookcase was filled with brochures on anarchism and Socialism. I forgot to tell you that I was an ardent follower of Stirner. I had studied not only Stirner but also Feuerbach, whose disciple Stirner had been before he rebelled. My own ideal was a 'community of egotists.' I wanted to become the 'perfect egotist'—a 'world history in itself,' ready 'to serve myself and everything that is mine.' Those were the Stirner phrases. For Proudhon, property was evil; for Stirner, property was the essence of humanism. What real tolerance was, none of us knew. Since I did not approve of the slogan over the door, I immediately fell into a debate with Maurice. That's all he wanted. He was always ready to argue. I went on quoting Stirner and he quoted Proudhon. I had taken the room without meals, but Libby made supper for me anyhow. We were all three sitting at the table, and Maurice was railing against property and everything connected with it. He foresaw that after the revolution the words 'mine' and 'thine' would be dropped from the dictionary. I asked him, 'How will you tell a man the good news that his wife has given birth to a son?' And Maurice screamed, 'The whole institution of marriage will disappear! It is all built on slavery. What right has one person to own another?' He became so wrought up that he almost knocked over the table. Libby said to him, 'Your plate —I mean our plate—will soon fall, and our belly will remain empty. In addition, we will make spots on our pants.'

"I laughed—the woman had a sense of humor. But Maurice was dead serious. He yelled, 'You are joking, eh? All injustice and wickedness come from property. Why are the imperialists at one another's throats? What is the cause of all exploitation?' In his rage he attacked Stirner, too: 'What a contradiction—a *"community of egotists."* ' I said, 'What about love? If a man loves a woman, he wants her for himself, not for others.' 'Jealousy is not a natural feeling,' Maurice answered. 'It is a product of feudalism and capitalism. In ancient times when people lived in communes, all children belonged to the commune.' 'How do you know this?' Libby asked. 'Were you there?,' and Maurice said, 'It's an established fact.' He mentioned Buckle or some other historian. We went on arguing until one in the morning. Meanwhile Libby washed the dishes. She opened the door from the kitchen and said, 'I am dead tired. Can't you put off the discussion until tomorrow? It won't get stale.' Maurice was so excited that he didn't even answer her. She said, 'In that case, I will go to sleep.' Then, turning to me, she added, 'Your bed —I mean *our* bed—is made.' "

"Did she become your lover?" I asked.

Max Peshkin lifted his eyebrows. "Really, you have intuition. But don't be in a hurry. One needs to have patience, too.

"I have forgotten to tell you that after supper I had a slight argument with Libby. I asked about the cost of the meal and she was insulted. 'I am not your cook,' she said. 'I invited you as a friend.' The next morning she gave me breakfast and I said, 'To be invited once is one thing, but to eat free of charge steadily is a different thing.' I was earning five dollars a week, and that was considered a decent salary. I told her that I would not eat with her again until she set a price for the meals. After some haggling we came to a decision. I could pay the cost of the food. In a few days we became like old friends. I went to the market on Orchard Street and bought bargains for her. I carried her bundles to and from the shops for which she worked. She knew Russian and Polish quite well but her English was bad, and I offered to give her private lessons. Now *she* wanted to pay *me*, and there was another argument. We were all young, but we didn't realize it.

"Since I am by nature a jealous person, I have never been able to imagine that someone else is not. I was careful not to make Maurice jealous. But he seemed happy that Libby and I were close. Once when I told him I wished to go for a walk, he proposed that Libby go with me. Libby blushed and said, 'What kind of business is this? Perhaps he wants to be alone.' 'Nonsense,' Maurice said. 'It's pleasant to have company.' Another time when I had two tickets to the Yiddish theater, he asked me to take Libby with me. 'She sits all day at the sewing machine,' he said. 'Let her have some diversion.' I took her to the theater and we saw Jacob Adler—the Great Eagle, as he was called—in a melodrama by Gordin. Then we went to Grand Street to eat knishes. The streets were crowded with people who bought next day's Yiddish newspaper and discussed the editorials as well as the Second Avenue plays. We came home late; Maurice was beaming with delight. He was preparing a speech about the exchange of products in a free society. Before Libby went to bed she said to me, 'Thank you for the evening.' 'Saying thank you is not enough,' Maurice said. 'What shall I do—fall at his feet?' And Maurice said, 'At least he has earned a kiss.' 'I was not brought up to kiss strange men,' Libby said, 'but since you order it I will do so.' She came over, put both hands on my cheeks, and kissed me on the mouth. I must tell you that I was still a virgin at the time. I had had affairs, but they were all romantic and platonic. On Attorney Street, right across from our house there was a brothel, but those females disgusted me. Besides, how can an idealist make use of white slavery? That was a capitalistic institution, a sport for Morgan and Company.

"That night Maurice was tired and went to bed at the same time as Libby. A gas lamp burned in my room. It had happened a few times that I had fallen asleep without extinguishing the lamp. My door opened and Libby appeared in a nightgown and slippers. Her hair was loose and fell to her shoulders. She said, 'If you are not going to read, I will turn off the lamp. It's a pity to waste gas.' And she smiled and winked.

"It's more than forty years since that evening, but it seems to me like yesterday. In those days, the minute I put my head on the pillow I slept. But this night I was too restless. Libby's kiss had aroused me—not so much the kiss as the way she had held my face. Her hands had been warm, almost hot.

"Just the same, after a while I did fall asleep. It was winter and the nights were long. I woke up not knowing whether I had slept one hour or six. The room wasn't completely dark; there was a glow from a street lamp. Suddenly I saw Libby. She was standing near my bed. Even though I considered myself a freethinker, I thought for a few seconds that it was a she-demon—one of the Lilith spirits who tempt yeshiva boys to sin. I said, 'Libby?' She bent down and there was both passion and mockery in her whisper, 'Take me into your bed. I am cold.' I almost died from fright. My teeth chattered. 'Where is Maurice?' I asked. 'He gave me permission,' she said. 'He doesn't wish to own any property.'

"If a thing like this should happen to me today, I would probably have a heart attack, but I was twenty-three years old and my blood was boiling. I forgot all prohibitions. Some time ago, I read that a man who was forced to fast forty days ate a rat. There is a kind of hunger that deadens all other feelings. Only when she left me a half hour later did I realize what we had done. But I was so exhausted that I couldn't stay awake.

"The next morning all three of us ate breakfast in the kitchen as usual, and Maurice seemed solemn, almost happy. He said, 'I cannot preach one thing and practice something else. Among us there is brotherhood.' In those years we did not know the things that we know today. But I had read Forel, or perhaps it was Krafft-Ebing—I don't remember exactly—and I understood that it wasn't all altruism. There are men, and also women, who have an urge to share. I was a lucky devil; I had everything all in one—a room, food, a mistress. Maurice became overwhelmingly friendly. He praised me to the skies. He also kissed me. When he made a speech, I had to sit with Libby in the front row. And he always found an excuse to quote me. He was ready to concede everything to me with the exception of Stirner. He still criticized him without mercy. At this time, Stirner had not yet been translated into Yiddish and our comrades knew little about him. But Maurice attacked him at every opportunity. He actually made Stirner known on the Lower East Side.

"Two years passed, and they seemed my happiest years. After a while I was bringing my paycheck—the *paydy,* they called it in our Americanized Yiddish—to Libby. And she did great things with those five dollars. I believe I even got a raise. She fed me, bought my clothes, and pampered me. There are no secrets. The Lower East Side is like a little village. Besides, Maurice did not conceal our affair. He actually boasted about it. Our comrades were busy discussing it. They all asked the same question: what will happen if there is a baby? But we were careful that there shouldn't be one.

"After a while the thing became routine, and I noticed that Libby was less ardent. The people on Attorney Street maligned us. Libby had *landsleit,* and they wrote to her relatives in the old country and told about our abominations. Some even threatened us with deportation. We made plans to settle in the West. Somewhere in Oregon there were the remains of the original communes founded by Socialists and utopians. They were falling to pieces because each member had his own ideas not only about how to liberate humanity but also about how to stack hay and milk cows. Many of the members became lazy and refused to work. Some went mad.

In the midst of all this there was a sensation: a Russian revolutionary who had been sentenced to twenty years' hard labor in Siberia had managed to escape, and after wandering for weeks and months through forests and over tundras had made his way to America. He had reached the Pacific and was said to have become a stowaway on a freighter bound for San Francisco. You will not believe me, but at this moment I have forgotten what he called himself. Was it Barushin? No. Kalushin? Also no. This is the trouble with old age—one forgets names. I mention him in my memoirs. It turned out that he was not a revolutionary at all but a criminal liar, a charlatan. He was sentenced not for throwing a bomb, as we had been told, but for robbery. But this is putting the cart before the horse. We believed then that a pillar of the Revolution was visiting New York and that he refused to divulge his true name because he planned to return to Russia. There was a notice in the Yiddish press that he was going to speak in one of the largest halls downtown. There even were hints that he was a rebellious son of the Russian aristocracy. All false. But one thing was true: he was a Great Russian, not a Jew— a huge fellow, blond, blue-eyed, and he spoke true Russian. With our comrades, this was a mark of distinction. So many guests from Russia had been our own brethren—small and dark—and they all spoke Russian with an accent. He received so much publicity that hundreds of the faithful who came to hear him had to be turned away from the hall. They remained standing outside—I among them. I happened to arrive late. Maurice was to introduce him and Libby had a front-row seat. Naturally, I could not hear what Maurice said, but that Muscovite had the voice of a lion. I remember that after he had spoken for ten minutes I said to someone standing near me, 'He is as much a revolutionary as I am a Tartar.'

"You might be able to write a whole novel about this, but

I will give the plain facts: Libby fell in love with him. She told me about it later: she glanced at him once, she said, and knew that her fate was sealed.

"Strange, I remember in all its details how our affair began, but I have forgotten how it collapsed. It seems to me that I did not sleep at all that night at Maurice's. It might very well have been that Maurice had taken the Muscovite home after the lecture and that I had to go somewhere else. It happened so suddenly. One day in Maurice's house I had everything—and the next day I had to pack my bag and go. They both were infatuated with him, Maurice and Libby—Maurice even more than she. Now that there is a Freud, we at least have the names for such behavior. Such is man that if he has the name for something it ceases to be a riddle. But then we didn't have the names. Or, if we did, I did not know them. I remember carrying my valise down East Broadway and stopping every few steps. I had been driven out of Paradise without even knowing my sin.

"After a few months, this impostor was unmasked. Letters came from Russia denying all his pretensions. But by that time I had awakened. I grasped that people like Maurice are hero-worshippers. Living with him, Libby had grown to be like him. I understood that since they could exchange me so easily for someone else, there had not been any substance there to start with. What good could come to a young man from staying with a perverted couple? Not long after, I met the woman who became my wife and the mother of my children. She died some time ago.

"What happened to Libby and Maurice? They were divorced. Heaven and earth conspire that such things do not endure. Libby married an elderly man, a druggist. Maurice went, if I'm not mistaken, to Oregon, where he lasted until the colony disintegrated. He came back with an ugly woman older than himself. Both he and Libby withdrew completely from the movement. I met him many years later in Miami Beach. I was looking for an efficiency apartment, and a building on Meridian Avenue had been recommended to me. I came into the lobby and saw Maurice. He was the landlord. A woman tenant was quarreling with him because she had no hot water. He had grown fat and flabby and was dressed in the Miami Beach fashion, in shorts and a pink flowered shirt. He had become bald, too.

"For a while I stood there and listened, and then I approached him and said, 'Maurice, my dear, "Property is theft." '

"He fell over me and cried like a child. He had been divorced from his second wife and had remarried. He offered me an apartment for a song. His wife boasted to me that her kreplech were famous all over the world. But I was not in a mood for nonsense. Besides, his third wife was even uglier than his second. They are both dead."

"What happened to Libby?" I asked.

Max Peshkin closed his eyes. "She too is already in what we all tried to make—a better world."

Translated by the author and Dorothea Straus

The Lantuch

"THERE *are* lantuchs," my Aunt Yentl said. "I wish there weren't. Actually, most of them don't do much damage —just the opposite. It all depends where they are and with whom."

Aunt Yentl blew her nose into a batik kerchief. Even though she was *telling* the story, not reading it from a book, she wiped her brass-framed glasses. She nodded her head, and her bonnet with all its ribbons and rhinestones wobbled. Aunt Yentl was not a blood relative. She came from generations of villagers—innkeepers, bailiffs, dairymen. She had the high bosom, broad shoulders, and high cheekbones of a peasant. Her amber-colored eyes were as mild as a dove's. Before Uncle Joseph married her, some gossiper told him that she was once a milkmaid. My uncle was supposed to have answered, So it will be an unkosher mixture of meat and milk.

Aunt Yentl polished her glasses until they shone and reflected bits of the afternoon sun. Then she put them back into their case.

"What were we talking about?" she asked. "Oh, yes. Lantuchs. There was a lantuch living in my parents' home. He kept house between the oven and the woodshed. After we had to leave, he stayed. Lantuchs don't wander; once they settle somewhere, it's forever. I never saw him. They can't be seen, you know. I was just a child when we packed up and left for Turbin, but my mother and my sister Basha treated him like one of the family. The Gentiles call him *'domowik'* —a familiar spirit. Sometimes when Basha sneezed, he whispered *Gesundheit.*

"We had a steambath in the yard that had two stones on the floor. The Polish maid who served us used to bring logs, light a fire, and when the stones got hot, she poured buckets of water over them until the vapor became as dense as farina. I had to stay in the house at bath time. Why should a baby sweat? But on that particular occasion I refused to stay with my nanny and I went with them. It was the only time I ever saw my mother and sister naked. I forgot to mention that the maid spoke Yiddish. When my mother called out, *'Shefele!'* she immediately poured a bucket of water on the stones and they sizzled and seethed. If it became too hot, my mother cried out *'Fire!'* and the woman opened the door a little so that a breeze wafted in. I cried and made a big fuss before they consented to take me to the baths, and in the confusion my sister forgot to bring towels with her. As for the maid, when she wasn't needed she went to the barn to attend to the cows. My mother scolded Basha about the towels and it occurred to my sister to call out in rhyme:

> Lantuch,
> Give me a Handtuch!

"Why draw it out? The lantuch brought the towels. I don't remember it myself, but I heard about it from my mother and from Basha more than once. Why should they have lied? Things like this happened in olden times. Now the world is so corrupted that the demons just keep hidden.

"But the story I want to tell you had nothing to do with our house. It happened in Turbin and it began years before we moved there. A man called Mordecai Yaroslaver lived there, and those who knew him swore that such a beautiful and saintly man had never existed before. He had a wife, Baila Fruma, and an only daughter, Paya. It is said in the Holy Book that those whom God loves he takes to himself. Reb Mordecai was still a young man, not yet forty. Suddenly he got a pimple on his chest—it wasn't a pimple, really, but a blister, as if he had been burned. That blister turned into many blisters and, God preserve us, he died. The greatest doctors couldn't save him. His house was just outside of town and it had a garden, sheds, an outhouse, a granary. He traded in grain, flax, and cattle. He was wealthy, but when a merchant dies, his debtors don't rush to pay their debts. In those days one dealt in faith. Reb Mordecai wrote down who owed how much in a notebook, but the notebook vanished.

"Baila Fruma was always ailing and she kept away from people. Just as her husband was close to everyone, she was remote. She called Turbin a godforsaken village. When the shining light of the family passed away, everything fell to pieces. After the funeral, Baila Fruma went to bed and she stayed there until she died—at least thirty years, if not more. She dismissed her servant and Paya became everything, maid, cook, her mother's nurse. Paya was blond, white-skinned, gentle. Most probably she took after her father, although she had some of her mother in her too. I barely knew her because when we moved to Turbin, things were already reaching their end. A girl must marry and the matchmakers showered Paya with suitors, but Baila Fruma ruled the roost from her bed. The candidates were brought to her bedside, and Baila Fruma would look them over and question them. None of them pleased her. What she really wanted was not a husband for her daughter but a son-in-law for herself, to wait on her like a courtier. She stipulated to all the matchmakers that after the wedding Paya must stay in her mother's house. For her own sake she made so many difficulties that

Paya eventually married a fellow who was supposed to be wealthy, with a drop of erudition, but was basically coarse. The whole of Turbin could see that Paya was falling into ugly hands, and they warned her. But Baila Fruma contended that they were envying her good luck. Paya, she should forgive me, was a slave to her mother. If Baila Fruma had told her to dig a ditch and bury herself alive, she would have done it. There are such daughters—who knows why? The strong ones always rule, even in the poorhouse. Baila Fruma was sure that her son-in-law—Feitel was his name—would play her tune, but he didn't care a hoot about her. What he could sell he sold, and what he could steal he stole. He emptied out the house like a locust. Paya became pregnant and gave birth to a girl, Mirele, and everyone agreed that she was the spitting image of her grandfather. She lit up the house. But her father, that vulgar bumpkin, had his own calculations. When he realized that there was nothing more to rob, he divorced his wife and went God knows where.

"A divorcée with a child is not always unwanted merchandise. But now Baila Fruma was not inclined to share her daughter with a man. She wanted her entirely for herself. Paya lost her courage. There are people who once burned never try again. Besides, what man would have wanted to be Baila Fruma's toady? A man wants a wife for himself, not a handmaid for his mother-in-law. To make it short, Paya never remarried. Feitel had squandered everything and for a while mother and daughter began to sell their knitting. Paya worked as a seamstress. They owned their house and in those days food was dirt cheap. They had apples, pears, and cherries from the orchard. They rented a few acres of land out to a farmer and he gave them part of the vegetables he grew as rent. Nobody died of hunger in those days, but what sense is there to such a life?

Suddenly Paya got sick and she did exactly what her

mother had done—she took to bed. It happened years later.
By then Mirele was seven or eight years old. And here begins
the story of the lantuch. They had a lantuch in the house
and he became the boss. You are laughing? This is no laugh-
ing matter. The whole of Turbin knew it. How else could a
house with two sick women and a young child keep going?
Even now when I talk about it, ants run up and down my
spine."

Aunt Yentl shuddered. She looked at the shawl that was
lying on the sofa and said, "Don't make fun of me, children,
but I'm cold."

Aunt Yentl wrapped the shawl around her, and for a while
she was silent. She drew her brows together and seemed to
consider whether or not she should go on with the story. She
looked at me from the corner of her eye as if to say, "How
can a little boy understand these things?" My mother said,
"Tell, Yentl."

Aunt Yentl stirred.

"I wasn't there, but the whole town couldn't have been
crazy. There *was* a lantuch in their house and he took over.
He chopped wood, carried water from the well—at night,
never during the day. In the winter he heated the stove. I said
before that they aren't visible, but this one was seen. That
winter, there was a blizzard in Turbin. Even old people
couldn't remember anything like it—snow dry as salt falling
in heaps. Roofs collapsed. It was actually more like hail.
Houses were snowed under and it took days to dig them out.
Turbin had a charitable group which called itself the Guard-
ians of the Sick, made up of strong men—coachmen, butch-
ers, horse dealers. When someone got sick and needed care,
they would go and help out. During the storm, the towns-
people suddenly remembered Reb Mordecai Yaroslaver's
family. Motl Bentzes, one of the Guardians, a giant of a man,

went to see what was going on. The whole house was buried
in the snow. Only the chimney stuck out. What a job! He
started to dig his way toward the house. As he dug he heard a
grating sound from the other side of the snow. Someone was
digging his way out. Who could it be? Finally he cleared a
space and saw a little man, broader than tall, wearing a tas-
seled cap, wielding a shovel three times as tall as he was.
Dusk had fallen. Motl Bentzes tried to talk to the little man,
but he stuck his tongue out and it stretched to his navel. In a
second he vanished and his shovel fell on Motl Bentzes. It was
the lantuch. Later Motl Bentzes went to the rabbi and told
him what had happened. The event was recorded in the com-
munity ledger.

"Somehow Mirele managed to grow up. Don't ask me
how. Children survive in gypsy wagons, in robbers' caves.
One day she was a child; the next day she shot up and was
a grownup. Her mother Paya had been known to be a rec-
luse from girlhood. She never mixed with the other girls,
and besides, Baila Fruma had discouraged any socializing.
But Mirele was gay and outgoing. She sang and danced. In
the winter she and her friends got together to chop cabbage,
pickle cucumbers, and shell peas. In the summer they went to
pick mushrooms and berries from the forest. She taught her-
self to sew and crochet, as well as to embroider on canvas.
They asked her, 'Is it true that a lantuch lives in your
house?' And she would ask, 'What's a lantuch? I've never
even heard the word!' They asked her, 'Who manages your
household?' and she would reply, 'We manage.' The girls
asked to be invited to her house for dancing, and of course
they wanted to see what went on. But Mirele would say
laughingly, 'My grandmother doesn't like to entertain!' The
townspeople tried to figure it out: even if they had tucked
away a nest egg, it should have been used up a long time ago.
Who did the cooking? And who was taking care of Mirele's

clothing? She was dressed like the daughter of a squire and her cheeks bloomed. Someone must have been giving her pocket money. She often went to Brina the Baker and bought herself buckwheat pretzels. She always had a few groschen for games with her girl friends.

"Their house was built so that you couldn't look through the keyhole or the windows. To get to the door you had to go through a yard and walk up a stoop. There were always stray dogs around their yard. Probably they belonged to the tenant farmer or they were mongrels the dogcatcher had missed. Mirele answered anything you asked her, but no one ever got the truth. 'Who cooks for you?' she would be asked, and she'd answer, 'My mother.' 'Does she get out of bed?' 'Once in a while,' she would say. 'Why doesn't she go to a doctor?' Mirele would answer, 'She's too lazy,' smiling as if it were a joke. In a small town everyone knows what is cooking in every pot. Everyone knew that uncanny things happened in that house.

"Well, Mirele grew up to be a dazzling beauty. The boys went into fits about her. Matchmakers flocked around, but they could never get to Baila Fruma or Paya. The door was always locked and chained. The matchmakers tried to speak to Mirele herself, but she replied, 'What do I know?'

" 'So how will the cat ever cross the water?' they asked, meaning, how would she ever get married? And she replied, 'So the cat will stay on the other side.'

"In a little town—maybe in a big town too—you can't cut yourself off from everyone. If you set yourself apart from the community, they start maligning you. People began to say that the Evil One was actually the head of the family. If he chopped wood, carried water, and was able to dig the house out of the snow, then maybe he was more than just a servant. Mirele was not the innocent girl she appeared to be. My dear ones, people began to draw away from her. The girls refused

to walk with her on the Sabbath. The matchmakers stopped
proposing matches. She wasn't invited to engagement parties
or weddings. I was still a child then, but I listened and I
understood. Mirele walked alone on Lublin Street, where we
lived, dressed like a princess; her shoes glittered on her feet,
but the girls wouldn't even look in her direction. The tailors'
apprentices and the butcher boys followed her—they didn't
dare approach her. Every time she passed the marketplace,
people stared at her from the windows. Where was she going?
What was on her mind? How could she exist with those two
dismal creatures, her mother and grandmother?

"Soon Mirele stopped going out. Once in a great while
she appeared in the shops to buy something. It was dis-
covered that the postman sometimes delivered to the family
a letter sealed with wax. No one knew where it came from.
In the cold months they were completely forgotten. I don't
know why, there was more snow around their house than in
any other part of the town. Whirlwinds blew in drifts from the
fields. As a matter of fact, no one was sure if Baila Fruma
was still alive, but since she hadn't been buried in the ceme-
tery, she was counted among the living. If things can be this
way in a village, God only knows how it is in a big city. Once
my father, peace be with him, brought a poor man to have the
Sabbath meal with us. A wandering beggar sees all sorts of
things and tells all kinds of tales. We asked him about Lublin
and he said, 'It's a city full of corpses.' 'What do you mean?'
my father asked. The beggar said, 'When someone dies in a
little town, everyone knows about it and the body remains in
its grave. But in a big city everyone is a stranger, and the
dead get lonely and rise up. I myself,' he said, 'met a man
in Lublin who had been dead for years. His name was
Shmerl Srotsker. I was walking on Levertov Street and he
came up to me. I stopped and he stopped too. I was so
astonished I couldn't open my mouth. Then I said, Shmerl,

what are you doing here? And he said, Do you know? So do I. Then he walked away and disappeared.'

"Where am I? Oh, yes. The lantuch. If things go well, these imps hide in the cellar or between the stove and the wood-shed, but when people loosen their grip, they take the upper hand. Perhaps he wasn't a lantuch but a hobgoblin or a mooncalf. They grow on rot, like toadstools. That witch Baila Fruma had consumed Paya and both of them set about destroying Mirele. Surrounded constantly by her mother and grandmother, Mirele too became morbid. It was said that she slept all day and was up all night. Zalmon, the night watch, used to go past their house and he heard Mirele laughing madly. The Evil One was tickling her, yowling like a tomcat."

"Do you mean to say that the lantuch had sinful dealings with them?" my mother asked after some hesitation.

Aunt Yentl put two fingers to her lips. "I don't know. How should I know? But lantuchs are male, not female. There is a story in *The Right Measure* about a goldsmith who lived in a cellar with a she-demon and he had five children by her. These things do happen. Why would three females stay alone without husbands? And if Turbin was too small for them, why didn't they sell the house and move somewhere else? God spare us—what people can get used to! That Baila Fruma was wicked. Even while her husband was alive, strange things were said about her. She kept two black cats and was seen gathering herbs in the fields at full moon. She could cast spells too. Poor Paya had no will. But that Mirele succumbed surprised me. The truth is that if you offer the Devil a finger, he grabs the whole hand. It was said that the lantuch danced and sang for them and did somersaults. Someone heard him reciting rhymes like a wedding jester. They had a huge bed and it was said they all slept there. I don't even want to think about it. Baila Fruma and Mirele never visited the synagogue. Paya used to come on Rosh

Hashonah for the blowing of the ram's horn. Once I saw her there. Her face was covered with warts. One of her eyes was as large as a calf's and the other was half closed. She seemed to have become deaf, because people talked to her and she didn't answer.

"One night after Succoth, someone knocked at Wolf Kashtan's door. Turbin had a fire brigade and Wolf was their chief. They had a wagon, a worn-out mare, and a beat-up water barrel. It was in the middle of a cold, wet night. Wolf Kashtan opened the door and outside stood a freak, neither man nor animal—half dog, half monkey, with elflocks and matted fur. 'What do you want?' Wolf asked, and the freak squeaked, 'There's a fire at Baila Fruma's.' Then he dissolved into the fog.

"By the time Wolf Kashtan harnessed the horse and filled the water barrel, Baila Fruma's house was a heap of ashes. All three women were burned to coal. There was nothing to bury. From what Wolf Kashtan said about that monster, it was clear that it was the lantuch."

"How did the fire start?" my mother asked.

"Who knows?"

"Maybe the lantuch kindled it," my mother said.

"If he did," Aunt Yentl asked, "why would he have gone to the firehouse?"

My mother pondered for a long while and then she said, "Demons, like people, get caught in their own traps. Maybe the lantuch had had enough."

Translated by the author and Laurie Colwin

The Son from America

THE VILLAGE of Lentshin was tiny—a sandy marketplace where the peasants of the area met once a week. It was surrounded by little huts with thatched roofs or shingles green with moss. The chimneys looked like pots. Between the huts there were fields, where the owners planted vegetables or pastured their goats.

In the smallest of these huts lived old Berl, a man in his eighties, and his wife, who was called Berlcha (wife of Berl). Old Berl was one of the Jews who had been driven from their villages in Russia and had settled in Poland. In Lentshin, they mocked the mistakes he made while praying aloud. He spoke with a sharp "r." He was short, broad-shouldered, and had a small white beard, and summer and winter he wore a sheepskin hat, a padded cotton jacket, and stout boots. He walked slowly, shuffling his feet. He had a half acre of field, a cow, a goat, and chickens.

The couple had a son, Samuel, who had gone to America forty years ago. It was said in Lentshin that he became a millionaire there. Every month, the Lentshin letter carrier brought old Berl a money order and a letter that no one could read because many of the words were English. How much money Samuel sent his parents remained a secret. Three times a year, Berl and his wife went on foot to Zakroczym and cashed the money orders there. But they never seemed to use the money. What for? The garden, the cow, and the goat provided most of their needs. Besides, Berlcha sold chickens and eggs, and from these there was enough to buy flour for bread.

No one cared to know where Berl kept the money that his son sent him. There were no thieves in Lentshin. The hut consisted of one room, which contained all their belongings: the table, the shelf for meat, the shelf for milk foods, the two beds, and the clay oven. Sometimes the chickens roosted in the woodshed and sometimes, when it was cold, in a coop near the oven. The goat, too, found shelter inside when the weather was bad. The more prosperous villagers had kerosene lamps, but Berl and his wife did not believe in newfangled gadgets. What was wrong with a wick in a dish of oil? Only for the Sabbath would Berlcha buy three tallow candles at the store. In summer, the couple got up at sunrise and retired with the chickens. In the long winter evenings, Berlcha spun flax at her spinning wheel and Berl sat beside her in the silence of those who enjoy their rest.

Once in a while when Berl came home from the synagogue after evening prayers, he brought news to his wife. In Warsaw there were strikers who demanded that the czar abdicate. A heretic by the name of Dr. Herzl had come up with the idea that Jews should settle again in Palestine. Berlcha listened and shook her bonneted head. Her face was yellowish and wrinkled like a cabbage leaf. There were bluish sacks under her eyes. She was half deaf. Berl had to repeat each word he said to her. She would say, "The things that happen in the big cities!"

Here in Lentshin nothing happened except usual events: a cow gave birth to a calf, a young couple had a circumcision party, or a girl was born and there was no party. Occasionally, someone died. Lentshin had no cemetery, and the corpse had to be taken to Zakroczym. Actually, Lentshin had become a village with few young people. The young men left for Zakroczym, for Nowy Dwor, for Warsaw, and sometimes for the United States. Like Samuel's, their letters were illegible, the Yiddish mixed with the languages of the countries where they were now living. They sent photographs in which the men wore top hats and the women fancy dresses like squiresses.

Berl and Berlcha also received such photographs. But their eyes were failing and neither he nor she had glasses. They could barely make out the pictures. Samuel had sons and daughters with Gentile names—and grandchildren who had married and had their own offspring. Their names were so strange that Berl and Berlcha could never remember them. But what difference do names make? America was far, far away on the other side of the ocean, at the edge of the world. A Talmud teacher who came to Lentshin had said that Americans walked with their heads down and their feet up. Berl and Berlcha could not grasp this. How was it possible? But since the teacher said so it must be true. Berlcha pondered for some time and then she said, "One can get accustomed to everything."

And so it remained. From too much thinking—God forbid —one may lose one's wits.

One Friday morning, when Berlcha was kneading the dough for the Sabbath loaves, the door opened and a nobleman entered. He was so tall that he had to bend down to get through the door. He wore a beaver hat and a cloak bordered with fur. He was followed by Chazkel, the coachman from Zakroczym, who carried two leather valises with brass locks. In astonishment Berlcha raised her eyes.

The nobleman looked around and said to the coachman in Yiddish, "Here it is." He took out a silver ruble and paid him.

The coachman tried to hand him change but he said, "You can go now."

When the coachman closed the door, the nobleman said, "Mother, it's me, your son Samuel—Sam."

Berlcha heard the words and her legs grew numb. Her hands, to which pieces of dough were sticking, lost their power. The nobleman hugged her, kissed her forehead, both her cheeks. Berlcha began to cackle like a hen, "My son!" At that moment Berl came in from the woodshed, his arms piled with logs. The goat followed him. When he saw a nobleman kissing his wife, Berl dropped the wood and exclaimed, "What is this?"

The nobleman let go of Berlcha and embraced Berl. "Father!"

For a long time Berl was unable to utter a sound. He wanted to recite holy words that he had read in the Yiddish Bible, but he could remember nothing. Then he asked, "Are you Samuel?"

"Yes, Father, I am Samuel."

"Well, peace be with you." Berl grasped his son's hand. He was still not sure that he was not being fooled. Samuel wasn't as tall and heavy as this man, but then Berl reminded himself that Samuel was only fifteen years old when he had left home. He must have grown in that faraway country. Berl asked, "Why didn't you let us know that you were coming?"

"Didn't you receive my cable?" Samuel asked.

Berl did not know what a cable was.

Berlcha had scraped the dough from her hands and enfolded her son. He kissed her again and asked, "Mother, didn't you receive a cable?"

"What? If I lived to see this, I am happy to die," Berlcha said, amazed by her own words. Berl, too, was amazed.

These were just the words he would have said earlier if he had been able to remember. After a while Berl came to himself and said, "Pescha, you will have to make a double Sabbath pudding in addition to the stew."

It was years since Berl had called Berlcha by her given name. When he wanted to address her, he would say, "Listen," or "Say." It is the young or those from the big cities who call a wife by her name. Only now did Berlcha begin to cry. Yellow tears ran from her eyes, and everything became dim. Then she called out, "It's Friday—I have to prepare for the Sabbath." Yes, she had to knead the dough and braid the loaves. With such a guest, she had to make a larger Sabbath stew. The winter day is short and she must hurry.

Her son understood what was worrying her, because he said, "Mother, I will help you."

Berlcha wanted to laugh, but a choked sob came out. "What are you saying? God forbid."

The nobleman took off his cloak and jacket and remained in his vest, on which hung a solid-gold watch chain. He rolled up his sleeves and came to the trough. "Mother, I was a baker for many years in New York," he said, and he began to knead the dough.

"What! You are my darling son who will say Kaddish for me." She wept raspingly. Her strength left her, and she slumped onto the bed.

Berl said, "Women will always be women." And he went to the shed to get more wood. The goat sat down near the oven; she gazed with surprise at this strange man—his height and his bizarre clothes.

The neighbors had heard the good news that Berl's son had arrived from America and they came to greet him. The women began to help Berlcha prepare for the Sabbath. Some laughed, some cried. The room was full of people, as at a wedding. They asked Berl's son, "What is new in America?"

And Berl's son answered, "America is all right."

"Do Jews make a living?"

"One eats white bread there on weekdays."

"Do they remain Jews?"

"I am not a Gentile."

After Berlcha blessed the candles, father and son went to the little synagogue across the street. A new snow had fallen. The son took large steps, but Berl warned him, "Slow down."

In the synagogue the Jews recited "Let Us Exult" and "Come, My Groom." All the time, the snow outside kept falling. After prayers, when Berl and Samuel left the Holy Place, the village was unrecognizable. Everything was covered in snow. One could see only the contours of the roofs and the candles in the windows. Samuel said, "Nothing has changed here."

Berlcha had prepared gefilte fish, chicken soup with rice, meat, carrot stew. Berl recited the benediction over a glass of ritual wine. The family ate and drank, and when it grew quiet for a while one could hear the chirping of the house cricket. The son talked a lot, but Berl and Berlcha understood little. His Yiddish was different and contained foreign words.

After the final blessing Samuel asked, "Father, what did you do with all the money I sent you?"

Berl raised his white brows. "It's here."

Didn't you put it in a bank?"

"There is no bank in Lentshin."

"Where do you keep it?"

Berl hesitated. "One is not allowed to touch money on the Sabbath, but I will show you." He crouched beside the bed and began to shove something heavy. A boot appeared. Its top was stuffed with straw. Berl removed the straw and the son saw that the boot was full of gold coins. He lifted it.

"Father, this is a treasure!" he called out.

"Well."

"Why didn't you spend it?"

"On what? Thank God, we have everything."

"Why didn't you travel somewhere?"

"Where to? This is our home."

The son asked one question after the other, but Berl's answer was always the same: they wanted for nothing. The garden, the cow, the goat, the chickens provided them with all they needed. The son said, "If thieves knew about this, your lives wouldn't be safe."

"There are no thieves here."

"What will happen to the money?"

"You take it."

Slowly, Berl and Berlcha grew accustomed to their son and his American Yiddish. Berlcha could hear him better now. She even recognized his voice. He was saying, "Perhaps we should build a larger synagogue."

"The synagogue is big enough," Berl replied.

"Perhaps a home for old people."

"No one sleeps in the street."

The next day after the Sabbath meal was eaten, a Gentile from Zakroczym brought a paper—it was the cable. Berl and Berlcha lay down for a nap. They soon began to snore. The goat, too, dozed off. The son put on his cloak and his hat and went for a walk. He strode with his long legs across the marketplace. He stretched out a hand and touched a roof. He wanted to smoke a cigar, but he remembered it was forbidden on the Sabbath. He had a desire to talk to someone, but it seemed that the whole of Lentshin was asleep. He entered the synagogue. An old man was sitting there, reciting psalms. Samuel asked, "Are you praying?"

"What else is there to do when one gets old?"

"Do you make a living?"

The old man did not understand the meaning of these

words. He smiled, showing his empty gums, and then he said, "If God gives health, one keeps on living."

Samuel returned home. Dusk had fallen. Berl went to the synagogue for the evening prayers and the son remained with his mother. The room was filled with shadows.

Berlcha began to recite in a solemn singsong, "God of Abraham, Isaac, and Jacob, defend the poor people of Israel and Thy name. The Holy Sabbath is departing; the welcome week is coming to us. Let it be one of health, wealth, and good deeds."

"Mother, you don't need to pray for wealth," Samuel said. "You are wealthy already."

Berlcha did not hear—or pretended not to. Her face had turned into a cluster of shadows.

In the twilight Samuel put his hand into his jacket pocket and touched his passport, his checkbook, his letters of credit. He had come here with big plans. He had a valise filled with presents for his parents. He wanted to bestow gifts on the village. He brought not only his own money but funds from the Lentshin Society in New York, which had organized a ball for the benefit of the village. But this village in the hinterland needed nothing. From the synagogue one could hear hoarse chanting. The cricket, silent all day, started again its chirping. Berlcha began to sway and utter holy rhymes inherited from mothers and grandmothers:

> *Thy holy sheep*
> *In mercy keep,*
> *In Torah and good deeds;*
> *Provide for all their needs,*
> *Shoes, clothes, and bread*
> *And the Messiah's tread.*

Translated by the author and Dorothea Straus

The Briefcase

C onstant rushing is supposed to be a peculiarly American disease. Although foreign-born, I am one of its victims. There are times when I am in such a rush that I have to make an effort to remember that my name is Kohn. I'm always in a hurry, even when I sleep.

That winter I worked on a newspaper, wrote books, went on lecture tours, and also agreed to be visiting professor of creative literature at a Midwestern university. Though I spent only two days there every other week, I rented an apartment and had a telephone installed. The university supplied me with an office, and that was equipped with a telephone. Both phones kept ringing; the din greeted me each time I opened either door. Professors wished to get acquainted, their wives invited me to lunch or dinner, students had papers for me to read, journalism majors wanted interviews, members of the local Jewish community asked me to give a talk at their center.

Since I'm incapable of saying no, I agreed to everything. The little notebook in my pocket was so crammed with telephone numbers and addresses that I could hardly decipher my own handwriting. Since I had an apartment in Manhattan and an office at the newspaper, I was receiving mail and books at four addresses. There was no time to go through the bundles of papers that accumulated everywhere. Sometimes I didn't even open envelopes. People like me have secretaries, but I was never in one place long enough. Besides, I couldn't possibly have anyone know my crazy relationships with women. Over years of a long bachelorhood, I had assembled an invisible harem of has-beens and might-have-beens. I made promises to all of them. Some were still comparatively young, others had grown old. One had cancer. Some had married—several even a second or third time. Their daughters treated me like a stepfather. I was expected to send congratulations and gifts on their birthdays and other anniversaries. I neglected most of them and woke up nights feeling guilty. I often communicated with them by telepathy, and they seemed to respond. Telepathy, clairvoyance, and premonitions became substitutes for letters, telephone calls, visits. I wronged everybody, but all these women continued to shower me with love. Maybe because—in my thoughts, at least—I was still devoted to them. Before I fell asleep, I'd pray for them.

In February of that winter, I had a week without any commitments. The rabbi of a California congregation where I was to speak died suddenly, and my appearance was postponed. As soon as I heard the news, I decided to spend the free days with Reizl. I had been with her the night before in the Bronx. My plane was to leave at noon and I was up at six o'clock. Reizl's sick mother, Leah Hinda, slept late. Reizl had prepared breakfast for me. When I reached home at eight, I found a wire under my door canceling the lecture.

Before I left Reizl, she had complained, "You used to stay with me for days. Lately, you never deal out more than one night."

All of a sudden I had a whole week!

First, I lay on the couch and tried to make up for the night of broken sleep. We had come home from the theater at 1 a.m. The telephone rang and I let it ring. I thought of Esau's words when he sold his birthright for a mess of pottage: "Behold, I am about to die: and what use is my birthright to me?" The kind of life I led made me feel that I was slowly committing suicide. I had reached the point where I never bought more than five razor blades at a time. To purchase ten seemed to dare fate—I might have a heart attack or a nervous breakdown.

About eleven I woke up as tired as when I had lain down. I looked around the apartment. My cleaning woman had had an operation and gone home to her old mother in Puerto Rico to recuperate. The place was filthy. Books, magazines, shorts, ties, handkerchiefs lay scattered on the floor. The desk was littered with papers. Though I tried to be orderly, I lived in perpetual confusion. I couldn't ever find anything. I lost bills. I misplaced my pen and my glasses. I'd put one shoe on and not be able to locate the other. One day I discovered that my cashmere coat was gone. I looked for it, even in crannies too small for a vest, but it had vanished. Had I been robbed? There was no sign that my apartment had been broken into. And why would a thief take only that coat? I opened the closet again and found it among my other clothes. Can absentmindedness make a man blind?

I called Reizl and told her the happy news that I had a free week.

"Come up here right away!" she cried.

"No. You come and spend the day with me. We'll go to your house later."

"You know I can't leave Mother."

"You can for a few hours."

After much haggling, Reizl agreed to "come into town," which was how she described a trip to Manhattan. Leah Hinda had an old neighbor who would look in on her. Leah Hinda suffered from high blood pressure and half a dozen other illnesses, yet somehow she managed to stay alive. She took countless pills and kept the strictest diet I'd ever heard of. Having survived ghetto life and concentration camps, she was determined to live to be ninety.

Although Reizl had promised to come in an hour, I knew it would take her three. At home she ran around half naked and in worn-out slippers. But when she ventured into town she put on her Sabbath best. Before leaving the house, she would lay out the pills her mother needed: heart restoratives, diuretics, vitamins. Leah Hinda never knew how to take these American medicines.

Now there was time to shave, have a bath, maybe even look over a manuscript. But the telephone gave me no respite. I had lost my razor and spent over a quarter of an hour searching for it. Suddenly I remembered putting it in the valise to take to California. As I began to unpack, the phone rang again. The voice was the voice of an adult imitating a child, and I guessed that it was Sarah Pitzeller. Though she suffered from cancer, she had remained playful. "Did you know your Sarah had died?" she said, in the childlike voice.

I was speechless.

"Why don't you answer? Are you afraid of the dead? They do no harm. You can't even hurt them any more. Isn't that wonderful?" She hung up.

The doorbell rang three times. That must be Reizl. She always arrived in turmoil. She brought with her the tensions of ghetto life, of secret frontier crossings, of the D.P. camp. She was blond, blue-eyed, and slim and, though almost forty, looked like a girl in her twenties. A dressmaker by profession, she had been asked to be a model. But she knew no English. Besides, in the ghetto she had developed the habit of drinking.

Before she closed the door, she was shrieking, "I won't ever go anywhere by subway again! I'd rather die!"

"What happened?"

"A bum attached himself to me. I said to him, 'Go, mister. I no understand English.' But he wouldn't stop pestering me. Drunk like Lot. A cutthroat's eyes. When I got out, he did, too. Dear Father in Heaven! I thought any minute he'd take out a knife."

"Your dress is too fancy, and so—"

"Are you justifying him? You're always on the side of my enemies. You could be Hitler's advocate. Anyway, this is a plain dress. You'll never believe it, but I bought the material for one dollar off a remnant table . . . I've forgotten my matches. I need a cigarette."

I brought Reizl matches.

She inhaled, blew out a cloud of smoke, and said, "I have to have a drink."

"So early in the day?"

"Give me a glass of brandy. I've brought you some lunch."

Only now I noticed that she was carrying a basket. I had asked her many times not to bring me food. Her dishes attracted cockroaches and mice. But she did as she pleased. She ignored my warnings that her smoking and drinking would make her sick. She used three packs a day. She even smoked in the middle of the night. I wanted to give her a small glassful, but she snatched the bottle from my hand and filled a tumbler. She gulped it down with the speed of an alcoholic, and for a moment her features were oddly distorted. Then she became cheerful.

Though she had brought lunch for the two of us, I had to eat it almost all myself. Cigarettes and liquor satisfied Reizl. She had cooked the dishes she knew from her home town: potato kugel, noodle pudding, mushroom gruel, and prune dessert. While I ate, she complained, "I didn't even dare to dream of a meal like this in the ghetto. All we prayed for was dry bread. I once saw two Jews beat each other up on account of a moldy crust. They were both whipped by the Nazis for disturbing the peace. Where is the God you scribble about? He's a murderer, not a God. If I had the power, I'd hang anyone who babbles about Him."

"Then you'd send me to the gallows?"

"Not you, dear. I'd muzzle you, that's all. You don't know what you're saying—you're like a tiny tot without any sense. How a little boy like you can write books is a miracle. The truth is you don't do the writing—a dybbuk has entered your body. He is the writer. If you don't eat that kugel down to the last crumb, I'll go home and never look at your face again. Pour me another drink."

"I won't give you any more—not even if you stand on your head."

"Oh, come on! I want to forget this stinking world for a few seconds. Who did you take to the theater to see *The Turkish Wedding*?"

"No one."

"But you spoke of a woman companion in your review."

"Oh, that's just my style."

"What style? Don't use fancy words with me. I know you run around with women. I hope they all burn up. Don't I satisfy you? You went to *The Turkish Wedding* with some bitch. Let Pharaoh's plagues strike her. She probably wallowed in luxury here in America while I was rotting in a bunker with rats and lice. Now she steals my man. I hope she roasts in Hell!"

"You're damning someone who doesn't exist."

"She exists, all right, along with the others. I wish they didn't. That's why I drink. Give me another drop."

"No."

"You won't? Then you're a cold-blooded murderer. You may be descended from rabbis, but my guess is that your mother gave birth to a bastard. Don't look at me like that. It's happened in our accursed history. How else do you account for the blond heads and snub noses among us? We're not Jews. It's Gentiles persecuting Gentiles! The real Jews perished long since. Maybe a handful have survived in Jerusalem. Give me a little liquor or I'll die."

"Go ahead."

Reizl fixed her light-blue eyes on me. "I don't know why I love you. What do I see in you? For years I yearned for a man. Finally I found one. Crazy and wicked."

We embraced and I tried to lift her up and one of her shoes fell off. The telephone rang. They were calling from my university. The chairman of the English Department wanted to remind me of a lecture I was to give the following day. Heavens, I'd completely forgotten! I asked him whether it could be put off. He said a special hall had been reserved for it, and a change would be out of the question.

As I spoke, Reizl's face grew flushed. She wrenched herself from my arm and limped over to get her shoe. On the way, she fell. Lying there, she began screaming, "That's how all our plans end up! I curse the day I—"

"Come with me."

"You know I can't, you conniver. Unless I poison my mother first."

"But I have to go."

"Go then, but when you come back you'll find two corpses. I've earned this fate for wanting to stay alive. No one should survive what I have—it's a sin. They died around me like flies, and I had fantasies about meat cutlets and love. That's why I'm being punished. Don't come near me again. You're my worst enemy."

I looked at her and saw a bony nose, a pointed chin, sunken cheeks. When she came in, she had looked like a young girl. Now middle age had caught up with her. I noticed wrinkles at the corners of her eyes. Her nostrils flared.

She yelled, "Give me the bottle! I'm going to get dead drunk."

"Not in my apartment."

"Hand me that bottle. There's nothing else for me to do but drink. Why did God create the world? Answer me that. He's no God. He's a devil. He's a Hitler, too—and that's the bitter truth."

"Shut up!"

"So, you've turned pious, eh? You're afraid of my blasphemies? He sat in His seventh heaven, watching children being dragged off to gas chambers. Angels sang Him songs of praise and He basked in heavenly glory. Give me the bottle. If you don't, I'll kill myself right now."

The title of my lecture was "Is There a Future for the Literature of the Subconscious and the Absurd?" Even while I spoke I could tell that the audience disagreed with me. There was mumbling and coughing, followed by hostile silence. One woman tried to interrupt me. I did not realize it but I had attacked the psychologizers and the sociologizers of modern fiction. At the discussion period, the students used Kafka and Joyce in their arguments against me. And how about the symbolists? Did I mean to turn the clock of literary history back to the realism of Flaubert? Some of my class had written long, obscure stories portraying the "inner man." Others were trying in their writing to rebuild society—or at least to tear it down. A professor pointed out that my theory of literature did not tally with my own writing, which is symbolical, often mystical. I tried to clarify my views, but the chairman announced that it was time for refreshments. We went to a hall where liquor and punch were served. This reception had been arranged in my honor, but the professors of literature ignored me and chatted among themselves. They told each other "in" jokes. I withdrew to a corner, sipping my punch— an outsider.

A woman came up to me. I recognized her, but I couldn't think of her name or where and when we had met. She looked both young and aging, as if she had just emerged from an illness or some crisis. Was she a graduate student, a professor, I wondered. She had black eyes, black curly hair, a high forehead, and a slightly hairy chin. Her black dress did not suit her. The glass she held was almost empty. She spoke in the hesitant manner of the tipsy. "Don't you recognize me?"

"I know you," I said, "but I haven't any notion who you are."

"Rosalie Kadisch."

"My God!"

We made a motion to kiss each other, but our glasses got in the way. I was afraid of drenching her in punch. She said, "I've grown old, but you haven't changed."

"What else is there besides growing old?" I said. "But what are you doing here? Where have you come from? What's been happening to you?"

She smiled shrewdly, showing her poorly spaced, yellowed teeth. "I've come from the Holy Land and am giving a course in contemporary Hebrew literature. I'm also writing my thesis."

"What happened to your Gentile boy friend?"

"You do remember, then. He married a rich divorcée."

"Has he stopped wanting to redeem humanity?"

"His wife has a tight hold on him. She has four children by her first husband and is pregnant now."

"Where do they live?"

"In California, like all crackpots."

"How about you?"

She winked. "What about me?" Then she told me about herself. In Jerusalem, she had fallen in love with a young professor who was to get his divorce any day but stayed with his wife. She had had an affair with an Italian student years her junior, but marriage with him was out of the question. She had had a liaison with an Arab. Now she rejected love entirely.

"What do you do instead?"

"I smoke pot."

"Is it enough?"

"Better than listening to the confessions of impotent men."

"Have things gone that far?"

"Yes, I've grown cynical," she said. "I'm totally disillusioned about everyone and everything. But I have to get my doctorate. Without it you earn next to nothing."

"How are your parents?"

"They've given up expecting anything good to come of me."

It had grown late. Rosalie said, "I have an apartment here. Would you like to come over for tea or coffee? I never go to bed before two o'clock. I don't have to teach tomorrow. Don't worry, I won't seduce you."

I wanted to say goodbye to people, but the chairman and his wife had gone. I didn't know the other guests. This university was like a city. As we left, Rosalie took my arm. The temperature outside was freezing. An icy wind blew. I had bought myself specially warm boots, thick gloves, and a mask to protect my face. Peering through the openings, I felt like a member of the Ku Klux Klan. We walked along dimly lit, snow-covered alleys, the wind forcing us backward. It penetrated my clothes, chilling me to the ribs. Drifting snow whirled around us. I remembered the descriptions of journeys to the North and South Poles I had read as a boy. The snow-laden street lamps diffused a dim glow. The pavement was slippery and we hung on to each other so as not to fall. A greenish-blue star sparkled above a roof. Down here it was eleven below zero; up there it might be a hundred million degrees above.

Rosalie Kadisch and I climbed three flights to her apartment. There were books and magazines everywhere—on her Hide-a-Bed, her chairs, the floor, even on the refrigerator and the gas range. Quickly she cleared them away and put on the teakettle. She offered me liqueur and cookies. I'm no great drinker, but I wanted to warm up after the walk. We drank "*l'chaim*" and she said, "I never forgot you. I wanted to write my thesis on your work, but I couldn't find enough reference material."

Suddenly I remembered that I was supposed to call Reizl. There she was in the Bronx, waiting. She might try to phone me. When I told Rosalie, she said, "You needn't be embarrassed. Call her."

I dialed and heard Reizl's voice. It was harsh. She had not forgiven my leaving her.

She asked, "How was the lecture?"

"So-so."

"You've forgotten that it's an hour later here. I wanted to go to bed."

"There was a cocktail party for me. I couldn't call from there."

"Are you in your apartment now?"

"Yes," I lied, regretting it at once.

"You're not. You're a cheat and a liar. I called your apartment five minutes ago."

"I just walked in," I said, knowing I was making matters worse.

Reizl said, "O.K. Hang up. I'll call you right back."

I was about to answer, but she had already rung off. I sat there dumb. I could hear the phone ringing in my empty apartment. I could hear Reizl's furious tirade. Well, I thought, this time I've lost her. It's all over between us.

Rosalie gave me a sidelong glance. "Don't worry," she said. "She'll make up with you."

"Never."

"Try a reefer. You won't get hooked on one."

"No. I'd rather have another glass of liqueur."

I tried to console myself. This wretched love, I thought; the entire romantic claptrap wasn't worth a chipped penny. How right the younger generation was—they no longer demanded faithfulness and were putting an end to jealousy. Ninety-nine and nine-tenths of our so-called instincts are inculcated by social hypnosis.

Rosalie served tea and cookies. There was no sense in rushing home. She was cultured, not bad-looking. In any case, we both belonged to a tribe that was destroying itself.

A week or more passed. I went on another lecture tour. The weather continued to deteriorate. Newspapers announced snowstorms and unprecedented cold waves across most of the country. Trains couldn't get through, and help had to be sent to the half-frozen, hungry passengers. In the winter, I usually traveled by train rather than by air. My little notebook indicated that I was to be in the town of M——, in the Midwest, by evening, and the hotel where I was to stay. Somewhere I had a letter from the organization that had invited me, but I had packed it in my briefcase with my lecture notes. Ordinarily I had no need of addresses or directions. As soon as I checked in at the hotel, I'd be called by whoever was in charge of the program. He would take care of me from that moment until my departure. I gave the same talks at synagogues and universities, to Hadassah ladies and librarians.

In Chicago, I tried to get a sleeper or roomette, but none was available. Because of the weather, I had to get to my destination some fifteen hours before lecture time. My train was to arrive at 4 a.m. No harm in that, I decided. I could stay in the hotel and work. The organization's representatives would most certainly invite me to lunch and to dinner. I was no longer accustomed to travel by coach, but it's not my nature to brood about trifles. I found a window seat. The car was warm. In Chicago, I had picked up a newspaper, a magazine, and the autobiography of a sex maniac. I had also bought a sandwich and an apple, in case I got hungry in the night. I was afraid that some bore might sit down by my side, but the coach was half empty.

We passed through a city hidden by snow and dense fog. Trucks and cars inched along the road. Factory stacks spewed smoke. Here and there a chimney belched flames. After a while I lowered the shade and began to read. As usual, the newspaper told of murders, rapes, fires; the editorials dealt with the Mafia, the danger posed by drug addicts. The magazine caried a long piece about an actress who had suddenly become famous and was getting $20,000 for an appearance. The sex maniac described the circumstances leading to his psychosis: a broken home, an alcoholic father, his visits to brothels, his mother's lovers. It was all both shocking and tiresome. I began to ponder the future of literature: what could a fiction writer add to the naked facts? Sensationalism and melodrama had become our daily diet. The unbelievable was all too believable.

I yawned and turned pages. Though I wasn't hungry, I ate the sandwich and apple. For a quarter I rented a pillow from a porter, leaned back, and tried to nap. Gradually darkness enveloped the car. I closed my eyes, half dozing, half musing. I had surely lost Reizl. Whenever I called her, she hung up. Someone will turn up, I thought. I started dreaming, though I could still hear the conductor calling out the stations. I must have fallen asleep later, for he had to rouse me. We had arrived at M——.

I took down my coat, my garment bag, and briefcase. I was the only passenger to get off. The wind was freezing. It was quite a walk from my coach to the platform. For a hundred years or so, the station had been a symbol of hurly-burly and noise; now it was dark and empty. A black man was snoring on a bench. I went out to look for a cab. It seemed hopeless, but at last one turned up. The driver took my things. I told him the name of my hotel.

"Where is that? I never heard of it."

I put my hand in my breast pocket to check. My notebook wasn't there. The driver got out a little book of his own, and a flashlight to read directions. I was surprised. Reservations were usually made for me in well-known, first-class hotels. We passed through brightly lit streets, then drove around dark, narrow lanes. Suspicion came over me. Was he intending to rob me? The taxi stopped in front of a shabby, third-rate hotel. I was furious at the group that had invited me. I decided to go back to New York early the next morning. I paid the driver, who rang and knocked at the locked door. After a while, a sleepy fellow came out. He had on a sweater. I asked whether there was a reservation in my name.

He shrugged. "A reservation? No."

Something was wrong. This place didn't even have an elevator. The fellow led me up a narrow staircase. It stank of gas and coal fumes. He opened a door and turned on a single bulb hanging from the ceiling. The room had peeling wallpaper, torn linoleum on the floor, a metal bedstead, and a rickety chest of drawers. It reminded me of the furnished rooms I had occupied during my poverty-stricken years. Soon the clerk left. Only now I realized that a real calamity had struck me. The briefcase I had carried off the train was not mine, and mine contained my speeches and other important papers; I must even have squeezed in my little notebook. As luck would have it, I had packed my traveler's checks, too. I don't know to this day why I did that, unless the forces that direct a man's life intended to cause me the greatest possible anguish. All I possessed was two dollars and some change.

I looked around for a telephone, but there wasn't one in the room. Anxious as I was, something inside me mocked at the trap I was caught in. I had one hope—that my hosts would come for me the next day. But I began to doubt whether I had gone to the right hotel. No organization would put up its speaker at a shambles like this. It was all a mistake. It became clear to me that I was being punished for disappointing Reizl. Her curses were coming to pass. As usual in times of trouble, my faith reawakened.

I became aware that the room was cold. The radiator was covered with dust, and the paint was cracking; it gave off no heat. I turned down the bed and caught sight of a gray sheet and dirty-looking pillowcase. There was a whiff of bedbug spray. I closed my eyes and tried to listen to the unconscious in me, the power that according to von Hartmann can never be mistaken. Who and what drove me into this pitfall? It had all the signs of self-sabotage.

I undressed, got into bed, using my coat as an extra blanket. If only I had my little notebook! I couldn't remember a single telephone number except my own and Reizl's. My apartment in New York was empty, of course, and Reizl wouldn't talk to me. I was afraid I wouldn't be able to sleep, but I went off in a heavy slumber.

The next morning I went to a public telephone and called Reizl's number collect. There was no answer. I tried again after an hour, then two and three hours later, without any luck. As a rule, when Reizl was out her mother would pick up the phone. Had she murdered her mother and done away with herself? I tried to remember other telephone numbers but was plagued with amnesia. There was only one thing to do—track down some Jews and find out where my lecture was to be given that evening. But I must eat first. I had had no breakfast, and hunger gnawed at me. I walked into a cafeteria and had pancakes, two rolls, and coffee. That came to eighty-five cents. My wealth now consisted of $1.58. A taxi was out.

I walked till I found some shops. Among the names was a Morris Shapiro. I'll find out something here, I thought. Maybe Morris Shapiro was planning to go to my talk tonight. I entered the store. It was big, but the merchandise was shoddy. Tables were covered with nightgowns, blouses, dresses, sweaters, scarves, hosiery—all kinds of cheap odds and ends. It was broad daylight, yet the lights were on. I thought of the tale about King Solomon. Asmodeus had had him flung out four hundred miles from Jerusalem. The King of Israel went about shouting, "I am Solomon!" At least he was a king. Who was I, after all? One of thousands of writers in America—a Yiddish writer, to boot.

I looked for someone who might be Morris Shapiro but could see only lady customers and saleswomen. I walked over to one of them. "Is Morris Shapiro here?"

Smiling, she took stock of me. "Mr. Shapiro is out."

"When will he be back?"

"What do you want him for?"

Stammering, I began to explain. She half listened. Occasionally, she called to another saleswoman. Her doll's face was framed by curly hair dyed blond.

"Mr. Shapiro is in Chicago today," she said finally.

"Could you direct me to a synagogue or to a rabbi?"

"I'm not Jewish. Hey, Sylvia!"

She pointed to a little woman with black hair, who was wearing the same light-blue smock as the other saleswomen. Sylvia was busy with a customer. I waited while a middle-aged woman twice tried on an apron, unable to decide whether to buy it. Sylvia stood beside her absentmindedly, chewing gum. Eventually the customer said, "I'll go look in the mirror."

I started to tell Sylvia about my dilemma.

She looked annoyed. I was wasting her time. She said, "There are several synagogues here, but I think they're open only on the Sabbath."

"Would you know where one of the rabbis lives?"

"No. Look in the phone book."

"Where can I find one?"

"At the Western Union office."

"And where's that?"

"Across the road."

I thanked her and left. I couldn't see a Western Union sign. Had she fooled me, or was I going blind? It was two-fifteen by my watch. My speech was scheduled for six hours from now.

In spite of the cold, the street was packed with pedestrians, and cars and trucks moved bumper to bumper, as in New York or Chicago. The people all looked sullen and impatient. An elderly woman dragged a dog on a leash. He had stopped at the trunk of a tree and would not budge. The woman swore at him. "Lord of the universe, what did You need all this for?" I mumbled. At that instant I saw the Western Union sign. I stepped into the office, got hold of a telephone directory, and turned the pages to "J." There was no organization beginning with the word "Jewish." Jews in the Midwest were probably not keen about advertising their affiliation. What was a man to do in these circumstances—lie down and die? I had a publisher in New York but couldn't recall the telephone number there. Anyway, the business was on the verge of bankruptcy. Recently, one of the secretaries had complained that she had not been paid for five weeks. Besides, my editor was getting a divorce and was somewhere in Reno.

I searched the yellow pages under the heading "Churches." I found two synagogues listed. I was about to make the calls, but I had no dimes. Meanwhile, someone had entered the only telephone booth. From the way he settled himself, I could see that he wouldn't be out soon.

I had forgotten the taste of poverty during the years I'd been earning my living by writing and lecturing. It came back to me now. I'd had a late breakfast, but I was hungry again. I waited for the Western Union operator to give me change; he sat at his telegraph key without glancing in my direction. I thought that writers should never get rich. They shouldn't even have a regular income. The well-fed can never understand the hungry. People with homes cannot identify with those who sleep in the streets. Memory, imagination aren't enough. Perhaps Providence wanted to remind me of my mission as a writer?

After I had waited ten or fifteen minutes, the telegraph operator changed my quarter. I called both synagogues. No response at the first number. A secretary answered the second and informed me that the rabbi was not in town—he was in England on a sabbatical. As far as she knew, no lecture was scheduled in the Jewish community that evening. She sounded irritable, so I decided it would be useless to tell her my story.

I made a sacred vow: if the Almighty saved me from my plight, I'd show more kindness toward anyone who came to me for help. Once more—"for the last time," I told myself—I called Reizl. No answer. It was obvious that some disaster had occurred there. Leah Hinda had died or had suffered a heart attack. Or had Reizl ordered her not to touch the telephone?

I went back to the hotel and hunted through my three suits. Maybe another address book would turn up. I might find money in my pockets. But there was only a stick of gum, which I began to chew to still my hunger. Then I tackled the briefcase I had carried off the train. Venting all my frustration on it, I broke the lock. What I had suspected was true—it belonged to a woman. I took out a nightgown, a plastic cosmetic bag, stockings, lingerie, a blouse, a sweater. No trace of a name or address. My briefcase contained my address as well as my New York phone number, but even if the woman were to call, there would be no one to answer. Besides, I couldn't be sure that she had my briefcase. She might have taken it to a lost-and-found office. I should call the railroad station, but strength failed me.

I stretched out on the bed and considered suicide. If a man's life and peace of mind depended on a briefcase full of paper, living wasn't worth a pinch of tobacco. You had only to lose a few scraps of paper to find yourself an outcast.

Should I pawn my suits? Or my watch? It was 3:20 p.m. In an hour or so, night would fall. The radiator pipes were barely lukewarm. I hadn't shaved or even brushed my teeth. A prickly stubble covered my face. Should I go to the police? Was there an institution devoted to cases like mine?

I began to doze off and pulled myself up sharp. I must try to call Reizl again. It occurred to me that I could call Information for telephone numbers of people whose addresses I knew. Why hadn't I thought of that before? My trouble is that I lose my head the second something goes wrong. Anyone else in my situation would have found a way out by this time. I felt ashamed to be so helpless and reproached myself for having remained essentially a yeshiva student. If only it hadn't been so cold, perhaps I, too, could have shown more initiative. The cold paralyzed me.

I put on two sweaters and another scarf before going out. I was afraid of nightfall in this strange, chilly town. I went into a drugstore near the hotel. Without looking, I started counting the money in my pocket. I made a mental note of those who might be willing to help me. I picked a discarded envelope off the floor and jotted down the names of friends and acquaintances whose addresses I thought I remembered. The trouble was that I wasn't sure of any of them.

There were four telephone booths in this drugstore, all occupied. While I waited, I beseeched the Lord, whose commandments I had broken, to deliver me from my plight. I vowed to give eighteen dollars to charity. A little later, I

added another eighteen. I must do penance, I decided. I was
being punished for not obeying the precepts of the Torah.
The scoffer in me made fun of my piety and predicted that I
would be my usual self the moment I returned to New
York.

Apparently God heard my prayer. I called Information in
the town where I was visiting professor, got Rosalie's num-
ber, and—I could hardly believe my ears—she answered the
telephone. Upon hearing my name, she accepted the charges.
I explained what had happened to me, talking with the in-
tensity of someone in mortal danger.

"I'll do all I can, my dear," she said. "I'll wire you some
money. I'd bring it myself, but I have an appointment tomor-
row with the professor who has to pass on my dissertation."

"Rosalie, I'll never forget this till I draw my last breath.
Of course I'll repay you immediately."

"Why are you so scared? Just find out where you are sup-
posed to lecture."

"How?"

"Go to the police. They can trace anything they want to."

I gave Rosalie the address of my hotel. Again I swore
eternal gratitude.

She said, "Wish I could come out to you. I'm sick of my
thesis."

I replaced the receiver with a trembling hand, overwhelmed
by my success, as if I'd just been saved from death. I was
filled with love for Rosalie. She was dissolute and smoked
marijuana, but the divine spark was still in her, for she was
ready to help another human being. She is a thousand times
better than Reizl, a voice screamed inside me. I was ready to
marry Rosalie there and then. Her past was none of my
business. New attitudes were needed between the sexes. There
must be an end to the boredom and deceit of present-day
family life.

My dime had dropped down, and I reinserted it to try Reizl once more. Some supernatural power told me that she would be at home this time. I could almost see her standing near the telephone. I heard the ringing and then her voice. Breathlessly I said, "Reizl, I implore you by all that's sacred to you to accept this call!"

"Will you accept this call or not?" the operator asked, impatient.

After a moment's hesitation, Reizl said yes. Her voice sounded hoarse, as if she had been quarreling or crying.

"Reizl, something awful's happened to me. I've lost my briefcase, my traveler's checks, my little notebook. I'm penniless and stuck in a cold, suspicious-looking hotel in this town. Listen to me, if there's a spark of humanity left in you."

"Where are you—you murderer, you dog, you beast?"

"Reizl, this is no time for settling accounts. Unless you want me to die."

Since Rosalie had promised me speedy help, I realized I need no longer despair. But I wasn't sure she would keep her promise. I told Reizl my whole story, puffing and shaking, ashamed of the way I was exaggerating my peril.

Reizl said, "You were probably meeting one of your sluts, and she left you high and dry."

"I swear I'm telling the truth."

She let a moment pass. "What shall I do?" she said then. "I can't leave Mother alone."

"At least wire me money for expenses. I have to get out of this rathole."

"All right. I'll take your address."

I told her where I was staying. If the women kept their word, I'd be getting two money wires, but one could never be sure how people would behave or what might happen. In any case, fate had helped me reach Reizl and Rosalie by telephone —a sure sign that I was not to perish yet.

Once outside, I felt utterly exhausted from the cold, the wind, and my agitation. I went into a supermarket and bought a container of milk and a loaf of bread. That left me ninety-four cents. Dusk had fallen when I came out. In spite of the marks I had made for myself, I had difficulty finding my way back to the hotel. It got colder and my nose turned wooden. A foggy haze blinded me. Every few minutes I checked in my pocket for my room key and the slip of paper with the hotel's address on it. Near the curb of the crowded sidewalk, pigeons were tossing around a bread crust that someone had dropped or thrown them. They couldn't cope with it or let it be. These creatures filled me with both compassion for them and rage against their Creator. Where did they spend the nights in this severe weather? They must be cold and hungry. They might die this very night. I wanted to pick up the piece of bread and crumble it for them, but I knew they'd fly off as soon as I came near their food. I took out my loaf, scratched and broke up bits of it, and scattered them. Passersby pushed and jostled me, but the pigeons accepted my offering. I bit off chunks and chucked them to the birds.

A policeman came up to me. "You're obstructing traffic," he said. "There's a law against feeding pigeons in the street."

"But they're hungry."

"Not that hungry." He gave me an angry look.

I moved on, but as soon as he had turned away I threw down another piece of bread. Startled, the pigeons flew off. The cabalists are right: ours is the worst of all created worlds. Satan rules here. I stopped someone to ask my way. It turned out that I was standing right next to the entrance of the hotel.

The clerk called me over. "How long will you be staying?"

"A day or two. I'll be receiving money by telegram."

He looked me up and down in disbelief. "Your room is taken starting the day after tomorrow."

I went upstairs and sat down to eat my dinner. How I relished the fresh bread and milk. Each swallow filled me with vitality. I ate in semi-darkness. I was tasting the holiness of poverty. Suddenly I realized that I had no proof of my identity. Even if the money arrived, they might not be willing to let me have it. What would I do then? At that instant, I heard the sound of steps, followed by abrupt knocks on my door. I jumped up. My fingers fumbled as I tried to turn the knob. By the hall light I could see the clerk and several other men.

One of them said, "Why is it so dark?" Then he spoke my name. Everything was cleared up within minutes. The organization that had invited me had been searching the town. I turned on the light. I saw the faces of well-to-do community leaders. Everyone talked at once. They had looked for me all day. They had made inquiries at hotels, railroad offices, airports. The police had been informed. The woman who had my briefcase had telephoned. It occurred to one of them that I might have gone to the wrong hotel. The miserable place I was in had a similar name to the luxurious hotel where a room had been reserved.

Proudly someone said, "You can't hide from us."

"He's a Sherlock Holmes," said another, indicating the first speaker.

They cracked jokes and laughed. One of them introduced himself as president and pointed disparagingly at the half-eaten bread and milk. "Come with us right now!" he cried. "The hall is sold out."

"I don't have my speech. It's in my briefcase."

"We'll send someone to pick it up. It's only fifteen miles from here. The woman who has it is one of our members."

"But I've had money wired to this address."

"They'll forward it to the hotel we're taking you to."

One of the men picked up my garment bag, another grabbed

the briefcase, which would no longer close. I remarked that I hadn't paid my hotel bill, but the president said it had been taken care of. Downstairs, the baffled clerk stared at me. He nodded and apologized. A photographer's bulb flashed. I should have welcomed the turn of events but felt sad instead. Demons had been playing with me. I knew it wouldn't be their last game, either.

I was driven to a first-class hotel by limousine. I barely had time to shave and shower and change before I was whisked off to a restaurant for dinner with a large group of people. While I was eating, someone brought my briefcase. Then a reporter from the local newspaper came to interview me.

Late that night, back in my room, I telephoned Reizl and Rosalie. How easy it was to make calls from a luxury hotel, one's pocket full of traveler's checks and an additional sum for a lecture just delivered. Both women were out. I went to bed and fell into a heavy sleep. I awoke at about ten the next morning, bathed, and ordered breakfast. I would have to wait at the hotel for the money to arrive. I no longer had to have it, but it mattered to me to know if they had keep their word. Besides, I needed to recover from my painful experience.

At one o'clock the president came to take me to lunch. Then he drove me around the town. We passed Morris Shapiro's store. I looked over at the Western Union office and recognized the cafeteria where I had eaten breakfast. The president kept twisting a cigar in his hand and repeated that M—— was a small town. He seemed to be apologizing for its size.

I said, "Yet one can easily get lost here."

"Impossible!"

He wanted to show me everything his town boasted: the museum, schools, agricultural college. But I had no patience for all of this. I was still tired and hoped to take a nap before being picked up for dinner by the chairman. Eventually, the president drove me back to the hotel. It was dusk. The windowpanes were turning blue. I lay down in my clothes. From time to time I tapped my back pocket with the traveler's checks. I slept.

A knock woke me. Night had fallen. I sat up, startled. I couldn't remember where I was. My legs felt flabby, as after an illness. I opened the door. In the light of the hall I saw two faces I knew well: Reizl and Rosalie. I stood there gaping. Reizl wore the shabby fur coat she had acquired in a German D.P. camp. She had a white shawl over her head. Rosalie also wore a fur coat. Both carried tote bags. I was too sleepy even to be amazed.

Rosalie said, "Well, aren't you going to invite us in?"

They must both have decided to come personally to extricate me from my predicament. They would have met at the other hotel, I thought, or perhaps in the plane that made a stopover in Chicago, but I was too weary to ask for an explanation or try to justify myself. I was numb. I stared at them for a long time. The imps had played a new trick on me —they didn't intend me to have repose. Rosalie's eyes were laughing. Reizl looked at me with a sort of mocking compassion. Was this my final downfall? Or had the powers that be answered a prayer I did not dare to utter?

I heard myself say, "Come on in. *Mazel tov.* This is a night of miracles."

Translated by Shulamith Charney

The Cabalist of East Broadway

As happens so often in New York, the neighborhood changed. The synagogues became churches, the yeshivas restaurants or garages. Here and there one could still see a Jewish old people's home, a shop selling Hebrew books, a meeting place for *landsleit* from some village in Rumania or Hungary. I had to come downtown a few times a week, because the Yiddish newspaper to which I contributed was still there. In the cafeteria on the corner, in former times one could meet Yiddish writers, journalists, teachers, fund raisers for Israel, and the like. Blintzes, borscht, kreplech, chopped liver, rice pudding, and egg cookies were the standard dishes. Now the place catered mainly to Negroes and Puerto Ricans. The voices were different, the smells were different. Still, I used to go there occasionally to eat a quick lunch or to drink a cup of coffee. Each time I entered the cafeteria, I would immediately see a man I'll call Joel Yabloner, an old Yiddish writer who specialized in the cabala. He had published books about Holy Isaac Luria, Rabbi Moshe of Cordoba, the Baal Shem, Rabbi Nachman of Bratslav. Yabloner had translated part of the Zohar into Yiddish. He also wrote in Hebrew. According to my calculations, he must have been in his early seventies.

Joel Yabloner, tall, lean, his face sallow and wrinkled, had a shiny skull without a single hair, a sharp nose, sunken

cheeks, a throat with a prominent Adam's apple. His eyes
bulged and were the color of amber. He wore a shabby suit
and an unbuttoned shirt that revealed the white hair on his
chest. Yabloner had never married. In his youth he suffered
from consumption, and the doctors had sent him to a sana-
torium in Colorado. Someone told me that there he was
forced to eat pork, and as a result he fell into melancholy. I
seldom heard him utter a word. When I greeted him, he barely
nodded and often averted his eyes. He lived on the few dollars
a week the Yiddish Writers Union could spare him. His apart-
ment on Broome Street had no bath, telephone, central heat-
ing. He ate neither fish nor meat, not even eggs or milk—
only bread, vegetables, and fruit. In the cafeteria he always
ordered a cup of black coffee and a dish of prunes. He would
sit for hours staring at the revolving door, at the cashier's
desk, or the wall where, years ago, a commercial artist had
painted the market on Orchard Street, with its pushcarts and
peddlers. The paint was peeling now.

The president of the Writers Union told me that although
all of Joel Yabloner's friends and admirers had died out here
in New York, he still had relatives and disciples in the land of
Israel. They had often invited him to come there to live. They
would publish his works, they promised (he had trunks filled
with manuscripts), find an apartment for him, and see that he
was taken care of in every way. Yabloner had a nephew in
Jerusalem who was a professor at the university. There were
still some Zionist leaders who considered Joel Yabloner their
spiritual father. So why should he sit here on East Broad-
way, a silent and forgotten man? The Writers Union would
have sent his pension to him in Israel, and he could also have
received Social Security, which he had never bothered to
claim. Here in New York he had already been burglarized a
few times. A mugger had knocked out his last three teeth.
Eiserman, the dentist who had translated Shakespeare's son-

nets into Yiddish, told me that he had offered to make Ya-
bloner a set of false teeth, but Yabloner had said to him,
"There is only one step from false teeth to a false brain."

"A great man, but a queer one," Eiserman said to me while
he drilled and filled my own teeth. "Or perhaps he wants to
atone for his sins this way. I've heard that he had love affairs
in his youth."

"Yabloner—love affairs?"

"Yes, love affairs. I myself knew a Hebrew teacher, Debo-
rah Soltis, who was madly in love with him. She was my
patient. She died about ten years ago."

In connection with this, Eiserman told me of a curious epi-
sode. Joel Yabloner and Deborah Soltis saw each other over
a period of twenty years, indulging in long conversations,
often discussing Hebrew literature, the fine points of gram-
mar, Maimonides, and Rabbi Judah ha-Levi, but the pair
never went so far as to kiss. The closest they came was once
when both of them were looking up the meaning of a word
or an idiom in Ben-Yahudah's great dictionary and their
heads met accidentally. Yabloner fell into a playful mood and
said, "Deborah, let's trade eyeglasses."

"What for?" Deborah Soltis asked.

"Oh, just like that. Only for a little while."

The two lovers exchanged reading glasses, but he couldn't
read with hers and she couldn't read with his. So they re-
placed their own glasses on their own noses—and that was
the most intimate contact the two ever achieved.

Eventually, I stopped going down to East Broadway. I sent
my articles to the newspaper by mail. I forgot Joel Ya-
bloner. I didn't even know that he was still alive. Then one
day when I walked into a hotel lobby in Tel Aviv I heard
applause in an adjoining hall. The door to the hall was half
open and I looked in. There was Joel Yabloner behind a lec-

tern, making a speech. He wore an alpaca suit, a white shirt,
a silk skullcap, and his face appeared fresh, rosy, young. He
had a full set of new teeth and had sprouted a white goatee. I
happened not to be especially busy, so I found an empty
chair and sat down.

Yabloner did not speak modern Hebrew but the old holy
tongue with the Ashkenazi pronunciation. When he gesticu-
lated, I noticed the sparkling links in his immaculate shirt
cuffs. I heard him say in a Talmudic singsong, "Since the
Infinite One filled all space and, as the Zohar expresses it,
'No space is empty of Him,' how did He create the universe?
Rabbi Chaim Vital gave the answer: 'Before creation, the
attributes of the Almighty were all potential, not actual.
How can one be a king without subjects, and how can there
be mercy without anyone to receive it?' "

Yabloner clutched his beard, glanced at his notes. Once in
a while, he took a sip from a glass of tea. I observed quite a
number of women and even young girls in the audience. A
few students took notes. How strange—there was also a nun.
She must have understood Hebrew. "The Jewish state has
resuscitated Joel Yabloner," I said to myself. One seldom
has a chance to enjoy someone else's good fortune, and for
me Yabloner's triumph was a symbol of the Eternal Jew. He
had spent decades as a lonely, neglected man. Now he seemed
to have come into his own. I listened to the rest of the lecture,
which was followed by a question period. Unbelievable, but
that sad man had a sense of humor. I learned that the lec-
ture had been organized by a committee which had under-
taken to publish Yabloner's work. One of the members of
the committee knew me, and asked if I wished to attend a
banquet in Yabloner's honor. "Since you are a vegetarian,"
he added, "here is your chance. They will serve only vege-
tables, fruits, nuts. When do they ever have a vegetarian
banquet? Once in a lifetime."

Between the lecture and the banquet, Joel Yabloner went out on the terrace for a rest. The day had been hot, and now in the late afternoon a breeze was blowing from the sea. I approached him, saying, "You don't remember me, but I know you."

"I know you very well. I read everything you write," he replied. "Even here I try not to miss your stories."

"Really, it is a great honor for me to hear you say so."

"Please sit down," he said, indicating a chair.

God in Heaven, that silent man had become talkative. He asked me all kinds of questions about America, East Broadway, Yiddish literature. A woman came over to us. She wore a turban over her white hair, a satin cape, and men's shoes with low, wide heels. She had a large head, high cheekbones, the complexion of a gypsy, black eyes that blazed with anger. The beginnings of a beard could be seen on her chin. In a strong, mannish voice she said to me, "*Adoni* [Sir], my husband just finished an important lecture. He must speak at the banquet, and I want him to rest for a while. Be so good as to leave him alone. He is not a young man any more and he should not exert himself."

"Oh, excuse me."

Yabloner frowned. "Abigail, this man is a Yiddish writer and my friend."

"He may be a writer and a friend, but your throat is overstrained. If you argue with him, you will be hoarse later."

"Abigail, we aren't arguing."

"*Adoni*, please listen to me. He doesn't know how to take care of himself."

"Well, we shall talk later," I said. "You have a devoted wife."

"So they tell me."

I took part in the banquet—ate the nuts, almonds, avocados, cheese, bananas that were served. Yabloner again made a speech, this time about the author of the cabalistic book *The Treatise of the Hasidim.* His wife sat near him on the stage. Each time his voice became scratchy she handed him a glass of white fluid—some variety of yogurt. After the speech, in the course of which Yabloner demonstrated much erudition, the chairman announced that an assistant professor at the Hebrew University was writing Yabloner's biography and that funds were being raised to publish it. The author was called out on the stage. He was a young man with a round face, shining eyes, and the tiniest of skullcaps, which blended into his pomaded hair. In his closing words, Yabloner thanked his old friends, his students, all those who came to honor him. He paid tribute to his wife, Abigail, saying that without her help he would never have been able to put his manuscripts in order. He mentioned her first husband, whom he referred to as a genius, a saint, a pillar of wisdom. From a huge handbag that resembled a valise more than a lady's purse, Mrs. Yabloner took out a red kerchief like the ones used by old-fashioned rabbis and blew her nose with a blast that reverberated throughout the hall. "Let him intercede for us at the Throne of Glory!" she called out.

After the banquet I went over to Yabloner and said, "Often when I saw you sitting all alone in the cafeteria I was tempted to ask you why you didn't go to Israel. What was your reason for waiting so long?"

He paused, closing his eyes as if the question required pondering, and finally shrugged his shoulders. "Man does not live according to reason."

Again a few years passed. The typesetter on the newspaper for which I worked had lost a page of my most recent article, and since the article had to appear the next day—Saturday —there wasn't time to send the copy by mail. I had to take a cab to deliver it to the composing room myself. I gave the

missing page to the foreman and went down to the editorial
department to see the editor and some of my old colleagues.
The winter day was short, and when I came back onto the
street I felt the long-forgotten hustle and bustle of the oncom-
ing Sabbath. Even though the neighborhood was no longer
predominantly Jewish, some synagogues, yeshivas, and Ha-
sidic study houses had refused to leave. Here and there I saw
in a window a woman lighting her Sabbath candles. Men in
wide-brimmed velvet or fur hats were going to prayers, ac-
companied by boys with long sidelocks. My father's words
came to my mind: "The Almighty will always have His
quorum." I remembered the chants of the Sabbath-eve lit-
urgy: "Let us exalt," "Come my bridegroom," "The temple
of the King."

I was not in a hurry any more, and I decided to have a
cup of coffee in the cafeteria before I took the subway home.
I pushed the revolving door. For a moment I imagined that
nothing had changed, and I thought I could hear those
voices of my first years in America—the cafeteria filled with
Old World intellectuals shouting their opinions of Zionism,
Jewish Socialism, the life and culture in America. But the
faces were not familiar. Spanish was the language I heard.
The walls had been painted over, and the scenes of Orchard
Street with its pushcarts and peddlers had disappeared. Sud-
denly I saw something I could not believe. At a table in the
middle of the room sat Joel Yabloner—without a beard, in a
shabby suit and an unbuttoned shirt. He was emaciated,
wrinkled, and disheveled, and his mouth again appeared
sunken and empty. His bulging eyes stared at the empty wall
opposite. Was I mistaken? No, it was Yabloner, all right. In
his expression there was the desperation of a man caught in a
dilemma from which there is no escape. With the cup of cof-
fee in my hand, I stopped. Should I approach him to greet
him, should I ask permission to sit down at his table?

Someone pushed me, and half of my coffee spilled over. The spoon fell on the floor with a clang. Yabloner turned around and our eyes met for a second. I nodded to him, but he did not respond. Then he turned his face away. Yes, he recognized me, but he was not in a mood for conversation. I even imagined that he had shaken his head in refusal. I found a table against the wall and sat down. I drank what was left of my coffee, all the while looking at him sideways. Why had he left Israel? Did he miss something here? Was he running away from someone? I had a strong desire to go over and ask him, but I knew that I would not get anything out of him.

A power stronger than man and his calculations has driven him out of Paradise, back to Hell, I decided. He did not even go to the Friday-night services. He was hostile not only to people but to the Sabbath itself. I finished the coffee and left.

A few weeks later, I read among the obituaries that Joel Yabloner had died. He was buried somewhere in Brooklyn. That night I lay awake until three o'clock, thinking about him. Why did he return? Had he not atoned enough for the sins of his youth? Had his return to East Broadway some explanation in the lore of the cabala? Had some holy sparks strayed from the World of Emanation into the Evil Host? And could they have been found and brought back to their sacred origin only in this cafeteria? Another idea came into my head— perhaps he wanted to lie near that teacher with whom he exchanged eyeglasses? I remembered the last words I heard from him: "Man does not live according to reason."

Translated by Alma Singer and Herbert Lottman

The Bishop's Robe

JACOB GETZELLES was the editor of a publishing company founded by a millionaire named Bernard Neihaus, mainly for prestige. He had made a fortune in real estate and other businesses. The company published not more than five or six books a year on Judaica—mostly translations from the Hebrew. Jacob Getzelles had been ordained by the Hebrew Union College, but he never became a rabbi. For some time he taught Hebrew in a small college in the Midwest. Then for years he had a position in a philanthropic organization in New York. Those who knew him joked that Jacob Getzelles's only talent was eating lunch with his boss. Jacob was a little man with dark skin, round, reddish cheeks, wavy hair without a sign of gray, though he was over sixty. He had a broad nose, curled brows, and brown eyes that sparkled like a child's. It was rumored that in his youth he had affairs with women. A few years after his marriage, his wife died of cancer and he never remarried. At that time he became the editor of Bernard Neihaus's publishing company.

Bernard Neihaus did not publish books like other publishers. He played with them. First he had to fall in love with the original text. Then he spent a lot of time finding the proper translator. If the work was to be illustrated, he made a long search for the right artist. Bernard Neihaus was as small-statured as Jacob but blown up like a barrel; he weighed 250 pounds. Eating lunch with Bernard Neihaus was a lengthy affair. All business decisions were made at these heavy meals. The doctors warned Neihaus that his blood was almost all cholesterol, but Bernard would say, "There is no cholesterol. The doctors invented it."

The day after his seventy-ninth birthday, Bernard Neihaus had a heart attack and died. Whether it was the fault of the cholesterol no one ever learned. Shortly afterward, his sons liquidated the publishing company and Jacob Getzelles was jobless. But the powers that took care of Jacob Getzelles sent him Bessie Feingevirtz, the widow of a hotel builder. She was the ex-president of an organization formed to help students in Palestine and a hotel builder in her own right. A few years older than Jacob, she had a fleshy, pimpled nose and the voice of a man, and ever since her own hair had fallen out she wore a red wig. After her husband's death, Bessie was on the verge of marriage a few times, but the candidates withdrew, complaining that they could not put up with her despotic character. However, Jacob Getzelles was used to complying. When they were married, Bessie boasted that at her first meeting with Jacob she told him, "Jacob dear, you will be my husband." And her husband he became.

In the beginning, they talked of reviving the publishing company—Bessie had a yen for culture and famous people. But she soon learned that Jacob lacked the initiative to be a publisher. Besides, publishing could eat up hundreds of thousands. They talked and planned to no purpose, until they finally decided that the best thing for them would be to spend the balance of their lives somewhere in California. Sam Feingevirtz left no children, and Bessie maintained that she had enough for the two of them to live in luxury even if they reached the age of 120, and she could leave a nice penny for charity besides.

First the couple took a five-month around-the-world trip. Then Bessie began to look for a home in California. She soon found what she wanted: a richly furnished house with a garden and a double garage in Hollywood Hills. As always, Bessie had come across a bargain; a week after the papers were signed, she was offered a large profit over what she had paid for the place.

Moving to California was difficult. It took a long time to get things the way Bessie wanted them. When that was done, she had time to devote to Jacob. She had decided that Jacob should write a book and also collaborate with her on her autobiography, which would describe her first years in the Polish town of Pishnitz, her coming to America, working in the garment shops, studying English, marrying Sam Feingevirtz, her activities in the organization where she became president, and her struggle with the jealous ladies who finally forced her resignation. Bessie had worked out a rigid schedule for when and what Jacob should eat, when and what type of clothing he should wear (she liked silk shirts, gaudy ties, velvet jackets, and pompon slippers), and for the hours of his work. But in California Jacob became lazy and apathetic. He yawned, dozed. He developed writer's cramp and a tic in his left eye. On their honeymoon trip Jacob had written Bessie a love poem every day. He had told her anecdotes about writers, translators, the celebrities he had met, funny stories about Bernard Neihaus and his whims. But now Jacob turned silent; Bessie had to pull words out of him. The garden around the house needed a man to tend it, but Jacob showed no interest in gardening. He walked around in his bathrobe all day long and neglected to go to the barber. In Los Angeles and its suburbs to drive a car was essential. Bessie ordered Jacob to take driving lessons. After the third lesson the instructor called Bessie and told her, "I am sorry, but it is hopeless. Your husband would kill someone on his first trip."

Bessie began to consider divorce, but then she met Phyllis Gurdin, a Jewish woman from Philadelphia, the widow of the spiritualist bishop Thomas Delano Gurdin who perished in an airplane crash. He had left his wife a house not far from Bessie's. She was a hypnotist, a medium, a wonder healer, an expert in reading tarot cards, and the head of a group that spoke in tongues. An intimate friendship sprang up between the two women. Some of the trees in Bessie's garden developed a blight that resembled spider webs, and Phyllis Gurdin recommended a spray as well as a special prayer that kills fungus. Bessie grew warts on her chin, and Phyllis gave her a potion and an incantation to make them wither away.

After a while Phyllis Gurdin invited Bessie and Jacob to a service of those who speak in tongues. This took place in Phyllis Gurdin's parlor. She kissed all the men and women as they arrived. The parlor filled up with men with gray hair and women with dyed hair. Phyllis Gurdin had a dark face, black eyes, bushy brows. She wore thick-lensed glasses. Her hair was colored a bright orange. On her upper lip she had a white fuzz. For the service she wore a white robe and a red turban. Phyllis Gurdin led the congregation in the singing of hymns. She danced and the congregation danced with her. The singing became louder. They danced in a frenzy, clapped their hands, cried out words of praise to God, to Jesus, and to Phyllis Gurdin. Suddenly they began to shout words that Bessie had never heard before. This was not a language but gibberish: sounds like "charopakitcichi," "hatchomarumbi," "leptchocalduku." All eyes radiated joy. Men embraced women. Women embraced men. A drummer drummed. A trumpeter blared into a trumpet that had a huge horn. They screamed, jumped, shook, and went into a state of exaltation. Bessie watched in astonishment. Was this madness? Sorcery? An orgy? A bacchanalia? Bessie became hot. She drank no liquor but she felt drunk. For years she had suffered from arthritis and varicose veins—now her feet became strangely light.

Suddenly Bessie, too, began to hop, clap, and yell in a language she did not understand. Was it Greek, Persian, Tataric? Had a dybbuk entered her? The floor rocked under her feet. The walls turned. Bessie heard herself scream, "Mutchiefalkosy! Sappolachia! Rinchiehoppler! Saltalafonta!" She was overcome with love for the whole crowd, as if they were all her brothers and sisters. She ran over to Jacob, who stood in the corner near the door, pressed him to her bosom, laughed, cried, and howled, "Katcharololshy! Poladumbka! Zakafier!"

Jacob started, smiled, and in a hoarse voice replied in a mixture of Yiddish, Hebrew, and Aramaic, "Pitchapoi! Yegar Sadussa! Otz koytzetz ben koytzetz!"

Bessie feared that Jacob might sabotage her spiritual rebirth just as he had her other plans and programs. In that case she was ready to go to Reno for a quick divorce. But this time Jacob cooperated. He developed a close relationship with Phyllis Gurdin. He sat with her and Bessie for hours at the ouija board and helped decipher the messages that Phyllis Gurdin's control, an Indian who called himself Red-Eyed Chief, sent from the other world. Jacob and the two women laid their hands on a table without nails and felt it vibrate, clap out answers, and try to raise itself. He attended meetings of those who spoke in tongues and began to jabber a balderdash that astounded Phyllis with its bizarre consistency. She assured Jacob and Bessie that this was a language spoken on a planet beyond the solar system and that, if a key to it could be found, humanity would gain an insight into the secret of the universe. Jacob was amazed to see that Bessie, who had formerly stinted, now became generous on a large scale. The congregation of those who spoke in tongues needed a church, and Bessie contributed a huge sum. Phyllis Gurdin was in need of a station wagon to transport the old and the crippled to meetings, and Bessie undertook the cost herself. Both women kissed whenever they met and called one another "baby," "darling," "honey," "sweetheart," "blessed soul," and such pet names.

Bessie, who on their trip around the world had been jealous and made scandals when Jacob so much as spoke a friendly word to a waitress, now demanded that he treat Phyllis like a sister—even closer than a sister. Bessie scolded him if he forgot to kiss Phyllis when she arrived at their house or left. When Bessie had to go to Los Angeles—she had a broker on Wilshire Boulevard with whom she conducted business— Phyllis prepared Jacob's lunch, consisting of watercress, mushrooms, long-grain brown rice, and yogurt. She reminded him to take his medicines and to rest after his meal. She told him of the sublime love that had existed between her and the late bishop and described the most intimate details. At every opportunity Phyllis spoke about her Jewishness and said that she did not forget her origins. She fasted on Yom Kippur. She had a grandmother who emigrated to America from Russia and who never learned English. Phyllis used to speak Yiddish to her; she still remembered many words. Whenever she had to go East, she didn't fail to stop in Philadelphia and prostrate herself at the graves of her parents and grandparents and recite prayers in Hebrew and leave flowers. Once when Phyllis went into a trance, their spirits appeared to her, assuring her that they approved of her conduct and were prepared to welcome her when she passed over. Where they were, such divisions as Jew, Gentile, white, black, American, European didn't exist. All souls dwelled together, seeking spiritual development, ascending from mansion to mansion, and helping newly arrived souls to begin their spiritual habitation.

One evening Phyllis stayed at Bessie's house later than

usual. The table vibrated, eager for levitation. Bessie and Phyllis had to apply force so that it would not rise to the ceiling. Under the table Phyllis's knee pressed Jacob's and he felt a tremor along his spine. The planchette wrote quickly and precisely, revealing mysteries and conveying greetings from many deceased relatives. In a trance, Phyllis announced that Jacob's mother was present and that she had not forgotten her beloved son; she watched over him from Heaven and interceded on his behalf. His mother spoke through Phyllis's mouth in a Yiddish mixed with English, calling him *"Yankele, little dove,"* and kissing him with Phyllis's lips. Later on, the bishop spoke. He announced in a deep voice that Bessie and Jacob's move to Los Angeles and their acquiring a house in Phyllis's neighborhood was not an accident. It was all arranged by the Heavenly Masters, because both Bessie and Jacob were destined to play an important part in the religious renaissance brought about by the merger of Judaism and Christianity—a new epoch in the Evolution of Redemption.

About one o'clock, Jacob became so sleepy that he could not keep his eyes open. Bessie and Phyllis helped him to bed, covered him, tucked him in, kissed him good night, and wished him blissful visions. He soon fell into a deep sleep. When he awoke it was still dark. He reached for Bessie, but it was a strange bosom that he touched. He listened and heard the snoring of two noses. Bessie awoke also. "Dearest, don't be afraid. It became very late and I didn't want Phyllis to go home. I insisted that she sleep with us because . . ."

Phyllis stopped snoring. "I will go to the sofa."

"No, Phyllis, my husband is your husband," Bessie said solemnly. "Jacob, be it known to you that we made a covenant tonight. We two are like Rachel and Leah, and you are our Jacob. Embrace her, kiss her, caress her. One sister is not jealous of the other. The opposite."

"I bought you from her for a bunch of mandrakes." Phyllis the scholarly paraphrased the story in Genesis. She spoke with a choked laughter.

Jacob Getzelles was silent. Passion he thought extinguished rekindled itself. "Am I dreaming?" he said.

"No, Jacob, my beloved, it's the truth." Bessie spoke in a tremulous voice. "Phyllis's husband, the bishop, has chosen you. He materialized to us and said—"

"Jacob, his soul entered you," Phyllis interrupted. "You will take his place in our congregation."

The things that are happening to me, and in my old age to boot, Jacob thought, bewildered. He quivered, overwhelmed by the eternal masculine fear of helplessness. He hugged Phyllis and she pressed herself to him. He kissed her, and she bit into his mouth with such ardency that in an instant all doubts ceased. He was overcome by lust. Bessie was screaming, "Take her! Do her will!"

"Spouse, lie in my lap," Phyllis implored him.

It was daybreak when Jacob silently left the bed. After lengthy murmuring and giggling, Phyllis and Bessie had fallen asleep again. Now Jacob went to the bathroom on shaky legs. The night of abandon was over and had left him with a weakness in his loins and a stabbing in his bladder. Jacob Getzelles had suffered from an enlarged prostate for years. With the help of massage and medications he had avoided an operation, but the doctor in New York had warned him that postponing surgery could bring about complications. Now he stood at the mirror—disheveled, wrinkled, with a yellowish face. "Am I happy?" he asked himself. "Was I happier before?" He felt an ache in his head and in his knees. He went to the toilet to urinate but his urine came with interruptions and in droplets. He said to himself, "It's too late for such blessings."

asleep and wake up with a start. He dozed off and his eyes would blink open, stunned by a dream he would instantly forget. Things stopped bothering him—the heat, the humidity, the stabbing in his bladder. His doctor's warning that he was in danger of uremic poisoning did not frighten him. Jacob had read a murder report in a newspaper, but he could no longer feel pity for the victim or hate for the murderer. When the telephone rang, he did not pick up the receiver. The mailman brought him a special-delivery letter, but he let it lie unopened. His insomnia did not irritate him any more. Bessie did not sleep either. She sighed, scratched herself, and mumbled. Although she and Jacob slept together in their large bed, she seemed far away and he kept forgetting her. Sometimes she spoke to him, but he was unable to pay attention to what she was saying. He heard her say, "Jacob, our life is one big mistake. I see no way out."

That morning Bessie did not call Jacob to eat breakfast in the kitchen with her. She left the house without telling him where she was going. She did not come home for lunch. For some reason Jacob's thirst and his frequent need to urinate had ceased. From sheer habit he now opened one of the books Phyllis had left with him—he could barely see the words. "Is it twilight already or am I developing cataracts?" He was aware that he was thinking about himself as he would of a stranger.

Suddenly the door was flung open and Bessie staggered in. "She ran away, the charlatan, the criminal! She locked the shutters and didn't even say goodbye. It's your fault. Yours, yours, yours!" Bessie cried out hysterically. "You were the one who led me to all those maniacs and crackpots. She has absconded with my fortune. I am left naked and penniless. Even the house no longer belongs to us. She hypnotized me into insanity!"

Bessie tore the book from his hands and threw it to the

floor. She overturned the coffee table, which was heaped with magazines, and screeched, "What nonsense are you reading, burying yourself in this garbage? It's all lies. She's as much a saint as I'm the Pope. Her husband was a faker. It's all swindle! Bishop Jacob Getzelles, my eye! Woe to my miserable life. Murderer!" The last word Bessie uttered in Yiddish: *"Rutseach!"* She kicked the books, spat on them. "Where do we go now? God has punished me and taken away my reason. That witch bedazzled me with her sacred babble and phony love. A bandit, a racketeer, a gangster. I don't want to live any more! Do you hear me or not?" Bessie moaned. "I want to die—this very minute." She clenched her fists and leaped at Jacob. Her red wig fell off and she stood with a bare skull from which only a few wisps of white hair hung down.

Something tore inside Jacob. "Be quiet. If we are going to die, let's die in a dignified way."

"There's nothing to live for. Everything is lost. Cursed be the day when I first saw your face and her face. She has made me a pauper. If *you* want to live, go to an old-age home."

"Bessie, I don't want to live."

"I'm going to the kitchen to turn on the gas."

"Yes, do so."

"Get up. I don't even have a cemetery plot. Let them throw me to the dogs."

Bessie ran over to the air conditioning and turned it off. She grabbed the cushions and the cover from the sofa, and ran toward the kitchen.

Jacob followed her. How strange: for the first time he felt a sort of love for this wild woman. In the kitchen Bessie shut the door, locked the windows, extinguished the pilot lights, and opened all the jets of the range. Jacob gaped at her. He didn't realize it but the fear of death had left him. He felt like one of those astral bodies he had read about—weightless, submissive, yielding to a power beyond his choice. Is this how one dies? he wondered. But he wasn't even curious. He was a child, and Bessie was putting him to sleep. She spread the sofa cover on the floor and threw down the cushions. "Let's not die on the hard tile."

Bessie helped Jacob lie down. She stretched out near him and kissed him. Her face was hot and wet. "If there is a God or whatever He is, we will soon know."

"There is nothing there," Jacob replied, baffled by his own words. The telephone rang in the corridor and Bessie started. "Who can it be? Never mind." The phone rang for a long while. Then it became silent.

Bessie embraced Jacob. She asked, "Shall I recite 'Hear O Israel'?"

And Jacob murmured, "Not necessary."

Those were his last words.

The next day he and Bessie were found dead. Months later, when Bessie's lawyers in New York were settling her estate, it came to light that she was still worth about $400,000, in addition to the properties that she had turned over to Phyllis and that the lawyers were trying to reclaim.

"She certainly did not die from want," said one of the attorneys, a little man with a pointed skull, pointed nose, pointed eyes. "Why didn't she leave a letter?" As he spoke, he began to sharpen a pencil that already had a long point. The other lawyer, a big fat man with yellow brows and a flabby double chin, pondered awhile and said, "I have read scores of letters from suicides, but none of them ever told the truth."

Translated by the author and Ruth Schachner Finkel

A Quotation from Klopstock

THOSE who have to do with women must boast. In literary circles in Warsaw, Max Persky was known as a woman chaser. His followers contended that if he hadn't spent so much of his time on females, he might have become a second Sholem Aleichem or a Yiddish Maupassant. Although he was twenty years older than I, we became friends. I had read his work and listened to all his stories. That summer evening we sat in a little garden café, drinking coffee and eating blueberry cookies. The sun had already set and a pale September moon hung in the sky above the tin roofs. But remnants of the sunset were still reflected in the glass door which led to the interior of the café. The air was warm and smelled of the Praga forest, freshly baked babkas, and the manure that peasants gathered from the stables to dump into the fields. Max Persky smoked one cigarette after another. The tray filled with ashes and butts. Even though he was already in his forties—some maintained he was nearly fifty—Max Persky looked young. He had a boyish figure, a head of black shiny hair, a brown-complexioned face, full lips, and the penetrating eyes of a hypnotist. The two lines at the sides of his mouth gave him an air of fatalistic awareness. His enemies gossiped that he took money from wealthy women. It was also said that a woman had committed suicide over him. Our waitress, middle-aged, with a young figure, kept staring at him. From time to time she smiled guiltily at me as if to say, I can't help it. She had a short nose, sunken cheeks, and a pointed chin. I noticed that the middle finger was missing from her left hand.

Max Persky suddenly asked me, "What happened to that woman who was twelve years older than you? Do you still see her?"

I wanted to answer him but he shook his head. He said, "There is something about older women that the younger ones cannot supply. I, myself, had one, not twelve years older than I but thirty. I was a young man of about twenty-seven and she must have been in her fifties. She was a spinster, a teacher of German literature. She also knew Hebrew. In those years the rich Jews in Warsaw wanted their daughters to be versed in Goethe, Schiller, and Lessing. If they weren't, they lacked *kultur*. A pinch of Hebrew did no harm either. Theresa Stein made a living teaching these subjects. You most probably have never heard of her, but in my time she was well known in Warsaw. This was a woman who took poetry very seriously, which proves that she was not too clever. She certainly was no beauty. To enter her small apartment on Nowolipki Street was an experience. Poverty hovered all around it, but she had turned her rooms into a kind of old maid's temple. She spent half of her earnings on books, mostly gold-embossed with velvet bindings. She bought paintings also. When I was introduced to her she was still a kosher virgin. I needed a quotation from Klopstock's *Messiah* for one of my stories, and I telephoned and she asked me to visit her that evening. When I arrived, she had already found the quotation I needed and many others. I brought her my first book, which had just been published. She knew Yiddish quite well. She worshipped Peretz. Whom did she not worship? She spoke the word 'talent' as solemnly as a pious Jew mentions God. She was small and roundish with brown eyes, from which radiated goodness and naïveté. Women like that don't exist any more. Since I was young and played the part of a cynic, I immediately did everything I could to shock her. I denounced all poets as imbeciles and told her I was having affairs with four women at the same time. Her eyes filled with tears. She said to me, 'You are so young, so talented, and already so unhappy. You don't know yet what real love is, and therefore you torture your immortal soul. True love will come to you and you will find treasures that will open the gates of Heaven to you.' To comfort me for being so misled, she offered me tea with jam cake she had baked herself and a glass of cherry brandy. I did not wait long before I began to kiss her—almost out of habit. I will never forget her expression at the first kiss. Her eyes lit up with a strange light. She clutched both my wrists and said, 'Don't do it! I take such things seriously!' She trembled and stuttered and tried to quote Goethe. Her body became unusually hot. I practically raped her, although not exactly. I spent the night at her house, and if someone could convey in a book all she said that night, it would be a work of genius. She promptly fell in love with me—with a love that endured to her last minute. I am far from being holy even today, but in those years I didn't have a trace of conscience. I considered the whole thing a joke.

"She began to telephone me every day—three times a day —but I had no time for her and invented countless excuses. Nevertheless, I used to visit her from time to time—mostly on rainy nights when I had no other engagements. Every visit was literally a holiday for her. If she could manage it, she prepared a festive supper, bought flowers in my honor, and dressed in fancy gowns or kimonos. She showered me with gifts. She tried to persuade me to read the German classics with her. But I tore them all to pieces and confessed to her brazenly all my sins, even about the brothels I had visited in my youth. There are some women who can be shocked constantly, and for her I never lacked material. Just because she spoke gently, with flowery phrases and noble quotations, I used the language of the streets and called everything by its name. She used to say, 'God will forgive

you. Since He bestowed talent upon you, you are His favo-
rite.' The truth is that it was impossible to spoil her. Figura-
tively speaking, she remained a virgin to the end. She pos-
sessed a purity and love for humanity not to be erased. She
defended everyone, even that famous anti-Semite, Purish-
kevitch. She said, 'The poor man is deluded. There are souls
who sink in darkness because they never have the chance to
see the divine light.' I did not realize it then but I slept
with a saint, like the Saint Theresa whose namesake she was.

"She was so pure that the things I forced her to do shat-
tered her. I have a large bundle of her letters and they are
stained with her tears—not false ones but true. A time is
coming when no one will believe that such women existed.
Meanwhile, years passed, she grew older and her hair became
white, but her face remained young and her eyes shone
with all the illusions of romanticism. I had less and less time
for her. The rich Jews of Warsaw slowly lost their interest in
German culture and Theresa earned less and less. But I could
not completely sever our relationship. I always had the feel-
ing that, if everything went wrong and I was forsaken by
everyone, I could depend on Theresa to be my mother, my
wife, my protector. She had developed the tolerance charac-
teristic of such natures. I was allowed to do anything. I never
had to defend myself. In my situation one has to be a chronic
liar, but to Theresa I could tell the truth no matter how
brutal. She always had the same answer, 'You poor boy! You
great artist!'

"The years, meanwhile, did their job. Theresa became bent
and wrinkled. She began to suffer from rheumatism. She had
to lean on a cane. I was ashamed of myself for my charity, if
it could be called that, but to leave her completely meant kill-
ing her. She clung to me with her last strength. At night in
bed she became young again. Sometimes in the dark, words
escaped her which astounded me. Among other things she

promised me that after her death she would appear to me, if it were possible. I don't want to disappoint you, so I am telling you in advance that she never kept that promise. But my story is just beginning."

Max Persky signaled the waitress and she came over at once, as though she had been waiting impatiently for this call. He spoke to her with caressing familiarity, "Panna Helena, I am beginning to get hungry."

"My God, today we have what you like—tomato soup."

"What are you going to have?" he asked me.

"Tomato soup, also."

"Panna Helena, make it two." He winked at her and I understood that he had the same conspiratorial relationship with her that he had had with Theresa Stein. Max Persky was in his own way a philanthropist—not with money but with love.

After the soup Max Persky lit a cigarette and asked, "Where did I stop? Yes, she grew old. She had to move out of her apartment and become a boarder with other people. This was a real tragedy, but I could not help her. You know, I never had a penny. I could not even lend a hand with the packing and moving, because Theresa Stein had a spotless reputation in Warsaw and the slightest gossip would have caused her to lose her last lessons. To tell the truth, no one would have really believed that Theresa was capable of doing what she actually did. The older she became the more guilty she felt about it and, nevertheless, shamefully asked for her due. As long as she had her private apartment, it was not difficult to keep the conspiracy. I always came to her early in the evening, and never failed to carry a book with me to pretend I was her pupil. If the neighbors ever saw me, they certainly did not suspect that I was Theresa's lover. But when she boarded with other people, I could not visit her any more.

This should have been the end, but with women such as The-resa it's as difficult to end as to begin. She kept calling me and writing me long letters. We began to meet in cafés in the faraway Gentile streets. Every time I met her she brought me some kind of present—a book, a tie, even handkerchiefs and socks.

At this time I was having an affair with a niece of the Biala Rabbi whose name was Nina. I think I've told you already about this Nina. She ran away from the rabbi's court and tried to become a painter in Warsaw. She kept threatening her uncle the rabbi that if he refused to help her with money, she would convert. She was half crazy. The love between us was what pulp novels call stormy. She burned with jealousy and always suspected the women who were most innocent. Every few weeks she attempted suicide. Until then I had never hit a woman, but Nina's hysteria was the kind that could be quieted only with blows. She admitted it herself. When she began her wild antics, tearing her hair, crying, laughing, and trying to throw herself out the window, there was no other remedy but to give her a few fiery slaps in the face. It worked like a charm. After the slaps she usually started to kiss. Until then I knew well how to manage my women. But Nina harassed me with her jealous behavior. If she caught me with another woman, she grabbed her hair and tore at it like a fishwife. She drove all my girls away. To get rid of Nina was impossible. She carried poison with her. I fell into such despair that I began to write a play—the one they ruined later in the Central Theater.

"One night, it was in the winter, Nina had to go to Biala to see her uncle. Whenever she went on a trip, she waited to let me know at the last minute to prevent me from making other rendezvous. The insane are very sly. This evening when she told me she was leaving, I began to telephone all my victims. But it was one of those nights when everyone was either busy or sick. There was an epidemic of grippe. Since I had been promising Theresa for weeks and months that I would meet her, it occurred to me that this was the right opportunity. I telephoned her and invited her for supper in a Gentile restaurant. Then I took her to my home. Even though we had been lovers for years, each time she behaved like a frightened virgin. She had to find an explanation for her landlord about not coming home to sleep. She was so alarmed and she stammered and sighed so on the telephone that I regretted the whole business. She was never much of an eater, but that evening she could not swallow a bite. A withered old woman sat opposite me at the table. The waiter thought she was my mother and asked, 'Why isn't your mother eating?' I felt awful. After supper she wanted to go home. But I knew that if I consented she would be bitterly disappointed. I also noticed that she had a nightgown in her bag. To make it short, I persuaded her to go to my apartment. When a young girl fusses too much it's bad enough, but when an old woman behaves like a frightened virgin, it's both comical and tragic. We climbed up the three flights of stairs and a few times she stopped to rest. She had brought me a present, a suit of woolen underwear. I made tea. I tried to cheer her up with a glass of cognac. But she refused to drink. After much hesitation, many apologies, and quotations from Faust and Heine's *Buch der Lieder,* she went to bed with me. I was sure that I wouldn't have the slightest desire for her but sex is full of caprices. After a while we both fell asleep. I had already decided that this night was the end of our miserable affair. Even she had hinted that we shouldn't make fools of ourselves any more.

"I was tired and fell asleep soundly. I awoke with an uncanny feeling. At first I did not remember with whom I was in bed. For a moment I thought it was Nina. I stretched out my hand and touched her. At that instant I knew the truth: Theresa was dead. To this day I don't know if she became sick and tried to wake me, or simply died in her sleep. I have gone through many tragedies, but what I experienced that night was sheer terror. My first impulse was to call an ambulance, but all Warsaw would immediately have known that Theresa Stein had died in Max Persky's bed. If the Pope had been caught stealing from an attic in Krochmalna Street, it would not have created a greater sensation. A man fears nothing as much as ridicule. Half of Warsaw would have cursed me, and the other half jeered. When I lit the lamp and looked at her face, I was frozen with horror. She appeared not sixty but ninety. I wanted to run to the end of the earth so that no one would ever learn what had happened to me. But I had spent all my money in the restaurant and for the droshky. I realized that coming home with me and walking up all those steps had killed her. I had actually committed a murder and I had done it out of pity.

"I lit all the lamps, covered the corpse with a blanket, and began to look for a way to end my own idiotic life. To die near her would create the impression that it was a double suicide. One is ashamed of what people will say and think even after one has gone. Prestige, not love, is stronger than death. I looked at my watch and it was ten minutes after three. As I stood there bewildered, cursing the day of my birth, the doorbell rang. I was sure it was the police. They could easily have accused me of murder. I did not answer, but the ringing soon became insistent and loud. I was sure that the next step would be breaking down the door. I did not ask who it was and opened. It was Nina.

"She had missed her train. Nina was an expert at being late for trains, theaters, rendezvous. She said there was no other train that night and she had gone home. But in the middle of the night she was assailed by the desire to be with me. Or perhaps she thought she would catch me with someone else and scratch out her eyes. How strange that I felt overjoyed to see Nina. To be alone with a corpse in such circumstances is so painful that all other suffering and shame is pallid by comparison. Nina said, 'Why are all the lamps burning?' She looked at the bed and exclaimed, 'There is no use hiding her!' She ran to the bed and wanted to tear off the blanket, but I held her hands and said, 'Nina, a corpse is lying there.' She saw from my face that I was not lying. I expected her to make a terrible rumpus and to wake the neighbors. Nina could be thrown into a panic at the sight of a little mouse or a beetle. But at this moment she became calm and seemed cured of all her madness. She said, 'A corpse? Who is it?' When I told her it was Theresa Stein, she began to laugh, not hysterically but in the way a healthy person would break out laughing at a good joke. I said, 'Nina, this is no joke. Theresa Stein died in my bed.'

"Nina knew Theresa Stein. The whole of intellectual Warsaw knew her. She still did not believe it, until I opened Theresa's pocketbook and showed Nina her passport. With the Russians everyone had to carry a passport, even women."

"How does it happen that you never wrote about this?" I asked Max Persky.

"No one has heard the truth until now. There are still too many people who knew Theresa Stein."

He lit another cigarette. It was now night. The moon was as yellow as brass.

"What a story it would make," I said.

"Perhaps I will write it someday, but only in my old age, when no one in Warsaw remembers Theresa Stein. It's still too soon. But let me tell you the rest. Nina was ready to help me, and even had a plan. We could easily have ended up in Siberia or on the gallows, but at such moments one becomes strangely courageous. We dressed the corpse in all her clothes. We decided to tell the janitor that the woman had had an attack of gallstones and we were taking her to the hospital. This janitor was an old drunkard and he never turned on the light when he opened the gate. Taking off Theresa Stein's nightgown and dressing her in her bloomers and other things almost killed us. Her body was a ruin. When she was dressed I lifted her and carried her down three dark flights of stairs. She did not weigh much but still I almost ruptured myself carrying her. Nina helped me by holding her feet. How Nina the hysteric could do all this is still a riddle to me. Never before or since was she so normal—or perhaps I should say supernormal. In the dark passageway to the gate, I stood Theresa up, propping her against the wall. Her head fell on my shoulder and for a moment I imagined she was alive! Nina knocked on the janitor's window and we heard a squeaking door and the typical growling of a man awakened in the middle of the night. He opened the gate, sighing and cursing, as Nina and I dragged the corpse along upright, holding her under the arms. I even managed to tip the janitor. He asked no questions and we told him nothing. If a policeman had happened to come along, I wouldn't be sitting here with you. But the street was empty. We pulled the corpse to the nearest corner and set her carefully on the pavement. I put her pocketbook near her. The whole business did not last longer than a few minutes. I was so dazed that I didn't know what to do next. But Nina took me to her home.

"There is an old saying that there is no such thing as a perfect murder. What we did that night had all the elements of a perfect crime. If we had actually strangled Theresa, the whole thing could not have gone more smoothly. It's true we probably left fingerprints, but the technique of discovering fingerprints was not known then in Warsaw. Little the Russian police cared that an old woman had been found dead in the street. She was taken to the morgue. When the Jews learned that Theresa Stein had been found dead, the community leaders arranged for her to be taken to the cleansing room at the Gęsia Street cemetery without an autopsy. Of course I learned all this later. You will not believe it, but that night—

or what was left of the night—I slept with Nina and every-
thing went as usual. At that time I still had good nerves. I
also drank half a bottle of vodka. There is really no rule
about how nerves will react.

"I don't have to tell you that Warsaw was shocked at the
details of Theresa's death. Our Yiddish newspapers gave the
event full coverage. Theresa had told her landlady that she
was spending the night with a sick relative. But who was that
relative? No one ever learned. My janitor could have told
the police we carried out a woman in the middle of the night,
but he was half blind and never read the newspapers. Since
her pocketbook was found near her, it was assumed that she
had dropped dead from natural causes. I remember that the
feuilletonist of *Today* developed a theory that Theresa Stein
went out to help the poor and the sick. He compared her to
the saint in Peretz's story who, instead of going to night
prayers, went to heat the oven of a sick widow.

"Our Warsaw Jews adore funerals. But such a funeral as
Theresa Stein had, I never saw before. Hundreds of droshkies
followed the hearse. Women and girls cried as if it were Yom
Kippur. Countless eulogies were spoken. The rabbi of the
German synagogue preached that the spirits of Goethe, Schil-
ler, and Lessing were hovering over Theresa's grave, as well
as the souls of Judah ha-Levi and Solomon Ibn Gabriol. I
wasn't too sure about Nina's power to keep a secret. Hysteria
and denunciation often go together. I was afraid that at our
first quarrel Nina would go to the police. But a real change
had taken place in her. She stopped bothering me with her
jealousy. We actually never again spoke of that night. It
became our great secret.

"Not long afterward the war began. Then Nina developed
consumption, which she had really had for years before. Her
family put her in a sanatorium at Otwock. I often visited her.
Something in her character seemed to have altered. I never

needed to stifle her hysteria with a slap again. She died in 1918."

"She never tried to appear to you?" I asked.

"You mean Nina or Theresa? Both had promised, but neither kept her word. Even if such an entity as a soul exists, I don't believe it cares to come down with messages from the other world. I really hope that death is the end of all our nonsense.

"I forgot to add one fact. It has no real connection with my story but it is interesting just the same. During all these years Nina had threatened her uncle, the Biala Rabbi, with conversion. The rabbi was terribly afraid of having a convert in his family and sent her money. After her death, when the family was going to bury her and documents were necessary, they learned that she had been a Catholic for years. It created a commotion among the Hasidim. Warsaw was already under German occupation. They bribed the authorities and buried her in the Jewish cemetery. As a matter of fact, she is lying not too far from Theresa Stein, in the first row. Why she converted I will never know. She often spoke about the Jewish God and mentioned her holy ancestors."

Max Persky became silent. The night grew cool. Around the lamp above the door flies, moths, butterflies, and all kinds of gnats had a summer night's orgy. Max Persky nodded his head over a truth that hung on his lips. "In love you don't do favors," he said. "You have to be an egotist or else you destroy yourself and your lover."

He hesitated awhile and then he looked at the waitress. She came to the table at once. "More coffee?"

"Yes, Helena. Tell me, how late are you working today?"

"As usual we close at twelve."

"I will wait for you outside."

Translated by the author and Dorothea Straus

The Magazine

I FIRST met Zeinvel Gardiner in Warsaw in a soup kitchen for intellectuals. He sat across the table eating mushroom-and-noodle soup that had peas and carrots and parsley in it. I watched as he rummaged around in the dish—he seemed to be looking for something—and then absently added salt and pepper. He left more than half of his portion, and I could barely stop myself from asking him to let me have what remained. In those days my appetite was strong.

He seemed to be in his twenties—dark, with a broad face, high cheekbones, and a head of black, disheveled hair. His eyes were set too far apart. He must have known me from stories I had published in the little magazines—the ones that don't pay anything and demand a contribution from the author. Every once in a while he raised his curly eyelashes and gave me a fluttery look that said, "Since we're bound to get acquainted anyhow, why wait?" The moment we began to speak, he tried to persuade me that we should publish a magazine together. "By profession, I'm a typesetter," he said. "I have a box of type at home. We could print it for practically nothing. If we sell two hundred copies, we get back our expenses. I can distribute a hundred copies myself—maybe more."

"But there are too many of these magazines already."

"What are you talking about? Their publishers are all literary prostitutes. For three zlotys they'll print the worst hacks, and they're a clique: you praise me, I'll praise you.

You and I could bring out a pure magazine. We could elevate literature to new levels."

The word "magazine" had a magic power over me; I had dreamed of having a journal of my own to publish my writing, so that I would not be dependent on the whims of editors. One of them used to take out any part that in his opinion was too sexy. Another complained that I indulged too much in mysticism. A third simply liked to cut and change my style. My stories and articles appeared with spelling errors, with lines reversed, and sometimes with the pages in the wrong order. What could be better for a writer than to be his own publisher? I went with Zeinvel Gardiner to his attic on Nowolipki Street, and climbed four flights of stairs. On every landing there were open doors. Tailors sat at sewing machines singing Socialist ballads. Girls peeled potatoes and sang love songs. Mothers rocked babies. A carpenter planed a long board, his gray beard full of shavings. From the kitchens came the smell of fried onions, diapers, and garlic. On the fifth floor, we passed through a dark corridor and entered a room with a slanting ceiling. High up just under the ceiling was a little window. Pictures of Spinoza, Kropotkin, Mme. Blavatsky, Nietzsche were tacked on the walls. Over the bookcase, on a sheet of paper, Zeinvel Gardiner had printed in huge letters: THOU SHALT LOVE THY NEIGHBOR AS THYSELF.

It didn't take me long to find out Zeinvel Gardiner's brand of idealism. He didn't eat meat or fish or eggs—just bread, vegetables, and fruit. He belonged to a group that spoke Esperanto and to a circle that followed Stirner's theory of anarchism. He offered me a raw turnip and said, "The world is waiting for the pure word. We will tell our readers the truth. Every line will be polished. We will practice what we preach—experiment on ourselves first."

Soon we announced our magazine at the Yiddish Writers

Club. It was to be called *The Voice*, and we were immediately
flooded with manuscripts and congratulatory letters from the
provinces. Established writers we thought wouldn't be in-
terested in a fledgling journal sent us stories, chapters from
novels, and "fragments from larger works." As I read them,
I realized that in the whole heap of manuscripts not one
represented the pure word for which the human race was
waiting. Zeinvel Gardiner's contribution was an essay on
Nietzsche's *Thus Spake Zarathustra*. He used a great number
of dots and dashes, and he seldom finished a sentence. He
was trying to say something, but I could not fathom what it
was. He complained that Georg Brandes didn't understand
Nietzsche, but as far as I could tell, Zeinvel Gardiner didn't
even understand Georg Brandes. His writing was a hodge-
podge of allusions and obscurities, and countless quotations
from Ibsen. Whole pages were devoted to Maeterlinck's
The Blue Bird, which was still having a vogue with the in-
tellectuals of Warsaw. It was Zeinvel's contention that after
Zarathustra reached the summit of the mountain he would
find not only the Eagle and the Snake but the Blue Bird as
well, and that would enable the Superman to redeem himself
and humanity to boot.

I packed all the manuscripts into a paper bag and carried
them to Zeinvel Gardiner's attic room. When I got there, I
found him putting type into a justifier. He was setting the
introduction that we had written together. I put down the
bag and said, "Zeinvel, I'm no longer an editor."

He became pale. "Why?"

"*The Voice* isn't a voice, the word isn't a word. There's
nothing to work with."

Zeinvel Gardiner tried desperately to persuade me to stay.
He argued in the name of humanity, culture, and progress. In
his agitation he knocked over the justifier, and the type fell

on the floor. He warned me that all the writers in Warsaw would turn against me when they found out that I had abandoned the magazine.

We went out into the street and began to walk. After each few steps, Zeinvel stopped and gave me a new argument. The manuscripts could be edited. Our meeting was not just an accident. Literature was waiting for young men like ourselves. A chance and a combination like this might never occur again. Zeinvel began to tell me about his past. His father was a Hebrew teacher in a small town and his mother had died young. His sister had committed suicide. He had left the town because of a girl who didn't understand his ideals, his problems, his spiritual crises. To spite him, she had taken up with the bookkeeper of a sawmill. Zeinvel Gardiner lapsed into silence. His black eyes were sad. Suddenly he said, "Hamlet was right."

A few days later, another young writer took my place as editor. The first number of the magazine was three months late. The binder was keeping back several hundred copies because he hadn't been paid in full. It appeared without a cover and was printed on two different kinds of paper: one gray, one yellowish. Not only the text but the names of the contributors were full of misprints, and already there were quarrels and intrigues. An essayist whose manuscript had been rejected accused Zeinvel Gardiner of cheating him out of twenty-five zlotys. The wife of a poet whose poem was printed on the last page slapped Zeinvel. He was called a thief and a sellout. The Communist magazine *Aufgang* came out against *The Voice* with a three-page attack. According to *Aufgang*, *The Voice* was the swan song of dying capitalism, rotten imperialism, and Jewish chauvinism. Zeinvel had ignored the class struggle, the needs of the masses, and the shining light of the Soviet Union. What Zeinvel Gardiner meant by the Blue Bird was Mussolini's Fascist regime.

After Zeinvel read this attack, he sat up all night and wrote a rebuttal, but *Aufgang* refused to publish it. Instead, it launched a fresh attack and warned that the day of revenge was near. Zeinvel became sick. He got cramps in his stomach and couldn't keep his food down.

One day I heard that Zeinvel had gone back to the small town he came from. Someone told me that he had married his former girl, who had given up the bookkeeper at the saw-mill for him. Her father had a small plant that manufactured seltzer water and Zeinvel had gone into business with him.

Twenty years passed. In that time, I had gone to America and Hitler had destroyed Poland. In 1947, I got two months' vacation from the Yiddish newspaper in New York where I worked, and I went to Paris. There I found the remnants of the Polish Yiddish literati. They lived in a house that the city of Paris had given them temporarily on Rue de Patay. Some had fled the Nazis and gone to the Soviet Union. Some had managed to escape to Morocco and Algeria, and some had hidden in France during the Nazi invasion. Former Communists had become anti-Communists. Husbands had different wives, wives different husbands. Boys who were beginners in my time were now gray-haired men and spoke with authority.

For whole days and half nights I sat with them, listening to stories of Nazi murders and Bolshevik insanity. They spoke of Asiatic cities and villages in which they had found refuge between 1940 and 1945, and of all varieties of rightist and leftist bands. A number had been in Auschwitz, others in Soviet slave camps. Still others had fought in the Red Army or with Sikorski's Polish troops. All their tales were of hunger, murder, lice, epidemics, lechery, and senseless brutality.

Paris itself looked like a dead city. American tourists threw cigarette butts into the gutter and shabby pedestrians picked them out. The stores were empty, and in my hotel the elevator functioned only a few hours a day. Often the electricity failed and the bath had no hot water. I had to buy my food on the black market.

One morning someone knocked on my door. As a rule my visitors telephoned first, but this one came unannounced. I opened the door and saw Zeinvel Gardiner. He had not changed much. He stood there, swarthy, badly shaved, his hair unruly and knotted. His clothes were rumpled, as if he had slept in them.

"Zeinvel, come in!"

"You recognize me, huh?" His voice was muffled. He walked unsteadily and sat in a chair. There was something stiff and dramatic in his manner. His eyes twitched. He reminded me of the bearers of bad tidings in the Book of Job.

When I began to question him, he answered haltingly. Yes, he had been through the holocaust, first in the Ghetto, then in Russia. Where hadn't he been? In Bialystok, in Vilna, in Moscow, Tashkent, and Jambol . . . Exiled? . . . Yes, he had been exiled. . . . Forced labor? Yes, in barracks and factories . . . Starved? . . . What else? . . . His wife? The children? . . . Wiped out by the Nazis. . . . Married again? . . . After the war, in a German camp.

I asked him why he didn't live in the house that the city of Paris had given to the Yiddish writers. For a long while he was silent. Then he asked, "What for?" All at once he became talkative. I could barely believe my ears, but Zeinvel Gardiner wanted to publish a magazine—here in Paris—in Yiddish! He was saying that the whole misfortune would never have happened if the intellectuals had not turned traitor. The German writers had all become Nazis. In Russia they capitu-

lated to Stalin. What happened in Bialystok in the first weeks
of the war was impossible to describe. The writers from Po-
land jumped on the Communist bandwagon. They became
Bolsheviks overnight—the Labor Zionists, the Bundists, the
Folkists, and the Independents. To pacify those in power,
they denounced each other. They discovered in the writings
of their former friends Trotskyite deviations, Menshevik ren-
egation, traces of Zionism. He, Zeinvel, had told the truth,
and they forced him to leave Bialystok. He was put into
prison—forty people in one cell. The stench from the latrine
was enough to kill you. Day and night they deloused them-
selves and debated. In the middle of the night, prisoners
were dragged off to be grilled. Many died from the tor-
tures and others went mad. Trials were held in which hun-
dreds of the accused stood in a row to be sentenced wholesale
to slave camps, to jail, to work in the gold mines—all in the
name of Socialism. How strange, the editor of *Aufgang* was
one of the first to be liquidated.

Zeinvel recounted this in a low monotone, in unfinished
sentences, staring at a corner of the ceiling. Although I was
too familiar with such events, I was shocked by his matter-
of-fact account. I asked, "And you want to cure all this with
a little magazine?"

"Someone has to tell the truth."

"To whom?"

"To the few."

"Who's going to read a little magazine in Yiddish?"

"Someone will read it."

Zeinvel told me that he had an apartment—a room with a
kitchen in Belleville. He could get a set of type. His present
wife was a dressmaker and she earned a decent living. She had
lost her husband and children in Poland. She loved Yiddish
literature and had read my articles in the New York Yiddish
newspaper, which had been sent into the camps after the war,

as well as some of my books. She was ready to help financially. The name of the magazine could be the same as it had been in Warsaw: *The Voice*.

I asked the same question I had asked in Poland twenty years before: "Whom do you have to work with?"

"There are still honest people. The trouble is that the wicked make all the noise and the just sleep."

"They'll always sleep," I said.

"They can be woken up."

"If they're woken up, they'll become wicked."

"It doesn't have to be that way."

I should have given Zeinvel a flat no. He lived in Paris and I in New York. I had neither the time nor the energy to devote to a little magazine. But before I had a chance to refuse him he made me promise that I would come to his apartment for dinner.

That evening I bought a bottle of wine and a tin of sardines and went to see Zeinvel Gardiner. I walked up four flights of narrow, crooked stairs. Walking behind me were two suspicious-looking couples, and I guessed that rooms in the building were let out to streetwalkers. Zeinvel opened the door and there was a homely smell that even the holocaust had not eradicated.

Zeinvel's wife was small, with a young face, a short nose, and full lips. There was something playful in her eyes. It was hard to believe that this woman had gone through a concentration camp and lost a husband and children. She gave me a small, firm hand. She spoke as if she knew me. Zeinvel had told her a lot about me, she said, and of course she was familiar with my writing. She said, "Maybe you can get this magazine nonsense out of my husband's head."

"Friedele, this isn't nonsense," Zeinvel said. "The world is based on the word."

"The world is based on the fist, not the word."

"Long after all the fists have disappeared, the Ten Commandments will still be remembered."

"They may be remembered but no one will keep them."

As she set the table, she said to me, "You don't know me, but I know you. You writers disclose all your secrets."

"What do you know?"

"That's my secret."

For dinner she had cooked a Warsaw soup of potatoes and brown flour, and as she put the plate down in front of me I saw the blue concentration-camp number on her wrist. She noticed my looking at it and said, "If you die, you die, but if you live you have to go through the whole comedy. There are too many magazines already. If Moses himself descended from Heaven today, he'd just be laughed at."

"So what should we do, Friedele?" Zeinvel asked. "Look and keep quiet?"

"Who's going to read your magazine? The victims, not the murderers."

"Not even the victims have easy consciences."

"Your magazine won't make them any easier."

During dinner, Friedele told stories from the concentration camps, and although they were about hunger, plague, and murder, she made me laugh. It was the first time I had ever heard jokes about the camps. Even while the Nazis cracked their whips, Jews were joking. There were jesters even in the camps.

In the middle of the meal the door opened and a round little woman came to have a dress fitted. Friedele took her behind a screen. After a while Friedele reappeared and whispered, "When the Allies found her at Maidenek, she weighed sixty pounds. She was in the hospital for four or five months and no one thought she would live. Now she has a rich husband who's in the black market." Friedele opened a drawer and took out a fashion magazine. "If you published something like this, the world would listen to you."

Another twenty years passed. I had gone to Europe a few times, but somehow I never got around to revisiting Paris. The Yiddish publishers in Paris sent their magazines to me in New York, and occasionally I came across a poem or an article by Zeinvel Gardiner. He was still raging at society and condemning the immorality of the human species, though between the lines I thought I discovered a note of quiet resignation. Once, I saw his picture in a journal. He was no longer the Zeinvel Gardiner I had known but a hunched-up, paunchy old man. From time to time visitors from Paris told me about him. He and his wife had opened a lingerie shop, which had quickly expanded. It seemed unbelievable, but the Gardiners had got rich in France. They had an elegant apartment and had bought a summer house in Robinson. Friedele had been pregnant at the time of my visit, and several months after I left Paris she gave birth to a daughter.

Over the years my books had been translated abroad. I had publishers in Paris, in Milan, in Lisbon. On my next trip to Europe, after spending a week in Lisbon and two weeks in Switzerland, I went to Paris to meet my French editor. The Yiddish writers had heard that I was coming and had arranged a little reception for me. One morning the telephone operator in the hotel called to tell me that a M. Kaplan was waiting for me in the lobby. I asked that he come up to my room. A young man with curly hair and darting eyes appeared. I had never heard of him or his writing, but he told me that in addition to being on the staff of a Yiddish newspaper he was a poet. He had been through the Hitler catastrophe, he said, so he was older than I thought. He had acquired the style and gestures of a Parisian. He sat down, lit a cigarette, and made notes on a pad as he questioned me.

I asked, "How's Zeinvel Gardiner?"

His eyes suddenly became solemn. "Didn't you read the Yiddish press today?"

"Not today."

"Today is Zeinvel Gardiner's funeral."

I was silent for a long while and then I asked, "Was he sick?"

"No, actually not. A strange thing happened. His death was a sort of suicide."

"What happened?"

"Oh, it's a peculiar story. He and his wife had a big lingerie shop and they were pretty rich. From time to time he'd have something in a Yiddish magazine. All of a sudden he got the crazy idea of publishing a magazine in French. I say 'crazy' because he didn't really know any French—just enough to make himself understood. I don't know the facts exactly, but they say he sold the shop without his wife's knowledge, rented an office, and got a staff together. The result was that his wife chased him out of the house. Then some swindler sold him a nonexistent printing shop. Zeinvel was never a practical man. What did he need a magazine in French for? He literally died in the street. They found him dead, and today's the funeral."

After the young man finished interviewing me, I asked him when and where the burial was to be. Three in the afternoon, he said, and he was going. I suggested that we go together and invited him to have lunch with me. During lunch he said, "The situation with Yiddish writers in Paris is so bad that the cemetery is almost the only place they meet. They're old, many are sick, and the city has spread out. They don't come to the cafés in Montparnasse or Montmartre any more. After a funeral everybody goes to a café for a snack, and for some of the older writers that's their only social life. I hear that in New York things aren't much better."

"In New York they don't even go to funerals."

The Paris cemetery wasn't as far away or as barren as cemeteries are in New York—it looked like a huge garden. At the gate were a number of people, some of whom I recognized immediately; others seemed complete strangers, but when they told me who they were, their faces became instantly familiar. All of them had survived the Hitler destruction. They made the disjointed kind of conversation that is usually made at funerals. As we walked to the grave, they gave me a few details about Zeinvel: yes, the magazine had been his mania; his daughter, Jeannette, was studying literature at the Sorbonne and she had published poems in French magazines; she was engaged to a Frenchman. One of my colleagues from the old days told me quickly about a former lover of mine. He had met her in a village in Central Asia, where she worked as a seamstress. She had married a lawyer from Lodz, who had died of beriberi. Now she was married again, in Israel, and her daughter was a professor at the Hebrew University in Jerusalem.

We reached the Jewish section of the cemetery. Zeinvel Gardiner's grave was open. A red-cheeked rabbi with a sparse goatee recited prayers in French and Hebrew. He droned half his words and swallowed the others. I expected eulogies, but no one had prepared any. There wasn't even anybody there to say the Kaddish. Then, according to what must have been French custom, the relatives formed a receiving line and we shook hands, kissing and comforting them. I saw Mme. Gardiner, her daughter and her fiancé, and another woman, all in black. I recognized Friedele—she was older, but she still looked fresh. The years had given her eyes the determined expression of a woman who has carried the responsibility for a household and a business. I offered my hand, and she turned her face to me so that I could kiss her. I looked at her daughter and saw the Zeinvel Gardiner I had met in the soup kitchen for intellectuals forty years ago—the same high cheekbones, the same pallor, the same wide-set eyes. Even her short-cut hair reminded me of Zeinvel's disheveled head. Her mother murmured to me, "She's a writer . . . out to save the world . . . wants to continue Zeinvel's magazine. . . . Please come to see us."

The daughter spoke in a mixture of Yiddish and French. *"Oui, Monsieur,* pay us a visit . . . I have translated a story of yours into French . . . *Mon papa* recommended it . . . I plan to write my dissertation about Mendele Mocher Seforim . . ."

"Yes, I'll come."

"In our epoch, a journal can elevate literature to new levels . . . modern writing is all corrupted. *Mon professeur* said that—"

She stopped in midsentence. Others waited behind me. Her fiancé put a card in my pocket. Someone nudged me toward the group of Yiddish writers who were waiting for me. We were all supposed to go to La Coupole for a drink.

An old friend of mine, Feivel Mecheles, a humorist from Warsaw, was leaning against a tree. His once red hair had turned a yellowed white. Someone had told me that a tragedian had gone off with his wife while they were both fleeing the Nazis. He wrinkled his forehead and drew his brows together. I knew he wouldn't move until he had come up with a joke. I said, "Feivel, you can't force humor. Let's go."

He shook his head, smiled, revealing a new set of false teeth, and said, "Really, it doesn't pay to leave. We'll soon be back anyhow."

Translated by the author and Laurie Colwin

Lost

W HEN I was counseling readers for the Yiddish news-
paper where I worked, all kinds of people used to
bring their problems to me: betrayed husbands and wives;
relatives with quarrels from the old country; immigrants
who had come to America many years before and wanted
to apply for citizenship but did not know the dates of their
arrivals or the names of their ships. In most of the cases, my
help consisted in listening and offering words of comfort.
Sometimes I gave them the address of the HIAS or of an
organization that provided legal assistance. Usually, these
advice seekers came in the middle of the week—almost never
on Friday. During the years I held this job, I learned that
even Jews who worked on Saturday looked upon Friday as a
day of preparation for the holy Sabbath. Whether this was a
matter of tradition or of atavism is of no consequence here.

But one particular man came to me on Friday, late in the
day, when I was ready to go home. He appeared to be
in his seventies. His back was stooped. He had a white goatee
and bags under his eyes. He wore a long black coat, and I
thought he must be a new arrival to America. But the mo-
ment he sat down at my desk he said, "Do you see me? I
began to read your paper more than sixty years ago on the
first day I came to this country."

I asked him where he came from, and he mentioned a town
in Poland. He told me that he had studied in a yeshiva and
had tried to pass examinations to enter the university. Here

in America he became a teacher in a Talmud Torah, and later, with training, a dental technician. Of course, he was retired now.

He said, "I know your job is to give advice, but I did not come to ask that of you. What advice can you give to a man of eighty-three? I have everything I require, and when I die there is a cemetery plot that my *landsleit* have prepared for me. I came to you because I thought that what happened to me might interest you. You often write about the mysterious powers. You believe in demons, imps—what have you. I am not going to argue with you about their existence. Neither you have seen them nor I. Even if demons do exist, they are not in New York. What would a demon do in New York? He would get run over by a car or tangle himself in a subway and never find his way out. Demons need a synagogue, a ritual bathhouse, a poorhouse, a garret with torn prayer books—all the paraphernalia you describe in your stories. Still, hidden powers that no one can explain exist everywhere. I am not speaking just about theories. I have had an experience with them. The Yiddish newspapers wrote about it, and the English ones too. But how long do they write about anything? Here in America, if the Heavens would part and the angel Gabriel were to fly down with his six fiery wings and take a walk on Broadway, they would not write about it for more than a day or two. If you are in a rush to go light candles and bless the incoming of the Sabbath, I will come back some other time," he said, smiling and winking. "Though with a man my age one cannot be too sure."

"I am in no rush," I said. "Please sit down and tell me."

"Where shall I begin? I will begin where it all started— on the boat. I did not come here the way the other greenhorns did, a pauper. My father was wealthy. I was his oldest son. He wanted me to become a rabbi, but in those times the Enlightenment had slowly spread from Lithuania to Poland.

I secretly read Sokolov's *Morning Star*, and the new ideas enticed me. When I was about to be drafted into military service, my father wanted me to maim myself: cut off a finger, or—forgive the expression—rupture myself. But I was a healthy boy—tall and strong—and I told my father plainly that I would not make myself a cripple. 'So what do you intend to do?' he asked me. 'Serve the czar and eat army rations?' And I replied, 'I will go to America.'

"In those times, to have a son in America was considered a blight on the family—like having a convert or a suicide. But I insisted, and my parents had to consent. My father gave me five hundred rubles for travel expenses, which was a fortune in those days. Most immigrants came to America penniless. They traveled below deck. I traveled second class on a German ship. I discarded my long caftan before I left Europe. I brought a copy of *Do You Speak English?* with me. In comparison with other immigrants, I journeyed like a count.

"There was a special table in the dining room for those who ate kosher food. I sat there. There were only five or six of us. There were a German rabbi and a rich merchant also from Germany. Right across from me sat a girl who was traveling alone as I was. She came from Kovno. She was about my age. I was bashful, but when a boy and a girl sit together for seventeen days, they are bound to get acquainted. She had finished Gymnasium, and a Jewish girl who studied at a Gymnasium was such a rarity that I regarded her as a princess. She behaved like one, too. She kept aloof and seldom spoke. She was blond, slim, and quite tall for a girl. She dressed elegantly and spoke both Russian and German. After a few days we began to greet one another and even took a walk on the deck together. She told me that although she did not believe in the dietary laws, she had given her grandfather a holy promise to eat kosher food. I learned that she was an orphan. Her father had been a rich lumber merchant, and her grandfather owned a number of houses in Kovno. I asked her why she was going to America. In the beginning, she avoided answering; then she confided to me that she was on her way to her fiancé—a student who had become active in the revolutionary movement and had to escape from the police. The fiancé lived in New York and was supposed to be studying there in a university."

"What was her name?" I asked.

"Anna Davidovna Barzel. One morning she came to breakfast late, and the moment I saw her I knew that something terrible had happened to her. She was as white as the wall. She did not eat the food she was served. The others at the table also noticed that she was miserable and questioned her, but her answer was inaudible. That is how she was—exceedingly proud. After breakfast, I saw her standing at the railing, and she leaned over so far I feared what she might be going to do. With some hesitation, I approached her and asked, 'Anna Davidovna, what do you see there below?' She started and almost fell. At first, she looked annoyed because I had interrupted her, and I was afraid that she might be angry. Then she grew calm. She had undergone a drastic change—she seemed emaciated, sick, and dejected. Somehow I gained courage, and I said, 'Anna Davidovna, I beseech you by all that is holy to tell me what has happened. Perhaps I could help you.'

" 'No, you can't help me,' she said.

"In time she told me the following story. Before she left Kovno, her grandfather had given her one thousand rubles. She had changed the rubles for dollars in a bank, and she carried them in a little pouch around her neck, along with a small notebook with her fiancé's address in it. He had an unusual name—Vladimir Machtei. The night before, when she undressed, she found that both the money and the notebook had vanished from the pouch. Instead, she found the stub of a ship's ticket there and other trivial papers that had been in a valise. She had a cabin to herself, not wanting to share one. She remembered for sure that the previous morning when she had dressed she had the banknotes and the notebook in the pouch. She was also positive that she had not taken the ticket stub and other papers from the valise. What for? A ticket stub had no value.

"In our thoughts we are all a little cynical, and it occurred to me that perhaps she was playing around with some young man and that he might have stolen her possessions. I suggested this idea lightly, and Anna turned even paler than she was already. 'You are rude and I don't want to have anything more to do with you,' she said, and she turned her back on me. I felt ashamed. Actually, there was not one young man in the second class with whom she could have become intimate. I never saw her talk to anyone. She did not have a deck chair. Wherever she went, she carried a book with her. She was a reticent *barishnia* of a type that no longer exists.

"From that day till the end of the trip, Anna did not speak a word to me. When I greeted her, she did not answer. I went so far as to ask the waiter to take her a note in which I apologized for my discourtesy. The waiter told me that when she saw my name she tore the note to pieces. I have forgotten to tell you my name. In the old country, they called me Shmuel Opalovsky. Here, I am Sam Opal. After the waiter told me about the note, I maneuvered it so that I would come to the table when she had finished eating. I also stayed away from meals. I was fearful of the disdain she showed me.

"We finally arrived in the land of 'the streets paved with gold.' As a rule, immigrants were taken to Ellis Island, but when I showed the money I had brought with me, I was allowed to enter without delay. I was about to leave the ship, when I saw Anna. She was crying. She tried to speak to the immigration officers in Russian and then in German, but they did not understand her. I asked her what had happened, and when she saw me her eyes showed relief. It seemed that Vladimir Machtei had not come to meet her. Whether she was in despair because they wanted to take her to Ellis Island or because she had no money and no place to go, I don't remember. She was in distress, and this was my chance to correct my stupidity. I helped her get through customs, hired a carriage—there were no cars in those days—and I took her to a hotel on Avenue C. We began at once to search for Vladimir Machtei, but we never found him. As far as we could learn, no person with such a name existed in the United States.

"I must confess to you that at the time these things were happening, I suspected she had invented everything—the fiancé, the money, and the address book. But later I convinced myself that it was all true. She showed me Vladimir Machtei's letters, although she had thrown away the envelopes. She told me that he came from Poltava. Anna wrote to his aunt there, and the aunt answered that she hadn't heard from her nephew for a long time and did not have his address. My dear friend, I know that you are a busy man, so I will give you the bare facts. We got married. I have a daughter by her, grandchildren, and great-grandchildren. The baby was born two years after we married.

"But the story that I want to tell you begins only now. I lived with Anna for six years. In this period I became persuaded that I was the husband of a person not of this world. First of all, she was the most silent creature I have ever met. She did not even say yes or no—she merely nodded her head. She became talkative only when she lost something, and this happened so often that even now when I speak about it I shudder. Years later, I discussed it with psychiatrists and they presented me with all kinds of theories: Freud, Shmeud; complex, shmomplex. The fact is that things literally disappeared before her eyes and sometimes before mine. I would bring her a book from the library—a Russian book, for she never learned English. Suddenly it would vanish. I brought her a diamond ring and shortly there was no ring. I gave her household money, and I myself saw how she put the ten dollars into her purse. A half hour later, the money was gone. Each time she lost something, she became hysterical. She literally turned over everything in the house. She went so far as to rip open the mattress. I am by nature a social person, but as long as I stayed with her I remained practically in isolation. I almost never brought anyone into the house. She refused to speak Yiddish, or perhaps she really couldn't speak it. There was no lack of young people who spoke Russian, but the few times I invited some of them into the house, she ignored them. We lived in a state of crisis and constant turmoil because Anna was forever losing things. She would say to me, 'A demon follows me—a fiend.'

"I had read many books of the Enlightened ones and I was far from believing in demons, imps, sprites—the whole lot. I was born a rationalist. After all that has happened to me, I still can't believe in the supernatural. Let's not fool ourselves. Planes fly, trains move, and if you press the right button you can hear Caruso. No demon has ever stopped a plane or a train. But living with Anna made me so jittery that I would wake up in the middle of the night to make sure that my watch, my money, and my first papers had not dissolved. We were not compatible in other respects as well. A silent love is perhaps possible among animals, but to me, love involves conversation. She was pregnant for nine months and I don't recall her speaking about it once. The nurse in the clinic where she gave birth told me that she never so much as let out a groan. I had hoped that having a baby would change her character, but no. She did everything a mother should do, all in silence. My daughter began to prattle when she was a year old. At two and a half, she asked her mother innumerable questions. Anna just shrugged. I was still a teacher in the Talmud Torah, and the moment I came home I would devote myself to the child, trying to answer her questions and playing with her. I must tell you that in her own way Anna loved the child. When toys were lost—it happened often, too often—Anna became frantic. The baby herself also seemed frightened. One day I brought her a teddy bear. Almost at once the bear disappeared. Our apartment was small, and there was really no place where it could have got to. I was afraid that the child had inherited her mother's dismal fate. Thank God, she is a normal woman.

"I remember the scene with the teddy bear as if it had happened yesterday. I had gone into the kitchen to make tea— Anna was not much of a housewife and I had to prepare things myself. I heard the baby screaming. I went back to the living room, and Anna stood there, white. 'The teddy bear is gone,' she said. 'The fiend tore it from her little hands.' I felt furious and I yelled, 'You're a liar! You threw it out of the window.' She said, 'Look out and see.' I did, and of course the teddy bear was not there. We lived in a decent neighborhood. Things could lie outside for days and nobody would touch them. 'You threw it into the garbage!' I yelled. 'Go and look in the garbage,' she said. I took the house apart, but there was no trace of the teddy bear. Even today, I say to myself that Anna must have hidden it somewhere—but where and for what reason? Anna seldom cried. This time tears streamed down her cheeks. In all the years, I never spoke about these things—people would have considered me mad. Even after what I am about to tell you occurred, I never told the whole story to anyone. Some time ago you discussed in an article the case of a farmer who vanished before the very eyes of his wife and children. Do you remember that article?"

"Yes, I remember. I read about it in a magazine and a number of other publications."

"What was the name of the farmer? When did it happen?" Sam Opal asked me, with the glint of a reader who prides himself that he remembers what was written better than the writer himself.

"Really, I've forgotten."

"I knew that you wouldn't remember, but I do. The farmer's name was David Lang, and the farm was a few miles from Gallatin, Tennessee. I even remember the date—September 1890."

"You have a remarkable memory."

"I remember it because it interested me immensely. I decided then that you were the person who would not consider me insane. I even tried to investigate the case myself, and I wrote to the mayor of Gallatin. I never got an answer. I want you to know that precisely the same thing happened with my wife," Sam Opal said. 'She vanished in broad daylight here in Manhattan. I wasn't there, because I had left her standing at the window of a shoe store and gone home. But I might just as well have been—it wouldn't have made any difference. She never returned to the house. They wrote about her disappearance in your newspaper, and in others as well. The New York police should have a record of it—they have records of thousands of missing persons. For them, this is an everyday occurrence. Their explanation is always simple: ran away, was kidnapped. Lately, they also use the word 'amnesia.' None of these answers fits the case. Could you treat me to a glass of water?"

I went to the faucet and brought the man a paper cup filled with water. All the journalists had left, even the reporters who worked in the city room. Friday they closed the press a little earlier than other days of the week. Sam Opal drank half the contents of the cup and asked, "Do you have any details about David Lang's case?"

"No, but I have read about it in a number of occult anthologies."

"How do the psychologists interpret an occurrence like this?"

"Psychologists pay no heed to such matters. What cannot be explained is considered unscientific."

"It happened in 1898, in June," Sam Opal went on. "Our girl was already more than three years old. I've forgotten to mention an important point. Anna was always afraid that she might lose Natasha—that was our little girl's name. You must understand that I did not choose this name. Anna was in her own way a Russian patriot, although we had no cause to be in love with czarist Russia. Yes, she always dreaded that the child might disappear. I feared it myself. If it can happen to a teddy bear, why not to a child? Anna almost never left Natasha alone, and when it was absolutely necessary to go somewhere, she took her along.

"That day it was cool and rainy. Anna decided that she had to buy shoes. We were going to a hotel in the Catskill Mountains and she needed a pair of summer shoes. We had a neighbor who had a daughter of fifteen. This girl loved our little Natasha. Her name was Dorothy. Anna had complete confidence in Dorothy, and she left Natasha with her. Because of Anna's lack of English, I accompanied her. She would never enter a store without buying something, so as not to disappoint the merchant. But when it comes to footwear one cannot be too considerate. I was supposed to see to it that she didn't buy shoes that would be too tight or a pair that the salesman wanted to get rid of. We lived on Second Avenue and Eighteenth Street, which was then considered uptown, and many wealthy people had moved into this neighborhood. By this time I had become a dental technician. It was a new profession in America, and it paid well. There were many shoe stores on the avenue and we window-shopped, passing from one to the other. After a while I tired of the whole business. I had a laboratory in my apartment and I wanted to return to my work. Anna had already bought socks and panties for the baby, and she gave them to me, saying, 'If I don't find the shoes I want, perhaps I will try Fifth Avenue.'

"Those were her last words to me. That was the last time I saw her. Many hours later, I informed the police. It was evening. The Irish policeman considered the whole affair a joke and he advised me to wait until later that night, or until the next morning. About one o'clock I returned to the station, and the policeman on the night shift suggested that my wife was probably visiting her boy friend. Just the same, he wrote down everything and told me to come the next day if she had not returned. I went back for days and weeks. Anna had disappeared like a stone in the water. People came up with the theories you would expect. Perhaps she had a clandestine lover. Perhaps she had found her lost fiancé, Vladimir Machtei, and the old love had rekindled. Perhaps she had decided to return to Russia and throw a bomb at the czar. From the police I had learned that not only men ran away in America but women as well. But none of the cases about which I heard compared to mine. Anna had no lovers. The baby was dear to her. If Vladimir Machtei wanted to know Anna's whereabouts, he could have written to her grandparents. In all the years we had been in America, he never showed a sign of life. Deep inside me, I knew the tragic and unbelievable truth: that Anna was by nature or fate—call it as you like—a person born to lose and to be lost. She lost her money, her possessions, her fiancé. She might have lost the child, too, if she had not got lost herself. I say 'deep in me' because my reason would never accept anything so irrational. What does it mean? How can a thing become nothing? The Pyramids have stood in place for six thousand years, and unless there is an unusual earthquake, they may last for another six thousand—or sixty thousand. In the British Museum and here in the Metropolitan, you find mummies and artifacts that have endured for many centuries. If matter can turn to nothing, all of nature is a nightmare. This is what my logic dictates to me. In the case of that farmer in Tennessee, some believed that the earth had opened its mouth and swallowed him the way it is described in the Bible of Korah and his congregation. But if the earth had opened that day on Second or Fifth Avenue, it would have swallowed more than just Anna."

"So you believe that a demon or demons took her?" I asked.

"No, I don't believe this, either."

For a long while we sat in silence, then I asked, "Did you remarry?"

"No, I could have got a divorce easily, but I remained alone all these years. I mean, I did not marry."

"Why not? Were you so much in love with Anna?"

"This was not the reason. The most faithful men and women remarry after the death of their spouse, but what had happened to me kept me back. I hoped that I would live long enough for the riddle to be solved, but I am at the end of my road and I have found no answer. A person who has witnessed what I did can no longer make plans, build a house, attach himself to people. Spiritually, I became lost myself."

"It's quite possible that she still lives somewhere," I said.

"Where? A woman in her eighties. Yes, it is possible. Somehow, I had hoped that you could give me an explanation. I would be satisfied even with a theory, but it would have to make sense."

"In Genesis it is mentioned that Enoch 'was not; for God took him.' "

"Do you believe in this?" he asked.

"I don't know what to believe in."

"Well, I won't take up any more of your time. But I wonder

what a scientist would say if I were to press this story upon him? He would have to find some solution."

"He might say that your wife was a pathological liar, or possibly insane."

"But where is she?"

"In the Hudson, in the sea, back in Russia, or perhaps even here with Vladimir Machtei."

Sam Opal rose from his chair and I rose with him. For a minute we stared at one another and neither of us spoke. Then I said, "Since I am not a scientist I will give you my own unscientific theory."

"What is it?"

"Vladimir Machtei was the demon who stole Anna's money on the ship, took away little Natasha's teddy bear, and later kidnapped Anna. She was engaged to a demon to begin with."

"Why would the demon pick on her?"

"They are said to be attracted to the shy and the beautiful."

"But he had an aunt in Poltava."

"A demon's aunt is also a demon."

Translated by the author and Rosanna Gerber

The Prodigy

A T THE BEGINNING of the present century, around 1907 or
1908, not long after the war with Japan, news spread
throughout Warsaw of a prodigy named Kopel Rashkes. Ko-
pel was the youngest child of Reb Tanhum Rashkes, a clever
Hasid of the court of Kotzk, a building owner, and a topsy-
turvy scholar, of whom it was said that he recited the
morning prayers at night and the evening prayers in the
morning. At the age of seventy, Reb Tanhum had married a
nineteen-year-old girl who had borne him Kopel. By the time
he was four, Kopel had already studied the Pentateuch with
Rashi's Commentary, and by five—the Gemara. At six, he
played twenty members of the Warsaw Chess Club simulta-
neously and won seventeen of the games. He taught himself
mathematics, could in his mind multiply numbers into the
six figures within minutes, and was also expert at quickly
calculating the square root and the cube root of large num-
bers. Articles about him appeared in the newspapers. A
special commission came from St. Petersburg to test Kopel and
investigate his abilities.

In the summer of 1914, Reb Tanhum, his wife, and Kopel
had gone to Carlsbad for the mineral water that was so bene-
ficial to the older man's liver, and when the war broke out
they were caught in Austria and couldn't get back. Reb Tan-
hum died in 1915 and the widow settled with her son in
Berne, Switzerland. The professors at the local university

took an interest in Kopel, arranged stipends for him, and made it possible for him to study. The mother, a product of a Hasidic family, hired a teacher to study Jewish subjects with Kopel. Following the Polish–Bolshevik War of 1920, Reb Tanhum's widow came back to Warsaw, but Kopel stayed on in Berne. The mother boasted that he became a mathematics professor there—the youngest professor in the whole world. The Warsaw chess players read accounts in chess magazines of how Kopel played in international tournaments, and they predicted that he would grow up another Schlechter or Lasker. Following Pilsudski's revolution in 1926, Kopel Rashkes returned to Warsaw. He had quarreled over something with the Swiss professors and had also suffered a defeat in a chess tournament. He was remembered as a handsome little boy, but now he had a black beard and a hunched back besides. The mother had kept it a secret, but in Switzerland his back had suddenly begun to twist and no braces or massages helped. He spoke a mixture of Yiddish and German. In Warsaw he had instituted a lawsuit against his half sisters and brothers from Reb Tanhum's earlier marriage, who had robbed him of his inheritance. In the meantime, Kopel's mother had married a wine merchant from Lodz, and Kopel didn't approve. He turned away from his family.

For a while he was a lecturer on the mathematics faculty at Warsaw University. He could have been a full professor, but he was hindered by the fact that he spoke a broken Polish. He had won his suit against his sisters and brothers, and the court had awarded him a house on Ceglana Street; but due to the rent control, it brought him a scant income. At a lecture at the student club in 1928, Kopel met Gina, or Genendel Shapiro, who had left her rabbinical family to study literature at the free Polish university, Wszechnica. Gina was tall and dark, with black eyes and an unusually pale skin that was as smooth as satin. She had been elected beauty queen at a ball organized by the Yiddish press. Gina was living with an aunt who had left a Hasidic home years earlier to become a nurse at the Warsaw Jewish Hospital.

Kopel Rashkes's lecture had been called "The Human Intellect and Cosmic Knowledge," and it had attracted a huge throng. In Switzerland Kopel Rashkes had been drawn into mysticism. Here in Poland, he became involved with a group of spiritualists who used to hold séances under the famous medium, Kluski. Kluski specialized in summoning spirits who left their handprints in vessels of paraffin. Professor Ochorowicz and a number of psychic researchers in England, France, and Germany considered Kluski the greatest medium of all time. Kluski was dead now and his disciples sought a leader. Kopel Rashkes (or Konstantin Rashkes, as his followers called him) enjoyed the prestige of a prodigy and scholar. He lived in a large apartment in his house on Ceglana Street, which was inhabited mostly by old and prosperous families.

Although Rashkes conducted his lecture in a mixture of Polish and German, it was attended by a great number of Poles who were interested in psychical research. Gina Shapiro came two hours early and took a seat in the front row. She had read an essay by Rashkes on the same theme in a magazine. Kopel Rashkes was barely twenty-seven but he looked forty. He was small, with a broad brow; long tufts of hair growing out of the middle of his skull, and dark eyes. His skin was sallow and scarred from acne. He wore a black velvet jacket, a high collar, and shoes with spats. He cited instances of scientific discoveries that had evolved in a second. He spoke of current prodigies and of past ones. He mentioned a mathematical formula that had revealed itself to him in a dream. He related an event that had occurred within his own family and which had been told him by his grandfather, Reb Baruch Amshinaver. It was the story of a boy who at the age of five had preached a sermon on the Great Sabbath at the synagogue; at seven, he already had a long beard, and at ten he grew as gray as a patriarch. He became senile at twelve and died a few years later of hardened arteries and old age. He could recite pages of the Talmud that he had never even read! When his father, an Alexandrow Hasid, took him to Alexandrow for the first time to meet his rabbi, the boy knew every street in the town. He even pointed out a spot where a well had once been located before it had been filled in and the ground paved with stones. Kopel Rashkes's lecture lasted more than two hours, and although he stammered, confused his notes, coughed, drank water, and often took lengthy pauses, the audience remained silent. When he finished, stormy applause erupted. Gina pushed her way through to Kopel Rashkes and kissed his head, his eyes, his cheeks. She fell to her knees before him and cried, "My teacher, Master, God! . . ." And she tried to kiss his feet.

A few months later, Kopel Rashkes and Gina Shapiro were married. It was a quiet ceremony with no in-laws present. Rashkes had questioned Gina extensively about her past— whether she had had other men and whether she had ever loved anyone before. Gina had assured Kopel that he was her first love and that she was a pure virgin. But Kopel Rashkes demanded that Gina submit to an examination by a gyne- cologist, one of his admirers. Only when the doctor had pro- vided written confirmation of Gina's virginity did Rashkes consent to the wedding.

Right after the wedding, Kopel began to plague Gina with his jealousy. Someone had told him that in order to be chosen beauty queen of the Press Ball, a girl had to submit to the members of the panel. Gina swore the holiest oaths that no one on the jury had even touched her, but this didn't satisfy him. She had to provide him with a list of the judges and Kopel Rashkes conducted a thorough investigation of each of them—whether they led a respectable family life, whether they had mistresses, and whether they were honorable members of their profession. Gina argued that a person of Rashkes's clairvoyant powers should have known the truth without such probing, but Rashkes warned her, "Better confess!"

"Dearest, to what shall I confess? I wouldn't even recognize one of them in the street, God is my witness."

"Something about this doesn't smell kosher . . ."

At the university, intrigues were hatched against Kopel Rashkes. He published essays in occult periodicals and surrounded himself with people who were a disgrace to a serious scholar. The regent issued Kopel an ultimatum: to either part from the spiritualists or leave the university. Kopel Rashkes was forced to resign. He now lived solely on the rents and the small fees that he earned from articles in occult magazines. He forced Gina to give up her studies at the Wszechnica. He didn't want her to sit next to male students who lusted after her, nor did he trust the younger professors. Rashkes suffered from stomach trouble and Gina prepared special soups and groats for him. In the evenings, Gina played hostess to the visitors who came to the séances. Rashkes didn't possess Kluski's powers, but the circle had discovered a young woman, a medium who displayed greater miracles than Mrs. Hardinge Britten, Cora Tappin-Richmond, and even Mrs. Piper and Eusapia Palladino. Her name was Halina Walewska, and she had as a control a fifteenth-century Polish squire, Zdzislaw Brzeski. Brzeski spoke an archaic Polish in a male voice through her lips. Halina Walewska sat between two men who held her hands and controlled her legs, but the trumpet on the table blew anyway and the piano played all by itself; little flames flashed and cold winds blew. An invisible hand wrote on a planchette. In a small "tent" constructed of curtains materialized a woman who at the time of Kosciuszko's uprising had dressed as a man, given herself the name of

Stach Mlot, fought alongside the soldiers, and been killed by a czarist bullet. She now hovered in the air and kissed Rashkes on his scalp.

Rashkes had started writing a book that would prove through logic and mathematics the existence of God, the immortality of the soul, the authenticity of mind reading, premonition, and other such psychic powers. His case for telepathy took this track: if one accepted the fact that there was a central intelligence or brain that controlled the universe, then this power had to have the opportunity to issue orders to every part of the universe. If these orders were to be dispatched with the help of electromagnetic waves, then the farthest stars wouldn't receive them until thousands or millions of years after they had been issued. Therefore, there had to exist a force that could relay the information immediately, regardless of the distance it had to travel, and this could only be a psychic force.

A publisher in Cracow had given Rashkes an advance. A portion of the book had been printed in *Light*. The Kluski circle predicted that Rashkes's work would once and for all convince the honest skeptics.

But instead of working on the book, Rashkes wasted his time wrangling with Gina. It happened like this. One night after long hours of grilling Gina, and demanding that she swear to the truth about her past, Gina confessed that once when she had been traveling through a town in Poland and had gone into a pharmacy to buy pills for a headache, she had felt something akin to desire for the pharmacist or for his clerk.

Rashkes quickly seized upon this. How had he looked— young, old, blond, dark, Jewish, Gentile? Did he have blue eyes or black eyes? Gina didn't recall his appearance. She remembered only that he had a reddish mustache and a gold tooth. Rashkes began to quiz her: had she felt love toward him or lust? Would she have sinned with him had he proposed it? Would she have married him if he were single? That night, the couple didn't sleep a wink. Gina got up with a migraine. Rashkes spent the whole day dozing on the couch. The next night, the couple again didn't get to sleep. Rashkes talked so much about the pharmacist and asked so many questions that Gina felt she would suffer a nervous breakdown.

She already doubted if such a person as the pharmacist had actually existed or whether the whole thing hadn't been a dream or a hallucination. When she dozed off for a while, the pharmacist came back to her in a dream; he screamed at her and sprayed her with some burning liquid.

One night, Rashkes decided to go to that town with Gina to see if the pharmacist was still there. Gina complained, "Lunatic! You'll bring us both to grief!"

But Rashkes replied, "I must know the truth!"

The couple first took the train, then a bus. Gina recognized the pharmacy, but the present owner was an elderly man. The couple began to inquire whether the shop had once been owned by a person with a reddish mustache and a gold tooth. The old pharmacist drew up his white brows suspiciously and asked, "Why do you want to know?"

After lengthy discussion, the old man admitted that he had once had a clerk who fit the description. His name had been Morris Lopata. That was all the old man remembered.

Back in Warsaw, Rashkes made up a list of all the pharmacies in the city and the couple went from one to another, but Morris Lopata was nowhere to be found. There was a Morris Lopata in the telephone book, but he was a pastry baker. Rashkes made plans to search for Morris Lopata throughout Poland. He went to the municipal archive where address and telephone books were kept.

He stopped having relations with Gina. He demanded of

Halina Walewska that she summon up Morris Lopata if he were dead. Halina Walewska fell into a trance and said, "I see a man in a white smock . . . Is he a doctor? No, a pharmacist . . . He is saying something but his voice comes from afar . . . He speaks of a woman that he loves . . . loved deeply . . . But she broke his heart and married someone else . . . He sends her his blessings from the spheres he now inhabits . . . He hopes to unite again with her soul . . ."

As she heard these words, Gina burst into tears. Kopel Rashkes muttered, "Everything is clear . . ."

Rashkes had ceased to search for Morris Lopata among the living, but relations between the husband and wife remained strained. Rashkes grew impotent. He spent the nights speaking only of Morris Lopata. Gina complained, "What's the point of it all? He actually never even looked at me."

The couple went to the Jewish communal office in Warsaw and searched for the name of Morris Lopata among the dead. They did find such a name, but it was of a man who had died thirty years before. Kopel Rashkes demanded that Halina Walewska again summon up Morris Lopata's soul. She did it, but his words were contradictory.

Living with Kopel Rashkes became so difficult for Gina that she packed her things and went back to her aunt, the nurse. Gina began to study nursing herself. At first, the couple still conversed on the telephone. Later, Gina stopped calling altogether. Rashkes threw jealous fits over the telephone. He called her aunt a slut and a madam. He suspected Gina of having relations with her teachers and with the doctors at the hospital.

Three-quarters of a year went by and Kopel Rashkes didn't hear a word from Gina. Halina Walewska materialized Polish women for him from earlier centuries, and they kissed him and whispered intimacies in his ear. The séances lasted far into the night, and during the day Rashkes tried to analyze all these phenomena and to arrive at some kind of conclusion. Did the dead live on? Did they have bodies? Was nothing lost at death? He had fallen in love with these extra-terrestrial women and it didn't bother him that they caressed the other men at the séances. At times when he sat alongside Halina and clamped her leg, he felt waves of passion emanating from her. Once when he had inadvertently put his head against hers, she licked his ear with the tip of her tongue. Another time, he saw that the man who was controlling her leg from the other side had placed his hand on her knee.

That winter was supposed to be one of the coldest in Poland's history. Warsaw lay half buried in snow and the frost didn't let up for weeks. The people who took part in the séances were nearly all sick. One evening, only Halina Walewska showed up. She wore a fox-fur coat, a fur hat, and fur boots. Her face with the high cheekbones and snub nose was red, and her eyes gleamed like a seventeen-year-old maiden's. As usual, Rashkes had arranged a "tent" in the living room and lit a red lamp for the séance. But would the spirits appear without the appropriate hymns and without the hands linked on the table to provide the energy? Halina said, "We can try."

She sat down next to Rashkes and placed her knee against his. Their hands touched on the table. She began to sing the hymn "Sisters of the Night" and her voice had never seemed so pure, sweet, and mysterious as on this night.

The glowing oven threw off heat. The table began to vibrate, and Rashkes actually felt its wooden legs trying to rise and tear loose from the floor like some beast that has just awakened from a deep sleep. He himself was as if asleep while awake. He pulled Halina around and she pressed her breast against him. An unearthly heat emanated from her body. Her mouth seared his. Without a word he led her to the sofa and she gave herself to him in ecstasy. Each time that Rashkes thought that he had satiated his desire, he was seized by a new surge of passion. She clasped his hunchback with such force that he felt his spine cracking. She said to him, "You're stronger than any man I've ever possessed."

"Have you had many?"

She laughed. "At the least, a hundred."

Rashkes put on the light and they ate a second supper together: bread, cheese, halvah. Halina brewed coffee. She put on Gina's apron. They drank the hot coffee and ate the pretzels that Rashkes kept for his guests. He said, "All those females that you materialized were yourself."

"Yes, they were all me."

Later in bed, Rashkes questioned her and she confessed. Yes, she had copulated with a number of the men who took part in the séances. She had given birth to a child, a girl, whom an old woman in Powazek was raising. Halina went to visit the child every other Sunday.

Rashkes asked who the father was and Halina shrugged. "I'm not completely sure."

And she began to laugh and yank his tufts of hair. "What are those, earlocks?" she asked.

"Shiksa! Hussy, *nafka!*" Rashkes both scolded her and showered her with kisses.

"What's a *nafka*? Is that Hebrew?"

"Aramaic."

"Oh, mother!"

And as Halina uttered these words she was asleep. Rashkes had never seen anyone fall asleep that quickly. She became as white as chalk. Her lips trembled. It was all supernatural and what Nietzsche called beyond good and evil.

A week passed or more. One night at three o'clock the phone rang. Rashkes had fallen asleep and he awoke with a tremor. He got out of bed and, wearing only his nightshirt, went to the telephone in the hall.

"Gina, is that you?" he said.

He heard Gina's voice on the other end. She emitted a sound that was a half laugh, half cry.

"How did you know that it was me?"

"I know everything!" Rashkes said.

"If you know everything, tell me why I'm calling in the middle of the night."

"You found Morris Lopata."

Gina burst out crying. "Are you a prophet, or what?"

"I don't know myself what I am."

Gina coughed and choked. She spoke in the lamenting tone of pious women who relate the miracles of wonder rabbis. "I came home from school and I felt a soreness in my throat. With me, if my throat acts up, it can drag on for weeks. A pharmacy had opened down the street and I went down to buy some aspirin. I went in and I recognized him. It's a miracle I didn't faint dead away."

"Did you speak to him?"

"I was with him until an hour ago at the Café Metropol. We had to leave because they closed up."

"Is he single?"

"He has a wife and children."

"Did you tell him everything?"

"Yes, everything."

For a long while, neither spoke. Then Rashkes asked, "Ginele, are you still on the wire?"

"Yes, sure."

"Do you feel any desire for him?"

"I won't become involved with a married man."

"So what will you do?"

"Keep going to school."

"Come back to me."

She didn't reply at once. "You'll start tormenting me again."

"No, Ginele, from now I'll be good to you."

"Kopel, I hear you trembling. Put on your warm bathrobe. I'll wait," Gina said with concern.

Rashkes went to find the bathrobe. As he stood there by the open wardrobe poking around in the dark for the bathrobe, his lids closed and he dozed off for an instant and even began to dream. He started and came awake. He draped a coat over himself and went back to the telephone. Gina spoke at length. She repeated Morris Lopata's every word, even what he had said to the waiter about the tea and cookies. She remembered all the compliments that he had paid her, all his druggist's jokes and expressions. She described him as she had once before, that night in bed: small, round, with a reddish mustache and ruddy cheeks. His hair had already thinned in the middle, but blond curls dangled all around the bald spot. Gina even remembered the kind of shirt he wore, the tie and cuff links. Rashkes listened wide-eyed. A remarkable memory! he thought or mumbled. When a female is in love it rouses cosmic powers within her. His stomach ached and his heart fluttered in anticipation of meeting this Morris Lopata and of holding a long conversation with him.

"Ginele, since you desire him, you must have him," he argued. "The will is not just a phenomenon but the noumenon, the thing-in-itself. That's what Schopenhauer says. Everything comes from the cosmic depths. *De profundis*—"

"So what shall I do?"

"Bring him here."

Day was already dawning when Rashkes hung up the receiver. He went back to bed, covered himself with the down coverlet, and lay there in deep contemplation. Along with the winter sun there emerged within him a secret that he had apparently always known but had never truly acknowledged—a truth hidden in those recesses of consciousness where the ego and the non-ego flow together; the superconscious and the unconscious, the personal and the uni-

versal. Rashkes fell asleep and dreamed about Morris Lopata.
They were playing chess. Suddenly Rashkes saw that Morris
Lopata was the white queen. He wore a veil over his face
and lace-edged drawers. How is this possible? Rashkes won-
dered. How can the player himself be a chess figure? He
awoke frightened, drenched in sweat, filled with a lust that he
had never before experienced.

A few days later, Gina came back to Rashkes. In mid-March,
Morris Lopata started to take part in the séances. He was
small and round, with a potbelly and a bald spot on his head.
The blue eyes behind the gold-rimmed spectacles were al-
ways smiling—sweetly, artfully, slyly. Each time that he came
he brought a present for the others—cookies, liqueur, halvah.
He patted Gina's cheek in front of everybody and gave her
advice on how to keep her hands soft in the wintertime, how
to use powder and cream, how to polish her nails; and even
gave her recipes for cooking and baking. He also kissed
Halina Walewska. When those present sang hymns, Morris
Lopata's thin little voice could be heard.

Morris Lopata had many relatives that had gone "over to
the other side," and Halina summoned them all up and
brought greetings from them. It always came out that Rash-
kes and Lopata sat on either side of Halina Walewska and
controlled her legs. Gina sat between Morris Lopata and
another man. When Halina went into a trance, throwing back
her head and fixing her eyes on the ceiling, Rashkes's and
Lopata's hands would meet on her lap. They lifted the hem of
her dress, tickled her thighs, played with her garters. After-
ward, their fingers intertwined with each other's. Rashkes
knew quite well that with the other hand Morris Lopata
was stroking Gina's calves and even fondling her belly.

In the red shine of the lamp, all the faces glowed, all the
eyes gleamed. The ancient squire Brzeski revealed secrets
of the other world in a deep voice and in the archaic Polish

of King Sobieski's times. Brzeski was fraternizing with all kinds of big people on high, with the Holy Kinga and the Priest Skarga; with Jagelo and Wanda, with King Kazimierz and Stefan Batory. The Jewish patriot Berek Joselevicz also found himself in this exalted company. Brzeski broke heavenly bread with them, drank the divine wine, and probed the mysteries of immortality. Brzeski met with Kluski and brought messages from him.

At times, Brzeski discussed the situation in Poland. He predicted a holy war in which the Polish military would drive off the godless Bolsheviks and march all the way to Moscow. The new Poland would again stretch from the Black Sea to the Baltic Sea. Brzeski also brought tidings to the Jews. Their Messiah would come, redeem them from exile, and rebuild the Temple in Jerusalem. Zdzislaw Brzeski constantly brought up the fact that love, like the soul from which it stemmed, could never die. It existed in all the spheres. It created its own bodies, both astral and flesh and blood. Those who crossed over to the other side weren't vain and didn't know about such things as jealousy.

The winter had passed and spring had come. Morris Lopata was now spending the nights at Kopel Rashkes's house. His wife came running to Kopel Rashkes, crying and threatening that if Morris didn't return to her, she would go to the police and charge that they had led her husband astray.

Not long afterward, Rashkes received a summons to appear before an investigating judge. The tenants in his house had complained to the authorities that their landlord had turned the building into a den of iniquity where there was singing at night, black magic was performed, and indecent acts were committed. Most of the tenants stopped paying their rent. Morris Lopata admitted to Gina and Kopel Rashkes that he was longing for his children. Besides, the séances were having such an effect upon him that the whole day afterward he walked around dazed and literally didn't know what he was doing in the pharmacy. Once he gave a woman rat poison when she asked for bicarbonate of soda; she barely escaped death from poison.

Morris Lopata came to say goodbye to Kopel, Gina, and Halina Walewska. He brought the ladies roses and eau de cologne.

One night as the people at the séance sang the hymn "Heaven on Earth" by the glow of the red lamp, the table vibrated and tried for levitation, the piano tinkled, the trumpet groaned, and the ancient squire Brzeski was speaking about Kosciuszko's heroic uprising of 1794, a shot was heard. The sitters around the table assumed that this came from the female soldier Stach Mlot, who had served with Kosciuszko's troops and fallen in the battle at Maciejowice. They kept on singing. But then a dull thud was heard along with an outcry from Gina. A chair toppled. In the midst of the séance Kopel Rashkes had put a bullet into his brain.

Translated by Joseph Singer

The Third One

I T WAS sweltering outside, but the cafeteria was cool. During the day, between three and five, it was almost empty. I took a table near the wall, drank coffee, nibbled a piece of apple cake, and looked into an occult magazine. In the letters to the editor, a woman wrote that her cat had been run over by a car and she had buried it but still it came to visit her every night. The woman gave her name and her address in a Texas village. There was sincerity in the letter; surely it could not have been made up. But does the astral body really exist? I wondered. And do animals possess it, too? If so, my whole philosophy must be revised.

Before I could undertake so large an order, I went to the counter and got another cup of coffee. "One reality has nothing to do with the other," I said to myself.

I looked at the few people sitting around me. A young man in a pink shirt was studying a racing form, smoking one cigarette after another; his ashtray overflowed with butts and ashes. Two tables away a girl was reading the want ads in the daily paper. To the left near the door sat a tall man with a white beard and long white hair—a relic of old America. I often saw him. He looked poor but clean, and he always carried a book with him. Was he religious? Was he a free-thinker of the old school, a pacifist, a vegetarian, a spiritualist, an anarchist? I had been curious about him for some time, but I never made an effort to find out who he was.

The door opened and in came someone I recognized, although I could not recall his name or where I had met him. He was a small man with a shock of hair the color of sand. His head was too big for his body. He could have been anywhere from forty to fifty-five. There was a withered haggardness in his face. He had high cheekbones, a flat nose, a long upper lip, and the tiny chin of a baby. He wore a sports shirt and linen trousers. At the check machine he hesitated. His yellow eyes darted from right to left as if he were searching for someone. Then he saw me and his face lit up. He pulled a check out vigorously, and the machine gave a loud ring. He approached my table with mincing steps. He was wearing sandals with two straps. He seemed to have adjusted to the heat of New York, while I wore a suit, hat, and tie. When he got to my table, he said in the familiar Polish Yiddish of the Lublin region, "What are you doing here in the middle of the day? Cooling off? May I sit with you? Can I bring you something?" His voice was slightly nasal.

"Thank you. Nothing. Sit down."

"You once promised to call me," he said. "But that's how things are in this city—no one has the time or the patience. You probably lost my number anyway. I do it myself—I write down addresses and numbers and they disappear. Do you come here often? I used to be a steady customer, but not lately. My wife has asked about you several times. Do you live nearby?"

Before I could answer him, he ran over to the counter with quick little steps. "Who is he?" I asked myself. The truth was that I had hoped to be alone.

He came back with a glass of iced coffee and blueberry pie. "I wanted to go to a movie," he said, "but who wants to go alone? I don't know what they're playing, but perhaps you'd like to go with me. You'd be my guest."

"Thank you, but I haven't the slightest desire for a movie."

"No? As a rule I don't go to the movies unless my wife forces me, but today I was ready to sit for a few hours and forget the daily grind. I don't even look at the screen most of the time. I let them talk, shoot, sing, or whatever they please, without me. Since you know that you can't change anything that goes on up there, you become a fatalist. Sometimes I imagine that reality is just another movie. Do you ever feel that?"

"Yes, but in the real movie we all take part and have a little choice—we can play either right or wrong."

"So you believe in free will. I don't believe in it—absolutely not. We are marionettes—nothing more. Someone pulls at a string and we dance. I'm a complete determinist."

"Just the same, when you cross the street and a car is coming you run."

"That's determined, too. I read in the paper once that a young man and his girl had supper and then sat down to play Russian roulette. Between yes and no, he killed himself. Everyone wants to test fate. Why haven't I seen your name in the papers lately?"

"I haven't had anything published."

"That's the reason I became a landlord, if you can call it that. I bought a building with furnished rooms and make my living from it. Some weeks are better, some are worse, but at least I don't have to listen to the opinions of an editor. People pay me in advance. I get all kinds. The man may be a murderer, a thief, or a pimp, but he gives me the five dollars and I give him the key. Today I wanted one of the rooms for a few hours myself, but they were all taken. You never know." He took a sip of his coffee, raised his eyebrows, and said, "You don't know who I am, do you?"

"I know you, but I'm sorry to say I don't remember your name. It's a kind of amnesia with me."

"I saw it at once. Fingerbein—Zelig Fingerbein. This is my pen name. No one calls me by my real name any more. We were introduced at the Café Royal."

"Of course. Now I know everything," I said. "You have a very pretty wife—Genia."

"So you do remember! I often forget faces and events. I used to write poems and I published, too, but who needs poetry today? It's unnecessary merchandise. Still, there are emotions that only a poem can express. Imagine the Song of Songs in any other form! But it's obsolete: Love is strong as death. Jealousy is cruel as the grave. Othello, too. To be jealous and strangle someone isn't such an accomplishment any more. True love is forgiveness. Civilized man has to learn the greatest of all arts: to overcome jealousy. Do you smoke?"

"No."

"Why not? A cigarette helps sometimes. Women had to suffer for generations—polygamy, harems, men who came back from war with concubines. Now men will have to take their medicine. Women have the same appetites as we do— maybe bigger. Don't laugh at me, but the underworld is a lot more advanced about these things than we are, though I hear that Europeans have made big steps forward. When a king of England gives up his throne to marry an American divorcée, it isn't just stuff for a headline but a symbol of the new time and the new men."

Zelig Fingerbein put his little fist on the table. He tasted the blueberry pie and pushed the plate away. He asked, "Do you have some time?"

"Yes, I have time."

"I know I'll regret what I'm going to do. But since I didn't go to the movies and met you here, I want to tell you something that has a connection with you."

"With me? How?"

"Actually with your writing—not with you personally."

The little man who called himself Zelig Fingerbein turned his head, as if suspicious of being listened to. His yellow eyes watched me, half smiling, half questioning. He said, "No one else must ever know what I'm about to tell you. We all need to confide in someone. If no one knows your secret, it's not a secret but just a hidden thing. It has to do with my wife. There's a great love between us. When I was a bachelor, I always thought there could not be any love between people who stood under the wedding canopy and shared a bedroom. No institution is so much spat on and laughed at as the institution of marriage. But most of these jokers sooner or later go to a rabbi or a pastor and tie the knot. If one marriage fails, they try a second, a third—a fifth. Of course, there are a lot of old bachelors and spinsters, but they want to marry, too. They keep searching until they die.

"You just said that my wife is beautiful. Thank you. I cannot tell you how beautiful she was as a girl. We both come from Kielce. We belonged to the Youths of Zion—that's how we met. All the young men were in love with her—some desperately. I'm not much of a man physically—that's obvious—but I was more intelligent than the others, and Genia and I developed a strong love for each other. I would not serve in the Polish Army, so we came to America in 1924, the very day before America closed its doors on free immigration. We were poor as the night, and Genia went to work in a shop so that I could scribble my poems. She thought I was going to become a second Slowacki or Byron. Well, as my mother used to say, 'Those who think fool themselves.' I don't have to tell you what it means to be a Yiddish poet in New York. In my circumstances, Lord Byron would have become a landlord, too.

"I grew disenchanted with my creative powers slowly. But

our love didn't suffer from this. What a woman sees in a man and what a man sees in a woman no third person can ever make out. No matter how difficult the day was, our evenings were always a holiday. No matter where we lived—Broome Street, Ocean Avenue, Brighton Beach—our apartment was always lovely. We both liked pretty things, and in those days you could get antiques on Third Avenue for a song. To our regret, we had no children. I became a Yiddish teacher and I earned a decent living. Once in a while, when an editor had to fill a hole, I got something published in a magazine. Genia became a forelady at her shop. We didn't spend every penny we earned. In the summer, we went to a hotel in the Catskills. We traveled through the United States. We even went to Europe. Still, I never made peace with my failure as a poet, and Genia suffered from it. One of our great pleasures was reading. I loved literature, and Genia couldn't exist without books. In the beginning, we read Yiddish and Polish, and later English, after we learned the language. I'm not boasting, but we both have good taste—remember the cantor who said, 'I can't sing, but I understand singing'? Genia's taste is even better than mine. It's curious how people who are dull and deaf are critics and professors of literature, while Genia, who has a perfect ear for words, is a shop worker. Well, it's all part of the hypocrisy of this world. Actually, neither Genia nor I overworked; her job left her plenty of free time, and in a Yiddish school there's not much to do. We had people for supper; we had little parties, usually with the same few friends. But we liked to be together best of all, and we often thanked God when our guests left. How many couples have such a life?

"But no matter how much I loved my wife, I was never indifferent to other women. I don't have to explain it to you. What defense do modern people have against indulgence? I wasn't pious, and even if I had been, having more than one

woman was not a real sin according to the Jews. The inter-
diction against polygamy was forced on us by the Christians.
I might not have been a Byron, but my appetite for women
was as strong as his. You know our milieu. There were al-
ways opportunities. I never got seriously involved, but from
time to time I made love to another woman. In the beginning,
I kept it a secret from Genia, but Genia's instincts are sharp
—sometimes I think she's a mind reader. When I finally
confessed, she didn't make a big tragedy out of it. 'Do what
you like, only come back to me,' she said. 'No woman can
give you what I can.' Typical feminine talk. I also began to
realize that my so-called adventures aroused a new desire in
her. Nothing new in that, either.

"This is how it was for a good many years. Our evenings
and nights were spent talking—fantasies, facts, the things
we read in books. Like most men, I wanted my freedom when
it came to other women, and at the same time I wanted my
wife chaste. In the beginning Genia warned me that if I ran
around she would try it, too. But time passed, and everything
remained as it was. By nature, Genia is shy—the shyness
that's inherited from God knows how many grandmothers.
The thought of having anybody else made her shudder—she
told me herself. 'What would happen if—' was a game we
used to play. 'Suppose you found yourself in this situation—
what would you do?' We often drew the situations from
your stories in the Yiddish papers. I wonder if you realize
how much literature influences life. We probably pondered
your heroes more than you did yourself.

"I could sit with you until tomorrow and not tell you a
thousandth of what happened. But I'll keep it short. Genia
began to insist that there was no basic difference between
the psychology of women and men, and she even talked about
finding herself a man. I didn't take it seriously. Her banter
excited me, and it's good to be stimulated. She wanted to

know how I would feel if she met someone who attracted her and she succumbed in a heated moment. Would I run away from her—stop loving her? If I did, wouldn't that prove that I had a double standard? I assured her that I would not; as they say in English, what's sauce for the goose is sauce for the gander. But it didn't mean anything—Genia was constantly being propositioned and she constantly said no. She confessed that she had decided to get even with me—once, at least—just to convince herself that she was a modern woman and not a sleepy yenta from behind the stove.

"She developed a real complex. Why couldn't she do what Mme. Bovary, Anna Karenina, or your Hadassa and Clara did? In her shop, the girls kept boasting about their successes. Nowadays Satan doesn't need to strain his voice to tempt us. The nine muses do his work for him. And there was Genia, walking around like a sort of holy virgin. She started talking in a jargon she picked up from books by doctors and love experts about how backward she was.

"Don't laugh, but Genia demanded my help in getting a lover. Isn't that crazy? She said, 'I can't do it without you. Find someone for me.' She wanted just once to taste what being 'progressive' is like. One night we sat down and actually wrote out a whole list of candidates. It was a game. I'm already past fifty and Genia's not much younger. We could be grandparents. Instead, there we were, awake at night making lists of possible lovers. Funny, isn't it?"

"Not so funny."

"Wait. I'm going to get myself a coffee."

Zelig Fingerbein brought two cups of coffee, one for himself and one for me. He took a sip and said, "In my reading, I often came on the word '*Hausfreund*'—the wife's lover. I could never get the sense of it. Why would a man allow his wife to betray him? Why let him into the house to begin with? An invention of novelists and playwrights, I used to think. In Kielce, no one had this kind of arrangement. But here in America I saw that it exists—actors, doctors, businessmen. There actually are men who make friends of their wife's lover. They eat together, drink together, and go to the theater together. It was beyond my wildest imagining that it could happen to me, but I have a *Hausfreund* now, and that's why I'm sitting here with you. That's why I wanted to go to a movie. When he comes, I leave. I even leave before he comes. Perhaps he's not exactly a *Hausfreund*, but he comes to the house and I know about it.

"It began like this. A few years ago, a refugee from Poland turned up. You might know him, so I'll just use his first name —Max. He was supposed to be completely Polandized, but he spoke good Yiddish. He's a painter—that's what he claims, anyway. He makes a few smudges on a canvas and it's supposed to be a sunset in Zakopane or a bullfight in Mexico. The main thing is that people buy it. The modern consumer is as much a charlatan as the producer. If a figure stands on its feet, it's banal. But if you put it on its head it's original. I met him in the Café Royal. He's a slippery fellow, with eager eyes that beg for love, friendship—the devil knows what. We were introduced and he fell over me as if I had been his long-lost brother. Right away he wanted to paint my portrait. He told me he had family in Kielce, and it came out that I was a distant relative. As a rule, when men act overly friendly to me it's because of Genia and they don't make a secret of it, but Genia wasn't around when Max and I met, and when he finally saw her he acted indifferent. Genia was insulted. She's not accustomed to being ignored by men.

"Max painted my portrait and made me look half ape, half crocodile. That's all they can do. It turned out that he was a shrewd businessman. He dealt in antiques and jewelry. He'd come to America only yesterday, and already he knew everybody and everybody knew him. He started offering us bargains: silver spice salvers, ivory pointers, ethrog boxes, snuffboxes, whatnot. Genia's crazy for bric-a-brac, and he sold them unusually cheap. Gradually, I realized that something wasn't right about him. It took him months to finish my portrait. He looked at me with longing eyes, and every chance he got he touched me. Once, he tried to kiss me. I was shocked. After a while, he told me straight out that he was in love with me. I wanted to vomit. I said to him, 'Max, don't make a fool of yourself. I'm as far from that sort of madness as Heaven is from Hell.' He began to sigh like a rejected lover.

"I told it all to Genia and she didn't know whether to laugh or cry. You read about such things, but it seems unbelievable when you meet them. Now we had a new topic to chatter about at night. Genia was outraged that I could be more attractive to a man than she. I decided to get rid of him—but how? Max is not a man to let go. He kept coming to see us, and every time he came he brought a present. He knew all the theater people—Broadway, not just Second Avenue— and he got us theater tickets. There we'd be, the three of us, sitting together in the first row watching a play we would have had to wait months to see. He took us to Lindy's, and every place else. Is this the way one becomes a *Hausfreund*, I wondered. He tried to take my hand in the theater, but I told him that if he did anything like that again I would be through with him. The whole business disgusted me.

"But suddenly a kind of competition arose between me and Genia. It almost amused me. Here was a beautiful woman trying to get that goon's attention, and he kept gaping at me. When Genia spoke to him, he pretended not to hear; when I said even the most trivial thing, he cried out with enthusiasm. Can you imagine anything more ridiculous? But I began to realize that he was spoiling our family life. Every night, Genia and I figured out different excuses for getting him out of our lives. We made firm decisions. The next day, Max would call to say that he had a gift or a great bargain for us or some sensational story we had to hear. Before I could say no, Genia would have asked him for supper. I found out later that his antiques came from a factory that turned out reproductions. I also learned that most of his paintings were copies. This man was a fraud all the way through.

"I'm not going to draw it out. Genia started to meet him alone. She had given up her full-time job and worked only two days a week. In the meantime, I'd bought the building with the furnished rooms, and that took my attention. I no longer had any patience for that phony with his lovesick gazes. Genia still said terrible things about him, but apparently she wanted to steal him away from me. Actually, he acted like a woman. He gossiped, he loved gadgets, he wore rings with stones on almost all his fingers. His hair was long and shiny from hair oil. He was obsessed with clothes. I am the short one, not he, but he wore shoes with lifts. And his ties! What woman could put up with this? You'll say I'm naïve, but it never occurred to me that Genia would have an affair with him."

"An affair? Even though he's a homosexual?" I asked.

"The devil knows what he is. Since everything else about him is a fake, maybe that is, too. Maybe his flirtation with me was only a way of getting to Genia. He's a sly fox. Slowly, as I drew away from him, Genia and he became cronies. They had lunch, supper; they went to the theater and the movies together, to exhibitions. If I protested, Genia said, 'Who are you jealous of? He's more interested in you than he is in me.' The truth is, every time they went anywhere, I was invited, but I always refused. Genia swore to me that he never touched her, and I believed her. It went on like this for months. It's astonishing how capable men are of self-deceit.

Besides, I was tired of all these movies, theaters, bargains. The apartment had to be painted, and where were we going to put the junk? Millions of things have been invented, but no one has found a way to avoid the crisis of painting an apartment. Suddenly all your belongings are moved out. Your paintings are taken down. Your books are in heaps on the floor. You become a stranger in your own house. The stench of the paint makes you sick. You see the bitter truth: that a home, like everything else, is just illusion.

"I began to feel that everything was falling apart, and then one night Genia confessed to me that she was having an affair with him."

Zelig Fingerbein finished off his cold coffee in one gulp. He looked at me reproachfully. "Why are you so shocked? You write like a modern man, but here you are with the old morals and prejudices. I had them once, but I freed myself. You can't condemn a modern woman to live her whole life with the same man even if she adores him. You couldn't find a more retiring woman than Genia, but she's living in the twentieth century and you can't require her to believe that Zelig Fingerbein is the only male in New York. Just the same, when Genia told me about her affair, it made me sick. I felt as if my whole life was destroyed. If I could, I would have dragged her to the Sanhedrin and had her stoned—the way it was done in ancient times. But there's no Sanhedrin in New York. I could have packed my belongings and left— but where would I have gone? And who would I have gone to? The night she told me, I lay in bed with Genia and she cried like a little girl. 'What should I do? If you are ready to die, I'll die with you—just to show you that I belong to you and not to anyone else.' She wailed and trembled so that the bed shook and—you can call me an idiot—I comforted her. I told her it was no tragedy, but my teeth were chattering.

"That night, we swore that our association with Max was over and done with, but I knew it wasn't. The creators of religion did not know God, but human nature they did know. It's written in Aboth that one sin drags another sin after it. One step off the accepted path and all taboos are broken.

"You write about religion, marriage, and sex. You seem to understand modern man with all his complexities and pitfalls. But all you can do is criticize—you can't show the way back to faith. It's impossible for us to conduct ourselves like our parents and grandparents without having their piety. I will tell you something, though I'm ashamed to admit it. That night, Genia finally fell asleep after she took a couple of pills, but I couldn't sleep a wink. I put on my robe and slippers and went into my study. I looked at my books and I knew that not one of them could give me direction. How can Tolstoy or Dickens or Balzac teach you? They had talent, but they were as confused as we are. Suddenly I saw a volume of the Talmud, and I thought, Since worldliness has failed me so miserably, perhaps I should return to God. I took out the tractate of Betzah, opened it, and began to hum as in the old times. 'If an egg was laid on festival day, the school of Shammai say: It may be eaten. And the school of Hillel say: It may not be eaten.' I kept on nodding and humming like a yeshiva boy for a good half hour. In the beginning, it was nostalgically sweet, but the more I went on, the heavier my spirit felt. As long as one believed that these laws were given to Moses on Mount Sinai, there was meaning. Without this faith, it's all sheer scholasticism. I got tired and went back to Genia. We have one bed. That night, I came to the conclusion that men must kill in themselves their strongest instinct: the possession of a woman as a piece of property. If there is a God, maybe He's leading us in this direction."

"And what happened later?"

"There was no later. Genia had promised, although I hadn't

demanded it of her, that she would never see Max again. But she still meets him. She has given up her work entirely. She doesn't need it any more, and I can't be with her day and night anyhow. Lately, I lost patience with everything: with Genia's guilt and with what we call culture. I can't make a fetish out of plays on Broadway and Picasso's paintings. Even good literature doesn't interest me any more. The wall that separates the world from the underworld has become too thin. The judge, the lawyer, and the murderer all nurture the same ideas, read the same books, visit the same nightclubs, talk the same gibberish. We're returning to the cave, even though it's a cave provided with telephone, electricity, and TV. I used to think that I knew Genia through and through, but since this freak invaded our house I keep discovering new traits in her. Even her voice doesn't seem the same. As for Max, I can't even hate him, and this really surprises me. I don't know what he is, and I don't care. All I know is that he wants the same thing we all want—as much pleasure as possible before disappearing forever."

"He's not a homosexual?"

"Who knows what he is! Perhaps we're all homosexuals. I've forgotten to tell you the main thing: Genia began to go to a psychoanalyst. Max has been going to him for years. They wanted to make me a member of the club with them, but I'd rather study about the egg that is laid on a festival day."

I hadn't noticed that the cafeteria had filled up. I said to Zelig, "Let's go. They'll throw us out."

We walked out on Broadway and the heat hit me like a furnace. It was still daylight but the neon signs were already lit, announcing in fiery language the bliss to be brought by Pepsi-Cola, Bond suits, Camel cigarettes, Wrigley's chewing gum. A tepid stench came up from the subway gratings. Over a movie house hung a billboard of a half-naked woman four stories high, lit up by spotlights—her hair disheveled, her eyes wild, her legs spread out, a gun in each hand. Around her waist was a fringed scarf that covered her private parts. A mob had collected to gape at her. Men made jokes, women giggled. I looked at Zelig. Half his face was green, the other red—like a modern painting. He stared, moved his lips, one eye laughing and one tearing. I said to him, "If there is no God, she is our god."

Zelig Fingerbein shook as if he had been awakened from a trance. "What *she* is promising she can deliver."

Translated by the author and Laurie Colwin

The Recluse

THE SNOW had been falling for three days. The winter
night was too long; the beggars in the study house
could not sleep through it. They woke up at about three
o'clock. One carried in wood from the shed for the stove. An-
other had a few potatoes in his bag to be roasted on the
coals. A third looked into a volume of the Mishnah by
candlelight. He appeared younger than the others, had a small
beard, bulging black eyes, and a dark complexion. His
clothes were not as tattered as the others'. A heavyset beggar
with a red face, who was wearing a sheepskin hat over flax-
colored hair, called out to him, "Hey, big shot! You want a
hot potato?"

The dark man answered without lifting up his eyes. "I
don't eat in the middle of the night."

"Are you afraid of spoiling your delicate stomach?"

The other did not reply.

"A fancy gentleman, hah? You think you'll get a white
tablecloth in Hell?"

A young man from the village who was spending the night
in study came to the defense of the man under attack. "What
do you want from him? He's just not hungry."

"He's hungry, all right. I got my supper at the house of
Reb Motl Bentzes. I ate so much that my belly almost burst.
That doesn't stop me from feeling empty now. Cold weather
keeps you hungry."

"A man's desire should be honored," the young man from

the village said, quoting the Talmud. "There's no reason to blame a person for not wanting to eat."

"He wants, all right, but he's too proud to eat with us. He thinks he's a scholar."

The dark man studying the Mishnah got up without speaking, took the candle in its holder and the volume of the Mishnah, and walked to the far corner of the study house. There he sat before a lectern. He must have been near-sighted, because his eyelids almost touched the page he was reading. The village student returned to the long table where he had left his volume of the Talmud with a sash placed across it to symbolize the temporary nature of the interrupted reading. He was small and of light complexion, with a round face. On his chin a small red beard sprouted. While he read he nodded his head, humming softly to himself, curling one of his sidelocks. After some time he got up and walked over to the stranger in the far corner, who raised his head from his text.

"Aren't you cold?" the village student asked him.

"Cold, no."

"What is your name?"

"Mine? Nachman."

"Where do you come from?"

"What's the difference?" Nachman asked back.

"Why are you afraid to tell me? It can't hurt you."

"There is a reason."

"My name is Zorach. I'm from Izbitza but I married a local girl. Since you're a scholar, why didn't somebody take you in? This place is only for vagabonds."

"I don't go to anybody's house."

Zorach sat on a bench at right angles to Nachman's bench. "Didn't you have supper at someone's house?"

"I don't eat in other people's houses."

"Are you fasting?"

"When I'm hungry I eat."

Zorach took one strand of his small beard and began to pull at it. "I see that you're fond of secrets."

After some hesitation the stranger took a handkerchief from his coat pocket and placed it on the volume of the Mishnah. This too was a sign that the interruption was momentary. "I don't like secrets, but you can't tell everything. It is written, 'Silence is good for the wise, and even better for the stupid.' "

"You don't look stupid to me," Zorach insisted.

"How can you tell? Everyone acts stupidly at times. One thinks one is clever and knows the world. Suddenly you see that you don't even know yourself. Jochanan served as a high priest for eighty years and then he became a Sadducean."

Zorach paused as if to think it over. "The Evil Spirit respects no one. Even when a man lies in the throes of death it tries to persuade him to deny God and serve idols."

"I know. Please forgive me if I don't tell you where I come from. I was born somewhere on the other side of the Vistula. Then I came to study in a yeshiva on this side of the Vistula, in a town I prefer not to name. I left that place to become a wanderer."

"Are you collecting money for a yeshiva?"

"No."

"Subscriptions for a book you're writing?"

"Not that either."

"Maybe you're trying to get the signatures of a hundred rabbis to be allowed to remarry?"

Nachman straightened. He pushed the lectern away. "I'm divorced and I'm a recluse."

"Is that so? The Lithuanians have many recluses. But I've never heard of one in Poland."

"It happens."

"Well, I'm not going to disturb you or your studies. Since

you are a recluse your soul must yearn for the Torah. Every minute is precious."

Zorach made a move to get up from his bench. Nachman raised a small hand, the nails of which were bitten down to the quick. He spoke in a reluctant tone. "Sit. I'm not all that studious. But the night is long. Lying awake on a bench to brood is not the right way to spend it. With a chapter of the Mishnah one forgets all worldly vanities. You always find something new in it. This is the power of the Torah. How about you, do you study all night long?"

"Only Mondays and Thursdays."

"And your father-in-law doesn't object?"

"I don't ask him."

"It's the right thing. My father-in-law was a prince of the Torah. And when a prince loses his dignity he becomes less than a common man. You know the story about the fallen angels."

"Is this why you are divorced?"

For a long while Nachman did not reply. He tried to bite the nail of the thumb of his right hand but there was nothing left to bite. He threw a side glance at the volume of the Mishnah and moved the lectern still farther from him. He said, "I've never talked about this to anyone. How could I? In the same town it would be slander. On the road you don't have long conversations. But since you ask, I'm going to answer you. There is a saying that 'telling the story lightens the worry.' I myself am a man without great qualities. But I've understood what greatness is since I learned the alphabet. My father died even before I was born. I bear his name, Nachman. Those who knew him say he was a saint. A scholar too. My mother, may she live long, remarried a simple man a year later—a grain merchant and—may God forgive me for saying so—an ignoramus and a ruffian. My mother had five more

children by him and they all take after their father. I was the
only Talmud student in the family; my stepfather made me
suffer for it. From childhood I began to observe people, their
behavior, and I saw things it was better not to see. Today I
know that it was all wrong for me to have been so critical.
Why pay heed to blood and flesh if you can contemplate the
majesty of the Creator? When my stepfather left the house on
business my mother used to tell me about my own father,
peace be with him. The truth was that her second husband
persecuted her. She came from a good home and he con-
stantly reproached her for it. Of all our sins envy is the worst.
What is the cause of all wars? One king envies another. I
always craved a guide. I couldn't find anyone I really looked
up to in our town. To make it short, at fifteen I left home and
wandered from one yeshiva to the next. I starved, I had to
eat at other people's tables. Everywhere I went I tried to find
a truly great teacher. But how do you go about that?

"Our way of study in Poland is all based on casuistry. But
that wasn't what I wanted. The Torah was not given to us to
exercise the brain, but to serve the Almighty. I went as far as
Vilna. There the learning is more basic. But a real mentor
was yet to be found. They all preached nicely, but preaching
and doing are not the same. There was a yeshiva master
whose very words were pearls. But among his pupils he had
his favorites and his scapegoats. He would send the ones he
liked to houses where the food was good, and the others could
barely fill their stomachs. All these teachers loved flattery.
I'm not a flatterer by nature, and I paid for it.

"There was one yeshiva head who liked me and tried to
help me. But it happened that while delivering an oration on
the Sabbath before Passover he misquoted one of the Com-
mentaries. Afterward I called him aside and pointed out his
mistake. That's all I needed. He became my blood enemy. I
began to think that the very essence of man is false. I don't

have to tell you that this way of thinking is only a step from heresy. I was already on the way to becoming a recluse. But how do you run away from the world when you're already without a woman or food? I prayed to God for one favor: if there is a higher man, let me have the good fortune of meeting him. I lay awake at night and prayed only for that. My yearning for a guide consumed me.

"Prayers are sometimes heard. In an inn I met a young man and we began to talk. In the conversation he told me of a small yeshiva in a village in Poland. There were only about ten students there. The head of it, a rabbi, was an undiscovered genius, and saintly in the bargain. The young man said to me, 'Small men, pinheads, become famous, but there in an out-of-the-way village lives a man who is a giant, yet nobody knows it.' The moment I heard these words I realized that destiny had led me to this inn. I didn't have enough money to get to that village. It was summer, so I decided to go on foot. The road was long. Here and there I was given a ride on a cart. Even Gentile peasants picked me up, and I saw in that the hand of Providence.

"I arrived at my destination emaciated and in rags. Immediately I went to the yeshiva. The rabbi was lecturing. The moment I looked at him I knew that this was the man. Every word he said stirred me. What he was saying sounded simple enough; he was only interpreting a passage of the Gemara. But beneath the simplicity was great depth. I was seized by such love for him that I could hardly restrain myself from falling forward to kiss his feet. He was already approaching his sixties, slight, lean, a little bent, with a high forehead and a white beard. I learned later that his first wife died childless. He married again and his second wife bore him a daughter, who later became my wife. But let me not put the cart before the horse.

"After the lecture I approached and I said, 'Rabbi, I heard

the lecture. You're the greatest of them all.' I repeated the fine points of his exposé and dwelled on their pertinence. In a few words he had answered questions which the greatest Talmudists of the past and present could never have explained. In Poland Hebrew grammar is utterly neglected, but I saw from his exegesis that he had a great command not only of Hebrew but also of Aramaic. When I finished talking he put his hands on my head and kissed my forehead, saying, 'You were sent to me from Heaven. All my life I longed for a student like you.'

"When the other students saw how he kissed the forehead of a stranger in rags, they were resentful. They pointed me out to one another with hostile gestures. Some of the community elders were also present. They immediately offered me board in their homes, but the rabbi invited me to stay with him. I was beginning to regret that I had showered so much praise on him. It is known that virtue is never re-warded in this world. Since I got my reward so quickly, this was a sign that God didn't approve of my act. But once a thing is done you can't undo it.

"To make it short, I joined the rabbi's household. I ate there on the Sabbath and also on weekdays. There was a man in town who was called the 'pious little tailor.' He fasted twice a week. He made me a coat and trousers without ask-ing for payment. I could tell that the rabbi's wife didn't ap-prove of her husband's generosity toward me. Such things one cannot hide. Her daughter was at the proper age for marriage, but I certainly didn't dream that I might ever be-come the rabbi's son-in-law. Three months later we were engaged. Half the town came to the engagement party. There was immediate talk that I should someday—'in one hundred years'—take over the rabbinical chair. The rabbi did not want to ordain me himself because I was a relative, so I was sent to another town to be confirmed. It's been some years since that took place, but even then, I swear to you, it was not my wish to be a rabbi.

"My mother came to the wedding with my stepfather and with a crowd of brothers and sisters whom I barely knew— they had grown up in my absence. When my stepfather became aware of my achievements he began to act like a father to me. This is how the mob is; it worships success. But not only the mob. There is pettiness in every man."

The beggars had fallen asleep again. Their snoring could be heard all over the study house. Beside the candle on Nachman's desk a memorial candle was sputtering in a candelabrum. The pillars of the podium threw trembling shadows on the walls and ceilings. Occasionally the wind outside made a noise like wheels on paving stones. Nachman nodded as if affirming a truth which one cannot become accustomed to. "What weather, hah? What do animals do in such cold? I once walked through a forest where I came upon a bevy of wolves. If they had seen me I wouldn't be sitting here with you now. There's a touch of the animal in every one of us, even in saints. Yes, we were married, and my father-in-law took me in to live. I say father-in-law but actually I could call him only 'Rabbi.' My wife was a female like all females, but because she was his daughter she appeared to me like a holy scroll. As for my mother-in-law, she was a simple person. Even though she could barely read the prayer book, she called other rabbis ignoramuses. She complained that her husband remained stuck in an obscure village while young men who couldn't reach his ankles got posts in cities. Often she talked to me about this, calling her husband an unworldly schlemiel. She said to me, 'Other rabbis publish a book every year. Mine has been scribbling away for forty years but not a word of his is printed.' I explained to her that one line of his was worth more than all their writings, but she

insisted, 'Who knows that? Only you.' She hinted that if
her husband had been more of a worldly person, his daughter
would have married the son of a rich man, not a poor yeshiva
boy. She should forgive my words, she was full of thorns.
One moment she flattered you, the next she nettled you. She
was stingy with food too. She kept the bread locked in the
pantry. My father-in-law remained aloof so that she was
the contact with the community elders. Most of them were his
enemies. When there was a lawsuit he did not like com-
promises—his verdict always conformed strictly to the letter
of the law. On ritual matters he was unbending. Often he
would declare an ox unkosher, so the butchers maligned him
and even had the temerity to threaten him. I looked on with
resentment that a great man was being mistreated and for-
gotten while midgets played the role of giants. But this is an
old story. Heaven seldom endows the same person with
spiritual and material blessings. Once in a while I tried to per-
suade my father-in-law to publish a book, but he would say,
'Who needs new books? The Pentateuch and the Psalter are
enough.' He contended that nowadays an author has to go
around asking for subsidies, and was seldom judged on his
merits. I could see that this situation hurt him. He had too
much insight not to be aware of his value.

"A few years passed. My mother-in-law was eager for a
grandchild, but my wife did not become pregnant. My
mother-in-law forced me to go to doctors and even to wonder
rabbis. My father-in-law was an anti-Hasid. He used to say
that the Hasids were sectarians, a clique. But my mother-in-
law took her daughter to a Hasidic quack who gave her herbs
that didn't help.

"Now hear what happened. Near the village there was an
estate which belonged to a man named Reb Todrus. I
shouldn't have mentioned his name, but you won't know him
anyway. He had little erudition but he was rich, so he became

the head of the community. He was one of the few men in town who sided with my father-in-law. On Purim he would always send him an expensive gift. He did the same for me when I got married. Just because he was so generous my father-in-law was careful never to praise him. But my mother-in-law flattered him outrageously. Todrus had a few sons but only one daughter, the youngest child. She married a young man from a big city. I was at the wedding; in fact, the whole village was there. My father-in-law performed the ceremony and was paid well for it. Two groups of musicians played. The young man—I'll call him Simon, though his real name was different—was tall, handsome, and of a wealthy family. As custom requires, he delivered an exegesis on the Talmud for the male guests at the banquet. May he forgive me, what he said was not only pointless but without foundation. It didn't matter, since he had a rich father-in-law.

"I'll try to make it short now. Simon became a frequent visitor of my father-in-law's. His father-in-law, Reb Todrus, wanted him to take lessons from the rabbi, not in the yeshiva with the others but privately. He paid well for it, and my father-in-law was barely able to provide for his family. Actually Simon didn't need such an important teacher; even the yeshiva would have been too much for him. I had more than once listened as my father-in-law explained things to him. He had to go over details again and again as with a schoolboy. For my father-in-law it was a waste of time, but my mother-in-law was in seventh heaven. She fawned upon the young man and bestowed so many nonexistent qualities on him that it revolted me. True, they needed the few rubles, but why indulge in such exaggeration? As a rule, when my mother-in-law began to talk about things she knew nothing about, her husband reprimanded her. He could be as sharp as a knife. But in this case he didn't react and even seemed to agree. I was astonished. No one could deceive him. He found blemishes even in the very great. I once heard him make mincemeat of the famous Rabbi Isaac Meir of Gur. It is true that it was Purim and he had had one drink too many, but he was only a little exuberant, not drunk. If Rabbi Meir of Gur wasn't good enough, how could he listen in silence while so much praise was being showered on Simon? For Simon it would have been an honor even to shine Rabbi Meir's shoes.

"It didn't take long before something new came out. Simon was sorting my father-in-law's manuscripts and preparing them for publication. When I heard this I was dumfounded. Only a short time before, my father-in-law had reminded me what Ecclesiastes said about making books. Then if he wanted to publish one himself, why ask the help of an illiterate? I couldn't contain myself, and I asked my father-in-law the meaning of this. He heard me out but did not reply. He clutched at his beard and nodded. I understood that my mother-in-law was behind all this. Simon had enough money and needed no subscriptions to finance the work. But that my father-in-law should change his ways so suddenly was incredible. Also, the fact that he didn't answer my reproaches upset me. It was not in his nature to keep silent when asked a question. He often replied even before he was asked. Sometimes I felt that he was a mind reader. When we studied together and I made a gesture, he would say, 'I know what you're thinking,' and he would meet my objection.

"The book came out and I don't think there are ten scholars in the whole of Poland who can understand it. His commentaries are shorter than short—not more than footnotes. In the introduction my father-in-law wrote that the book would never have seen the light if his esteemed pupil, the erudite, sharp-minded Simon the son of so-and-so, had not helped him select the material and contributed indispensable advice. When I read this preface my brain shook."

"Your idol had fallen?"

"From a high tower into a deep ditch."

"Did Simon cause your divorce?"

"In a way."

"Did he ever become a scholar?"

"An author."

The beggar with the flaxen hair woke up and rose to a sitting position. "Why are you two babbling all night? Either study or go to sleep."

"How do you like the low-life's insolence?" Zorach asked.

"This world is based on insolence. What was Simon's power if not insolence? To this day I don't know why he hated me. The first time I looked at him I knew he was my enemy. From the beginning he began to intrigue against me. My father-in-law was not a man to carry gossip, but my mother-in-law repeated everything Simon said about me and perhaps she added something of her own. I asked her not to be a bearer of calumny, reciting the law to her, but it didn't help. What Simon said to the mother she probably repeated to her daughter. I was a ne'er-do-well, a bookworm, and other such talk. He maligned me before the elders. People who used to be friendly became hostile to me. I learned that Simon wanted to become rabbi of the village. What did he need this post for? You will soon hear.

"The town had no assistant rabbi. My father-in-law didn't need an assistant. Suddenly I heard the news that Simon had become assistant rabbi. This was meant to be a slap in the face for me but I kept silent. My mother-in-law rejoiced. According to common sense my father-in-law should have opposed this appointment, but the opposite happened. In the sermon he preached on the Sabbath of Repentance he praised Simon to the skies. My father-in-law himself ordained him, and this bordered on improper procedure. I never saw Simon study the Shulhan Arukh. With his lack of erudition he might well have misled people to eat food that was not kosher. I could not restrain myself and I spoke to my father-in-law. For the first time he scolded me, assuring me that Simon had all the qualifications to be a rabbi, and he added, 'And you're not going to be punished for my sins, anyway.' I was flabbergasted. Had I been deluded? Had my father-in-law lost his discernment? I blamed myself and began to fast, abstaining from other worldly pleasures too. Until then I had been studying in my father-in-law's yeshiva, but that day he said to me, 'A yeshiva is for bachelors, not for married men.'

"So I began to study by myself.

"When one is excommunicated no one is allowed to approach him, but there is also such a thing as unspoken excommunication. People began to avoid me. I was as the proverbial broken vessel which is forgotten by everyone. All this time I kept asking myself the same question: how could it have happened? Even if justice is disregarded, how can a father allow his daughter's husband to be passed over for a post while it goes to a stranger? And how about the mother? Such behavior goes against nature. I could have understood it if Simon had been a bachelor or a widower but he was a son-in-law in a wealthy household. There are all kinds of tortures but the worst is when one is persecuted without knowing why. When I came to the study house everyone turned his back on me."

"How about your wife?" Zorach asked. "On whose side was she?"

Nachman grimaced. "I don't know to this day. Just as her mother was garrulous she was close-mouthed. You rarely heard a word from her. All day long I sat in the study house. When I came home my mother-in-law gave me dinner. I lived with my wife for years but I doubt if we spoke ten words together.

"One day I heard that Simon went out of town. A few

days after that my mother-in-law brought me the tidings that my father-in-law had accepted a rabbinical post in a large town. Simon had gone to that town to act as a go-between. It was all his plot. He wanted to take my father-in-law's chair as rabbi. How he convinced the elders of the other town that my father-in-law was right for them I don't know. He was a cunning schemer. Perhaps he had bribed someone. He could have gotten the job himself but he wanted to stay near his father-in-law's estate. I was told that Simon became a chum of the squire, who allowed him to rent a flour mill. He also sold him a forest. So a rabbi's post could have meant only prestige for Simon. It would also help him get his first book accepted.

"As long as Simon's book did not appear I could reproach myself with the thought that perhaps I was mistaken about the man. But when I had that miserable book in front of my eyes, I became convinced that the genius and the saint to whom I had gone on foot was no more. For Simon's book began with a preface by my father-in-law—the praise which he poured on him in it I am ashamed to repeat to you. Transmigration of the soul doesn't occur only after a man's death. Sometimes it takes place during his lifetime. The old soul leaves him and a new soul enters. How ironical, but my father-in-law's great book can't be found anywhere today, while Simon's hodgepodge is studied all over Poland."

"When were you divorced?" Zorach asked.

Nachman placed a hand on his forehead as if trying to recall.

"The time approached when my father-in-law was to go to his new post. My mother-in-law began to nag me. 'What will you do there? You're a small-town person, unworldly, while everyone there will be up-to-date and sophisticated. It's a new world. Today a rabbi has to know Russian.' It seemed that Simon had obtained a large advance payment for their moving expenses to the new community. My mother-in-law ordered a silk robe, a coat lined in fox fur, a sable hat for her husband. She and her daughter dressed in fancy capes. The tailors came and went. My father-in-law suddenly looked younger and I could barely recognize him. When the soul changes so does the body. He became taller and straighter. His former enemies began to show respect for him.

"One night I recited the prayer before retiring but I could not close an eye until morning. My mother-in-law often teased me by saying that I was not of this world. That night it became clear to me that she was right. I was fit neither for a village nor for a big town. I really had no desire to be a rabbi, and certainly not a merchant. The next morning when my mother-in-law served my breakfast, almost throwing the food in my face, I said to her, "Mother-in-law, you are right. I'm not for this world.' 'You want a divorce?' she asked me. And I replied, 'If you agree, so be it.' The divorce was served two weeks later."

"What did your wife say?"

"She said nothing."

"Didn't you have a talk with her?"

"She listened and did not answer."

"Did she remarry?"

"Yes, a relative of Simon, a widower without children."

"So."

"I went out into the world and somehow I manage to survive. What do I need? A piece of bread and an onion. Wherever I go I find sacred books, thank God. I carry *The Beginning of Wisdom* in my bag."

"What happened to your father-in-law?"

"I heard that he had trouble with the new congregation. His son-in-law became the assistant rabbi, but actually he acts as the rabbi. He's just waiting for the old man to die."

"Did he ever publish another book?"

"My father-in-law, no. But Simon has already published a dozen."

It became quiet, and on the south wall the old clock with the Hebrew dial and copper weights rang out five.

"I know who this Simon is," Zorach said.

Nachman rose. "In that case I have broken the Mosaic prohibition against slander. I'm going to take a vow of silence."

Translated by the author and Herbert R. Lottman

A Dance and a Hop

Houses sometimes bear a strange resemblance to those who inhabit them. Leizer, my uncle Jekhiel's former brother-in-law, owned such a house. Beila, Leizer's sister, was Uncle Jekhiel's second wife. She was no longer alive and my uncle had married for the third time after my parents brought me to Shebrin.

A man in his sixties, Leizer was tall and broad-boned. In his youth he was a giant, but in his later years he became bent and broken from troubles. His wife was dead. He was plagued by a hernia, and a bad leg caused him to walk with a limp. The granary he possessed had burned down and his grain business was gone. His two older daughters baked bread and flatcakes, and from their meager earnings he maintained himself. Actually, all his misfortunes stemmed from his three daughters, Rachel, Leah, and Feigel, who remained spinsters. How was it possible for three girls in a Jewish village not to be married? Everyone in Shebrin asked the same question, and I think that Leizer and his daughters were as baffled as the others, perhaps more so.

But let us go back to the house. Its brick walls were unusually thick, its roof green from moss, and the chimney, no matter how often it was swept, always spewed forth a mixture of smoke and flames. Grzymak, the chimney sweep, swore that he once saw an imp in the chimney: a creature black as soot, hunched both in front and in back, with an elflock in the middle of his skull and a nose that reached to his belly. He seemed to live there. A neighbor's daughter had also seen this monster. In the middle of the night, when she went to pour out the slops, she heard him giggling. As she glanced up at Leizer's roof, the creature, crouching on the tip of the chimney, beckoned her to come to him and stretched out his tongue that was the length of a shovel.

Why did the builder who constructed this house make the walls almost a yard thick, with no windows facing the front and with a long entranceway that was dark even in broad daylight? Why were the ceilings low and heavily beamed and the attic unproportionately high? No one knew the answer, as the building was about two hundred years old. The small, crooked windows looked out over a swamp which led to the river. On murky summer nights, mysterious lights hovered over the swamp and it was said that those who went toward the lights never returned.

Leizer's rupture caused his intestines to drop and there was one woman in Shebrin who could manipulate them back. If not for her, people said, Leizer would have died long ago. It was a disgrace for Leizer that a strange female should touch his private parts, but when it's a question of saving a life, such things must be overlooked. This woman refused payment. It was her good deed. She also specialized in warding off the evil eye and removing the pips from chickens, thus enabling them to eat again.

Leah was already past forty when my parents and I arrived in Shebrin. Tall and broad like her father, she had the hands of a man and a face that was as wide and as brown as the pumpernickel loaves she baked. It was difficult to get a word out of her. Her strength, too, was that of a man. She chopped wood, brought water from the well, and carried sacks of flour from the mill on her back. In spite of all this, one could see that she was quite good-looking, with regular features and black, fiery eyes.

I heard it told that one day when she carried a sack of grain to the mill, she was attacked by two brigands. One of them held a rifle to her chest. Leah grabbed the gun, broke it in two, and with the butt hit the brigands until they passed out. The culprits were caught, taken to the hospital, and later jailed.

Rachel, who was younger than Leah, resembled her physically; but all that was hard, strong, and resolute in Leah appeared weak, soft, and indecisive in her sister. No one dared ask Leah why she had never married but everybody asked Rachel. Her reply was always the same: "When you serve dinner, you serve the soup first, then the meat."

I remember my mother once said to her, "Is it so terrible if one serves the meat first? There's no law against this."

Rachel listened and replied, "It is the custom, first you serve the soup and then the meat."

Leah kneaded the dough, shaped the loaves, shoveled them into the oven, and then removed the finished baked goods. Selling was Rachel's job. On Thursdays she stood in the marketplace with a basket of loaves, flatcakes, bagels, and rolls. Fridays she sold hallah and Sabbath cookies.

Feigel, the youngest, was only twenty-nine years old at that time and the matchmakers had not yet given up on her. Her mother had died at her birth. Unlike her sisters, Feigel was fair, small statured, and bore no resemblance to the rest of the family. She was supposed to have taken after a great-aunt from Janów. Three times she was engaged. Her first fiancé died, she returned the engagement contract to the second, and the third one went to war and was never heard from again.

Leah and Feigel were not on speaking terms for more than ten years. They even avoided looking at each other. Feigel liked to sing. She had a cat. Her father bought her a sewing machine and she became a seamstress, making shirts, men's underwear, and brassières. She had long discussions with the matchmakers. From time to time introductions and meetings were arranged with a potential suitor, but somehow nothing came of them. Feigel often visited my mother. She told horror stories about the 1915 cholera epidemic and gossiped about the girls and young women in Shebrin who became smugglers during the war. The Austrian gendarmes frequently ma le them undress when they searched them, and they touched intimate parts of their bodies, where no decent woman allows herself to be touched by a strange man. My mother nodded her bewigged head. "It's all a result of our long exile."

Feigel accused Leah of witchcraft, saying that Leah didn't desire marriage herself and that she had prevented Rachel from getting a husband. Every time Feigel became engaged, Leah cast an evil spell. Feigel would say to my mother, "My dear aunt, that Leah is a male, not a female."

"What are you talking about?" My mother winced. "She has breasts."

"She has the feet of a Cossack. God made a mistake."

"How can you say this? The Almighty doesn't make any mistakes."

"If so, she's a mooncalf."

This family did not come up to our standards. My uncle Jekhiel had fallen in love with his second wife, though she was much beneath him, and when Feigel called my mother "aunt" it was like a slap in the face. But my mother had compassion for Leizer's daughters because they were orphans. She sent me to buy baked farfel from them and ordered my shirts to be sewn by Feigel. Her fingers tickled me when she took the measurements and I had to laugh. My mother's comment about Leah having breasts preyed on my mind. Until then I thought that only women who nurse children have breasts. Yes, Leah had a huge bosom, but she had the deep voice of a man. Could she be what the Talmud called androgynous? I was as fearful of her as of the dark gateway that was full of holes and ditches. From reading storybooks I knew that there existed sinful females who copulated with demons and gave birth to sprites and succubi. Perhaps Leah was having an affair with the demon who dwelt in her chimney. I was close to bar mitzvah age and I kept thinking more and more about what I had studied in the Gemara concerning relations between men and women. Novels, too, began to interest me. It was at about this time that my mother asked Feigel to make me several pairs of drawers and shirts.

I brought the linen to Feigel, and as I approached the house I noticed a thick black smoke issuing from the chimney. I pondered about the devil who lurked in his sooty lair. When I passed the bakery I saw Leah standing in a shabby skirt and huge boots. As she sprinkled water on the freshly baked loaves, the steam rose into the air.

The threshold of the gate was high and I tripped over it. It was a hot day and the door of Leizer's room was ajar. His white beard had turned brown in spots from the snuff tobacco he used. The thought that a female rummaged around with his genitals invoked in me feelings of curiosity and disgust. He had a workshop equipped with hammers, saws, pliers, screwdrivers, and knives. Boards and metal rods were stacked in the corner. I remembered my mother saying that when he was young he tried to invent a cradle that would be self-rocking with the force of weights and springs. This was the reason that his business went to pieces.

After a while I entered Feigel's room. It was the brightest in the house. Father and daughters did not live as a family. They were rather like neighbors. Some of the rooms were ruined and remained locked. Feigel had a mannequin in her room—a female without a head but with hips and breasts. Pieces of thread caught in Feigel's hair gave her a special

charm in my eyes. It was hard to believe that she was near-
ing thirty, as her appearance was that of a young girl. She
deftly stepped on the treadle of her sewing machine with her
small foot and quickly moved her index finger out of the way
of the needle.

"You are here, huh?" She smiled at me invitingly.

"Yes, my mother sent me."

"You love your mother?"

I stood there embarrassed. "Yes, why not?"

"Is a Hasid allowed to love a female?" she asked.

"A mother is not a female."

"What else?"

Feigel rose to take my measurements, being most careful
as my mother had pointed out to her that my neck had got-
ten thicker. Her knuckles touched my chin and I felt that her
fingers were warm and soft. Suddenly she bent her head,
and her hair brushed my cheek as she kissed me on the lips.
I was so perplexed that I could not utter a word. "Don't men-
tion this to anyone," she admonished me.

How peculiar: days in advance I knew that I was about to
commit some transgression. My brain teemed with sinful
thoughts. Several nights earlier I had dreamed about my
cousin Taube, naked, her body enveloped in a net. The follow-
ing day I fasted until noon.

In Shebrin word got around that Feigel was about to be
engaged again. The new suitor, a droshky driver from War-
saw, had a relative in Shebrin, Chaim Kalch, and it was
through him that the match was arranged. Everything went
quickly. One day we heard about it and two days later we
were invited to the engagement party. The affair was a quiet
one, the guests were few. Leibush, the bridegroom-to-be,
seemed like a man in his late thirties or perhaps early forties,
big, with a reddish-blue complexion, a large nose, thick lips,

and a deeply creviced and pimpled neck. I imagined that he smelled of horse manure and axle grease. Under flaxen eyebrows, his watery blue eyes had a look that suggested anger and mockery, as if the whole event were nothing but a sham. Rachel served chopped herring, freshly baked kaiser rolls, and vodka. Leah put in an appearance just for a minute, not even bothering to change her clothes. Leibush had the coarse voice of one who customarily shouts. I heard him say, "I'm tired of the Warsaw cobblestones." He drank three-quarters of the vodka and ate almost all the rolls while discussing business. He had had enough of the Warsaw tumult and stench, and he intended to buy a horse and wagon in She-brin to carry freight to Lublin. People in Warsaw didn't know how to cross the streets, and when an accident occurred, the driver got the blame. From his words I understood that he most probably ran over someone, with a resulting lawsuit, or perhaps he went to jail. Feigel, too, helped with the refreshments. My father drew up the engagement papers. He asked Leibush, "What is your full name?"

"Leibush Motl."

"Aryeh Mordecai." My father translated the name into Hebrew.

"What are you?" my father asked. "A Cohen, a Levi, or an Israelite?"

"Who knows what I am."

"Don't you attend synagogue? Aren't you called up to the reading of the Torah?"

"Once in a while."

"Here you will have to attend the synagogue. In a small town you must behave," Feigel interrupted.

"Well . . ."

Feigel's father, Leizer, appeared peeved, impatient, and barely able to wait until he could return to his hammers, saws, files, and screws. To everything that was said, he nodded in silence. Feigel smiled, joked, and even winked at me. She shrugged. "Marriage and death are unavoidable."

"What makes you say such things?" my mother asked. "You're still young and you will live till 120."

"Not so young. No one knows what the next day will bring."

"Exactly my words," Leibush agreed. "Last week as I sat drinking a mug of beer with my friend, his head suddenly fell to one side and he was a goner."

"God forbid the misfortunes that can happen."

"People creep right under the wheels."

The wedding date was set for a month later. Leizer and Leah wanted the wedding to be a quiet one, but Feigel demanded a ceremony with musicians and a jester. I heard her say to my mother, "What does a girl get out of life? A dance and a hop."

At the wedding, Feigel danced with her sister Rachel and then with another girl. She looked lovely in the bridal gown she had made herself. The gown opened out like an umbrella as she whirled around and I saw her lace-trimmed panties. After the virtue dance, two women led Feigel into a darkened bedroom. A few minutes later Leizer and one of the other men escorted Leibush to his bride.

Leah came to the wedding dressed in her Sabbath dress and high-heeled shoes. Under her heavy, masculine brows her black eyes were sad and resentful. When my mother went to wish Rachel *mazel tov,* she replied, "Whoever heard of serving the dessert before the main dish?"

"You and Leah will also bring joy to your father one day."

"Maybe."

The morning after the wedding, the whispering began. A boy who had hidden behind the window of the bridal chamber announced that Feigel and Leibush quarreled half the night. There was scolding, and blows were struck. In order to reach the window he had crept through the swamp, and he showed the mud and moss that still clung to his pants and boots. Feigel soon called on my mother to unburden herself. I was most eager to listen to Feigel's secret but she dismissed me. "Do me a favor," she said, "and leave the room. It's not for your ears."

From the other side of the door I heard muttering and stifled crying. When Feigel left, my mother's face had red blotches. I inquired as to what was wrong with the couple, and my mother said, "God spare us, how many madmen there are."

"They don't get along?'

"She has bad luck."

But the boys in the study house spoke clear words: "Feigel does not allow her husband into her bed."

Leibush came to my uncle Jekhiel to press charges, and they locked themselves in the study. Just as Leibush had previously maligned Warsaw and praised Shebrin, he now reversed himself. He stood in the marketplace surrounded by boys and men and kept repeating, "How can anyone live in this godforsaken village? One can lose one's mind just from seeing so much mud. Whatever else can be said about Warsaw, at least it's lively."

"For money you can get everything here also," called out a newly married young man.

"What can you get? There's not even a place to drink a decent glass of beer."

People tried to make peace between Feigel and Leibush. Horse dealers offered to sell Leibush a team of horses for a song. Merchants promised they would hire him to carry their merchandise to Lublin and Lemberg. But Leibush shook his head. Feigel didn't show herself. A girl who went to her shop to be fitted for a dress found the door locked. My aunt Yentl came to talk it over with my mother. They murmured and the ribbons of Yentl's bonnet shook. "I'm afraid there'll be no bread from this dough," Yentl said.

"A crazy ignoramus," my mother agreed.

The marriage was quickly dissolved. Divorce in Shebrin was not permitted because the river had two names and there was some doubt as to which name to use in the divorce papers. The pair went to Lublin to obtain the divorce. I watched both of them mount the wagon for the trip. Leibush seated himself near the driver and Feigel sat in the rear on a bundle of hay. She wore the same hat with the feather which she had worn on the Sabbath after the wedding when she was led into the women's section of the synagogue. She looked drawn and older. Rachel came out and handed her sister a package of food. Girls and women watched from behind drawn curtains.

Though Feigel was supposed to return soon afterward, weeks passed and she still remained in Lublin. When she did get back, winter had set in. Rachel paid us a visit and said, "Never serve the third course before the first."

"Forgive me, Rachel, but you talk nonsense."

"Men are wild beasts," Rachel spoke, half to my mother and half to herself.

"What's the matter with you? The greatest saints were men."

"Maybe in ancient times."

One afternoon Feigel appeared at our house. "It's all Leah," she confided to my mother. "She bewitched us. When she learned I was about to marry, hell broke loose. She put a curse on me. This is the truth."

"If one trusts in God, one need not fear evil."

"It doesn't help. She's got Rachel under her spell. Rachel repeats Leah's every word like a parrot. She would stand on her head if Leah told her to. The reason she's my enemy is because I refused to do her bidding."

"God will send you the right match."

"No, Auntie, my bridegroom will be the Angel of Death."

Feigel spoke the truth. Not long after this conversation, we heard that she was mortally ill. Though a doctor was summoned, he could not help her. Women reported that she was as emaciated as a consumptive and was failing more and more each day. When I went to buy farfel I no longer heard the sound of Feigel's sewing machine. One time I noticed that the door to Feigel's workshop was open and I looked in. She sat basting a seam. When she saw me, she smiled weakly and said, "Look at him, he's grown up."

"Feigel, I wish you a speedy recovery."

"If wishes were horses, beggars would ride. I'm already beyond help, but it's nice that you came to visit me. Come in, sit down."

When I sat on the stool she began to reminisce. "Only yesterday you were a child. Now you're an adult. There's one thing I want you to remember: never torture the woman who will fall into your hands!"

"God forbid."

"We are all God's children."

"The main thing is that you should be healthy."

"No, my darling. I'm not long for this world," and a knowing smile appeared on her lips.

A few weeks later Feigel died. She had sent for my uncle Jekhiel, recited her confession to him, and requested that her trousseau be given to poor brides. The village women said she died like a saint. I followed her hearse. Rachel wailed and pounded her head with both fists, but Leah walked silently. Leizer recited the Kaddish. Father and daughters sat together for the seven days of mourning.

After Feigel's death the family fell apart. Leizer contracted pneumonia several months later and passed away. Now the rumors spread that Rachel was losing her mind. She gave the customers more change than they paid for the items. It reached the stage where Leah no longer trusted her to sell. Leah herself wasn't good at selling. She had no patience with the peasants and their haggling. Her baking was limited to those who came to the shop—a few girls and matrons who liked her baked goods. The two sisters could not earn a living any more. Rachel, who used to make the household purchases, no longer came to the butcher shop. She became senile. When she visited with my mother, dates and facts were confused in her stories. As a rule she brought us bread and rolls every second weekday. One Sabbath the door opened and Rachel entered in workday clothes, carrying a bakery basket. My mother began to pinch her cheeks. "Rachel, what is the matter with you? It's the Sabbath!"

"Sabbath? I thought it was Sunday."

"But all the stores are closed. Carrying is forbidden."

"Shall I take the bread back home?"

"No, leave it. Didn't you prepare a Sabbath stew?"

"Maybe I did. I will go home."

Not long after this incident Rachel developed cancer of the breast. She lay in bed and Leah took care of her. Dr. Katz, the Shebrin physician, maintained that if Rachel went to Warsaw they might be able to operate and save her. Though the community was ready to pay her expenses, Rachel refused to go, saying, "Here I was born and here I will die."

In her pain and delirium she began to sing songs. Fragments of the Rosh Hashonah and Yom Kippur liturgies remained in her memory. It became obvious that she had a singing voice, though no one had ever heard her sing before. She even improvised words and melodies, as well as threnodies for her father and her long-dead mother—all in the plaintive tones inherited from generations. She now openly complained that Leah prevented Feigel and herself from marrying.

After Rachel's death Leah stopped baking. She rented out

two rooms and was somehow able to manage from the income. Her seclusion was complete. She went nowhere and didn't even come on Rosh Hashonah to the women's section of the synagogue to hear the blowing of the ram's horn. The chimney stopped spewing smoke and sparks, and in Shebrin it was said the imp now lived behind Leah's stove and slept with her in her bench bed. Although she was past her sixtieth year, her hair remained black as pitch.

When I left Shebrin, Leah was still alive. I heard that she died just before the Nazi invasion. For a long time I hadn't thought about the sisters, but yesterday when I dozed off for a minute at my desk, I dreamed about Feigel. I saw her in a bridal gown, silken shoes, her hair streaming down to her waist, her face pale, and her eyes alight with an other-worldly joy. She was waving a palm branch and a citron fruit as though it were Succoth and saying to my mother, "What has a girl from her life? Nothing but a dance and a hop."

Translated by the author and Ruth Schachner Finkel

Her Son

O NE day when I had been in New York only a short time,
a poet invited me out to Sholum's Café for lunch. He
had a reputation among the Yiddish writers as a dandy, a
cynic, a womanizer. He had a wife so fat that she could hardly
get through a door—or so someone had told me. She ate out
of anguish over her husband's love affairs. Although he was
close to seventy, his hair was still a golden blond. He had blue
eyes, a high forehead, and a nose and chin that gave the im-
pression of being worldly-wise. He wore an English suit and
smoked a Havana cigar. His shirt was striped red and gray,
his tie embroidered with gold. He had a diamond ring and
monogrammed links in his cuffs. It struck me that he resem-
bled Oscar Wilde. He wrote like Wilde too—with paradoxes
and aphorisms. I was twenty-nine, newly arrived from War-
saw, and he spoke to me like an older writer to a beginner,
offering advice. He said, "You look like a yeshiva boy, but
I can tell from your writing that you know about women."

The door of the café opened to admit a man in a crushed
hat. His face was pale, unshaven; his eyes looked bloodshot,
sleepy, and full of the gloom of the depressed. He came di-
rectly to our table. Without a word, my host—I'll call him
Max Blender—reached into his pocket, took out a check, and
handed it over. "Well, Bill, are you seeing your way clear
yet?" he asked.

"Things just keep getting worse," the man grumbled.

"The loan didn't help?"

"Nothing will help me any more." He spoke Yiddish with an

253

American accent. Although his voice was low, it had the quality of a muffled shriek. Bitterness hovered about his lips. One shoulder was higher than the other. The cheap tie he was wearing had twisted to the side. A button was missing from his coat. From a distance, he had appeared to be in his fifties, but up close I saw that he was much younger. "Well, I'll be going," he said.

"Maybe you'll have a glass of coffee with us? This young man is—"

"I have to go!"

"Where?"

"To kiss somebody's behind so I can borrow a hundred dollars to pay on the mortgage. If I can't get it, I'll lose the house and end up in the street with my family."

Max Blender bit down on his lower lip. "Wait. I'll give you the hundred dollars, and you won't have to kiss anyone's behind."

"It's all the same to me."

Max Blender opened his wallet and counted out a hundred dollars. He shook his head and winked at me. Bill scooped up the money, mumbled something that might have been goodbye, and left. He didn't glance at me.

"A relative, eh?" I said.

Max Blender smiled, showing a mouthful of false teeth. "A son, though not mine. He adopted me for a father, and he had the right to do it. But how did he know that he had this right? I'll tell you the story, if you like. I swear on Asmodeus's beard that I've never told it before. I wanted to write about it myself, but I'm a poet, not a prose writer. Wait—I'll order another plate of blintzes. Let's spend the day together."

"My pleasure."

"Just let me light up." He took out a cigar and rolled it between his fingers.

"I'll make it as brief as I can," he said. "I had a mistress forty years ago who was the greatest love of my life. She has been dead for thirty-seven years, but a day doesn't go by that I don't think about her. You might say, not an hour. I've had other big affairs. Even at my age I'm into this foolishness right up to here—" he held his finger to his throat— "but no one compares to what she was to me and no one ever will. She had a husband—what else? And not only a husband but a husband who loved her with a savage passion. And she hated him as intensely as he loved her. Her name was Sonia —the most common name a girl from Russia can have. And there was nothing extraordinary about her appearance—the usual dark eyes, the black braids, the whole claptrap that's described in Yiddish novels. But when I met her at the Szydlaw Society—my mother's people came from Szydlaw—and talked with her a few minutes, I fell desperately in love and, believe me, in this case 'desperately' isn't an exaggeration. I felt a burning in all my limbs, and what's more, I realized that she was going through the very same thing. We grew deathly afraid of each other and of what we were starting. Her husband was sitting up there on the dais—he was president of the society—pounding the gavel to keep the crowd quiet. I forgot to tell you the main thing—she was twelve years older than I and had four children. All girls. They lived on Avenue C, downtown, and he was—thank God for that—a traveling salesman. He sold textiles, and he often went to Fall River, Massachusetts, which is the Lodz of America. Chaskell Wallach was his name.

"Sonia was something of an intellectual. She had read Artsybashev's *Sanin* and could recite several pages out of *Eugene Onegin*. She had tried to write poems in Yiddish. She attended the opera when her husband was on the road. She read Socialist pamphlets. Chaskell Wallach both hated and admired her gentility. He had a huge nose, the bulging eyes of a golem, and the voice of an ox. He couldn't speak— only shout. Sonia told me that even when he was in bed with her he shouted. He had had the silly ambition to be head of the Szydlaw Society. At the society's meetings, they talked about only one thing—the cemetery. He attended the funeral of every member who died. To this boor, death had been the means for becoming president, for gorging himself on knishes and drinking liquor at the society's expense.

"He knew as much about sex and love as a eunuch. In time, Sonia told me that during all the years they had been together he had never satisfied her. She began to dream about a lover right after their wedding, but she was essentially a small-town, modest woman, although in moments of passion she could utter words that might surprise the Marquis de Sade.

"Our affair began at our very first meeting. Sonia said that she felt warm, and I took her to Houston Street for ice cream. Going down the stairs, we began to kiss and bite each other like two lunatics, and by the time we reached the ice-cream parlor we had made plans to run away together to California or Europe.

"There are fires that start spontaneously. Maybe you've heard of the Triangle Building fire? In a few minutes, tens or maybe hundreds of factory girls were burned to death there. A fatality doesn't need any kindling.

"I'm not a scientist, but I've read some science. I know the theories and all the babble about evolution. It's a big lie. The universe happened in one second. God alone, if He exists, simply became. There was nothing. Suddenly it was all there —God, the world, life, love, death. Oh, here are our blintzes."

"The blintzes didn't come all of a sudden," I remarked.

"Eh? Not at Sholum's Café. If this cook were God, we would still be in Genesis."

We ate the blintzes, and Max Blender went on. "All the talk about running away came to nothing. A mother of four doesn't run away. The old game of deception began. When Chaskell was on the road, there was nothing to stop us. She met me at a hotel or at a furnished room that I rented. I was married by then, but my wife and I had no children. When he stayed in town, that's when the trouble began. He didn't leave her side for a moment. He couldn't write or figure, and she served as his secretary. Besides, he insisted that she prepare his favorite dishes—stuffed derma, fat soups, and the devil knows what. She would sneak out for an hour and we would fall on each other with a terrible hunger. She told baffling stories. She had the most fantastic dreams and visions —or how should I call them—while awake. As for me, near her I became a veritable giant. The usual love affair cools off in time, but ours grew stronger with the years, and such affairs have no good end.

"My wife found out that I loved somebody else—she had learned to accept my minor affairs—and she used every means that a wife can employ to get me away from Sonia. She took her sister's daughter into our house—a young girl of nineteen—and tried to seduce her in my behalf. If I hadn't experienced such a thing, I wouldn't believe the lengths a jealous woman will go to. She threatened to be unfaithful to me, but those who betray don't threaten. She was one of those women who can have only one man. Whether this is biological or a kind of self-hypnosis, I don't know. Hypnosis is itself biological. The whole human history is a history of hypnosis.

"Why drag it on? Sonia's husband found out about us. When I learned that he knew, I was scared to death. He could kill me with one blow. He had a pair of paws like a coachman. I'm no hero, and it never was my ideal to die for romance. I was so scared I left town for a while.

"Sonia called to tell me what grief he was causing her. He broke all the dishes in the house. He beat her. He terrorized the children. He told the members of the society about us. But for some reason that I still don't understand, he never tried to take revenge against me. He didn't even telephone my wife, which is the least you'd expect. Perhaps he considered all writers charlatans, beneath him to bother with.

Anyway, you can't tell what goes on in someone else's brain. A person who has gone through as much as I have knows that psychology is not a science and never will be.

"He used another method—he made Sonia pregnant, so that she wouldn't have time for an affair. After the birth of their fourth daughter, they had exercised a kind of birth control. But now he insisted that she have another child. Sonia was in her forties and didn't believe that she could still get pregnant, but she did, and she gave birth to that fellow you just saw here. He's her son. I know what you're thinking. No, he isn't mine. He looks like his father, although his father was a bruiser and this one is a weakling. As a matter of fact, I suspect that I'm sterile. Anyway, Sonia became pregnant, and it was the hardest pregnancy I have ever seen. When she was in her fifth month, she looked like a woman in her ninth. She became yellow, as if she had jaundice. He had raped her physically and spiritually. We were both sure that she would die in labor. The few times that we managed to meet, she spoke only about death. She made me promise that when my time came I'd be buried beside her. Unfortunately, there's no way I can manage this. Chaskell is already lying there, next to her. The cemetery is so full of the *landsleit* from Szydlaw that I'll have to be buried somewhere else.

"No, she didn't die in labor. She lived nearly two years more, but it was a slow death. Her husband got her pregnant again, and this time she miscarried. I won't go into details. From the day I learned that she was pregnant, all physical relations between us ceased. We had neither the desire nor the opportunity. I had brought about her death, and the sense of guilt was so strong that it left no room for any other feelings. I also began to fear that my own end was close. I went to visit Sonia at her home when she was on her deathbed and she said to me, 'Don't forget Velvel.' Velvel is what his father had named the boy. Later, Velvel became Bill.

"I never liked this child. First, he had killed Sonia, although it hadn't been his fault. Second, he had something of his father's character, albeit none of his strength. A year following Sonia's death, Chaskell remarried and moved to Brooklyn. After the years of the bitterest guilt had passed, the old fire came back—I could only be with other women if I imagined, or forced myself to imagine, that they were she. In moments of intimacy I called them Sonia. For years I suffered from hallucinations. I saw Sonia walking on the street, riding the subway. Once I saw her in Central Park. I had forgotten that she was dead and I began to talk to her, but she disappeared before my very eyes. Sonia had willed me a whole packet of her poems that were written to me. I needn't tell you that they weren't poetry in the usual sense of the word, but they were full of sincerity and therefore had genuine power. Total sincerity is bound to all the forces of nature.

"I read these poems to this day. I know them by heart. A number are about this Velvel that she called Benjamin and Benoni, after Mother Rachel's son. Sonia loved the Scriptures. She had a translation of the Bible in Yiddish that was published by the Christian missionaries. In her poems, she calls him 'your son,' because I was the reason for his coming into the world. It's a kind of spiritual fatherhood.

"Years went by, and I never got in touch with Sonia's children. When she was alive, she told me that the girls—at least the two oldest—cursed my name. Chaskell had confided in his children and had planted a hatred toward me in them. It was because of me that they had a stepmother. Those romantic loves that the poets laud with such lofty phrases actually ruin lives. Our pious grandparents considered what we call love a crime, and that's what it is. If this kind of love were truly virtue, modern man wouldn't deify it so. It is the very opposite of free will—the most extreme form of hypnosis and fatalism. Our God-fearing mothers and fathers lived a decent life without this slavery, and believe me, they were more ready to do things for each other than the people who are involved in love affairs, and this includes myself. Much of the love of our time is sheer betrayal. It is often hatred, too.

"Yes, the years went by and I knew nothing of Chaskell. He was some twenty years older than I. Then I learned that he had died—most probably from overeating. One day the phone rang. It was his son. He said, 'My name is Bill—Velvel. I'm Sonia's son.'

"I didn't care for his voice. Even then I could hear a reproach in it. Nevertheless, I arranged to meet him. He told me that three of his sisters were married. The youngest had gone to England. After Chaskell's death, the family had drifted apart, as families will. Bill recited to me a whole parcel of woes. His father had persecuted him. His sisters both pampered and hated him. He hadn't finished high school. He had had many jobs, but he had been swindled out of each one. He needed money. He looked at me as a son looks at a father who has grown estranged from him. He didn't ask but demanded. Everything about him irked me and I wanted to tell him, 'I don't owe you a thing—get going!' Instead, I gave him everything I had. He took it and didn't even thank me. After he left, I swore not to see that miserable creature again. But I knew that I was helpless against him. I owed him a debt that I could never repay."

Max Blender stopped a moment to order more coffee. "I've seen lots of good-for-nothings in my life," he continued, "but there isn't another schlemiel like this Bill in the world. He did everything upside down. He wouldn't study, he wouldn't train for a profession, he wasn't suited for any business. He failed at whatever he tried. How does the saying go? 'If he was dealing in shrouds, no one would die.' Sometimes a man like that makes a good marriage and gets an energetic wife who helps him. But he married a lazy girl—some lump—and she started right off to spray with children. Five girls. Children get sick and grownups do, too, but his house was like a hospital. Half the income he had went for doctors and medicines. He had other misfortunes, too. Once, there was a fire. Another time, a leak in the plumbing and a ceiling collapsed. With every disaster, he came running to me in a sweat, and I did as much as I could.

"You may not know this, but for years I had a printing shop—my own books earned me next to nothing. I never figured up how much this Bill cost me, but it came to thousands of dollars. I helped him buy that house we spoke about just now. Naturally, he knew he had to make the mortgage payments, but each time one was due he came running to me —always on the last day. One thing I do regret—that I didn't write down all these mishaps of his and catastrophes. A book might have been put together out of them that would have been both tragic and funny.

"There were times when I wanted to rebel. After all, he wasn't my flesh and blood. If I could be sure that there is a hereafter and that Sonia—wherever she is—knows what I'm doing for her darling, then I would move Heaven and earth to take care of him. But if there is nothing on high and Sonia is only a heap of dust, for whom am I sacrificing? It has never even occurred to him to bring me some trifle for Hanukkah or for a birthday. When my books came out, my colleagues occasionally honored me with a banquet. I always asked that an invitation be sent him. He never showed up. You saw how he grabbed what I gave him without so much as a thank you. That's how he has been for years.

"This pipsqueak is my enemy because he somehow knows —call it subconsciousness or simply instinct—that I'm responsible for his being in this world. He carries a grudge against me. He seems to believe that his failures are also somehow connected to me. A cabalist told me that when a man rapes a woman or gives her a child against her will, he drags down from the Throne of Glory a soul that shouldn't be on earth and such a soul strays about as if in the World of Chaos. In the few conversations that I have had with this Bill, he has always said the same thing: that he wouldn't live for long. But this didn't stop him from hinting that I should remember him in my will. He is made up of contradictions. It may be that the whole universe is one big contradiction. God contradicted Himself, and from this the world evolved. How does that philosophy strike you?

"Now listen to this. I told you Bill has five girls—each one brighter than the next. With children, of all things, he did succeed. He didn't have the money to send them to school, but three of them worked their way through college. They got scholarships, too. I was interested in his daughters. I often asked him to let me meet them, but he kept me at a distance. You wouldn't believe this, but I was never invited to this house that I helped him buy. I assumed that he would name one of the girls after his mother, but he gave them all Gentile names: Jean and Beatrice and Nancy and the like. He doesn't want to know any Jewishness. He buys a tree on Christmas. That's actually what caused the fire at his house.

"I've made peace with the fact that as long as I live I'll owe him a debt, but I won't leave him a penny. Besides, I have little to leave. I liquidated my print shop years ago.

"Now comes the real stuff. A couple of months ago, my book *The Amber Idol* came out. Don't look so surprised. I like unusual names. Somewhere inside me I'm a Dadaist, a futurist—give it what name you like. Since there were idols of gold, silver, and stone, why couldn't there have been one of amber? And even if there weren't one in reality, why shouldn't there be one in poetry? You know better than I do that the cabala is based on combinations of letters. When you combine two things that never existed together before, they begin a new existence and perhaps the spheres become enriched from this.

"In brief, my good colleagues arranged an evening for me. They asked whom to invite, and I gave them the list of names and addresses my wife uses to send out New Year's greetings and such. We all ate dinner and we maligned other writers, the way these things go. As I sat there struggling with a quarter of a tough rooster, *Sonia* came to the table. Yes, Bill's daughter. Her name was Nancy, but it was Sonia as she might have looked at eighteen. I sat there speechless. She said to me, 'You don't know me, but I know you. On account of you I studied Yiddish, so that I could read your poems. I'm Sonia's granddaughter!' And she smiled as if the whole thing were a joke.

"I could hardly keep from crying. I said, 'You look exactly like your grandmother.' Just as if she were afraid to shatter my illusions, she told me right then and there that she was going out with a young man and that they were ready to marry. He was a student at Princeton University, and he came from somewhere in Arizona or thereabouts. She told me more: that her future husband—and probably her current lover—had taken an interest in my work too, and wanted to learn Yiddish. He was studying literature.

"I barely heard what she was saying. The pious speak of resurrection, and here was resurrection in front of me. Well, but Sonia was Sonia and this was Nancy. She lacked her grandmother's intensity. I asked her to sit down next to me. Little time remained before the speeches would begin. I heard her say, 'Why don't you ever come to visit us? We all consider you our grandfather. Now that we have a house in the country, you could rest up there or write. We have a guest room.'

" 'A house in the country?' I asked, and she said, 'My father didn't tell you? Imagine it. He can hardly pay off the mortgage on the old house, and here he buys a new house with new debts. My father has to have things to worry about and to rack his brain over. The old house is almost paid for, and we girls are already earning money. We could soon be independent. So he buys a summer house and now there'll be new crises. That's my daddy.'

"The whole thing upset me so that I didn't hear the speeches, and when it came my turn to respond I didn't know what I was saying. I'm considered a good speaker. On that evening I ruined my reputation.

"That night, I didn't sleep a wink. I swore the most solemn oath that when Bill showed up the next time I'd grab him by the collar and say, 'Get to hell out of here.' I called myself 'ox,' 'horse,' 'dumbhead.' A week didn't go by and there he stood before me again, with the twisted buttons, the ragged clothes, the pale face, the gloom in his eyes—an image of despair. He looked at me as the victim looks at the murderer and said, 'Only one way out for me—to hang myself.'

"I wanted to shout, 'Sell your summer house, you faker! You parasite. You lousy schnorrer!' But at the same time I thought, Why shouldn't he be allowed to have a summer house? Why shouldn't he have a place where he can go and rest up? And what if he kept his word and really hanged himself? I had seen idiots jump out of windows during the Wall Street crash of 1929 when their stocks fell. The rest you know already. I pay like a father. You were just a witness. What do you say to all this?"

"Spinoza maintains that everything can become a passion. 'Everything' includes all possible emotions," I said.

"Pity, too?"

"Pity, too."

"What about love?" he asked.

"Spinoza compares those in love to the insane," I said.

"Really? Well, he's absolutely right. But after all these years it's too late for me to become sane."

Translated by Joseph Singer

The Egotist

I N THE apartment house where I lived on Riverside Drive, I had a neighbor two floors above me—Maria Davidovna. Famous emigrants from Russia visited her—radicals, Socialists. She was tall and dark, with classical proportions and gray eyes behind thick-lensed pince-nez. Her hair was pulled into a bun. She always wore dark skirts and blouses with high collars. She reminded me of the revolutionary women of Russia who lived in attic rooms and printed illegal pamphlets by hand or put together bombs to throw on the czar's henchmen. I made her acquaintance when the elevator broke down and I helped her carry an old dog-eared Russian encyclopedia she had bought on Fourth Avenue. When we became more familiar, she invited me to come up to her place to play chess, and every time we played she checkmated me.

Slowly her friends became known to me, too—especially her three steady visitors. One of them had been the leader of a faction in the Russian Duma—Popov. He became a widower in New York and married a distant relative of Maria Davidovna's. Popov lived only a few blocks from us. His new wife was sick, and Popov used to buy the food and do the cooking. I met him many times in the supermarket, pushing a cart. He was short, with broad shoulders and a head of white hair like foam. He had a red face, a turned-up nose, and a white goatee. He always wore the same double-breasted suit and shoes with round toes. His tie had a wide knot. It seemed to me sometimes that he had been dressed like this forty years ago and had remained in the same clothes and with the same expression he wore in a picture I had seen of him in a book about Russia. Each time we met he stretched out his heavy hand and gave me a long grip followed by a short one. Since I knew no Russian, he spoke to me in broken English. He had a reputation in Russian politics as a peacemaker among the various factions—one who had averted many a split in the radical movement. The essence of his good-natured conversation was that in spite of all the difficulties we should be grateful that we were living in a free country.

The second visitor, Professor Bulov, had written a history of the Russian Revolution from the Decembrists up to Stalin. Bulov was tall and broad—a giant of a man—with a square yellowish face and the slanted eyes of a Mongol. He seldom spoke; he just shook his head. Maria Davidovna told me he came from somewhere in the north of Siberia and that when he was young he used to hunt bears with a cudgel. Later, he sat for years in solitary confinement in a Russian prison, and it was this that had made him so silent. He had a flattened nose, a low forehead, thick lips, a shock of hair like a brush. He hated the Bolsheviks with a passion that seemed to glow in his steely eyes. I imagined he held grudges that went back to the time of Genghis Khan. Maria Davidovna said that Bulov could never forgive Popov for opposing the arrest of Lenin. I was told that Bulov had managed to escape Russia after killing a G.P.U. man. Whenever he spoke about present-day Russia, he planted his fist on the table, and I always felt that the table could barely stand the pressure of that powerful fist and might collapse.

Kuzensky was the third visitor. He had been born a count. He entered the revolutionary movement when he was still young and played an important role in the nine months of Kerenski's regime. Kuzensky was tall, lean, with a high forehead and a pointed beard that remained black although he was already in his sixties. He had brown eyes that often smiled with a worldly-wise humor.

Kuzensky was known as a skeptic. a humorist, a ladies' man. He dressed more elegantly than the other Russians who visited Maria Davidovna, and wore spats summer and winter. I once saw Maria Davidovna ironing a silk shirt for him. A writer who knew this group told me that Kuzensky had the soul of a *feuilletonist*—not that of a fighter. His jokes made the others uncomfortable. Kuzensky and I had one thing in common: when he played chess with Maria Davidovna, she invariably checkmated him. Sometimes he and I played together against her. Kuzensky smoked a cigarette, hummed a Russian melody, ate the chick-peas and halvah that Maria Davidovna placed before us, drank many glasses of tea with lemon, and made one wrong move after another, all the while throwing out witticisms. Near him I became even more of a botcher at the game. When finally we were checkmated, Kuzensky would say, "Don't worry, comrade, the final victory is on our side. The day of vengeance is near." And he would wink at Professor Bulov and make funny grimaces. It was a parody of Bulov's faith that any day there would be a counter-revolution in Soviet Russia.

Kuzensky and Bulov were both bachelors. From remarks that Maria Davidovna let fall and from inscriptions on books that Kuzensky had given her on birthdays, I guessed that he had been in love with her. As for Bulov, he seemed to be enamored of her. He gazed at her avidly with his slanted eyes, under which were heavy pouches. He listened to every sound she made when she was in the kitchen preparing tea. Maria Davidovna assisted him in gathering material for his lengthy book. One thing I knew for sure—he never spent the night in her apartment. I sometimes met him going down in the elevator at two o'clock in the morning. Then he looked especially angry; he had a crooked wrinkle on his forehead and didn't answer when I greeted him. His wide face with the high cheekbones had a greenish hue. I believed that Bulov was constantly jealous, that he suspected every man of having an affair with Maria Davidovna and could barely curb his rage, which threatened to break out at any moment with Siberian ferocity.

Sometimes Maria Davidovna invited me to her apartment when there were no other guests. After I had been check-mated, we drank tea with jam and conversed about Zionism, the Talmud, Yiddish literature. Since we both spoke in a language foreign to us, our conversations could not go very deep.

Maria Davidovna had studied and read a lot and knew Russian and French literature, but she had the mind of a social theoretician. She tried to find logic in everything. There remained in her a youthful rawness that the years did not ripen. She was somehow still a student at the Gymnasium—a *barishnia* of the days before the First World War. I was sure that she kept a diary. She had brought out of Russia a thick album of faded photographs showing her with countless university students, girl friends, cousins. Most of the young men had beards; many of them wore black blouses with tasseled sashes. I often browsed among these photographs and asked Maria Davidovna about them. She would stare with shortsighted eyes, as if she herself were not sure any more who was who, and she would finally say, "Fallen in the war." "Shot by the Bolsheviks." "Died of typhoid fever."

I tried to question her about her friendship with Kuzensky and Bulov, but she answered evasively. Still, I learned some details. Maria Davidovna was the daughter of a rich lumber merchant. She had graduated from the Gymnasium in Kiev with a gold medal. While she was in the seventh class, she had entered a revolutionary group. The short term of Kerenski's regime was a period of personal triumph for her. She was close to all the Menshevik leaders; they entrusted her with important government missions. Every day of the year was full of surprises. That was a year without a winter, because the Revolution began in the spring and ended in the fall, when the Communists took over. Since then, Maria Davidovna had lived in a kind of prolonged mourning. She escaped from Russia, resided briefly in Warsaw, Vienna, Prague, and London, and could settle nowhere. She studied in a number of universities without ever completing any course. She had been in New York for years, but she could not stand this prosaic city with its noise, hurry, dirt, and greed for money. She contended that there was not a single beautiful building in New York, not one *gemütlich* restaurant or café, and that, in spite of all its electric lamps, at night the city was as dark as a jungle. The subway was a nightmare to her.

Once, unexpectedly, Maria Davidovna opened her heart to me. I had told her that she was actually a worldly nun in a private cloister. When she heard these words, she took off her pince-nez and her face became naked and grief-stricken. On both sides of her nose where the pince-nez rested were indentations, deep and bluish. She raised her reddened lids and asked, "Have you ever seen a living corpse? I don't mean it figuratively but literally."

"Literally, not."

"Since you write about ghosts and such topics, I want you to know that you are in the presence of a living corpse."

"When did you die?"

"After the Bolshevik Revolution."

"How?"

"Oh, there is too much to be said. As a matter of fact, I was dead even when I was young. I demanded too much from life, and those who demand too much get nothing. My father was seldom home. I don't know why he avoided my mother. She was a beautiful woman, although melancholy. She died when I was still in the Gymnasium. I was their only daughter. Every day when I took my schoolbag and went to school, I asked myself, 'What am I living for? What is the sense of it?' This wasn't just caprice. I always had a strong desire to die. I envied the dead. I used to go to the Greek Orthodox cemetery and stand for hours gazing at the photographs on the headstones. The February Revolution pulled me away from death. It intoxicated me. But I knew even then that such intoxication could not last. Kerenski's regime had all the symptoms of inebriation—a kind of carnival that was bound to end soon. Bolshevism was the bitter hangover that comes after—I am sorry . . ."

For a while we were both silent. Then I asked, "What kind of a man is Kuzensky?"

"An egotist—the greatest egotist I ever met. He has hidden from reality his whole life. All that remains of that carnival is a heap of rubbish, but for him it is still a holiday—the private holiday of a hedonist. Please, don't ask me any more. I have said too much as it is."

And Maria Davidovna put on her pince-nez again.

I began to realize that Kuzensky was not well. His face had become yellowish, his cheeks sunken. When he lit a cigarette, the match trembled between his long fingers. One evening when Kuzensky was visiting Maria Davidovna, Popov brought a pitcher of borscht that he had cooked himself. Kuzensky took only one spoonful.

Popov said, "This borscht is a remedy. It is cooked with lemon, not with sour salt."

"Well, the world knows you are a first-class cook—after the mess you cooked in Russia."

Kuzensky continued to make jokes, but everything else changed. When I played chess with Maria Davidovna, he no longer gave me advice. He even stopped humming his usual melody. Every few minutes he went to the bathroom and returned with shaky legs. His beard became white and I suspected that he had dyed it before. I was told that he was writing his memoirs, that he had a subsidy from a foundation.

In Maria Davidovna's books about Russia, photographs of Kuzensky could be found: as a Gymnasiast, a university student, a revolutionary, a political prisoner in exile, a speechmaker at a mass meeting in Petrograd. He was a part of the history of Russia, and therefore also of world history. But here he was, lying on Maria Davidovna's sofa, coughing into a handkerchief, dozing frequently, with Maria Davidovna chiding him for not keeping his diet, for being afraid to go to a doctor or the hospital.

Maria Davidovna's words that she was a living corpse had impressed me more than such phrases should. I began to imagine that there was a sweetish smell of decay in the apartment. Though all her lamps burned in the evening, the rooms remained in shadow, perhaps because every wall had bookshelves up to the ceiling. Each time I took out a book, pieces of dry paper broke off from the pages. I also noticed that Bulov and Kuzensky spoke to Maria Davidovna but not to each other. They even avoided looking at one another. Had they quarreled, or was it just that they had nothing more to say to each other? I developed a fear of Bulov. Sometimes when he sat in silence with his two slanted cracks for eyes, I felt that he was still in the forests of Siberia—a prehistoric man who by a caprice of nature had fallen into the twentieth century and become a professor. I stopped visiting Maria Davidovna.

One evening, I was sitting in my room reading a newspaper when someone knocked at my door. As a rule, only the exterminator knocked at my door unannounced. However, he always came in the daytime. I went to the foyer and asked, "Who is there?"

"I, Maria Davidovna."

I recognized her voice, but it was half choked. I let her in.

Maria Davidovna stood there without her pince-nez, her face pale and changed.

She said, "Please forgive me for disturbing you, but something terrible has happened and I don't know whom to turn to. Kuzensky just died."

"Died! How? Where?"

"In my apartment. I telephoned, but no one is home— neither Bulov nor Popov. Or maybe I didn't dial correctly— I've lost my glasses and I simply cannot see."

"Did you call the doctor?"

"He never would go to a doctor. Have pity and come up with me. Without my glasses I'm blind."

I was overcome by a boyish fear, but I could not refuse Maria Davidovna and leave her alone with a corpse. We did not use the elevators but climbed the stairs in silence. Maria Davidovna held on to my arm. We passed through the long hall of her apartment, through the living room, and entered the bedroom. On Maria Davidovna's wide bed lay Kuzensky in his suit, his bow tie, his shoes with spats. I barely recognized him. His straight nose had become hooked, his skin a deep yellow, his white beard turned up and shrunken. In the creases at the corners of his eyes there remained a congealed smile.

After some hesitation, Maria Davidovna asked, "Do you think I should call the police?"

"The police? Why? Perhaps you should call the Russian newspaper."

"No one is there at night. In my excitement I dropped my glasses. It's a miracle I managed to find your door. With him, my life is ended." Her tone changed. "Do you think you could find my glasses?"

I searched on the floor, on the night table, on the chest, but Maria Davidovna's pince-nez were nowhere to be seen. I said, "Perhaps you should call the English newspapers."

"They will ask for details, and I am too confused to remember anything now. The telephone is ringing—wait!"

Maria Davidovna left the bedroom. I had an impulse to follow, but I was ashamed to show such cowardice. I stood staring at Kuzensky; my heart pounded. His face was yellow and stiff as a bone. His mouth was small, half open and toothless. On the rug I saw his false teeth, strangely long, on a plastic palate. With the point of my shoe I shoved them under the bed.

Maria Davidovna returned. "Crazy—I was just told I had won two free lessons at a dance studio. What shall I do?"

"If you can remember the numbers, I will call Popov and Bulov."

"They're definitely not at home. Bulov is supposed to be here soon—any minute. We were drinking tea and playing chess. Suddenly he collapsed on the bed and was finished."

"A merciful end."

"He lived like an egotist and now he has deserted us like an egotist. What shall I do? Every second will be hell. Please sit down."

I sat on a chair, Maria Davidovna on another. I arranged myself in a position not to see the corpse. Maria Davidovna clasped her hands. She spoke in a singsong that reminded me of the keening of mothers and grandmothers.

"It was all selfishness. His going to the people, his imprisonment—all of it. He was a squire to the last second of his life. He never gave anything that wasn't an alm—even his love. He was too proud to see a doctor. As for me, I wasted my years for nothing. I forgot that I was a Jewish daughter. The other day I read in my Bible about the Israelites serving idols. I said to myself, 'My idol was the Revolution, and therefore I am punished by God.'"

"It is good that you understand it now."

"It is too late. He went when it was convenient for him and

left me to die a thousand deaths. Once, they put all their hopes in the Revolution. For the last thirty years they have been yearning for the counter-revolution. But what difference will it make? They are all old and sick. The new generation will not know the truth. The only ambition left to them is to prolong the agony. He, at least, admitted it."

The telephone rang. This time it was Popov. I heard Maria Davidovna telling him the news. She kept repeating "*Da, da, da.*"

It didn't take long for Popov and Bulov to arrive, and others followed—some with white beards, some with white mustaches. One old man leaned on crutches. Popov's suit was spotted; his cheeks were flushed, as though he had just left a hot stove. His childish eyes under his shaggy brows were reproachful. "See what he has done to us!" they seemed to be saying. Bulov took the corpse's wrist and felt for a pulse. He made a face, shook his square head from side to side, and his eyes were saying, "This is against all rules, Count. This is not the way to behave." Skillfully, he closed the corpse's mouth.

Women began to arrive, in long, old-fashioned dresses and low-heeled shoes, their sparse hair gathered into buns and fastened with hairpins. One of them wore a Turkish shawl over her shoulders—the kind my grandmother used to wear. In America I had forgotten that such wrinkled faces and bent backs existed. One old woman carried two canes. She took a step and I heard the crunch of glass. She had stepped on Maria Davidovna's pince-nez. Her hairy little chin shook as though she were muttering an incantation. I recognized her from a picture I had seen in a book. She had been an expert bombmaker and had been kept in solitary confinement in the infamous Schlisselburg prison.

I wanted to leave, but Maria Davidovna asked me to stay. She kept on introducing me to new visitors, and I heard names familiar to me from books, magazines, newspapers:

leaders of the Revolution, of the Duma; members of Keren-
ski's Cabinet. Every one of them had made historic speeches,
taken part in decisive conferences. Though I knew Polish, not
Russian, I could follow what they were saying.

The old woman with the canes asked, "Should we light
candles?"

"Candles? No," Popov said.

The one in the Turkish shawl cracked her rheumatic fin-
gers. "He is beautiful even now."

"Perhaps he should be covered," said the old man on
crutches.

"Who can take his place?" Popov asked, and then an-
swered himself, "No one." His face became apoplectic red,
and because of this his beard appeared even whiter. He mum-
bled, "We are passing away; soon no one will be left; Eternity
claims us—the great mystery. Russia will forget us."

"Sergei Ivanovich, don't exaggerate."

"It is written in the Bible: 'One generation passeth away
and another generation cometh.' Only yesterday he was
young and daring—an eagle."

One of the group, small, slight, with a pointed pepper-and-
salt beard, wearing thick glasses behind which his eyes looked
crossed, began to deliver a sort of eulogy. "He lived for Rus-
sia and he died for Russia," he said.

Maria Davidovna interrupted. "He lived for no one but
himself. The world will never know how great his egotism
was—never, never!"

There was silence. The telephone rang but nobody an-
swered it. They all looked perplexed, grieved, full of reproach,
full of forgiveness. The wrinkles at the corners of Kuzensky's
eyes seemed to laugh. Maria Davidovna covered her face with
both hands and began to cry in a hoarse voice.

Translated by the author and Dorothea Straus

The Beard

THAT a Yiddish writer should become rich, and in his old age to boot, seemed unbelievable. But it happened to Bendit Pupko, a little man, sick, pockmarked, with one blind eye and a game leg.

While he struggled with his physical handicaps, the plays he could not finish, the poetry which no one read, and novels which no one was willing to publish, he followed a relative's advice and bought a thousand dollars' worth of over-the-counter stock for two dollars a share. He got the capital in the first place from generous patrons and benevolent societies. The stock went up to almost one hundred times its original value in a matter of months.

Later on, the same relative advised him to buy some half-ruined buildings on Third Avenue in New York. A construction company wanted the land and paid him an enormous sum for it.

No one in the cafeteria which we all frequented ever learned the identity of the mysterious advicegiver, but we knew that Bendit Pupko became richer from day to day. He himself admitted that he wasn't very far away from his first million. Nevertheless, he wore the same shabby clothes he always wore. He sat with us at the table, smoked cigarettes, coughed, ate rice pudding, and complained. "What can I do with my money? Nothing."

"Give it to me," said Pelta Mannes, a writer of fables.

"What will you do with it? Take an egg cookie and a cup of coffee on my check."

Bendit Pupko was the kind of primitive writer who could never learn how to construct a correct sentence, had no notion of grammar, but was talented just the same. I often looked into his published works. They lacked any sense of organization, but on every page I found some lines to surprise me.

He described half-crazed people, chronic misers, old country quarrels which had gone on for so many years that no one knew how they began or what they were about, and complicated love affairs which started in the Polish villages and were carried over to the East Side tenement houses of New York and later to the hotels for old people in Miami Beach. His paragraphs went on for pages. He would insert himself into the middle of his hero's dialogue.

In the United States Pupko learned about Freud for the first time, and he tried to explain his characters according to Freudian theory. He needed an editor, but he never allowed anyone to correct even his punctuation.

Once, when I edited a small literary magazine, he brought me a story which began: "The day was cloudy and the sky loyal." When I asked him what he meant by "loyal," his good eye looked at me with anger and suspicion, and he exclaimed, "Don't bother me with this bookish nonsense. Either publish it or go to hell."

He grabbed his manuscript and ran away.

He had lived in America for forty years and never learned more than a handful of English words. He never read anything besides his Yiddish newspapers. Psychology he pronounced "pyschology." Someone told me that a dictionary could be compiled of Pupko's errors. But at times he spoke like a sage. He lived somewhere in Brownsville and had no children.

A man told me that Bendit Pupko's wife had a thick beard

which used to be black but had since turned gray. He never took her anywhere. Nobody knew why she didn't shave off her beard.

In my circle I learned long ago never to look for explanations. A comedian of the Yiddish theater who was known for his salty language suddenly became religious, let his sidelocks grow, and settled down in Jerusalem in the Mea Shearim quarter, where the most zealous Jews lived. An Orthodox rabbi divorced his wife, left his synagogue, and went over to the Communists. Two Hebrew teachers divorced their husbands and went to live together as lesbian lovers. Even Pupko's getting rich would not have surprised us too much, but he never let us forget about it. Every day he came and told us about his latest financial accomplishments. He began to advise us how to invest our savings.

One day he boasted to us that the critic Gabriel Weitz was writing a book about him. This we could not believe. Weitz had written unfavorably about Pupko's work at every opportunity. He called him an ignoramus, a village philosopher, and a contriver.

We all asked, "How is this possible?" Bendit Pupko winked with his bad eye and smiled cunningly. "When you grease the wheels, you ride well." Then he quoted a saying from the Talmud: "Money can purify a bastard."

Pupko spoke to us openly. "All these literary faultfinders can be bought for a pittance." He, Pupko, had talked business to Gabriel Weitz. "How much would it cost, buddy?" And the critic had given him a price—five thousand dollars.

We were all shocked. Gabriel Weitz had the reputation of a serious writer. We had all decided that Bendit Pupko was bluffing. But then a magazine appeared with an essay by Gabriel Weitz about Bendit Pupko, which was announced as a fragment of a longer work. In it Gabriel Weitz spoke of Bendit Pupko as a classic. He called him a genius. He was

eloquent concerning Pupko's importance to Yiddish litera-
ture. Bendit Pupko did not lie: Gabriel Weitz had let himself
be bought for five thousand dollars.

I said to Bendit Pupko, "What do you gain by paying for
such things? What is the value of such fame?" And Bendit
Pupko replied, "You must buy everything. If you have a wife
you have to provide for her. If not, she'll sue you. If you have
a mistress you have to take her to a restaurant, pay for her
hotel, and shower her with presents. Your own children would
become your enemies if you stopped supporting them.
Sooner or later everybody sends you a bill. In that case, why
should fame be different?"

He said to me, "You too will praise me one day."

These words made me shudder and I replied, "I have a
high opinion of you, but there isn't enough money in the
world to make me write about you."

He laughed and immediately became serious. "Not even for
ten thousand dollars?"

"Not even for ten million."

Someone at the table remarked, "Bendit, you spoil your
own business. He might have written about you sooner or
later."

"Yes, it may be," I said. "But now it's finished."

Bendit Pupko nodded. "Still, if you knew that writing a
favorable review of me would keep you in comfort for the
rest of your life, you wouldn't have to scribble your articles
and could live somewhere in California, you would think
twice. Why is it such a sin to say that Bendit Pupko has
talent?"

"It's not a sin and you do have talent. But since you have
begun to bribe critics, I wouldn't write about you for anything
in the world."

"What if somebody put a gun to your temple? Would you
give in then?"

"Yes, it certainly doesn't pay to die for something like this," I replied in our cafeteria style of conversation.

"Well, eat your rice pudding. I'm not offering you ten thousand yet. You'll make it a lot cheaper." And he laughed, showing his teeth, crooked and black like rusted nails.

A year passed, perhaps a little more or less. One day I entered the cafeteria and sat down at our usual table. For a while we chatted about a poem which a colleague had published in a magazine. One of us said it was a work of genius and another that it contained nothing but empty phrases. For a while we were engrossed in this controversial subject. Then the writer of fables asked, "Did you hear about Bendit Pupko?"

"What happened?"

"He has cancer."

"So this is the end of all his fortunes," someone remarked. We ate our rice pudding, drank coffee, and the question of whether the poem was excellent or a worthless compilation lost its importance. One of us said, "We are disappearing and younger writers don't appear. Twenty years from now no one will know we ever existed."

"And if they do know, how will this help us?"

After a while, I went home to my bachelor quarters. My desk was cluttered with manuscripts, stories, and novels I had never finished. Dust covered everything. I had a Negro woman who cleaned for me once a week, but I had forbidden her to touch my papers. Besides, she was old and half paralyzed. Often when she came I paid her for the day and sent her home because I saw that she had no strength to work. I worried that she might collapse while working in my apartment.

This time I lay down on the sofa and read a letter, the date of which showed that I had received it two years earlier. I found it while rummaging in my inside breast pocket. The sender's address could no longer be read. Then someone knocked at my door. I opened it and what I saw was like a nightmare. Outside stood a woman dressed in a shabby black dress, men's shoes and a hat, with a white beard. She leaned on a cane. I knew at once who she was—Mrs. Pupko. I was afraid my spying neighbors might see her and have something to laugh about. I said, "Come in, Mrs. Pupko."

She looked at me with astonishment. Her cane passed the door first. She said with a mannish voice, "Your elevator doesn't function. I had to climb five flights of stairs."

"I'm sorry, it's an old house. Sit down."

"May I smoke?"

"Yes, certainly."

She took out a cigar and lit it. Perhaps it's a man, I thought. But I saw that she had a large bust. Probably androgynous, I thought.

She said, "My husband is very sick."

"Yes, I heard. I'm very sorry."

"You are responsible for his illness," she said in a strong voice.

Shaken, I asked her, "What are you saying?"

"I know what I'm saying. You told him some time ago that you wouldn't write about him for all the money in the world. For you this was just talk to make yourself sound important. But there is a proverb, 'A blow is forgotten, but a word never.' You hurt him with those words more than you can imagine. How did he deserve it?

"My husband has great talent. Gabriel Weitz calls him a genius. Bendit has a high opinion of you. When you told him that you would never write about him, he took it very badly. You will never know how this affected him. He came home as yellow as wax. I asked him what was the matter and in the beginning he didn't want to tell me, but I got it out of him.

You won't believe me, but from that day on he was never the same. Sick as he was, he was always full of joy. He used to make plans for years in advance. But since that day he never lifted a pen. He began to suffer from cramps in his stomach—"

"Mrs. Pupko, this cannot be true," I interrupted her.

"God knows that it's the truth."

"I'm not a critic. Gabriel Weitz is writing a whole book about him."

"He doesn't think much of Gabriel Weitz. We all know who he is, an intellectual bore. All brain, no feeling. He understands literature like my left foot. Don't think that one can fool Bendit. He may deceive himself but he knows the truth. You are different. He reads every word you write. Sometimes we read you together. We are both insomniacs. We lie awake at nights, and whenever we talk about you he says the same thing, 'He's genuine.'

"Then you had to strike such a blow. He's more sensitive than you imagine. Literature is his whole life. I've been with Bendit for over forty years. Do you realize what it is to share a life for forty years? He reads me every line he writes. Whatever problem he has in his work he asks for my advice.

"We have no children, but his works are our children. You never shared anything with anyone, so you don't understand such things. You write about love, but you don't know what it is. Forgive me, but you describe passion, not love which makes sacrifices and ripens with the years. In this respect Bendit is ten heads taller than you. Do you have an ashtray?"

I brought her an ashtray and she shook the cigar ash into it. She lifted her bushy brows and I saw dark eyes, almost all pupil. I thought the witches who flew on brooms to attend Black Mass on Saturday nights and were later burned at the stake must have looked like this.

"Why do you stare at me like that? I'm a woman, not a man."

"May I ask you why—"

"I know what you want to ask. I grew a beard when I was still a young girl. You may not believe it but I was beautiful then. I tried to shave it or even to burn out the roots, but the more I tried the quicker it grew. Don't think that I'm the only one. Thousands of women grow beards. A beard isn't only a man's privilege.

"When I met Bendit and he kissed my cheek, he exclaimed, 'Zelda, you're growing a beard!' And he fell into a strange rapture. He was in love with my beard. Unbelievable? I didn't believe myself that this could be true. He spoke to me clearly. He was willing to marry me, but on one condition— that I let my beard grow. It wasn't easy to promise a thing like that. I thought he was insane."

"He must have homosexual inclinations," I said.

"Oh, I knew you'd say that. That is what everyone said. From you I expected something more original. He's not a homosexual. People have idiosyncrasies which can't be explained by any theories. It wasn't a small matter for me to comply. It meant complete loneliness. When my mother came to visit me in Odessa after our marriage and she saw me with a beard, she literally passed out.

"I became a hermit. But Bendit's wish was more important to me than any comforts. This is the kind of love which you cannot appreciate. Here in America my isolation became even more complete. I could tell you a lot, but I didn't come here to explain my beard but to warn you that you're killing Bendit."

"Please don't say such things. Bendit is my friend."

"In that case, you are killing your friend."

We continued to talk for some time. I gave Mrs. Pupko my word that I would write about her husband. She said to me, "It may be too late to save him, but I want him to have the satisfaction of seeing something written about him by you."

"May I ask why you smoke cigars?"

"*Nu*, one mustn't know everything."

In my mind I prayed to God that none of the neighbors would see her leave my rooms, but when I opened the door for Mrs. Pupko, I saw my neighbor the spinster lurking in the hall. The elevator was still not working, and Mrs. Pupko had to walk down the stairs. She called out to me, "Be a gentleman and help me down."

She grasped my arm and her breast touched my elbow. For some reason, all the neighbors on all the floors had their doors open as we descended. I heard children screaming, "Mama, look! A woman with a beard!" A barking dog ran out of one apartment and caught Mrs. Pupko's dress in his teeth, and I barely succeeded in driving him away.

That evening I sat down to reread Pupko's works. A few weeks later I had written an article about him, but the editor of the magazine to which I sent it delayed its publication so long that Bendit Pupko died in the meantime. He had just managed to read the proofs and on the margin of the last page he had written in a trembling hand: "Didn't I tell you?"

Once when I sat in the Automat on Sixth Avenue, not far from the public library, the door opened and Mrs. Pupko came in. She was supported by a cane and a crutch. Though a widow for two years, she still had her beard and wore a man's hat and shoes. She immediately limped over to my table and sat down as if she had an appointment with me.

All the customers in the Automat stared, winked at their neighbors, laughed. I wanted to ask Mrs. Pupko why, since her husband was no longer alive, she had kept her beard, but I remembered her words: "*Nu*, one mustn't know everything."

Translated by the author and Herbert R. Lottman

The Dance

WHEN I was a boy of twelve, Matilda Block was a woman in her late thirties or perhaps forty. She was a folk singer and had already acquired a reputation for herself in Warsaw for her talent as well as for her beauty. She performed in Hazamir, and I think that she also appeared at the Philharmonic. Her figure was slim, her eyes blue; she had unusually white skin and hair that was the closest to gold that I had ever seen. A descendant of rich Hasidim, she spoke fluent Polish, Russian, Yiddish, a little Hebrew, and even some French, which wealthy girls were taught in Gymnasium. She accompanied herself on the piano. Matilda married an artist, Adam Block, who exhibited at the famous Zacheta and whose pictures were purchased by museums abroad. He possessed an atelier with a skylight on Mazowiecka Street, was a steady habitué at the Ziemianska Café, and numerous articles appeared in the Polish press about his work. The tenderness of his lines, colors, and subjects was praised by the reviewers. But that tender artist began to beat his wife immediately after the wedding. According to Matilda's later accounts, he knocked out one of her teeth on their honeymoon. Once he hit her with a chair leg and an ambulance had to be called. She lived with him close to two years, bore him a son whom they called Izzy, and then they were divorced. Adam remarried soon after the divorce, but Matilda lived alone with her son. Adam Block's brutality was her constant topic of conversation. My older brother was well acquainted with

Adam Block, as he had studied painting with him. Adam almost never mentioned Matilda. He once said after a glass of vodka, "The fact that I did not kill her proves that I'm a saint."

When a beautiful woman is a divorcée and an artist to boot, men will seek her out, but Matilda gave no reason for gossip. All her energy was devoted to her singing and her son. When I first met Izzy (through my brother), he was a student at the Gymnasium and much older than I. Physically he resembled his mother, but he had his father's temperament. Studies did not interest him. He tried painting, singing, playing the violin in an orchestra, and even acting. A few weeks before the matriculation examinations he dropped out of school. At the age of twenty-one, in 1914, Izzy was called to serve in the czar's army but was released because of a rheumatic heart. My brother came home once and told us that Izzy hit his mother. Matilda had cried as she told him about this. She said, "What shall I do now? He's all I have."

In 1917 my mother took me and my younger brother to Bilgoray, which was then occupied by the Austrians. My older brother had gone to Russia. The only news I had about Matilda was what was printed in the advertisements in the Yiddish press. Once in a while there was a review about her performance. The reviewer always used the same phrase: "Matilda Block sang like a nightingale." She must have been close to fifty by then.

When I began to write and returned to Warsaw, I frequented the Writers Club and other cultural institutions, and there again I met Matilda Block. Adam was no longer alive. There was talk that he had committed suicide in Paris. After his death Matilda put on mourning clothes, which she kept wearing year after year. Though her figure was still slim, her golden hair was faded and her skin had many wrinkles. Only her eyes remained the same. Sorrow and goodness could be seen in them. Izzy was then past thirty, unmarried, and living with his mother. When I introduced myself to Matilda and told her who I was, she exclaimed, "The little Hasid with the red sidelocks! Why, I'm reading you in *The Literary Epoch.*"

She kissed me. I invited her to a café, and after the first few words she began to weep and blow her nose. Izzy isn't interested in marriage. He refuses to go out with girls and has no occupation. Of late he decided he wanted to become a dancer, but he lies in bed till noon, reads the novels of DeCobra and Margaritte, smokes numberless cigarettes, and is constantly listening to the chatter and singing on the radio. "What will happen to him? I'm not going to live forever. The impresarios complain that I'm too old and my engagements are fewer and fewer."

"How is it you never married? You are a beautiful woman."

"Marry? Whom? After living with a true artist you cannot put up with ordinary men like merchants or dentists. There's no spirit in them. Besides, I'm getting old."

"What really happened between you and Adam Block? I was a young boy at the time."

"What happened? I really don't know myself. I loved him too much. This was my misfortune. The more loving I was, the more vicious he became. He could not stand a good word. When I kissed him, he shuddered. Whatever I said made him nervous, and he found countless faults with me. I hope God forgave him, for I have forgiven him long ago."

For a while Matilda remained silent, repairing the damage the crying had done to her makeup. Then she said, "Izzy is the same. I never know what will infuriate him. I say an innocent word and he begins to scream like mad. He attacks me with his fist and constantly accuses me of killing his father. What did I do to him? I made myself a doormat for him. I suffered all his caprices. Even before he asked for something I gave it to him. I wanted only to serve him. Once when I handed him his slippers, he took one and smacked me in the face with it. The maid was there. It was my fault, not his. My hard luck."

And Matilda took out a lace handkerchief.

She insisted that I go home with her as she wanted me to get acquainted with Izzy. Matilda had a small apartment, the type that Warsaw women compared to a bonbonnière. It was crammed with vases, all types of figurines, pictures, bric-a-brac. There were a goldfish bowl and a cage with a canary. Matilda knocked at Izzy's door but there was no answer. His radio was playing. Matilda said to me, "This is the way he spends his days and nights. It breaks my heart."

She treated me to sweet liqueur, cake, tea, and jam. I tasted everything, still she brought more: chocolate, halvah, vishniak. I implored her not to give me so much, but she kept on bringing refreshments. I said, "You are too good. This is your trouble."

"I want to sacrifice myself, but there isn't anyone to do it for." She opened a closet and began to show me clothes: evening dresses, crinolines, furs, blouses, holding each garment up to her body. Then she removed jewelry from drawers and told me about each piece: where she got it, the identity of the jeweler, and other such details. I told her that I had to go, but she beseeched me to remain. From an ornate chest she extracted albums packed with photographs of herself, her relatives, her girl friends, Adam Block, Izzy—from the day of his birth up to the present. Suddenly the door opened and Izzy came out of his room in his pajamas, scuffed slippers, his blond hair disheveled, his face covered with yellow stubble, and looking as though he had just gotten out of a sick bed. He shouted, "What do you want from this young man?"

"Just wait. He will soon beat me up," Matilda said, and

cracked her knuckles. A gleam came into her eyes. She looked at Izzy with both love and terror.

"I'm not going to beat you," Izzy shrieked, "but that man has to leave. Ten times I heard him say that he has to go, but you attached yourself to him like a leech . . ."

"He strikes me, just the same as his father did, may he rest in Paradise. Once my darling son blackened my eye." Matilda pointed at Izzy with her index finger.

"I'm sorry, I must go," I said.

"Wait, you promised to take the cookies home." She began to put them into a paper bag, but her fingers trembled and the cookies spread over the tablecloth. Her pale double chin heaved up and down as if of its own accord. Two glistening tears rolled down her rouged cheeks. She addressed herself partly to me and partly to Izzy. "Adam Block all over again. The moment something is not to his liking he showers me with blows. I have deserved it all for offering him my life, my health, my very being. He will murder me. This will be my end."

"Liar, thief, nauseating martyr," Izzy bellowed at her. He tilted the table and knocked everything onto the floor: the food, teacups, bottles, and albums. Then he ran back into his room and slammed the door so hard that the windowpanes rattled and the chandelier shook. I rushed to the outside door, Matilda running after me, shouting, "The cookies, you forgot the cookies!"

About ten years passed. Matilda no longer sang professionally. She retained a girlish figure, but her face was a network of wrinkles, with blue eyes as sparkling as a child's. She applied her cosmetics badly. Her eye makeup ran down the sides of her nose; the powder on her cheeks was blotchy and uneven. Her clothing consisted of old-fashioned dresses and capes, worn-out stoles, and hats that looked like inverted pots.

I was told that she was receiving a subsidy from the Jewish community. Once a year she sang at a benefit performance put on for her by the Yiddish actors. I happened to attend one of these benefits where she sang a song that ended with the words "A noodle like this has never been and never will be."

One day I saw her in a soup kitchen for intellectuals. She sat with Izzy, and for some reason which I cannot explain even today, both ate out of the same bowl. Izzy too looked aged. He had become strangely thin, had bags under his eyes, and his blond hair was streaked with gray. He still had no occupation. Matilda became known as a *schnorrer*. She would eat on credit at the Writers Club and then the cashier had to pay the bill. She borrowed many a zloty from me which she never returned. Matilda became a sponsor of young poets from the provinces. They had wild faces, unkempt hair, and were raging with revolutionary zeal. They threatened us, the writers who managed to make a living, with the wrath of the masses and the revenge of the proletariat. Every one of them promised me that when the revolution came he would hang me from the first lantern—just because I had a job as a proof-reader at *The Literary Epoch* and did translations for three zlotys a page. Matilda scrounged around for food for these beginners, listened to their long poems, and praised their talents. I once heard her say to one of them, "Recognition comes late, but it always comes," and she quoted a Ukrainian proverb: "Suffer, Cossack, you will be an Ataman."

Hitler had already come to power in Germany and demanded the Polish Corridor. A Fascistic organization called Nara rose in Poland. Jews were being beaten in the Saxon Gardens. In order not to sit on the ghetto benches, Jewish students at university lectures remained standing. Senile Pilsudski gave interviews filled with obscenities. In the southeastern part of Poland, the peasants sat in darkness at night because they could not afford to buy kerosene and even had to split each match into four parts. The Ukrainians in Galicia were rebelling. In the Jewish streets of Warsaw the Zionists fought with the Revisionists, the Communists with the Bundists, the Stalinists with the Trotskyites. *The Literary Epoch* had closed down. The publisher, who went bankrupt, owed me a few hundred zlotys. No one was in need of translations.

That summer, Lena and I starved together. We had rented a summer apartment in a half-ruined villa in Swider, and I paid for the full summer in advance, but no money was left for food. One morning I sold my silver watch to a watchmaker in nearby Otwock, paid the grocer what I owed him, and went to Warsaw hoping to sell an article or story. But the literary editors were all on vacation. I called up friends, acquaintances, colleagues. No one was home. In my confusion I lost a five-zloty bill—my dinner and fare back to Swider: the demons seemed to be playing with me. All day I sat in the library at the Writers Club and read the Yiddish and Polish newspapers. Nowaczynski had again discovered that the Jews, the Freemasons, the Protestants, Stalin, Hitler, and Mussolini were all partners in a plot to destroy Catholicism and to bring about the dictatorship of the Elders of Zion.

Dusk had fallen. The library was now empty. A single lamp burned. I looked up from the newspaper and saw Matilda Block. She greeted me and said, "Darling, why are you sitting alone and what are you so absorbed in?"

I pointed to the article I was reading.

"Oh, he's a madman."

"Sometimes I think that the entire human race is out of its mind."

I had no choice but to tell her my situation. She pinched my cheeks. "My little dove, why didn't you speak up sooner? I owe you money. I don't even know how much myself. I'm sorry I have little with me, but . . ."

Matilda proposed that I go home with her. She would give me supper and I could spend the night. I stammered, "Your son . . ."

"What are you talking about? He reads you. You are his beloved writer."

We got into a trolley car and went to her house. It was the same building, but it had deteriorated. The steps were not lighted. The hall of Matilda's apartment smelled of gas and dirty linen. In the living room the wallpaper was peeling. The canary and the goldfish were no longer there. Matilda knocked at Izzy's door, but she got the same results as ten years earlier —he didn't answer. From the kitchen she brought me bread, Swiss cheese. We ate, and occasionally Matilda became tense and listened. In his room Izzy had turned on the radio and then turned it off immediately. We heard him making sounds as though he were talking to himself. Matilda shook her head. "So a life has passed. With what? For what? Women my age have grandchildren. I even lack the courage to put an end to things. What will become of him when I'm gone? He won't know where his next meal is coming from."

That day I had gotten up early, walked a good deal, and was now tired. Matilda gave me her bedroom and said she would sleep on the sofa. I offered to sleep on the sofa instead, but she explained that Izzy might come out of his room and I would be embarrassed. Her bed linen consisted of an overstuffed pillow and a heavy feather quilt. She brought me a sleeping gown which smelled of napthalene, and I suspected that it had once belonged to Adam Block. I fell asleep quickly but awoke with a start. I had the uncanny feeling that someone was blowing into my ear. From the other side of the hall I heard a scraping, a shuffling, and a tapping of feet. I sat up and listened. Was the apartment haunted? No matter how hard I tried I could not recognize the sounds I was listening to. They were too loud to be caused by rats. I had to go to the bathroom, and after much hesitation I entered the hall. The living-room door stood half open. In the light of the red night bulb, mother and son were dancing, both barefoot, he in only his underwear, she in a nightgown. I could discern Izzy's bony neck, pointed Adam's apple, rounded back. It seemed to me that both mother and son had closed eyes. No one uttered a sound, as if they were dancing in their sleep. I stood there at least ten minutes and perhaps much longer. I realized that I had no right to spy on my hosts, but I could not tear myself away. Most probably they were waltzing, though I couldn't tell what type of dance they were doing. Without music, in complete silence, it seemed a kind of midnight *anger dance*. I held my breath and stood there bewildered. Were mother and son having an incestuous affair? Had they both lost their minds? Perhaps it wasn't them but their astral bodies. I had already begun to dabble in the occult. Once I thought Matilda gasped as mediums do when in a trance. I forgot what I had gotten out of bed for and tiptoed back to the bedroom. The tapping and shuffling still continued for some time, then it finally quieted down. After a while I dozed off, though I feared that I wouldn't sleep a wink.

In the morning Matilda called me to have breakfast with her. We sat at the kitchen table. She poured my coffee and gave me stale bread and marmalade. In the light of the gas lamp she looked weary, and last night's cold cream gave her face a gelatinous appearance. While she sipped her coffee she complained about the high cost of living, the landlord's refusal to make necessary repairs. "Why should he do it?" she asked. "If I move out he will raise the rent and get key money in addition." This prosaic conversation sounded strange after what I had witnessed just the night before. I asked her, "Did you sleep well?"

Matilda shook her head. "Nothing is well with me any more. How did you sleep?"

"Like the dead."

"Well, you are young."

"What do you do when you can't sleep?" I asked. "Do you read?"

Matilda shook her head. A faint smile appeared on her lips. "I dance."

"Is this a remedy for insomnia?"

"It is my remedy. I learned it from Izzy. He too suffers from sleeplessness. How can he sleep if he lies in bed all day and broods? He once dreamed of becoming a dancer, and this is what remains of his dreams."

I never saw Matilda again. Soon after this incident I left for America. Matilda and Izzy perished in the Warsaw ghetto. I don't know the details of their last days, but I often imagine that one night when the Nazis bombed the city, while fires raged and people ran for shelter, mother and son began to dance and continued until the building collapsed and the two of them were covered with rubble and silenced forever.

Translated by the author and Ruth Schachner Finkel

t station. From there to Zamość
nd buggy. Ozer Mecheles got off
d stood for a moment on the plat-
warm and moonless. The conduc-
in the cars of the train as soon as
, and the only light came from a
y station. For a while, the loco-
motive puffed thick smoke, hissed, and poured water; then
it began to move backward. Ozer caught a glimpse of the
engineer. He stood at the window, half illuminated by the fire
in the box, his face smeared with soot, like a chimney sweep.
He made Ozer think of the black angels of Gehenna de-
scribed in the Nod of Punishment. The station was located a
few versts from the village, and the breezes that drifted from
the fields smelled of fresh-cut hay and the smoke of fires in
which shepherds were roasting potatoes. Frogs croaked.
Crickets chirped. A wagon drawn by one horse arrived from
somewhere, and Ozer knew that it would take him through
the night all the way to Zamość.

Another passenger waited on the platform—a woman from
the same train. In the light of the station lamp Ozer could
see that she was young. She wore a long skirt and a white
blouse, and her wide-brimmed straw hat was circled with
flowers. She left her bags on the platform and seemed to
hesitate before approaching Ozer.

"Are you going to Zamość?" she asked.

"Yes," Ozer said. "To Zamość."

"Is that your home town?"

"I am from Lublin, but my parents-in-law live in Zamość."

"Whose son-in-law are you, if I may ask?"

"Gabriel Danziger's."

"Nesha's husband!" the woman cried.

"Yes, Nesha's husband."

"Then I was at your wedding—and here I was standing asking myself, 'Is he or is he not from Zamość'! It's so dark I wouldn't recognize my own mother. I am a great friend of your sister-in-law Mirale. So you are Ozer Mecheles."

"That's right. May I ask whom I have the honor of speaking to?"

"Bella Felhendler. My maiden name was Bardulin. My husband is Feivel Felhendler, from the sawmill."

"I know your husband and your father-in-law quite well," Ozer said.

"Who doesn't know them? Zamość isn't Lublin, after all. But our coachman is waiting." And she called out, "Reb Zeinvel, are you ready?"

Zeinvel, a little man almost as broad as he was tall, wore on this summer night a padded jacket, a sheepskin hat, heavy boots. He smelled of axle grease and sweat. He cracked his whip. "Yes, ready!" he called back. "How many are you?"

"Only two."

"Two, eh—for that I will not have enough for the Sabbath. Well, what are you standing around for? Get in."

"Will you be so good as to take care of my luggage?" the woman said.

"Where is it? Without the moon, it's as dark as Egypt in this godforsaken hole. The Russian pig, curse him, is too stingy to pay for a half a quart of kerosene. Get in, get in. Yesterday, I had a full wagon. Today, nobody. Well, so be it.

If only it doesn't rain. The way my left leg twinges, we're in for nasty weather."

Ozer hurried to load the luggage himself and helped Bella into the wagon. There was a fragrance about her of perfume, chocolate, cookies. She leaned on his shoulder for support, and Ozer's hand inadvertently touched her breast. He apologized, and she laughed. The wagon had four benches, upholstered in horsehair. Hay and straw covered the floor. Bella sat down on the rear bench, which had a back. She pointed to the space beside her. "Sit near me," she said.

"Yes, thank you." It's a miracle it's dark, Ozer thought. He felt himself blushing. Although even before he left the yeshiva he considered himself enlightened, read modern books, and now in Warsaw spent time in museums and the observatory, he still grew red in the face when a girl or a young woman addressed him. Whenever he went to Warsaw, he realized how far he really was from worldliness. He got lost in the streets and had to ask his way. In the hotel, he had trouble finding his room. When he spoke on the telephone, he became deaf. All kinds of mishaps befell him. The shoelaces that he knotted in the morning kept coming untied. His black Hasidic tie hung always askew. His father-in-law was trying to make him a dry-goods merchant and had sent him to buy for the store, but he could not differentiate between wool and felt. Besides, he had an aversion to the Warsaw wholesale merchants— their vulgar jokes and salesmen's antics. Behind his father-in-law's back, he studied algebra, physics, philosophy. In one of his valises, he carried Darwin's *On the Origin of Species* and a book about astronomy by Flammarion, translated into Polish. It was too late for him to enter the university to become a doctor, an engineer, or a chemist. He studied only because of his desire for knowledge. But as Zeinvel the coachman had just said, from that one would not have enough for the Sabbath.

Zeinvel had disappeared. In the half darkness, the horse chewed oats from a burlap bag, spilling some grains. Every now and then it stamped the ground as though impatient. Bella Felhendler had taken off her hat and placed it on the bench in front of her. She smoothed her black hair, which was coiled at the nape of her neck, and settled herself comfortably. Ozer Mecheles tried to move over to give her more space, but she was spread out on the short bench in such a way that he could feel her hip. She opened her bag and took out halvah and biscuits, ate some herself and offered some to Ozer. She said. "Why do you move away? You'll fall out of the wagon." After a while, she added, "You are not so holy."

Zeinvel reappeared, bringing a sack and a crate. Ordinarily, he did not carry baggage, but as he had only two passengers he would make a gulden on the side. After the sack and crate, he loaded a pack of flax. This freight almost hid the horse and the driver's seat. Bella began to laugh softly. "Next thing, he'll bring a barrel of herring."

Zeinvel got in, waved his whip: giddap.

The horse walked slowly on the broken cobblestone road with its ditches and holes. In the fall and spring, the cart often overturned and threw its passengers into the mud. But after Pentecost the mud had dried. Now the road stretched between ripe fields, pastures where horses grazed through the night, haystacks, and sleeping hamlets. Dew was forming. A night bird cried. At the edge of the horizon there was lightning not followed by thunder. Ozer looked in silence from right to left. He had lived almost twenty-five years, he had read many scientific books, but the world remained as much a riddle to him as when he had started cheder. The wagon went over a bridge. Stars were reflected in the water. Where the river turned to the right, a mist rose, white as milk. There was no doubt about it—Bella pressed her foot against his deliberately. Her soft knee spoke to his knee independently and in a language that only the flesh understands. Ozer was amazed; she had a decent husband, wealthy, the owner of a sawmill—even somewhat worldly. What could she want from him, Ozer? Or was she just teasing?

Bella asked, "You come from Warsaw, eh?"

"Yes, from Warsaw."

"What do you do in Warsaw? Do you buy dry goods for your father-in-law?"

Ozer did not answer immediately. "My father-in-law wants to make a merchant out of me, but I am afraid nothing will come of it."

"Would you rather be a professor?"

"Too old."

"Mark my words, you will be a merchant. My Uncle Beinush was so unworldly as a boy he didn't know the difference between a kopeck and a ruble, but he became a shrewd businessman. He was even accused of filching money from a squire. Besides, Reb Gabriel Danziger will leave you a nice inheritance."

"Let him live 120 years."

"Why should anyone live so long? For myself, I'll be satisfied to reach forty-five."

"No longer than that?"

"What is a woman after forty-five? Old, sick, worn out. Trouble begins with daughters, sons-in-law, daughters-in-law, grandchildren. I could make peace with a short life, but it has to taste good."

"From what I know, you have a good life."

"Not bad. But what does a small town have to offer? No theater. No circus. Why, when so much as a performing bear arrives, the whole place goes wild. There isn't even anywhere to take a real walk. And who could I go walking with? Feivel is always busy with his business. Your sister-in-law Mirale can't leave her children. Your Nesha used to be a jolly girl, but she's not the same any more. Besides, she's younger than I am."

"What was she before?"

"A husband shouldn't be too nosy," Bella said, and gave a short laugh.

"I hope nothing bad."

"No, but she liked to enjoy herself. She was the best dancer in Zamość. We girls used to gather at Zalman Krosess'—he has a living room as big as a forest, and we used to dance there. He forbade boys and girls to dance together, but he went to sleep at nine and we did as we pleased until eleven. The boys would sneak in through the back door. Those were gay times —especially in winter. Your Nesha was always the life of the party. Half the young men in Zamość were in love with her, but she was madly infatuated with a cheap guy."

Ozer felt hot under his collar. "Who was that?"

"Oh, you know well enough. That kind of thing gets around. Don't play innocent with me."

"I swear I don't know."

"Well, men are funny! What difference does it make at this point? What happened happened."

"Please, do me a favor. Tell me who he is."

"Curious, eh?" Bella began to murmur. "All right, then, I'll whisper in your ear. I wouldn't want Zeinvel to listen." She leaned over, took Ozer's neck, and bent his head toward her. Her hand was warm, her lips touched his ear. "Mendele Shmeiser." And she did something to Ozer's ear that no woman had done before: she pushed her tongue into it.

Ozer was startled both by the name and by what she did. His ear burned and rang. He was overcome by anger and an unfamiliar feeling of shame. He knew Mendele Shmeiser—a musician and a barber. He had a round face, a head of curly hair, and a thin twirled mustache; his chin was cleft. Even though he never went riding, he carried a crop and wore highly polished riding boots. He was known in town for his spicy jokes. Ozer felt nauseated and his mouth filled with bile. He thought he was going to vomit, but using all his will, he managed to control himself. His left leg trembled, but his right, which Bella was pressing with hers, remained stiff. His forehead became moist. In spite of his doubts about God, he murmured a prayer. "Father in Heaven, let me not be disgraced."

He heard Bella speaking—her voice seemed to come from far away. "After all, it's not the Middle Ages," she was saying. "It's the twentieth century. It's high time humanity became civilized. Zamość is neither Bilgoray nor Tomaszów. A woman is just as entitled to enjoy herself as a man. We grabbed what we could. Was that so wrong? The minute you're married and then pregnant, everything is finished. Feet stop being so light for dancing. That Mendele is a no-good fellow, but he knows how to make a girl fall for him. He kissed everybody—a real sport. Your Nesha was terribly jealous! She wanted him all for herself, the poor girl."

Ozer bent his head in silence.

"I shouldn't have told you this. Give me your hand. Swear that you won't reproach her."

"No." Ozer's voice was barely audible.

"Some time before the marriage agreement was signed, she got sick and had to go to Warsaw. They said all kinds of things. But what does that mean? People gossip. Swear." Bella took Ozer's hand and put it on her breast. She held it there with her own. "What does it matter? Now she is your wife. Still, she hasn't forgotten Mendele. We were all standing around in Tsippe's Candy Store one afternoon not long ago when he came in. She looked at him and turned as white as chalk. And what do you think he did! He held out his riding crop and lifted up her skirt. To him a woman is worth nothing because they all throw themselves at him. A shameless rascal, even though he is handsome."

"Handsome . . . Well—"

"A big talker, that's all he is. An ugly mouth. But when he talks it does something to you. Still, a man can come from a Hasidic house and also have charm. I like you better than Mendele Shmeiser. You're quiet and gentle. Nesha doesn't appreciate you. This is the truth. If I had you, I wouldn't even look at Mendele."

"Does she meet him?"

"Who knows what a woman does when her husband is out of town! You can love your husband and still be interested in another man. Sometimes you want a change. A woman doesn't wear the same dress forever. You don't eat noodles with boiled beef every evening. Am I right?"

"Perhaps you are right," Ozer Mecheles mumbled. The bitterness remained in his mouth. Stealthily he withdrew his hand from Bella's breast.

The night had grown darker. Everything had merged: fields, road, sky. The horse moved slowly; once in a while it stopped and then moved forward again. Ozer remembered his mother's saying that animals see demons—a horse will halt to let one of the night creatures pass by. The wheels knocked against the cobblestones. The air remained warm, humid. Who knows, Ozer thought, maybe a comet is approaching the earth. Since the heavenly bodies have neither purpose nor consciousness, such encounters are possible. Zeinvel the coachman kept silent on the other side of the load, or perhaps he had dozed off.

Bella again took Ozer's hand and put it against her breast. "Please don't be a stick-in-the-mud." She spoke with a kind of insolence that was unknown to him. "Why should God care if young people enjoy themselves? And how do you know there *is* a God? The delegate from Warsaw said that everything was evolution. He said that the earth was hot and it cooled off, like the crust on a pot of buckwheat. Is that true?"

"Who knows."

"I love Feivel. But if you love butter cookies, can't you eat a few macaroons? Why should men have it all their own way? They chase after every skirt. I was sitting on the train, and in comes a traveling salesman. We got to talking. He had a wife and three children, but that didn't keep him from other men's wives. Wherever he goes, he'll find a woman, Gentile or Jewish. He propositioned me, but I didn't like him—small, fat, paunchy. If I take on someone, I want to enjoy it, too. Do you understand me?"

"Yes, I understand. Our fathers and mothers—"

"Fathers and mothers!" Bella half cried out. "What were they—fanatics! They wasted their years on the Talmud and the supplication books. What did my mother get out of life? At thirty-four she became a widow, and that was the end. The day before the new moon, she used to go to the cemetery and prostrate herself over my father's grave. She spoke to him as if he were alive, told him all the news about the children. Silly superstition! The world has awakened, but they don't even know they're living in the twentieth century. What's the matter?" Bella changed her tone. "Aren't you well?"

"Yes. No."

"Why do you tremble? Are you cold?"

"I think I have a fever."

"Is that so? Well—" Bella made a gesture that meant *"You can now take away your hand."* She even moved over. She was saying, "In the restaurants in Warsaw, they give you meat left over from the Flood. You probably upset your stomach. When you get home, take castor oil. There's nothing better. Remember, what I told you is our secret."

"Yes, certainly."

"Do you ever walk in the woods?"

"What woods?"

"In a small town like ours, everything is done in the woods. In the middle of the week, the woods are empty. Saturday, the rabble arrives and it's worse than the marketplace . . ."

Ozer Mecheles did not answer. He remembered that he had found a photograph of Mendele Shmeiser in Nesha's album. Nesha was making a fool of him. She was in love with a barber—an ignoramus, a scoundrel. She had told Ozer recently that she was pregnant. Who knew, it might be by Mendele Shmeiser. What was there to curb her? When these yokels become advanced, there is no limit.

Ozer was taking stock of his life. Yes, if one denies God, the Torah, and believes man has descended from an ape, why shouldn't one act like an ape? And if Nesha was so infatuated with Mendele Shmeiser, what value could he, Ozer, have for her?

When Ozer Mecheles became engaged to Nesha, he assumed she was a decent girl. At the engagement feast, she sat at the women's table and he hardly caught a glimpse of her. He was surrounded by Hasids, scholars, yeshiva boys. At the wedding, after the virtue dance, he was led into a dark bedroom. He knew from the Talmud that a girl ought to be a virgin, but he didn't know how a man could be sure. At dawn, the bride's attendants came to take the sheet, and they were supposed to dance a kosher dance outside the window. Later on, he noticed that Nesha was not pious. She combed her hair on the Sabbath and soaped herself. A few times he caught her drinking milk after she had eaten meat. She made jokes about the ritual bath. She told him to come to her bed on the nights when according to the law it was forbidden. She went to the lending library and borrowed novels in Polish and Russian. Ozer was pleased by this—he had an enlightened wife.

True, he had never felt spiritually close to her. Ozer aspired to knowledge, and she was concerned with money. She envied her brother-in-law, Benie, because he was established in business. Though she received a lot of jewelry for her wedding, she constantly complained that her sister had more. Nesha tried to persuade Ozer that he should ask for her dowry, start his own business, and move to a home of their own instead of boarding with her father. She was always ordering new dresses and would chat for hours with her sister Mirale about shoes, lingerie, lace, cakes and cookies, which both sisters baked, and about all kinds of creams and perfumes, which they ordered from Lublin. A box of chocolates stood on her bedside table and she nibbled them in the middle of the night. Ozer was aware that Nesha did not read the books she brought home. He tried many times to talk to her about science and philosophy, but she always interrupted him—a friend would call her, she had to say something to her mother, she had to do some chore in the kitchen. Ozer realized with bafflement that the doubts which had tortured him from as long as he could remember—time, space, eternity, the problem of the just who suffer—did not bother her at all. She did not even concern herself with death, about which he had begun to brood when he was still in the cheder for beginners. Ozer had decided that this was how woman is made—to indulge in petty things. In some way, a woman was like a child who needed toys.

Well, but to be dazzled by Mendele Shmeiser one had to be a Mendele Shmeiser oneself. If Mendele Shmeiser is all one can gain from the Enlightenment, then woe to the Enlightenment.

Ozer heard a snore. Bella had fallen asleep. He raised his eyes to the sky. He had read the theory of Kant and Laplace that the universe developed from a nebula. But how can a nebula bring out man, animals, trees, grain, flowers, eyes, ears, a brain? What is the suffering and shame that Ozer felt now made of? And since all being is a combination of atoms, what basis is there for the words of Isaiah, Lessing, Mendelssohn, Reb Nachman Krochmal? Somewhere Ozer Mecheles had made a false calculation, but where was the error? Could he become pious again? Could he believe that every commentary each rabbi has written in each generation was given to Moses on Mount Sinai? In what can he believe?

Hate? Was it Mendele's fault his atoms combined in this way instead of another? And how is it Nesha's fault? How can there be talk of good and evil if there is no God, no revelation?

Ozer Mecheles closed his eyes. He did not sleep but neither was he awake. A heaviness pressed on his heart, hanging there like a weight. He was cold, as though it were winter. He felt like a mourner: he had to sit shivah for his own illusions.

The wagon stopped, and with a start Ozer roused. Bella got off without a word. Her husband, Feivel, came out of the house in his night robe and slippers; he was not wearing a skullcap. It was daybreak. Ozer saw the silhouette of husband and wife embracing, shaking silently.

Soon the wagon approached Gabriel Danziger's house. Ozer took down his bags. The one with the books was especially heavy. In his father-in-law's house, everybody was asleep. A small kerosene lamp glimmered in the kitchen. In a coop behind the stove, chickens were clucking. Ozer listened. The whole household snored—his father-in-law, his mother-in-law, Nesha. Ozer heard her sigh. Verses from the Book of Proverbs came to his mind: "There be three which are concealed from me, yea, four which I know not: the way of the eagle in the air; the way of a serpent upon a rock; the way of a ship in the midst of the sea; and the way of a man with a maid." "Which forsaketh the guide of her youth, and forgetteth the covenant of her God."

Ozer left his luggage in the parlor and went outside. One half of the sky was still night; the other half glowed a deep red. Dew was falling as though from a sieve. Birds were twittering. Ozer moved like a sleepwalker. His legs took him to the yard of the synagogue. He passed the barrel where the worshippers washed their hands. The water reflected the gold of the sun breaking through.

Ozer entered the study house. Here the night still held sway. A single memorial candle spluttered in the menorah. The pillars of the reading table threw jumping shadows. The tables, the bookshelves, the candelabra kept a midnight silence. Ozer stopped and tried to read the Ten Commandments in the dusk, but the letters were hidden. "It's finished, finished," he murmured, not knowing what he meant. A weariness such as he had never experienced overcame him. He leaned against a stand in order not to fall. He remembered that this was the hour the corpses are supposed to pray in the holy places, before the first worshipper crosses the threshold.

Suddenly a purple light blasted through the windows and everything in the study house was illuminated as though from a heavenly lamp: the lectern, the benches, the stands, the lions on the cornice of the Holy Arc that were supporting the tablets with their curled tongues. Their beady eyes seemed alive. Ozer stood transfixed. It became clear as the rising day to him that the books he had brought from Warsaw and the Commandments on these tablets denied one another. If creation was a blind process and man a beast, it was allowed to deceive Ozer (or Feivel), steal from him, even kill him. Why didn't I understand it before? he wondered. He shuddered and his teeth rattled. For the first time in years, he had a desire to start the morning with a prayer, but how could he be sure that his prayer would be heard?

Ozer went outdoors. In the sky, a cloud like a fiery chariot rode toward the east. The windows of the synagogue shone and flickered. The water in the barrel had become greenish, and Ozer saw his image in it as in a mirror: a pale face, sunken cheeks, two sidelocks like hemp, a throat with a pointed Adam's apple. He barely recognized himself. The worldliness was gone. He was again what he had been before his marriage to Nesha—a poor scholar from Lublin, an orphan supported by strangers. He bent down and dipped his fingers in the water. Powers stronger than man had conspired to take everything from him this night: his wife, his dowry, his lodging. The Enlightenment had deceived him; Nesha and Mendele Shmeiser did the rest. Ozer knew he must again pack a bundle and make his way somewhere to a yeshiva. He was not angry, only astonished. He had to make a choice between God, Who may not exist, and creatures as loathsome as Mendele Shmeiser and his females.

Translated by the author and Dorothea Straus

Neighbors

THEY both lived in my building on Central Park West —he two floors below me, she one above. Greater contrast than those two would be hard to imagine. Morris Terkeltoyb was a writer of "true stories" for the Yiddish newspaper to which I also contributed. Margit Levy was the former lover of an Italian count. One quality was common to the two of them: I could never learn the truth about either. Morris Terkeltoyb assured me that his stories were invented, but when I read them I realized they couldn't be all fantasy. They contained details and odd incidents that only life itself could devise. Besides, I often saw him with elderly people who looked like the characters out of his tales. Morris Terkeltoyb was far from being a man of literary skill. His style teemed with clichés. I once saw a manuscript of his at the newspaper. He had no notion of syntax. He used commas and hyphens indiscriminately. Each sentence ended with three dashes. But Morris Terkeltoyb wanted me to believe that he was a creative writer, not a reporter.

In the years I knew him, he told me many lies. Countless women threw themselves into his arms—socialites, stars of the Metropolitan Opera, famous authoresses, ballet dancers, actresses. Each time Morris Terkeltoyb traveled to Europe on vacation, he returned with a list of fresh amorous adventures. Once, he showed me a love letter in handwriting I recognized as his own. He wasn't even ashamed to include in his stories scenes taken from world literature. Actually, he was a lonesome old bachelor with a sick heart and one kidney. He himself seemed unaware of the missing kidney; I knew about it from a relative of his.

Morris Terkeltoyb was short, broad-shouldered, with remnants of white hair that he combed into a bridge spanning his skull. He had large watery eyes, a nose like a beak, and a mouth almost without lips—a gash revealing a large set of false teeth. He said he was descended from rabbis and merchants and he must have studied the Talmud in his youth, because his conversation was filled with quotations from it. Yiddish was his language, but he also spoke a broken English, faulty Polish, and the kind of Yiddish-German that was used at Zionist congresses. Slowly, I managed to dig out some truths from his exaggerations. In Poland he had been engaged to the daughter of a rabbi: she died of typhoid fever a week before the wedding. He had studied in Hildesheimer's rabbinical seminary in Berlin but never graduated. He had attended lectures on philosophy at a university in Switzerland. He had published a few poems in a Yiddish collection and some articles in the Hebrew newspaper the *Morning Star*. Of his mistresses I knew only one—the widow of a Hebrew teacher. I met her at a New Year's party, and after a few drinks she told me that she had been involved with Morris Terkeltoyb for years. He suffered from insomnia and had periods of impotence. She made fun of his boasting. He had bragged to her that he had had an affair with Isadora Duncan.

The other neighbor, Margit Levy, seemed not to be a liar, but the events of her life were so strange and complicated that I could never figure her out. Her father was a Jew; her mother belonged to the Hungarian aristocracy. Her father was supposed to have committed suicide when he learned that his wife was having an affair with a member of the Esterhazy nobility—a relative of the Esterhazy who was a major figure in the Dreyfus affair. Her mother's lover committed suicide when he lost his fortune at Monte Carlo. After his death, Margit's mother became insane and remained in a clinic in Vienna for twenty years. Margit was brought up by her father's sister, who was the paramour of the Brazilian owner of a coffee plantation. Margit Levy spoke a dozen languages. She had valises filled with photographs, letters, all kinds of documents that testified to the truth of her stories. She used to tell me, "From my life one could write not one book but a whole literature. Hollywood movies are child's play compared to what happened to me."

Now Margit Levy lived in a single room as the boarder of an old maid and survived on Social Security. She suffered from rheumatism and could barely walk. She took mincing steps, supporting herself on two canes. Though she claimed to be in her sixties, I calculated that she was well over seventy. Margit Levy existed in a state of confusion. Each time she visited me she forgot something—her pocketbook, her gloves, her glasses, even one of her canes. Sometimes she dyed her hair red, sometimes black. She rouged her wrinkled face and used too much mascara. There were black bags under her dark eyes. The nails of her crooked fingers were painted bright red. Her neck made me think of a plucked chicken. I told her that I was poor at languages, but she tried again and again to talk to me in French, Italian, Hungarian. Though her name was Jewish, I noticed that she wore a little cross beneath her blouse and I suspected that she had been converted. Margit Levy had one time borrowed a book of mine from the public library, and after that she became a reader of whatever I wrote. She assured me that she possessed all the powers I described in my stories—telepathy, clairvoyance, premonition, the ability to communicate with the dead. She owned a ouija board and a small table without nails. Poor as she was, she subscribed to a number of occult magazines. After her first visit to me, she took my hand and said in a trembling voice, "I knew that you would come into my life. This will be my last great friendship."

And she brought me as a gift a pair of cuff links that she had inherited from Count Esterhazy—the same Esterhazy who lost eighty thousand crowns in one night and then put a bullet through his head.

It didn't occur to me to bring my two neighbors together. The truth is that I didn't invite either one of them. They used to knock on my door, and if I wasn't too busy I would ask whoever it was to come in, and I would treat him or her to coffee and cookies. Morris Terkeltoyb received Hebrew newspapers from Tel Aviv. When he found a review of a book of mine or even an advertisement, he brought it to me. From time to time, Margit Levy would bake a cake in the oven of the old maid where she boarded, and she would insist on stopping by to give me a piece.

But once it happened that both came in at the same time. Margit found among her papers a letter she had spoken to me about. Morris had discovered a monthly magazine from South Africa that reprinted a sketch of mine. I introduced my guests to each other; though they had been living in the same building for years, they had never met. Margit had become partially deaf in recent months. For some reason she could not pronounce "Terkeltoyb." She pulled at her ear, frowned, mispronounced the name. At the same time she shouted into Morris Terkeltoyb's ear as if he were the one who was hard of hearing. Morris spoke to her in English, but she could not understand his accent. He shifted to German. Margit Levy shook her head and made him repeat each word. Like a demanding teacher, she corrected his grammar and pronunciation. He had the habit of swallowing words, and when he became excited his voice was shrill. Without finishing the coffee, he got up and went to the door. "Who is that crazy old woman?" he asked me. He slammed out as if I were to blame for his failure to impress Margit Levy.

When he had left, Margit Levy, who as a rule was exaggeratedly polite with everyone, going so far as to shower compliments on the neighbors' dogs and cats, called Morris Terkeltoyb an uneducated idiot, a ruffian. Though she knew that I came from Poland, she couldn't contain her rage and spoke of him as "a Polish schlemiel." She apologized immediately and assured me that I was an exception. The spots that came out on her cheeks were so red they could be seen through the rouge. She left the coffee I had placed before her. At the door she took both my wrists, kissed me, and pleaded, "Please, my dear, do not let me meet that creature again."

I imagined that I heard her cry as she made her way up the steps. Margit had a fear of elevators. She had been stuck in one for three hours. Also, an elevator door had closed on her hand, causing her to lose a diamond ring. She sued the building.

After this encounter, I decided never to let one of the two enter my apartment if the other was already there. I had lost patience with both of them. When Morris Terkeltoyb wasn't boasting of his successes with women or the brilliant offers he got from publishers and universities, he complained about the rudeness he met with from editors, reviewers, officials of the journalists' union, secretaries of the P.E.N. club. He was accepted nowhere; people were always doing him in. The proofreaders on our newspaper not only refused to correct the mistakes he marked in his stories but they intentionally crippled his text. Once, he caught a makeup man in the composing room reversing lines of type in an article. When Morris protested to the printers' union, he received no reply. He called Yiddish literature a racket. He accused playwrights of the Yiddish theater of stealing from his stories. He said to me, "You probably believe that I suffer from a persecution mania. You forget that people really do persecute one another."

"No, I don't."

"My own father persecuted me." And Morris Terkeltoyb recited in a plaintive voice a long monologue that could have been serialized as a dozen chapters on his true-story page. Whenever I tried to interrupt to ask for details, he rushed on with such intensity that there was no way to stop him. He dismissed my questions with an impatient wave of his hand.

I decided that with all their differences Margit Levy and Morris Terkeltoyb had much in common. Just as he did, Margit mixed up names, dates, episodes. Like him, she accused people who had died years before of innumerable offenses against her. All the evil powers had conspired to ruin Margit Levy. A broker who had invested her money became a devotee of race tracks and squandered her capital. A physician who was supposed to cure her rheumatism gave her an injection that brought out a rash on her body and caused an illness that almost killed her. Often she slipped on ice in winter, fell on escalators in department stores. Her pocketbook was snatched. Once, she was held up in the middle of the day in a street crowded with passersby. Margit Levy swore that when she went on vacation the spinster who was her landlady wore her dresses and underwear, that she opened her letters, and even helped herself to her medicines.

"Who would use another person's medicine?" I asked her.

She replied, "If people could, they'd steal each other's eyes."

In the summer, I took a long holiday. I went to Switzerland, France, Israel. I left in the middle of August, when my hay fever begins, and came back at the beginning of December. I had paid my rent in advance, locking up my apartment before I left. There was nothing in it for thieves except books and manuscripts.

The day I returned, snow was falling in New York. When I got out of the taxi in front of my building, I was stunned by what I saw. Margit Levy was creeping along on a cane and a crutch, with Morris Terkeltoyb holding on to her arm. With his free hand he was pushing a cartful of food from the supermarket on Columbus Avenue. Margit's face was yellow from the cold and more wrinkled than ever. She wore a mangy fur coat and a black hat that reminded me of my childhood in Warsaw. She seemed ill, emaciated. Her eyes, too close together, had a piercing expression like those of a bird of prey. Morris Terkeltoyb had also aged. His beaked nose was red, and white whiskers sprouted on his face.

No matter how unusual an event may seem, my astonishment never lasts more than an instant. I approached them and asked, "How are you, my friends?"

Margit shook her head. "The facts speak for themselves."

Later, a neighbor told me that the old maid in whose apartment Margit boarded had given up her place to go to Miami. Margit would have been thrown out into the street. Instead, she had moved in with Morris Terkeltoyb. How this came about my neighbor did not know. I noticed that the name of Margit Levy had been added on Morris Terkeltoyb's letter box.

A few days after my return, Margit visited me. She wept, mixed German with English, and told me at great length how the selfish spinster had decided without warning to move away, how all the neighbors had treated her misfortune with indifference. The only one who showed humanity was Morris Terkeltoyb. Margit acted as if he had taken her in as just a boarder. But the next day Morris knocked at my door, and from his unfinished sentences and gesticulations it became clear that their relationship was more than that of tenant and boarder. He said, "One gets older, not younger. When you are ill, you need someone to bring you a glass of tea."

He nodded, winked, smiled guiltily and sheepishly, inviting me to come see them in the evening.

I went down after supper. Margit received me as a hostess. The apartment looked clean, there were curtains at the windows, the table had a tablecloth and dishes that could only have belonged to Margit. I brought flowers; she kissed me and wiped away her tears. Margit and Morris continued to address each other as "you" instead of the familiar "thou," but I thought that I heard Margit forget herself once and use "thou." They talked to one another in a mishmash of German-English-Yiddish. When Morris Terkeltoyb ate herring with his fingers and started to wipe his hands on his sleeves, Margit said to him, "Use your napkin. This is New York, not Klimontów."

And Morris Terkeltoyb replied in a typical Polish Hasidic intonation, "*Nu*, so be it."

That winter Morris Terkeltoyb had a long spell of sickness. It started with the flu. Then the doctor discovered that he had diabetes and prescribed insulin. He stopped going down to the newspaper and sent his manuscripts by mail. Margit told me that Morris couldn't read his own articles in the paper, they contained so many errors. He got palpitations of the heart every time he read one. She asked me to bring proofs uptown for him. I was willing to help, but I rarely had time to go to the paper any more. I lectured a lot, leaving the city for weeks. Once when I entered the composing room, I saw Margit Levy. She stood there waiting for proofs. She now took the subway downtown twice each week—first to pick up the proofs and the second time to return them. She said to me, "Aggravation does more damage to the health than any medicine can cure." She also said something that could only have come from Morris Terkeltoyb: "A writer doesn't die of medical errors, only of printing errors." Jake, the printer's devil, tossed the proofs to her hurriedly. Margit put on her glasses and began to look them over. Jake often ran off proofs so sloppily that letters were missing on the margins or lines were missing because the paper was too short to carry the whole column. Even though she didn't know Yiddish, she seemed to realize that some of the proofs were defective and she went to look for Jake among the humming linotype machines. The boy screamed at her and called her names, she complained when she came back. "Is this the way they treat literature in America?"

Toward spring, Morris Terkeltoyb began to go down to the newspaper again, but Margit had a gallstone attack and was taken to the hospital. Morris visited her twice a day. The doctors found all kinds of complications. They made many tests and took a good deal of blood for them. Morris claimed that American doctors had no respect for their patients; they cut them up as if they were already corpses. The nurses didn't come when they were called and the sick didn't get proper food. Morris had to prepare soup for Margit and bring her orange juice. He asked me, "In what way are doctors better than writers or theater directors? It's the same human species."

I left New York again for about three months. When I came back in the fall, I read in the newspaper that the Yiddish Writers Union was having a memorial evening on the thirtieth day after the death of Morris Terkeltoyb. He had been stricken with a heart attack while reading proofs. Perhaps he died of a printing error. In the evening, I took Margit in a taxi to the hall. It was badly lit, half empty. Margit was wrapped in black. She did not understand the Yiddish speakers, but each time the name of Morris Terkeltoyb was mentioned she sobbed.

A few days after that, Margit knocked at my door. For the first time I saw her without cosmetics. She looked to me like a woman of ninety. I had to help her sit down on a chair. Her hands trembled, her head was shaking, and she spoke with difficulty. She said, "I don't want them to throw Morris's manuscripts into the garbage after my death." I had to give her a solemn promise that I would find an institution which would accept his manuscripts and books, the thousands of letters he kept in trunks and even in a laundry hamper.

Margit lived on for thirteen months. During that time she kept coming to me with projects. She wanted to publish a collection of Morris Terkeltoyb's best writing, but he had left so many manuscripts it would have taken years to choose among them. There was no chance of getting a publisher. She kept asking the same question: "Why didn't Morris write in an understandable language—Polish or Hungarian?" She wanted me to find a Yiddish grammar for her so that she could learn the language. Even though she had never read anything he had written, Margit called him a talent, possibly a genius. Another time Margit found a manuscript that looked like a play, and she urged me to offer it to a theater director or to find someone to translate it into English.

Margit Levy spent the last months of her life more in the hospital than at home. A few times I went to visit her. She was in the general ward, and her face had changed so much that on each visit I had trouble recognizing her. Her false teeth no longer fit her shrunken mouth. Her nose had become hooked, just like Morris's. She spoke to me in German, French, Italian. Once, I found her with another visitor— her lawyer, a German Jew. I heard her telling him that she had bought a plot in the cemetery of the Klimontów Society, near Morris's grave.

She died in January. It was a frosty day and the wind was blowing. Two people came to the chapel—the lawyer and myself. The rabbi quickly recited "God Full of Mercy" and delivered a brief eulogy. I heard him say, "The privilege of leaving a good name is for villagers only. In a city like New York, a person's name often dies before him." Then the coffin was put into a hearse and Margit Levy rode into eternity without anyone to accompany her.

I wanted to carry out my promise to find a place for Morris Terkeltoyb's packs of manuscripts, but the institutions I called all refused to take them. I kept in my apartment one valise filled with his writings and two albums that belonged to Margit Levy. All the rest the superintendent threw out into the street. That day I did not leave the house.

In Morris Terkeltoyb's valise I found, to my surprise, bundles of faded love letters that women had written him—all in Yiddish. One woman threatened that she would commit suicide if he did not return to her. No, Morris Terkeltoyb was not the psychopathic boaster I had thought him to be. Women did love him. I remembered Spinoza's saying that there are no falsehoods, there are only distorted truths. A strange idea ran through my mind: perhaps among these letters I would find one from Isadora Duncan. For a moment I had forgotten that Isadora Duncan did not know Yiddish.

A year after Margit Levy's death, I received an invitation from the Klimontów Society to attend the unveiling of a monument to Malkah Levy—the Society had given her a Hebrew name. But that Sunday a heavy snow fell, and I was sure that the unveiling would be postponed. Besides, I woke up with a severe attack of sciatica. I took a hot bath, but there was no one for whom to shave and dress. Neither did I miss anyone. After breakfast, I took out Margit's album, some of Morris's letters, looked at the pictures, and read the texts. I dozed, dreamed, and forgot my dreams the moment I wakened. From time to time I looked out the window. The snow descended sparsely, peacefully, as if in contemplation of its own falling. The short day neared its end. The desolate park became a cemetery. The buildings on Central Park South towered like headstones. The sun was setting on Riverside Drive, and the water of the reservoir reflected a burning wick. The radiator near which I sat hissed and hummed: "Dust, dust, dust." The singsong penetrated my bones together with the warmth. It repeated a truth as old as the world, as profound as sleep.

Translated by the author and Herbert R. Lottman

Grandfather and Grandson

AFTER Beyle Teme's death Reb Mordecai Meir sold his store and began to live on his capital. Someone figured out for him with a pencil on paper that if he spent eight rubles a week it would last him seven years—and how much longer could he live? He had reached the age at which his parents had died. Every minute after that was a gift.

His only daughter had died of typhus several years ago and he had a few grandchildren somewhere in Slonim, but they would have to get along without his inheritance. Reb Mordecai Meir's daughter had married a Litvak, an opponent of Hasidism, an enlightened Jew, and her father had virtually cut her off as his child.

Reb Mordecai Meir was a small man with a yellowish-white beard, a broad forehead, bushy eyebrows beneath which peeped a pair of yellow eyes, like a chicken's. On the tip of his nose there grew a little beard. Wisps of hair stuck out of his ears and nostrils. In the course of time his back had become bowed and he always looked as if he were searching for something on the floor. He didn't walk but shuffled his feet. All year round he wore a cotton caftan with a sash, low shoes, and a velvet hat over two skullcaps. He spoke in half sentences, only to the initiated Hasidim.

Even among Hasidim, Reb Mordecai Meir was known as an impractical man. Though he had lived in Warsaw for years, he was not at all acquainted with the streets of Warsaw. The only road he knew was from his home to the Hasidic

House of Prayer and back. During the year, he occasionally traveled to the Rabbi of Alexandrow, but he always had difficulty finding the trolley to the railway station, changing cars, and buying tickets. In all this he had to be assisted by young men who knew their way around. He had neither the time nor the patience for such externals.

At midnight he arose for study and prayer. Very early each morning he recited the Gemara and the Tosephot Commentary. After that came Psalms, more prayers, delving into Hasidic books, and discussing Hasidic matters. The winter days were short. Before one had a bite to eat and a nap, it was time to return to the study house for evening prayers. Even though the summer days were long, there were not enough of them. First it was Passover, then the Feast of Omer, and before you could turn around it was Shevuoth. After that came the seventeenth of Tammuz, the three weeks of mourning for the destruction of the Temple, the nine days of refraining from meat, and then Tisha B'Av, the Sabbath of Comfort. These were followed by the month of Elul, when even fish in water tremble. Later there was Rosh Hashonah, the ten days of Penitence, Yom Kippur, Succoth, the Day of Rejoicing in the Law, and then, Sabbath of Genesis.

As a boy, Reb Mordecai Meir had already realized that if one wanted to be a real Jew there was no time for anything else. Praised be God, his wife, Beyle Teme, had understood this. She never asked him to assist in the store, to concern himself with business, to carry the burden of earning a living. He seldom had any money with him except for the few guldens which she gave him each week for alms, the ritual bath, books, snuff, and pipe tobacco. Reb Mordecai Meir wasn't even certain of the exact location of the store and the merchandise sold there. A shopkeeper had to talk to women customers and he knew well that it was only one short step from talking, to looking, to lecherous thoughts.

The street on which Reb Mordecai Meir lived teemed with unbelievers, loose women. Boys peddled Yiddish newspapers which were full of mockery and atheism. The saloons swarmed with ruffians. In his library, Reb Mordecai Meir kept the windows shut, even during the summer. As soon as he opened the transom of the window, he immediately heard the playing of frivolous songs on the gramophone and female laughter. In the courtyard, bareheaded jugglers often performed their tricks, which he felt might be black magic. Reb Mordecai Meir was told that Jewish boys and girls went to the Yiddish theater where they made fun of Jewishness. There emerged worldly writers, writing in Hebrew and Yiddish. They incited the readers to sin. At every turn the Evil Spirit lay in wait. There was only one way to defeat him: with Torah, prayer, Hasidism.

The years passed and Reb Mordecai Meir did not know where or how. Overnight his yellow beard turned gray. Because he did not want to go to the barber shop and sit among the shaven transgressors, Beyle Teme used to cut his hair. She took off his skullcaps and he quickly replaced them. She would argue, "How can I cut your hair with the skullcaps on your head?"

In later years he became bald and only his sidelocks remained. When Beyle Teme stopped having children (five of the children had died and they were left with just the one daughter, Zelda Rayzel), Reb Mordecai Meir separated himself from his wife. What more was needed after he had fulfilled the commandment "Be fruitful and multiply"? To be sure, according to the Law a man was permitted to have relations with his wife when she could no longer bear children. Some were even of the opinion that one must not become a recluse. But when was this said? Only when one could copulate without any desire for the flesh. If a person had intercourse for the sake of pleasure, this could lead to temptations and lust. Besides, in recent years Beyle Teme was not in good health. She used to return home from the shop exhausted, smelling of herring and valerian drops.

After Zelda Rayzel's death, Beyle Teme became melancholy. She wept almost every night and kept repeating the same words: "Why did this happen to me?" Reb Mordecai Meir reminded her that it was forbidden to complain against God. "All God does is good." The reason there was such a thing as death was because the body was only a garment. The soul is sent to be cleansed in Gehenna for a short time and after that it goes to Paradise and learns the secrets of the Torah. Were eating, drinking, urinating, and sweating such a bargain?

But Beyle Teme became sicker from day to day. She passed away on a Wednesday and was buried on Friday afternoon. Since it was just before the Sabbath she was spared the pressure of the grave, which those who are buried on weekdays suffer. Reb Mordecai Meir recited Kaddish for the repose of her soul, prayed before the congregation, studied Mishna. When the thirty days of mourning had passed, a relative took over the shop for four thousand rubles. Pesha, a neighbor who was a widow, came to Reb Mordecai Meir every day to clean and cook some food. For the Sabbath she prepared stew and a pudding for him. The Hasidim tried to arrange a match but he refused to remarry.

One summer morning, while reading *The Generations of Jacob Joseph,* he dozed off and was awakened by the sound of knocking. He opened the door and saw a young man without a beard, a head of long hair over which he wore a broadbrimmed black hat, in a black blouse tied with a sash, and checkered pants. In one hand he carried a satchel and in the other a book. His face was pale and he had a short nose.

Reb Mordecai Meir asked, "What do you want?"

Blinking his widely separated eyes, he stammered, "I am Fulie . . . You are my grandfather."

Reb Mordecai Meir stood dumfounded. He had never heard the name Fulie. Then he realized that this was most probably the modern variation of the old Jewish name Raphael. It was Zelda Rayzel's eldest son. Reb Mordecai Meir felt both pain and shame. He had a grandson who tried to imitate the Gentiles. He said, "So come in." After hesitating a moment, the boy came in and put his suitcase down. Reb Mordecai Meir asked, "What kind—is that—?" and pointed to the book.

"Economics."

"Of what use is that to you?"

"Well . . ."

"What's new in Slonim?" Reb Mordecai Meir asked. He didn't want to mention the name of his former son-in-law, who was an anti-Hasid. Fulie made a face as if to indicate that he did not fully comprehend his grandfather's question.

"In Slonim? Just like everywhere else. The rich get richer and the workers have nothing to eat. I had to leave because . . ." and Fulie stopped himself.

"What will you do here?"

"Here—I'll look around—I'll . . ."

Well, a stutterer, Reb Mordecai Meir thought. His throat scratched and his stomach started to turn. It was his daughter Zelda Rayzel's son, but as long as he shaved his beard and dressed like a Gentile, what would he, Reb Mordecai Meir, do with him? He nodded his head and gaped. It seemed that the boy took after the other side of the family with his high cheekbones, narrow forehead, and wide mouth. His bedraggled and famished appearance reminded Reb Mordecai Meir of the recruits who starve themselves to avoid conscription.

"Wash your hands. Eat something. Don't forget that you are a Jew."

"Grandfather, they don't let you forget."

In the kitchen the boy sat down at the table and began to leaf through his book. Reb Mordecai Meir opened the kitchen closet but found no bread there; only onions, a string of dried mushrooms, a package of chicory, a few heads of garlic.

He said to Fulie, "I'll give you money, go to the store and buy a loaf of bread or something else you might like to eat."

"Grandfather, I'm not hungry. And besides, the less I'm outside the better," the boy answered.

"Why? You're not sick, God forbid, are you?"

"All of Russia has the same sickness. Everywhere it is full of denouncers and secret agents. Grandfather, I am not altogether 'clean.' "

"Have you been called by the military?"

"That too."

"Maybe you can be saved?"

"All mankind needs to be saved, not only I."

Reb Mordecai Meir had decided not to get angry, no matter what his grandson did or said. Anger won't win anyone over to piety. There were moments when Reb Mordecai Meir wanted to spit on the impudent fellow and drive him out of his house. But he restrained himself with all his might. Even though Fulie spoke in Yiddish, Reb Mordecai Meir did not fully comprehend what he was saying. All of his talk boiled down to one complaint: the rich live in luxury, the poor suffer deprivation. He continuously mentioned the workers in the factories, the peasants who tilled the fields. He spoke against the czar. "He resides in a palace and lets others rot in cellars. Millions die of hunger, consumption. The people must wake up. There must be a revolution . . ."

Reb Mordecai Meir clutched his beard and asked, "How do you know that a new czar would be better?"

"If we have our way, there will be no new czar."

"Who will rule?"

"The people."

"All the people can't sit in the ruling chair," Reb Mordecai Meir answered.

"Representatives will be chosen from the workers and peasants."

"When they get power, they may also become villains," Reb Mordecai Meir argued.

"Then they'll be made one head shorter."

"It is written: 'For the poor shall never cease out of the land,' " Reb Mordecai Meir spoke. "To whom would one give charity if there were no paupers? Besides, everything is ordained in Heaven. On Rosh Hashonah it is decreed in Heaven who shall be rich and who shall be poor."

"The Heavens are nothing but air," Fulie said. "No one decrees anything."

"What? The world created itself?"

"It evolved."

"What does that mean?"

The boy began to say something, then got stuck. He mentioned names which Reb Mordecai Meir had never heard. He mixed Polish, Russian, and German words. The sum total of his talk was that everything was accident, chance. He babbled about a mist, gravitation, the earth tearing away from the sun and cooling off. He denied the exodus from Egypt, that the Red Sea was split, that the Jews received the Torah on Mount Sinai. It was all a legend. Each of Fulie's words pained Reb Mordecai Meir's insides, as if he had swallowed the molten lead which, in ancient times, was given to those who were condemned to be burned. A cry tore from his throat. He wanted to shout, "Blackguard, Jeroboam, son of Nebat, get out of my house, go to the devil!" But he remembered that the boy was an orphan, a stranger in the city, without means. He could, God forbid, become a convert, or commit suicide.

"May God forgive you. You are deluded," he said.

"You asked, Grandfather, so I answered."

From then on, grandfather and grandson stopped debating.

They actually didn't speak. Reb Mordecai Meir sat in the living room, Fulie stayed in the kitchen and slept there on the cot. When Pesha cooked something, she also gave him a plate of food. She bought him bread, butter, cheese. She washed his shirt. Fulie was given a key to the outer door. Though he was not registered, the janitor let him in at night. Each time Fulie gave him ten groschen. Some nights he didn't come home at all.

Reb Mordecai Meir slept little. Right after evening prayers fatigue overcame him and he went to bed, but after an hour or two he awoke. In the morning Fulie was gone before Reb Mordecai Meir began to recite the Shema. "One must not estrange them," Reb Mordecai Meir said to himself. "The birth throes of the Messiah have begun."

In the kitchen, in a box of books, Reb Mordecai Meir found a Yiddish pamphlet with frayed pages. He tried to read it but could understand little of what was written there. The writer seemed to argue with another writer of his kind. He mentioned such strange names as Zhelyabov, Kilbatchitch, Perovskaya. One, it said, was a martyr. A bitter taste came to Reb Mordecai Meir's mouth. In his old age he had to room with a heretic who was his grandchild. In the Alexandrow study house he asked what was going on in the world and was told things which utterly amazed him. Those who, years before, had murdered the czar had begun to arouse the populace anew. Among them were many Jews. Somewhere in Russia a bomb had been thrown, a train derailed, sacks of gold robbed. In some faraway city a governor had been shot. The jails were full. Many rebels were sent to Siberia. The Hasid who recounted these events said, "They kill and are killed. It is each man's sword in his neighbor!"

"What do they want?" Reb Mordecai Meir asked.

"That all should be equal."

"How is this possible?"

"Sons of the rich have joined their group."

The Hasid reported that the daughter of a wine dealer, a Hasid of the Rabbi of Gur, got mixed up with these instigators and was imprisoned in the Citadel. There she fasted for eighteen days and had to be fed by force.

Reb Mordecai Meir was stunned. The Redemption must be near! He asked, "If they don't believe in the world to come, why do they torment themselves so?"

"They want justice."

That evening, when Reb Mordecai Meir returned home after evening prayers, he saw Fulie seated at the kitchen table, his black blouse unbuttoned, his hair unkempt, chewing on a piece of bread and reading a book.

"Why do you eat dry bread? The woman cooks for you too."

"Pesha? She was taken to the hospital."

"Really? We must pray for her."

"She had an attack of gallstones. If you like I can make something."

"You?"

"I'll make sure it's kosher."

"You believe in it?"

"For your sake."

"Well, no."

From that day on grandfather and grandson ate only dry food. Fulie brought rolls, sugar, cheese from the store. He brewed tea. Reb Mordecai Meir was not sure he should trust such a one even with the making of tea. It was one thing to be a Gentile cook, who, the Talmud presumed, would not damage his livelihood and so could be trusted, and something entirely different to be a renegade Jew. However, bread and sugar could not be made unclean. Fulie bought the cheese from David in the dairy store across the street. If Fulie looked for a Gentile shop on another street, it meant he was an apostate out of spite, of whom it is said, "He knows his master and wants to defy Him." But so low he had not fallen.

The Sabbath meal was prepared by another neighbor. Reb Mordecai Meir lit the Sabbath candles himself. He sat at the table alone, in his threadbare satin coat, worn-out fur hat, chanting Sabbath chants, dipping a piece of hallah into the glass of ritual wine. The boy (which was what Reb Mordecai Meir called Fulie) didn't show himself on the Sabbath. The neighbor's daughter brought in rice soup, meat, carrot pudding. Reb Mordecai Meir half sang, half moaned.

If the old rabbi were still alive, Reb Mordecai Meir would have gone to live with him. But Reb Henokh was dead. The new rabbi was still a young man who cared more for the young Hasidim than the old. It was whispered that he was learned in worldly affairs. Many of the older Hasidim had died out and no new ones joined.

One Sabbath day, when Reb Mordecai Meir was sitting at the table murmuring, "I shall sing with praise," he heard the crack of a gun and a hideous scream. In the courtyard there was a din. Windows were thrown open. The sound of a police whistle pierced the air. A neighbor came in to tell Reb Mordecai Meir that the "comrades," the strikers, had shot one of their own, a bootmaker who was said to have denounced them to the police. Reb Mordecai Meir trembled.

"Who did it—Jews?"

"Yes, Jews."

"It is the end of the world." And Reb Mordecai Meir immediately regretted his words. It was not permitted to be sad or utter words of despair on the Sabbath.

Because Reb Mordecai Meir awoke for midnight prayers, he went to sleep early. At nine o'clock he was already in bed, often not undressed. He took off only his boots. That night he heard the kitchen door open and he recognized Fulie's steps.

He fell asleep again, but at exactly twelve he awoke, got up, performed the ceremony of ritual hand washing, put on a housecoat and slippers, and began to lament on the destruction of the Temple. On his head he smeared a bit of ash, which he kept in a small jar. He intoned a plaintive melody. When Reb Mordecai Meir came to the verse "Rachel laments for her children," the door opened and Fulie entered barefoot, wearing a pair of dirty underpants, without a head covering. Reb Mordecai Meir raised his eyebrows and motioned to Fulie to leave and let him finish his supplications, but the boy said, "Grandfather, are you praying?"

Reb Mordecai Meir was not certain whether he was permitted to interrupt his prayers. After some hesitation he said, "I am reciting midnight prayers."

"What kind are they?"

"A Jew must never forget the destruction of the Temple."

"And what are you trying to accomplish by this?" Fulie asked.

Even though Reb Mordecai Meir understood every individual word, he did not grasp their meaning. He wanted to ask Fulie where his fringed undergarment was, but he realized that the question was pointless. He thought a moment and said, "One must pray. With God's help, the Messiah will come and there will be an end to the exile."

"If he hasn't yet come," Fulie asked, "why should he come now?"

"The Messiah wants to come to the Jews more than they want him to come, but the generation must be worth it. The Heavens send plenty of blessings, but we block the channels of mercy with our iniquities."

"Grandfather, I must talk to you."

"What do you want to talk about? One is not allowed to interrupt midnight prayers."

"Grandfather, the world won't get anywhere from all these

prayers. People have prayed for nearly two thousand years, but the Messiah still did not get here on his white donkey. It's a battle, Grandfather, a bitter war between the exploiters and the exploited. Who incited the peasants to make pogroms on Jews? The Black Hundreds, the reactionaries. If the workers don't resist, we will be more enslaved. Grandfather, tomorrow there will be a big demonstration and I will be the speaker. If something should happen to me, I want you to give this envelope to a girl by the name of Nekhama Katz."

Now, for the first time, Reb Mordecai Meir noticed the boy holding a stuffed envelope.

He said, "I don't know any girls. I am an old man. Why are you involved with mutineers? You may be arrested, God forbid, and you will bring suffering on all of us. The czar has many Cossacks and he is stronger than you. Since you don't believe in the soul and the hereafter, why put yourself in danger?"

"Grandfather, I don't want to begin the discussion all over again. All of Europe is free and here the czar is a tyrant. We have no parliament. What he and his satraps want, they do. The war with Japan cost millions. Thousands of soldiers were lost. In the West they worry about the hygiene of the workers, but here a worker is worse than a dog. If we don't get a constitution, all of Russia will go down in blood."

Reb Mordecai Meir put down his prayer book. "Are you a worker?"

"What I am is not important, Grandfather. We are fighting for something, an ideal. Here is the letter. Put it in the drawer. Perhaps I will be back tomorrow. If not, a girl by the name of Nekhama Katz will come. Give it to her."

"Don't run, don't rush. He who is above governs the world. He determines that there will be wealthy and poor people. If there were no poor people, no one would want to do the ordinary work. One is a merchant and another a chimney sweeper. If everyone were a shopkeeper, who would sweep the chimneys?"

"We are striving to give chimney sweeps the same rights and the same means as merchants. Merchants aren't necessary. In a Socialist world, production will be apportioned according to need. We won't let a middleman skim off the cream for himself."

"What! We Jews must not interfere. Whoever rules will persecute Jews."

"Anti-Semitism was created by the capitalists to divert the wrath of the masses against the regime. The Zionists want to run to Palestine, to the Tomb of Mother Rachel, but it's all just fantasy. We Jews must fight, together with all other oppressed people, for a better tomorrow."

"All right, all right, give me the letter. Leave me in peace. 'Except the Lord build a house, they labor in vain that build it.' It is written: 'No one should be punished before he is warned.' The Gemara says: 'If you go into a spice shop you smell good, and if you go into a tannery the stench stays with you.'"

"Grandfather, what are you calling a stench, the people's fight for their rights? Are you on the side of the exploiters?"

"Give me the envelope."

"Good night, Grandfather. We'll never understand each other."

Fulie left. Reb Mordecai Meir took hold of the envelope by one corner and put it into a drawer. He began to recite anew: "A voice was heard in Ramah, lamentation and bitter weeping, Rachel weeping for her children, refusing to be comforted." A kerosene lamp was burning and Reb Mordecai Meir's figure cast a large shadow on the wall. His head climbed the rafters. Reb Mordecai Meir grimaced and swayed back and forth. Can they possibly be made to understand the truth? he asked himself. They read a few books and repeat the gibberish. Constitution, schmonstitution! It's a battle between good and evil, God and Satan, Israel and Amalek. Esau and Ishmael refused to accept the Torah. The slave enjoys being abandoned. But when Jews cast away the Law, they become like pagans and maybe even worse. How could the Messiah come? Possibly, God forbid, the whole generation would become entirely guilty. He wiped his brow. "Oy, Father. The water reaches up to the very neck!"

After finishing prayers, Reb Mordecai Meir went back to bed. But this time he could not fall asleep. He heard the boy moving about in the kitchen. He banged the dishes, turned the faucet on. It seemed to Reb Mordecai Meir that he heard a sigh. Could that be Fulie? Who knows, perhaps he had thoughts of repentance. After all, on his mother's side, he stemmed from righteous men. Even among his Litvak forefathers there were probably some devout Jews. Reb Mordecai Meir could not remain in bed. Maybe the boy could be persuaded to stay home. What he said that evening was like a last testament. Reb Mordecai Meir got out of bed with trembling feet. Once again he put on his slippers and robe. When he opened the kitchen door he saw something so bizarre that he did not believe his own eyes. Fulie was standing completely dressed, holding a revolver in his hand. Reb Mordecai knew what it was. On the Feast of Omer children were given such guns, not real ones, only toys.

When he noticed his grandfather, Fulie laid the weapon on the kitchen table. "Grandfather, what do you want? Are you spying on me?"

"What kind of an abomination is this?" he asked. He began to shiver and his teeth chattered.

Fulie laughed. "Don't be afraid, Grandfather. It's not meant for you."

"For whom is it?"

"For those who want to hold back progress, to keep the world in darkness."

"What? *You* will sentence them to death? Seventy judges were required in the Sanhedrin to condemn anyone to die. There had to be admonition and at least two witnesses. The Gemara says that a court which sentenced anyone to death even once in seventy years was called a court of murderers."

"Grandfather, these people have sentenced themselves. Their time is past, but they refuse to give up peacefully. So they'll be made to leave by force."

"Fulie, Raphael, you are a Jew!" Reb Mordecai Meir choked on the words. "Esau lives by the sword. Not Jacob."

"Old wives' tales. Jews are made of the same stuff as Gentiles. It's all foolish chauvinism. This business about the Chosen People is sheer nonsense. Grandfather, I'm going."

"Don't leave! Don't leave! If they catch you, God forbid, they might . . ."

"I know, I know. I am not a child." Fulie put the revolver into the pocket of his pants. He took a package wrapped in newspaper with him. Probably some bread for a bite. He let the door slam as he left. Reb Mordecai Meir remained standing on unsteady feet. He leaned against the wall to keep from falling. "Have things gone so far?" he asked himself. Sleep was out of the question, but it was too early for morning prayers. The morning star was not yet in sight. Night and day still ruled in confusion.

On wobbling feet, Reb Mordecai Meir walked over to the window. To the right the sky was still black. But to the left, in the east, it had become like daylight. All the stores on the street were shut. A baker's apprentice passed by, barefoot, in white pants, carrying a tray of cakes or rolls on his head. "Well, baked goods are needed," Reb Mordecai Meir murmured.

He expected to see Fulie appear on the sidewalk, but he didn't come through. The gate was probably still locked. He must have friends here in the yard, Reb Mordecai Meir decided. Woe, woe, what has become of my people! For the first time he was envious of Beyle Teme—she had not lived to see these calamities. By now she was certainly in Paradise. Until today, Reb Mordecai Meir had seldom thought of his wife during prayers. A Jew was supposed to pray directly to God, not to any saintly man or woman. But now Reb Mordecai Meir began to talk to Beyle Teme's soul. "He is your grandchild. Intercede for him. Let nothing evil happen to him, and let him, God forbid, do no harm to others."

To the right, the moon was still visible and Reb Mordecai Meir looked up at it, the lesser light which, according to the Talmud, begrudged the greater light, and as compensation was given the stars. That meant that there was envy on high, Reb Mordecai Meir half asked, half stated. He could not bring himself to leave the window, hoping to see Fulie once more. The thought crossed his mind that Abraham also had an Esau for a grandchild. He had Ishmael for a son and the sons of Keturah. Even the saints couldn't bring forth only good seeds. Suddenly the street was flooded with a reddish glow. The sun had risen over the banks of the Vistula. There was a clatter of horseshoes on cobblestones and the twittering of birds could be heard. Reb Mordecai Meir saw soldiers, their swords gleaming, riding on horses. The riders kept glancing at the upper floors.

Is it against them that Fulie went to wage war? Reb Mordecai Meir pondered. He felt cold and shuddered. Never before had he wished to be rid of this world. But now he was ready to die. How much longer would he have to wander in the valley of tears? Better to go through the pains of Gehenna than to see this futile turmoil.

The shouting and confusion began in the early morning.

Right here in the street, it seemed, the rebels tried to conquer the forces of the Russian czar. Youths stormed out of every gate, shouting, waving their fists, and singing. Policemen, their swords bared, chased them and fired shots. A red flag was raised with more singing and shouting. The stores remained shut. Gates were closed. The shrill sound of police whistles could be heard. First-aid wagons appeared, and for a while the street became empty. The red flag, which someone had just held aloft, now lay in the gutter, torn and dirty. The street soon began to fill up again. Another flag fluttered. There was renewed shouting and the stampeding of many feet.

Reb Mordecai Meir could not bear to watch any more. God's light certainly had to be dimmed and His face hidden before there could be free will, reward and punishment, redemption; but couldn't the Almighty find another way to reveal His power? These youths with their shaven beards and short coats bellowed like peasants. Once in a while the sound of female shrieks came through. A policeman was beaten up, a horse had fallen and lay on the pavement, apparently with broken legs. In what way was the poor animal guilty? Unless it was a soul in reincarnation, atoning for some transgression committed in a former life.

Reb Mordecai Meir began to pray. There was no possibility of going to the synagogue on such a day. He wrapped himself in his prayer shawl, kissed the fringes, placed the phylacteries on his arm and head. He could hardly stand through the Eighteen Benedictions. While he prayed, the din in the street grew louder. He heard the cries of those who were hit and injured. Blood was spattered on the wall across the way. Children, whom mothers had carried, borne, nursed, worried over their slightest whim, now lay in the mud writhing in the agonies of death. "Woe, my punishment is greater than I can bear!"

Usually after morning prayers Reb Mordecai Meir washed

his hands, had a bite to eat: a piece of bread, a slice of cheese, sometimes a bit of herring, a glass of tea. But today he could not eat; the food would stick in his throat. He reminded himself of the passage in the Midrash: "When the Egyptians drowned in the Red Sea, the angels wanted to sing songs of praise, but the Almighty said to them, 'My creatures sink into the sea and you want to sing!' " The Creator had pity even on the Egyptian oppressors.

Reb Mordecai Meir felt dizzy and lay down on the couch. To keep the light of day out he put the hat with the big brim over his eyes. For a time he was neither awake nor asleep. Finally he fell into the deep sleep of those who have not rested for many nights and are utterly exhausted. He dreamed, but later could not recall his dreams.

The tumult from the outside became even wilder. He awoke with a start. Screams and shots reverberated. Reb Mordecai Meir imagined that multitudes of women were wailing and dogs were howling. During a moment's lull, Reb Mordecai Meir heard the singing of birds, which in the midst of this total madness fulfilled their mission. These creatures ignored the humans with their schemes and ambitions even while they built their nests under man's eaves, ate his leftovers, hopped about on his telephone wires. People too are helped by beings they cannot comprehend.

Reb Mordecai Meir got up with the intention of brewing himself a cup of tea. He went into the kitchen, found some matches, filled a kettle of water from the spout. There was a quarter of a loaf of bread which Fulie must have bought last night, as well as a piece of stale cake. The old man was about to strike a match when he suddenly remembered that he had decided to fast. "Today it is Tisha B'Av for me. I'll eat and drink nothing," and he put the match down.

The living room had a book closet and he began to rummage through it. He had no strength to study the Talmud, but he wanted to look through a Hasidic volume. Maybe *The Generations of Jacob Joseph*? He pulled out a thin little book, *The Waters of Shiloh*, written by the first of the Radzyn dynasty. He was surprised; he didn't even know he owned this book. Reb Mordecai Meir turned to a page in the middle. There he read that the way to grasp the greatness of the Creator was to recognize one's own nothingness. As long as man considers himself important, his eyes are blinded to Heaven. Reb Mordecai Meir took hold of his beard. The flesh forgets. The Evil Spirit and the Lord of Forgetfulness band together. Perhaps they are one and the same?

Suddenly it occurred to him that it was strangely quiet outside. Were they tired? He went to the window and saw that the street was empty, the shops still closed. Dusk was setting in. "Have they already gotten, what do they call it, the constitution?" he wondered. It was weird to see the stores closed on an ordinary weekday. The square, which was usually teeming with boys, girls, assorted peddlers, and urchins, was as empty as in the middle of the night.

Then he heard the tread of heavy steps on the stairs and in an instant knew that they were coming to him, and that it was with bad news. He trembled and his lips began to move in prayer, even though he realized that it was too late now to ward off what had already happened. For a few moments there was no sound and the thought flashed through his mind that maybe he was mistaken. Then the thumping on the door and the bang of a boot made his legs buckle. It seemed to him he would not be able to reach the door. But he opened it and saw what he expected to see: four men were carrying a body on a stretcher, a dead man—Fulie. They entered without speaking, with the sullenness of pallbearers.

"The murderers killed him," one of them shouted. "Where should we put him down?" a second one asked. Reb Mordecai Meir pointed to the floor. The dead man was bleeding. A puddle of blood formed on the floor. A hand stuck out from under the cover—a lifeless hand, limp and pale, which no longer could take anything, no gift, no favor, no constitution . . .

Reb Mordecai Meir's belly swelled up like a drum. "Great God, I don't want to live any longer. Enough!" He was angry with God for the punishment which He had visited upon him in his old age. He had to vomit and dragged himself to the toilet, where he retched as if he had eaten and drunk all day and not fasted. Fires leaped before his eyes. Never in his life had he complained to God. He murmured, "I don't deserve this affliction!" And he knew that he was blaspheming.

Late that night there was again a knocking at his door. "Who is it, another corpse?" Reb Mordecair Meir asked himself in his anxiety. He was sitting beside Fulie's body reciting psalms. When he opened the door, first a policeman entered, followed by a civilian, and then by two more policemen and the janitor. They were saying something in Russian, but Reb Mordecai Meir did not understand their language. He pointed to the corpse but they turned away.

A search began. Drawers were opened, papers thrown around. From the dresser the person in civilian clothes took Fulie's thick envelope for Nekhama Katz. He opened it and removed several sheets of paper, a notebook, a nickel watch, other objects. He read a part of the letter to the others— in Russian. One of them smiled. Another stared silently. He then said to Reb Mordecai Meir in broken Yiddish, "Grandfather, come."

"What? Where?"

"Come."

"What will happen to the corpse?"

"Come, come."

Somewhere the janitor found Reb Mordecai Meir's coat.

Reb Mordecai Meir wanted to ask the one in charge why he was being arrested, but he could speak neither Polish nor Russian. Anyway, what good would it do to ask? The civilian took him by one arm, a policeman by the other, and they led him down the dark staircase. The janitor lit matches. He opened the gate. A small carriage with barred windows was waiting outside. They helped Reb Mordecai Meir get in and sat him down on a bench. One of the policemen sat next to him. Slowly the carriage began to move.

"Well, let me imagine that it is my funeral," Reb Mordecai Meir said to himself. "No one will say Kaddish for me anyhow."

A strange calm came over him and the complete surrender that accompanies misfortune so great that one knows nothing worse can occur. Before, when they had brought Fulie's body, he had rebelled in his thought, but now he regretted his resentment. "Father in Heaven, forgive me." There came to his mind the saying from the Talmud: "No one is subject to penalty for words uttered in agony."

"What time is it?" he wondered. Suddenly he remembered that he had not taken his prayer shawl and phylacteries. Well, it was too late even for that. Reb Mordecai Meir started to confess his sins. "We have transgressed, we have betrayed, we have cheated, we have deceived . . ." He raised his hand and tried to make a fist to beat his breast, but his fingers were rigid. Well, he has probably already atoned for his mistakes, Reb Mordecai Meir was thinking about Fulie. His intentions were good. He wanted to help the poor. He pitied the hungry. Perhaps that was his salvation. In Heaven everything is judged according to intention. Maybe his soul is already cleansed.

It was not customary to say Kaddish without a quorum or for someone who had not yet been buried, but Reb Mordecai Meir knew that he had little time left. He mumbled the Kaddish. Then he recited a chapter from the Mishna which he knew from memory. "At what time is it permissible to recite the Shema in the evening? From the time that the priests enter the Temple to eat their food offerings. So sayeth Rabbi Eliezer. And the sages say: Until midnight."

"Hey, you, Jew, old dog, who are you talking to, your God?" the policeman asked. Somehow Reb Mordecai Meir understood these few words. What does he know? How can he understand? Reb Mordecai Meir defended him in his thoughts. Since no evil can come from God, those created in His image can't be completely wicked. He said to the policeman, "Yes, I am Jew. I pray God."

Those were all the Gentile words Reb Mordecai Meir knew.

Translated by Evelyn Torton Beck and Ruth Schachner Finkel